GUARDIANS

By

Kaitlyn O'Connor

Futuristic Romance

New Concepts   Georgia

Guardians is a publication of NCP. This work is a novel. Any similarity to actual persons or events is purely coincidental.

New Concepts Publishing, Inc.
5202 Humphreys Rd.
Lake Park, GA 31636
ISBN 1-58608-728-2
© copyright 2005, Kaitlyn O'Connor
Cover art (c) copyright 2005, Eliza Black

NCP books are available at special quantity discounts for bulk purchases for sales promotions, premiums, fund raising, or educational use. For details, write, email, or phone New Concepts Publishing, Inc., 5202 Humphreys Rd., Lake Park, GA 31636;   Ph.   229-257-0367,   Fax   229-219-1097; orders@newconceptspublishing.com.

First NCP Paperback Printing: December 2005

We offer a 20% discount on all new Trade Paperback releases ordered from our website!

Be sure to visit our webpage to find the best deals in e-books and paperbacks! To find out about our new releases as soon as they are available, please be sure to sign up for our newsletter (http://www.newconceptspublishing.com/newsletter.htm) or join our reader group (http://groups.yahoo.com/group/new_concepts_pub/join)! The newsletter is available by double opt in only and our customer information is *never* shared!

Visit our webpage at:
www.newconceptspublishing.com

TABLE OF CONTENTS

GUARDIAN OF THE STORM

Chapter One

The first rock caught Kiran completely off guard and missed his head by mere inches. He looked up just in time to see his attacker launch another missile. This one, fortunately, was far smaller, for it caught him on the shoulder. "Throw one more rock, Earth born demon spawn, and I'll thrash you within an inch of your life when I get my hands on you!" he roared.

"This watering hole is mine!" the youth screamed at him, looking around for another rock to throw. "And I'll defend it to the death if need be!"

Kiran jumped back as a sizable rock screamed past his ear. It struck the ground near his foot, shattering, sending tiny missiles in every direction. One collided with his bare toe, sending a shaft of throbbing pain all the way up his leg. He let out a yelp of pain, then glared up at the ragged urchin above him.

The child's eyes widened in horror at the look he sent him.

Muttering under his breath, Kiran grabbed a handhold and hoisted himself rapidly up the short outcropping of rock. The face disappeared as he neared the top and Kiran braced himself, expecting to be met at the edge of the summit with more determined resistance.

Instead, he hoisted himself onto the ledge just in time to see his attacker beating a hasty retreat down the other side. A combination of satisfaction and renewed anger went through him. With a roar, he charged after the culprit. The youth was quick on his feet, but Kiran had a far longer stride and rapidly overtook him, catching the youth by the rags of his shirt. To the surprise of both, the fabric could not withstand the tug in two different directions at once. It separated from its wearer, who yelped with a combination of fear and anger and ran faster. Not to be outdone, Kiran launched himself at the youth. He twisted as he fell, knowing he would crush the scrawny creature if he landed on top of him.

The landing stunned them both for several moments, but Kiran had the youth tightly clutched to his chest. After a moment, he rolled over on top, pinning the youth to the ground. Straddling, him, he levered himself up and glared down at his captive.

He could count every rib ... except those beneath the two, very feminine, surprisingly full breasts. Mesmerized by the bobbing globes that undulated with every desperate heave the boy--girl made in her efforts to wriggle free of him, Kiran's mind went perfectly blank. His body, however, operating under its own agenda, burgeoned with lust.

Sucking in a deep breath, he curbed his instincts with an effort and dragged his eyes from the jiggling breasts to the face above them. He had, quite obviously, been wrong about pretty much everything else, but he had not been wrong about her origins, he saw.

The girl was Earthling, and from her condition, probably one of the few orphans to survive the disease that had swept through the Earth colony almost a year and a half ago, though she had not survived well. Her eyes were huge, dominating her thin face, glazed now with pure terror.

Irritation surfaced, but so, too, did sympathy. Neither completely subdued his desire, however. He closed his mind to it, willing his body to cool, but it would've been far easier if she had ceased heaving beneath him. He knew very well that she was only trying to throw him off, but his serpent smelled a nice warm hole and was resistant to his efforts to tame it when she continued to bump her female body against his groin.

"Be still!" he ground out harshly.

Instead of obeying, she swung at him. He caught her arms, forced them down, manacling them to the ground on either side of her head.

"I mean you no harm, grat! Cease and I will release you."

He wasn't certain whether she finally understood, and believed him, or if she simply ran out of strength to fight. She went still.

He eyed her warily. After a moment, when she remained perfectly still, he relaxed his hold on her wrists. The minute he released her, she snatched up a rock and jackknifed upright, swinging at him for all she was worth, snarling. He slammed his chest against hers as he dove forward to avoid the blow, flattening her. They wrestled briefly over possession of the rock. He tightened his hand around her thin wrist until her hand went numb and she dropped it.

This time when she went still, he moved far more cautiously.

Her eyes were closed when he rose up enough to see her face. He studied her for any telltale signs that she was pretending and finally, satisfied, rolled away. Touching his fingers to her throat, he was relieved to discover that he had not suffocated her when he'd thrown his weight upon her, but without doubt he'd crushed her lungs enough to make her lose consciousness.

She looked like a broken doll.

Guilt swamped him, but it was followed quickly by irritation. He'd told her he wouldn't hurt her. If she had not tried to kill him with the rock....

After a moment, he scooped her limp body into his arms and moved back to the small pool of water. Settling her gently beside it, he scooped up a double handful of water and dashed it into her face. She came up swinging and he jumped back.

"Zoe's truth! You are a demon spawn!"

Coughing, sputtering, Tempest glared at the bear of a man hovering over her, scowling as if *he* were the injured party! "Asshole! What'd you do that for!" she demanded.

He sat back on his heels. "To wake you," he said through gritted teeth.

Tempest eyed him with disfavor. "I wasn't asleep," she snapped. "You nearly crushed me!"

"You tried to hit me in the head with a rock!"

Tempest looked away uncomfortably, covering her breasts with her hands. "I thought you were trying to … you know."

Kiran ignored the movement with an effort. He let out a bark of laughter. "I would sooner mate with a grat!"

Tempest glared at him, but decided she'd had worse insults thrown at her than being compared to the desert cat-like animal the natives called a grat. For her own part, she thought them rather cute--of course they were vicious killers, but they reminded her a lot of the pictures she'd seen of the cougar that had once inhabited the mountain areas of earth in the *days before*. They were not nearly as big, of course, in fact, from what she'd read, not much bigger than one of the domestic cats *the people* had once kept as pets.

Looking around, she saw that he'd left her shirt where they'd struggled. With an effort, she got to her feet and went to retrieve it. To her relief, there remained enough salvageable material to wrap the shirt around her breasts and tie it. It wasn't much, but it beat the hell out of going around bare-chested.

When she was decently covered, she turned around and studied the man again. "Will you share the water?" she asked tentatively.

He glared at her. "You were not inclined to share," he said coldly.

Tempest's shoulders slumped. She'd feared as much.

He was Niahian, though, of the nomad race of Niah. He would not remain long. They never did.

It was the one thing about Niah that had truly set them apart, *the people* and the Niahians. From the time they had crashed here, long before her memories, *the people* had set about making a colony, something of permanence since they knew they would never leave the desert world they'd crashed on. The Niahians were nomadic, always moving, and could no more understand the Earth survivors' determination to put down roots than *the people* could understand having none.

Physiologically, they were much the same. The Niahians were giants compared to humans, on average nearly a foot taller than their human counterparts. They were dark skinned--not surprising considering theirs was a desert world--and remarkably handsome--apparently ugly people did not breed on this world.

Kiran was exceptional, even for a Niahian. Despite her fear, Tempest had noticed that. He was also shorter and far broader than most that she'd seen, probably no more than six foot six ... which still put him a good foot taller than she was.

Or maybe not. Maybe she had just gotten so used to the Niahians he didn't seem so tall? *The people* were gone ... probably all dead by now, so it wasn't as if she had anyone to compare him with anymore.

Something clutched at her heart at the thought. Resolutely, she ignored it. If she gave in to fear and sorrow for all who had died, she would die, as well.

She wasn't certain what she wanted to do beyond living, but she didn't want to die.

When she saw that Kiran was occupied setting up his camp for the night, she moved, as quickly and quietly as possible, toward the rocks where he had ascended. He didn't seem to be paying her any attention, but she wasn't about to take a chance on leading him back to her shelter. She cast a glance back up after she'd reached the desert floor. Her heart skipped a beat when she saw that Kiran had moved to the ledge and stood watching her, his hands on his hips.

Shaking her surprise off, she whirled and darted away, slowing only when she reached cover and saw that he hadn't followed her. A wave of dizziness washed over her and she had to lean against a boulder until the weakness passed. It had been stupid to run when there had been no need. She was as acclimated to Niah as she could get, having been born here, but she had not been born of Niahian parents. Her physiology was designed for the planet of her parents' birth, Earth. Moreover, she had had little to eat in days and had not dared compensate by drinking more water for fear her little pool would dry up.

After a few moments, she began moving again, making a wide circle around the jumble of rocks that formed a tiny island in a sea of unending sand. When she'd traversed perhaps two thirds of its circumference, she began to climb again.

She'd found the tiny cave by purest accident. The colony, ravaged by some disease *the people* had neither resistance to, nor medicine for, had ceased to be a place of security. So many had died so quickly it had rapidly reached the point where there were not enough living to bury the dead.

Knowing that she too would die if she stayed, she had gathered together what she could carry after her parents died and struck off into the desert with her younger brother and her best friend. The tiny oasis here was one of the few *the people* had known of ... that she had known of ... and she had headed for it.

Two days into their trek, her friend, Georgia, had become ill. They'd pressed on anyway, knowing they had no chance at all of surviving unless they reached a source of water. Dallas, her little brother, had become ill on the third day out ... too ill to help her scrape out a shallow grave for Georgia ... too ill to continue. She'd discarded most of the supplies so that she could help him walk, worrying all day that he would not be able to walk at all by the following morning.

He hadn't. Just as Georgia had, he'd died during the night.

Tempest had buried him the next morning and kept moving, reaching the oasis at last the following day.

The desert was cold at night. She'd thought she had the sickness at first, but then realized that she was just cold, not feverish. She'd left most of her supplies, however, and wasn't strong enough to return for them.

She'd discovered the tiny cave while she was scavenging for rocks to use to build a crude shelter.

She would be dead now if she hadn't found it, and she had not been able to bring herself to leave it for any length of time. It was shelter from the elements, and located near a source of water. The water drew food. Sometimes days passed before she managed to catch anything small enough to kill, but she could count on the water drawing food to her.

One day, she would return to the colony ... when she thought it had been long enough that it was safe.

Pausing cautiously every few feet to listen for any sound that seemed out of place and to look around for any sign that she was being followed, it was almost dusk when Tempest reached her shelter at last. She smelled smoke long before she reached it. Thinking it was the fire of the Niahian, she ignored it along with the smell of cooking meat, though her stomach rumbled in response.

She didn't dare try to make fire herself. The Niahian was far too close and would almost certainly notice.

The fire, she discovered when she was within sight of it, was directly in front of the entrance to the cave. She stopped as if she'd hit a wall, too shocked to assimilate the implications at first. Even as she looked for the Niahian, however, she was grasped from behind in a hold she couldn't hope to break. Wrenching her head around, she gaped up at the Niahian.

"I have food, little grat. You are welcome to share if you will refrain from trying to hit me with rocks."

Tempest was too stunned to do more than nod.

Kiran studied her a long moment and finally released her slowly. When she did nothing more than stare at him, dumbfounded, he moved away and returned to the fire he had built from niahten. It was the one thing that Niah had in abundance ... besides the dull red sand that seemed to go on forever. One had only to dig down a few feet most anywhere on their world and cut it from Niah.

The priests considered it sacred, a gift of the Great One, Zoe. The Keepers of the Memory said that it was the decaying remains of what had once been plant life in the time before the rains had ceased to fall, when their world had been full of growing vegetation.

Regardless of who was right, Niahians in general considered it precious, despite its abundance, and used it sparingly. He had not been pleased to find the cave of the little strange one and see the signs that told him she used it every night, most likely only to give herself comfort.

He studied her as she settled herself cautiously opposite the fire. She was a lovely creature despite her condition, but she would not last long if left to her own devices. She was painfully thin, showing obvious signs of slow starvation, and pity, unwelcome but impossible to ignore, welled inside him when he looked at the bones that threatened to protrude from her skin. He was amazed that she had survived as long as she had.

There had been other orphans that had escaped the death village the Earth people had built, but those had been taken in by Niahians to rear with their own offspring. This one would have been older than most at the time, for she was obviously grown into a woman now, but still so young she could not have been much more than a child.

He could not leave her here. It went against every belief of his people to leave a helpless one--and yet he did not welcome the burden, not now, when he was on Hymria, the sacred journey that he hoped would lead him to the One. He must remain chaste to be considered worthy by Zoe. He must focus mind, body and spirit upon Hymria or the way would not be revealed to him.

The priests had told him the time had come. He must find the Storm, the One who commanded the elements, and lead him to the sacred temple of Zoe that legend held was beyond the far mountains in a secret valley long forgotten by all Niahians of living memory, for only when ... *if* the two of them joined on the sacred alter could the rains be summoned to make their world green once more.

He had been told that he alone, of all those born on Niah at the time of the first sign, had been born with the mark of the Guardian.

The coming of the star people, the Earthlings, had been the first sign.

Chapter Two

Tempest eyed the Niahian with disfavor. He was a bossy bastard! He'd had the nerve to forbid her to build a fire of her own in the cave where she usually slept. As much as she appreciated the food--which was not only more than she'd had in weeks, but also better than she'd been able to cook for herself--she did not appreciate being told what she could, or could not, do. She'd managed quite well by herself all this time--Ok, so not so well, but she'd managed just the same.

In all honesty, she supposed it *was* wasteful to build a second fire. Conservation hadn't been something *the people* had been really big on, particularly when it inconvenienced them, and look what had come of that--their world had been dying even before the 'planet killer' meteor had hit and the Earth's life cycle had collapsed like a row of dominos. This world being so arid, it made sense that they'd be more environmentally conscious.

And it *was* his world, after all.

On the other hand, he hadn't taken into consideration that, unlike him, she didn't have so much as a thin blanket to protect her from the incessant breezes. The fire didn't do much to keep her warm when it only warmed one side of her body at the time. Facing it, her front was warm and her backside freezing, or vice versa if she turned over. She'd tried sleeping in the cave without a fire and discovered it was just as miserable. The cave walls protected her from most of the wind, but without a fire....

If he'd been any kind of gentleman, he'd have offered her his blanket.

If she'd been bigger and stronger, she'd have taken it.

"I will share the blanket and the warmth of my body," he said suddenly, as if he'd read her thoughts.

Not that he'd have to be much of a mind reader to figure out she was too cold and miserable to sleep. She stared at him suspiciously for several moments, but the truth was she was beyond caring whether or not he demanded the use of her body in return. How bad could it be, after all? Granted, she didn't know a whole hell of a lot about copulating, but she wasn't completely ignorant. It had never taken her parents that long to do it--fifteen or twenty minutes, tops, of being groped, slobbered on and stabbed by his blunt member, and then she could be warm the rest of the night.

She got up and moved toward him. As she knelt beside him, he lifted the edge of the blanket and after only a slight hesitation, she slipped under it.

It was absolute heaven. Warmth instantly enveloped her. Goose bumps covered her from the crown of her head to her toes, making it feel as if her skin had shrunk until it was too small for her body, but it began to subside almost at once as the warmth soaked into her skin, then into her muscles. Slowly, the tension seeped from her, and her muscles began to relax. As it did, she began to realize that she was still cold--warmer by far than she had been, but not comfortably so.

There were two sources of heat now--the fire, and the heat radiating from his body--and she wasn't close enough to either to be comfortable.

Surprisingly, he hadn't said another word, or made any attempt to collect payment for his offer. Maybe she'd been wrong? Maybe he didn't actually have any interest in copulating and was just being polite?

After a few minutes, she inched a little closer to him--casually, as if she was just shifting to get comfortable.

"Be still. I can not sleep."

Tempest stiffened and let out an irritated huff. "I'm cold," she complained.

With a growl of impatience, he grasped her around the waist and hauled her back until she was laying full length against him. She lay stiffly for a few minutes, more than half expecting that, now, he would seize the advantage and expect her to perform for her comfort. Instead, he merely rubbed her arms briskly, tucked the blanket more tightly around them both and settled back.

"Better?"

She hesitated. She was warmer, that was for certain, but an almost weightless feeling clenched at her belly. She felt really strange, almost dizzy feeling his skin brush against hers, feeling every taut muscle of his body pressing into her. "Uh huh," she finally managed.

"Then sleep, little grat, so that I may sleep. I must travel far on the morrow."

Irritation surfaced. She didn't know why she was irritated. She should have just been grateful. He'd offered food, and comfort, and neither asked, nor demanded, anything at all in return except that she be still and let him sleep, but she was irritated.

"I wish you wouldn't keep calling me a grat," she muttered irritably.

"I do not know the name you are called," he said with determined patience.

"Tempest."

"Sleep, Tempest. I have come far, and have far to go."

"You didn't tell me your name," Tempest pointed out.

He sighed. "I am called Kiran."

Tempest swiveled around to look up at him. "Cool. I like the sound of that."

It had been an impulsive act, but she saw at once that, like most impulses, it would have been better to resist it. They were almost nose to nose. Kiran merely stared at her for several moments, his gaze slowly moving down her face until it reached her lips, hesitating there for several moments and then dropping lower still, resting in the vicinity of her breasts, which were now pressed firmly against his bare chest. He swallowed convulsively.

"Sleep," he said, his voice suddenly rough.

Unnerved, Tempest turned over once more. She discovered, however, that there was a very long, very hard ridge snuggling against her buttocks now. Alarm went through her, but so, too, did a deep sense of feminine satisfaction. She'd gotten a rise out of him without even trying. Despite the fact that he'd been careful to treat her like an annoyance, he obviously found her attractive-- didn't he?

Oddly enough, the realization comforted her as much as it pleased her. He was obviously not completely immune to her and yet he had made no attempt at all to take advantage of her. Feeling more secure than she could remember feeling in a very long time, she relaxed, snuggled closer, and slept.

The sun had barely risen over the horizon when Tempest awoke, cold and uncomfortable. Unwilling to open her eyes, she wiggled backwards, searching for the warmth that had sustained her through the night. She opened her eyes when she discovered it was gone and turned over.

Kiran, she discovered with stunned surprise, was gone.

She sat up and looked around. The fire had died to ashes. Around her was nothing but the same bare rocks that had greeted her every morning since she'd arrived at the watering hole. The only thing that had changed was that she was still huddled in the bedding and blanket that Kiran had provided.

He'd left them for her.

He had risen while she was sleeping, gathered his belongings and left.

Tempest searched for a sense of relief and failed to find one. She was alone again. She should be glad that he'd gone, but a sense of desperation such as she hadn't felt since she'd first come here filled her. She hadn't realized how afraid she was of being alone until Kiran had forced his unwelcome presence upon her. Now, looking forward to waking day after day, alone, without a face to look at or a voice to listen to filled her with the most terrible dread.

She was going to go mad if she stayed here alone--assuming she didn't die of starvation first.

Leaping to her feet, Tempest rushed over the rocks until she found a vantage point and looked around for Kiran. She saw him at last, his back to the bright red, rising sun, his silhouette already greatly diminished by distance. In a blind panic, she rushed back to the campsite, bundled the blanket and bedding and scrambled down the rocks to the desert floor. Kiran had disappeared over a dune by the time she left the rocky outcropping and her panic rose. Too frightened even to consider calling out to him, Tempest took off at a trot in the direction she'd last seen him. By the time she'd caught sight of him again, her panic had given way to breathlessness and she had time to consider whether it was even wise to allow him to know she was following him--particularly when she wasn't at all certain she should--and she was absolutely certain that he didn't want her to.

She stopped abruptly, indecisive now. Should she follow a man she didn't even know to god alone knew where? Or would she be better off just to stay where she was?

She had a bad feeling that she was making a terrible mistake, but she could no more resist the urge to follow Kiran that she could stop breathing. She couldn't think at all beyond the fear of being completely alone again.

He did not stop to rest. She hadn't given herself time to consider all the ramifications of trying to follow Kiran. He was considerably bigger than she was, which meant his stride was longer. Not only had he had a considerable head start on her, but he was accustomed to walking great distances without stopping to rest. She had to take two or three steps to every one he took and, as the day wore on, she fell further and further behind.

She was too tired at first, and too driven, to be afraid. As Niah's great red sun began its downward arch, however, and exhaustion threatened to overwhelm her, fear lifted its ugly head.

She'd lost sight of Kiran. She wasn't even completely certain she was still following him, but she was fairly convinced that she wouldn't be able to find her way back to her safe haven. When she stopped at last to catch her breath and looked back, she could see nothing but endless sand in every direction. As high as the outcropping of rock that had provided her little cave had seemed when she was standing near its summit, it was little more than a bump in the landscape.

She stood indecisively for some time but finally realized that her choice had been made even before she had left. She must find Kiran now if she was to have any chance of surviving.

She was heartened somewhat when she realized she could still see faint impressions of his footprints in the shifting sand. Wishing she'd had the presence of mind to drink her fill of water before she'd charged off, she gathered as much moisture into her mouth as she could, readjusted her burden, and continued, scanning the sand ahead of her now for signs of his passing.

Fear again assailed her as the sun dipped below the horizon and it became harder and harder to see the faint impressions in the sand and finally impossible. She stopped, knowing it would be madness to keep going when she could no longer be certain of his direction. If she tried, she would be hopelessly lost and then she would die because she had no water and only Kiran would know where there was a watering hole.

Resisting the urge to weep, she lowered the bundle to the sand and sat, trying to catch her breath, trying to gather the energy to spread the bedding as one by one the stars winked through the darkening canopy of sky overhead. As the blackness of night surrounded her, however, she caught a glimpse of light quite near the ground and her heart leapt in her chest. A campfire!

It was small in the distance--at least another hour's walk, she thought, but, tired as she was she realized she would far prefer walking all night to sleeping alone in the desert. Then, too, she needed water. Besides, this might be her only chance to catch up to Kiran.

It occurred to her that it might not be Kiran's campfire at all, but she knew it was most likely his--and what choice did she have anyway?

The smell of food lightened her steps when she was close to flagging. Her stomach growling in anticipation, she hurried onward. Ahead, she saw a jumble of ragged shapes that told her she was nearing an outcropping of rock similar to the one she'd lived on for months. A couple of stunted, scraggly trees dotted the mound and even a few emaciated bushes and she realized this must be a far more luxurious watering hole than hers--which was probably why she hadn't seen a soul in months. The little pool she'd staked claim to was hardly worthy of any Niahian going out of their way for.

Caution overcame her as she reached the first of the rocks, stubbing her toes and sending loose scrabble in every direction. She stopped, listening. When she heard no sounds indicating that anyone had heard her clumsy arrival, she moved more carefully among the rocks, making her way toward the glow of the campfire and finally stopping behind a rock to peer over it.

Kiran was sitting beside the fire. What unnerved her, however, was that he appeared to be looking straight at her. Her heart skidded to a rough halt, then banged against her rib cage. Before she could dismiss it as pure imagination, however, he spoke.

"I should not have called you a grat. You are as clumsy as a hrzog."

Tempest glared at him, tempted to stay where she was considering his nasty remark. The hrzog was a rodent, and virtually blind and deaf, depending on its virtually impenetrable armor-plated hide to protect it from predators.

She stood up. "How did you know it was me?"

"I smelled you."

"I don't stink!" Tempest snapped indignantly as she stepped from behind the rock where she'd been hiding. She might be dusty--it was impossible not to be on such a planet--but she bathed regularly.

His lips twitched. "I did not say you smelled badly, only that I smelled you."

Tempest frowned. "It's the same thing ... isn't it?"

"It is not."

She was fairly certain she'd been insulted just the same, but she went to the campfire anyway, plunking her--his bundle down and then sitting on top of it. He nodded his head. "There is water there."

Swallowing convulsively, Tempest leapt to her feet and rushed toward it.

"Do not drink too fast or you will be sick."

She ignored him. She'd survived this long without him in the desert. She knew she could only allow herself a little water. Once she drank a little, his previous remark came back to her, however, and she splashed water over herself in a half hearted attempt at a bath. She was shivering when she returned to the campfire. He glanced at her and then looked away again just as quickly and frowned.

Tempest stared at him in confusion and finally looked down at herself. A blush rose in her cheeks when she realized she'd soaked the cloth tied around her breasts. Wet, it was nearly transparent and worse, her nipples were standing out like little pebbles.

She moved a little further from the firelight, pulling the wet fabric from her skin and sloughing the water off her arms and legs the best she could. She felt like a block of ice by the time she was dry enough to feel comfortable about moving closer to the fire again. Without looking at her, Kiran handed her a plate of food.

"You should not have followed me."

Tempest looked down at her food for several moments, uncomfortable. She couldn't very well say she hadn't been following him. "I'm sorry. I just didn't want to be alone anymore."

He shook his head. "I would have come back for you. Where I travel ... I must go alone."

Tempest gaped at him. "You would?" She thought it over for several moments and felt a surge of anger at the chastising note in his voice. "And I was supposed to know this?"

He frowned. "It is not the way of my people to leave the helpless to fend for themselves."

Tempest was insulted all over again. She was *not* helpless. "Well, I don't know your people so I could hardly be expected to know that about them, could I?" Settling in a bit of a huff, she turned her attention to her food, demolishing it in short order. She would say one thing for him. The man could cook. "Where are you going, anyway?"

"I am on Hymria, vision quest."

Tempest thought that over for a while, but it finally occurred to her that she remembered something from her history lessons that sounded a lot like that, some sort of ritual the ancient tribes of Earth had once practiced when they hoped for a sign from their gods. She asked him if that was what it was. He looked at her in surprise and finally nodded.

"The star people practice this ritual, as well?"

Tempest gaped at him, but fortunately it occurred to her that it would be rude to point out that it was the uncivilized ancients of her world that had practiced such customs. Not that she could see any reason not to be rude when he'd been rude to her--except that she wasn't completely certain that he'd been intentionally rude. She merely shrugged finally. "Once they did, but that was a long time ago. I don't honestly know that much about it--except from history lessons."

He nodded. "I must go alone to the sacred mountain. There I will purify myself --mind, body and spirit--and if I am worthy, the way will be shown to me."

"Oh," Tempest said, losing interest. "Well--maybe I could just go with you as far as the nearest village?" she suggested hopefully.

"What is village?"

"Where a lot of people live closely together … in shelters."

"Like the place of the star people?"

"Yeah!" Tempest said. It seemed odd to be referred to as the star people, but she had no doubt that he was talking about their colony.

He shook his head. "There are none on Niahian. The old ones tell that once there were such places, but that was long before living memory … before Niahian became as it is now. Now we must travel always, looking for water and food, and we must leave before it is depleted and allow it time to replenish before we return again to that place."

Tempest swallowed her disappointment with an effort. "I guess I'll have to stay here then."

He thought about it for several moments and finally shook his head. "This place is not safe. You must return to the other place. I will come for you there when I have done what I must do and take you to those who will be willing to care for you."

Tempest gaped at him. "But … why?"

"Life is abundant here. Many tribes visit this place, some who do not value life as we do. You will be safer at the other place."

"I think I should just stay here," Tempest said stubbornly. "Maybe somebody will come along that won't mind if I travel with them."

"And maybe not."

Tempest looked away, feeling a blush mount her cheeks again. "I can't find my way back," she confessed.

Kiran gaped at her for several moments as if she'd suddenly grown two heads. "You must follow your nose."

Tempest glared at him. "You must have a better sense of smell than I do, because I sure as hell can't sniff my way back to that place like a damned bloodhound."

Kiran looked at her with a mixture of suspicion and surprise. "You truly can not?"

Tempest gave him a look. "No, I truly can not," she said in a sarcastic tone of voice.

His lips tightened at her tone, but he said nothing else for some moments, apparently, from his expression, not terribly pleased about the options that left him with. "I will have to lead you back," he said finally.

It wasn't the solution Tempest had been hoping for and her disappointment made her angry. "That would be a real waste of time."

"Yes, but I can not afford to do otherwise."

"I won't be in your way. I promise," Tempest wheedled, deciding that it would probably not please him if she told him she'd just follow him again.

He shook his head, rising abruptly. "I must be pure of mind, body and spirit or I will not be shown the way. You are a distraction I can not afford."

Tempest gaped at him blankly. "I can be quiet."

He rolled his eyes, shook his head and stalked off toward the pool of water. Tempest stared after him, trying to figure out why he thought she would interfere with his purity. A thought occurred to her quite suddenly, but she dismissed it almost immediately. He couldn't be talking about sex … could he? Impure? She did another mental scan for references in her studies and finally concluded that, as archaic as it might seem to her, his people still undoubtedly considered sex, or the lack of it, in the light of pure, or impure. It struck her as funny, not just his view of sex, but the fact that he found her distracting. Why would a gorgeous creature like that find someone as ordinary as her attractive?

She frowned then. She hadn't really had the opportunity to experiment with her sexuality or even to begin to discover if males found her attractive. There had been a boy in school that she had really liked, but her parents had said that she was too young to be socializing intimately and before she'd reached the age they found permissible, disease had spread through the colony and everyone had died. Before, though, when it had seemed they had their lives before them, most everyone her age had been obsessed with the possibility of sexual encounters, the boys most particularly. Her friend, Georgia, who'd been a year older than her and allowed to socialize, used to giggle and tell her boys could think of little else.

She glanced at Kiran speculatively, but, try though she might, she simply could not picture him behaving at all the way the boys in the colony had behaved. Maybe she'd been mistaken and that wasn't what he'd meant at all? There was one way to find out, of course, but she was uncomfortably certain that she hadn't mastered the art of flirtation. Kiran was bound to think her ridiculous if she even tried any of the silly things she could remember the other girls doing.

She was still debating whether to join him beside the pool and try her hand at flirting when a scream tore through the night air that made her hair fairly stand on end.

Chapter Three

Tempest spun in a circle, wondering from which direction the threat would come, when something shot past her in a blur of motion. As her stunned gaze followed the movement, she looked up to see Kiran whirl to face the oncoming threat, his shock mirroring her own.

With another scream, the creature launched itself at him. Kiran let out a grunt of pained surprise as the animal's momentum threw him off balance and he crashed to the ground. The creature moved like lightning, clawing and biting at him in a blur of motion that made it almost impossible to deflect the animal's assault.

"Stop!" Tempest yelled, abruptly shaking her stupor as she saw blood oozing from dozens of wounds on Kiran's hands, arms and chest. To both her surprise and Kiran's, the grat jerked at the sound of her voice and whirled to look at her, its red eyes glowing in the light of the moons. Scooping up a handful of rocks, Tempest began pelting the small cat-like creature. "Shoo!"

It let out a cry of pain as several of her missiles found their mark, leapt off of Kiran and disappeared into the darkness as suddenly as it had appeared.

Gasping with a combination of effort and fear, Tempest stood stock still for several moments and finally rushed to Kiran as he pushed himself up to a sitting position.

"Are you hurt badly?"

He winced, but shook his head. "She did not reach my throat."

Tempest knelt beside him, looking him over worriedly, but she saw that he had not tried to minimize his injuries. There were a dozen or more deep scratches and several nasty looking bites, but none appeared particularly life threatening. Ripping a scrap from her tattered shirt, she dipped it into the water, grasped one of his hands and began to wipe the blood away so that she could see the injuries better. Despite her concern for him, or perhaps because of it, her heart jumped and her stomach clenched as she looked down at his hand, felt the warmth of his palm seeping into hers. The sharp contrast in their skin tones fascinated her almost as much as the difference in sizes, making her feel, strangely enough, dominated--fragile next to him even though he'd given no outward appearance of doing so.

"You do not need to do this," he said tightly.

She glanced up at his comment. There was pain in the taut lines of his face, but something else, as well, that made her feel suddenly self-conscious about the fact that she'd knelt virtually astride one of his hard, muscular thighs. She'd thought nothing about it when she'd done it, intent only upon getting close enough to him where he sprawled on the ground to examine his injuries. "Don't be silly. You're hurt. Do you have medicines with you?"

"Yes. In my pouch." He sounded relieved.

Smiling at him reassuringly, Tempest left him to bathe the wounds while she went to retrieve his pouch. He joined her near the fire while she was still searching for it. Settling beside her, he took the pack from her and emptied it beside the fire. His medicinal pack was at the bottom of the pack. They both reached for it at the same time, but Kiran was faster. "I can apply the salve myself," he said when she tried to take it from him.

Tempest sat back, torn between hurt and confusion. "You can't see to put it on yourself. I'll be careful not to hurt you."

He ignored her comment, dipping his fingers into the vial of salve and swabbing it over the abrasions. Tempest watched him critically, still feeling more than a little hurt and angry that he'd rejected her offer to help. When he'd finished and reached to place the vial back in his pouch, she took it from him and moved closer. "You missed more than you hit," she said chidingly as she carefully dabbed the spots he'd neglected.

To her surprise, he caught her upper arms in a grip painful enough that she winced. Immediately, he relaxed his hold, but he didn't release her, merely stared into her eyes for one long moment before he set her firmly away from him.

"Thank you."

Tempest's surprise gave way to hurt and confusion once more. She stared down at the salve on her fingers for a couple of moments and finally replaced the top on the vial and dropped it into his pouch. "You're welcome," she said, standing abruptly and moving to the pool to wash the salve from her hands.

When she'd finished, she stood, contemplating the reflection of the moons on the water's surface for a few moments and finally returned to the fire, settling on the opposite side from him and staring into the flames.

She hadn't fully appreciated the stupidity of following Kiran off until now and wondered what had possessed her to act without fully considering the matter. Her parents had often chided her for being impulsive, but she had learned better, or thought she had, in the time she had been alone, knowing her situation was so precarious that she couldn't afford to act without thinking everything through very carefully if she wanted to stay alive.

"I was … surprised, but grateful, that you were able to chase the grat off. This is strange. Ordinarily, they will turn and attack in such a situation."

Tempest merely shrugged. "Surprised me, too, but I couldn't think of anything else to do."

"Perhaps the grat sensed that you were as ferocious?"

He smiled when he said it and she realized he was trying to lessen her sense of discomfort. As much as she appreciated the effort, however, it didn't particularly make her feel better. She had encroached when she had no right to, made demands by following him off when she'd had no business doing so, and he'd slapped her hands. It would have been easier if she could've just disliked him and felt that it was her decision to leave and go back, if she could have blamed him for being a hateful bastard, instead of having to accept the fault as her own. "I should have bashed its head in," she said, willing to focus her anger on the animal.

Kiran frowned. "I am glad you did not. It was a young cat, and most likely starved to desperation or it would not have attacked."

Tempest immediately felt diminished in his eyes. She shrugged, trying to thrust the sense away, but felt a sudden empathy for the creature that had frightened her and pity as she realized that it had seemed terribly thin. She had never seen one of the animals at such close range. She supposed it might be the thick pelt of orange-red fur that ordinarily gave them the appearance of being fat and round. This one had had more of the look of an earth fox than a cat, and a hungry one at that, and she couldn't picture it as appearing fat and round even at a distance.

The poor thing! It must have been hungry to take on something as big as Kiran.

Now that she thought about it, it was strange that the animal had run right past her and focused on Kiran. Maybe, though, that had been because he was kneeling by the pool and had appeared smaller at that moment?

"I've been thinking about what you said earlier," she said, studying her toes instead of looking at him. "I think I will go back."

He frowned. "You said that you could not find your way."

Tempest shrugged, but refused to meet his eyes. "I lied," she lied. "Nothing to it, really." Not that she had any intention of going back. Regardless of what Kiran had said about this place, it was far better than the watering hole where she'd been and she thought she might survive far better here.

"It will be best if I take you."

"Not for you. And I don't need your help," Tempest said, keeping her voice carefully neutral with an effort. "You said you were on a quest."

Kiran frowned. "This is a matter of utmost importance or I would willingly take you with me."

Tempest nodded. "I got that impression. Look, don't worry about me. I've been fine all this time."

Kiran shook his head. "You are not fine, little grat. You are not much more than bones. I will have no peace in my mind if I leave you to find your way back alone. I will take you. When I am done, I will come back for you."

Tempest couldn't control the blush of embarrassment at his comment. The sense of hurt that had not diminished a great deal flooded through her with a vengeance. Bones? And she had flattered herself to think he found her attractive! Wishful thinking, she supposed. She ought to have known better. The pain and humiliation made her angry. She realized, however, that there was no point in arguing with him. He refused to see reason, and she certainly couldn't stop the big ox from doing whatever he wanted to.

There was no hope for it if she wanted to stay here. She'd have to wait until he fell asleep and slip away and hide. Otherwise, he was going to drag her back to that pile of rocks where she'd spent the best part of two years. Without another word, she got up and unrolled the bedding. Spreading the blanket over it, she crawled in and turned her back to him. All things considered, she doubted very much that he would expect to share the bedding with her. She hoped not, anyway. It would make it much harder to slip off if he was lying next to her.

"I regret that it must be this way."

Tempest didn't bother to answer, merely nodding that she understood.

He was silent for some moments. "I am curious about your name. Does it have meaning?"

Tempest was tempted to pretend she'd drifted off to sleep and ignore him, but decided she didn't want to appear too sullen. It might make him suspicious. "I doubt you'd understand if I explained it."

"Why?"

"Because you've probably never seen one. Actually, I haven't either, but I know my Earth history so I at least have some idea of it."

"Explain."

Tempest turned over and looked at him. "It's a storm. On Earth, water would fall from the sky. They called it rain, and when it was driven by hard wind, it was a tempest."

Kiran's face went perfectly still. "What?"

"I told you you wouldn't understand."

He shook his head. "It is the same as storm?"

Tempest shrugged. "I guess. I think it's more like the word for a particular kind of storm, though."

He said nothing and Tempest considered leaving it at that, but she was determined to act as if she had nothing important on her mind. "Does your name have a meaning?"

He frowned. "It means 'guardian of the storm'."

Tempest's brows rose. "Really? That's weird, huh?"

Kiran didn't answer, however. He seemed deep in thought and after waiting for several minutes to see if he would pursue the conversation, Tempest settled once more, this time facing him. He was still staring into the fire when she lost the battle against weariness and dozed off.

Kiran lifted his gaze from the dancing flames and stared at Tempest when he sensed that she slept. As the shock wore off, denial sprang up to take its place in his chaotic thoughts. It could be no more than a strange sort of coincidence, he assured himself, though uneasiness persisted and refused to be subjugated. The legend had been committed to his memory long ago and although he had repeated it over and over to himself as he sat staring into the fire, searching for truth, he could not recall a single passage that had led him to the conclusion that *the Storm*, like himself, would be a man, a native of his own world. And yet, everyone, even the ancient ones, the Keepers of the Memory, believed *the*

Storm the legends foretold would be a warrior such as himself ... greater even than himself.

This ... female ... was barely old enough to even be considered a woman. To his mind, she was more child than adult, and beyond that, as frail a creature as could be imagined. She was not even Niahian!

Was it at all possible that everyone had misinterpreted the prophesy?

He shook that doubt off. The Keepers had studied the prophesies endlessly, pondering each word, debating each meaning. They could not *all* be wrong.

He was to go to the sacred mountain so that he would be shown the way to *the Storm.* The prophesy had made that much clear ...and, that being the case, he knew he must simply be allowing his imagination to take hold of him.

Perhaps her family had heard the legend and had simply decided to name her that? He knew very little about the star people. Perhaps it was common to name females such names. She'd said the word was from her own world. Perhaps they had chosen names for their offspring to remind them of their world?

The uneasiness receded. Finally, realizing that he was weary and it was growing very late, he lay down next to the fire and forced himself to relax and seek his rest.

* * * *

Tempest wasn't certain what woke her, but she became abruptly wide awake. Sitting up, she looked around the campsite. Kiran, she saw, appeared to be sleeping. She studied him for several moments and finally decided that he really was asleep.

A faint sound caught her attention and she turned toward it, gasping when she saw two angry red eyes peering at her from the darkness beyond the firelight. She relaxed only fractionally when she realized it was the grat. For several moments they merely stared at one another. Finally, Tempest felt around on the ground for a good sized rock to pitch at the animal. She was on the point of doing so when she remembered what Kiran had said.

Well, she didn't feel sorry enough for the grat to allow it to gnaw on her!

They'd had food left over, however.

After a moment's debate, she moved quietly toward the bundled food and unwrapped it. Tearing off a piece, she tossed it toward the cat. The eyes disappeared, but she could see no sign of the animal moving to retrieve the offering. She shrugged. It was wild.

Most likely it wouldn't come near the meat, but at least she'd tried.

She was on the point of bundling the meat up again when it occurred to her that she'd probably be hungry herself before she managed to find food on her own. Tearing off half of what was left, she tied the bundle once more and tiptoed quietly away from the campfire, heading away from the grat.

One of the moons had set and it was a good deal darker than it had been earlier, difficult to see more than a few yards away. Tempest regretted falling asleep. If she'd only managed to stay awake, she would've had a far easier time of finding a hiding place. As it was, she had to move slowly and very carefully just to keep from making noise that might wake Kiran. Finally, she decided she had put enough distance between herself and the campsite to move more quickly and less cautiously and she began to scramble over the rocks more quickly. She did not have much time to find shelter. The small moon was dipping toward the horizon and, except for the feeble light from the stars, she would be left in total darkness before much more time passed.

Relief filled her when she reached the desert floor at last. She hesitated, wondering it Kiran would bother to look for her or only be satisfied that she had taken herself off and relieved him of any responsibility for her. Finally, she decided that being followed by Kiran was probably the least of her worries. There was no point in wasting more time to try to throw off a pursuit that was unlikely. She knew one grat inhabited the oasis. It didn't seem likely there would be another one since they were territorial, but there might well be other, even more dangerous animals. With that thought prodding her, she hurried along the desert floor, studying the rocks above her for some sign of a crevice or cave.

She had walked and searched for more than an hour and the small moon was already dipping below the horizon when she spotted what appeared to be the entrance to a cave about half way up the jumble of rocks. It was difficult to be certain from this distance and might be no more than a slight crevice, but since she was running out of options, she decided to climb and hope for the best.

It was almost pitch black by the time she reached the general area where she'd spied what she thought might be an opening in the rock. Almost blind now, she felt around, searching for it and finally discovered the opening by falling over a rock and into the mouth of the cave. She froze as she hit the ground, listening for any sounds of an inhabitant. When she heard nothing, she felt around for a handful of rocks. Backing away, she tossed the rocks inside before scrambling up onto one of the boulders at the opening. She could hear the dull thud of the rocks striking other rocks but, to her relief, no growls or sounds of scurrying feet. Satisfied, she crawled inside, feeling her way carefully and finally settled with her back against the smoothest, flattest stone she could find. It gave her the creeps, sitting in a darkness so thick she could almost feel it, but she was out of the wind and relatively warm. Once it was light she could explore the cave more thoroughly and decide if she wanted to remain or look for other shelter.

It comforted her to see that, now that she was inside the cave, the starlight made the world outside look far brighter. Dropping her cheek to her knees, she focused on the light outside. Her eyes were just beginning to drift closed when movement outside jerked her awake once more.

It was the grat ... and it was heading straight for her.

Chapter Four

The grat stopped just outside the cave entrance, sniffing the air and then dropping its head to sniff at the ground. A low growl rumbled from its chest and then it slunk forward until it was just inside the entrance of the cave, its red eyes glowing malevolently, staring unblinkingly into Tempest's.

Either her luck was running true and she'd managed to wander around the pile of rocks until she'd found the grat's cave, or the grat had followed her because of the meat she'd brought with her. At the thought of the food she'd brought, two things occurred to her simultaneously--she did not want to be holding something that was going to draw the thing closer, and, if it had followed the smell of the meat, then tossing it to the grat might appease it.

Tearing a small piece off, Tempest threw it. The tidbit landed almost directly between the grat's forelegs and it jumped back, startled. Cautiously, it eased forward again, sniffing the cave floor in tight little circles until it found what it sought. It looked up and directly toward her once more even before it had finished eating it.

The second piece Tempest tossed hit the grat on the forehead and bounced away, rolling to a stop only a few feet from

Tempest's foot and her heart skipped several beats as the grat scrambled after it. The idea had been to get the thing away from her, preferably away from the cave entrance altogether so that she could escape, not tempt it closer. She knew she had to wait until she had the grat's attention again before she threw the last of the meat, however, otherwise it might be hard to convince the thing that she didn't have it anymore.

The next time the grat looked up expectantly, Tempest hurled the remainder of her meat as far as she could send it. The grat ducked, apparently thinking she'd thrown a stone at it, but its nose automatically followed the arc as the scent of the meat whizzed past its head and, with a hopeful growl, it launched itself in pursuit. The moment the grat shot out of the cave, Tempest scrambled out behind it. Unfortunately, she emerged just in time to see the grat trotting back triumphantly with the meat in its mouth. Tempest froze, staring at it, but the grat stopped well before it reached her and focused its attention on devouring the meat.

Slowly, Tempest began inching away, her gaze fixed on the grat as it ate quickly and looked up at her hopefully once more.

"Do not move!"

As quietly as it was said, the voice was so unexpected Tempest jumped, glancing quickly toward Kiran as he emerged slowly from the predawn gloom. The grat's reaction was far more violent. It whirled toward Kiran, all four legs splayed in a stance that dared him to approach. The bristly hair that ran from the crown of its head to the tip of its tail stood straight up, making the small animal seem suddenly twice its size.

Tempest stared at it in amazement. For several moments she wondered if it actually had doubled in size. As it growled threateningly at Kiran, however, and she saw the bunching of its muscles that indicated it was about to leap toward him, she strode briskly toward it and popped it on top of its head. "Stop that!"

The grat jumped, cringing away from her, its head whipping in her direction. It stared up at her indignantly for several moments and then, to her surprise, trotted off a short distance and flattened itself against the rock, its bushy tail slapping angrily against the rock as it divided its attention between Kiran and Tempest.

Kiran, she saw when she looked at him once more, was studying her with a mixture of disapproval, surprise and something else she couldn't quite identify.

"Why did you leave?" he asked finally, both anger and confusion in his voice.

Tempest looked away. "Because I didn't want to go back and I knew you would make me if I stayed."

"You are a stubborn female."

Tempest looked at him indignantly. She was not appeased in the least by the faint smile that now played around his mouth, but it made her heart flutter strangely and the muscles in her belly clench. "Because what I want is not the same as what you want? Or because I am just as determined to do what I want to do as you are?"

He frowned. "Life is not always a matter of simply deciding what one wants for oneself," he said harshly. "I did not dismiss your needs only because I wished it. I have been given a task which is vital to all of Niah. It is mine by right of birth, and a great honor to be chosen. It is a destiny I wish to fulfill, but not one that I chose. The prophesy unfolds, and I must follow my destiny for the good of all."

Tempest was skeptical and made no attempt to hide it. She didn't doubt for a moment that Kiran believed what he'd told her, or that he was a capable warrior, but he was only one man, after all, no matter how great a warrior he might be. How could one man do anything that would affect the whole world?

Kiran flushed angrily at her expression. "I know you do not understand. You are a child of the stars. You do not understand our ways or our beliefs."

The comment irritated Tempest. "You didn't seem to think of me as a child the other night. Or was that something else I felt nosing around my backside?"

Kiran stared at her hard, his color slowly darkening. It was obvious from his expression that he was more than a little tempted to pretend he had no idea what she was talking about. After a moment, however, a hint of amusement gleamed in his eyes. "A serpent has no mind and can not consider its actions. It does not always obey my commands. It acts solely upon instinct, seeking a warm, dark place in which to hide."

From what she knew about the male of her own species which, granted, wasn't much, it was an honest answer--insulting, but true. Apparently, men were men, whatever part of the universe they hailed from.

There was nothing in his expression to suggest that he'd said it to be nasty. It was still a low blow, whether intentional or not, and one she would've liked to dispute. Unfortunately, her experience with the male of the species was virtually nil. There had been a painfully brief period of time when she had attained an age where she had begun to see boys in a new light, when she had made awkward attempts to gain their attention by flirting. With impatience and excitement, she had looked forward to the time when her parents considered her old enough to begin to experiment with her sexuality in her search for a compatible male to share her domicile.

The sickness that spread through the colony like wildfire had changed all that. It had banished all thoughts from everyone's minds except survival. She had not been able to think beyond surviving since that time, had spared little thought to a possible future when it was difficult even to get through each day. She had had no opportunity to begin to understand better.

His comments brought to mind something her best friend, Georgia, had once told her, however. She'd said boys rarely had another thought in their heads beyond sex, but was that only young males? Or all males? And would that include males of other species? And if it was true, then how was a female to know if a male was particularly interested in her?

She blushed, embarrassed to realize she had been ignorant enough to think that Kiran's reaction must mean he was interested in her as a woman. In spite of all that he'd said to contradict it, she'd been certain he must think she was attractive or he wouldn't have reacted in such a way. She should have known better, considering his comment about her bones.

She didn't know why it hurt. She ought to be glad. She *was* glad. At least now she knew, without a doubt, that she didn't have to worry about him sweating and grunting and slobbering all over her.

Not that it looked like that would be anything she'd have to worry about anyway, considering he'd made it clear she wasn't welcome. She didn't believe for a moment that he had any intention of coming back for her, or ever had. He'd just said it to make her feel better.

She shrugged. "Just so long as he doesn't take it into his head to wander around my.... Uh." She felt a blush brighten her cheeks and stumbled to a halt, horrified by what she'd almost said. "I never did like the idea of all the grunting and sweating and slobbering that...." *That* made it better! She looked away, unable for the moment to think of anything to say to redirect the conversation to something a little less uncomfortable.

Kiran closed his eyes, willing the images she'd conjured to leave his mind, fighting the urge to offer to teach her the joys of the flesh. His instincts had been right. He was going to have a hell of a time purifying mind, body and spirit if Tempest remained so temptingly close. He would have with most any female companion, but he found that, against all reason, he was drawn to Tempest far more powerfully than he could recall being attracted to any female of his own kind.

It was not something he wanted to explore ... not now, certainly, perhaps not ever, for she was not of his kind and it seemed doubtful that two who were so different could find harmony.

He did not want to leave her here, however, and she was just strong willed enough to follow him back if he did take the time to return her to the other place.

"You may come with me ... if that is what you wish. I will have no peace if I leave you here." He would have no peace in taking her, but at least he would know he had not left her in danger.

Tempest looked at him sharply, but she wasn't about to question the invitation, or spurn it only to save face. She would've preferred to stay at the oasis than return to the place where she had spent nearly two years of her life, but she far preferred being with him, however reluctant his invitation. After a moment, she nodded and they returned to their campsite of the night before, gathered Kiran's belongings and set out just as the great red sun of Niah crested the horizon.

They had been walking for several hours when Tempest cast a glance back, wondering if she could find her way back to the last oasis if she ever found herself in need. To her surprise and dismay, she saw an undulating movement and realized the grat, crouched low to the ground, was following at a cautious distance. She glanced at Kiran to see if he'd noticed, but he had not even stopped. Finally, she dismissed it, certain the grat would not follow them long before it realized she wouldn't be tossing out more food to it.

When the sun reached its peak, they stopped to rest, relieve themselves and eat. She discovered then that she'd underestimated the little grat's determination. The long, coarse red hair that covered the animal blended surprisingly well with the dull red sand of Niah's great desert as it flattened itself against the ground, but she saw it slink down the side of the dune behind them before flattening itself at the bottom of the shallow trough that separated the two dunes.

Finding she'd lost her appetite at the reminder of how desperately starved the poor little thing was, Tempest casually tossed the remains of her meal over her shoulder.

"She will continue to follow if you continue to feed her," Kiran said without glancing at her, a frown of disapproval drawing his dark brows together.

Tempest flushed, but there seemed no point in trying to deny that she'd just thrown the remains of her meal to the grat. "She's hungry."

"She is a wild thing. She must learn to fend for herself, or die. It is the word of the Great One, Zoe."

Tempest glared at him. "So, only the strong are worthy of surviving?" she demanded tightly.

Kiran nodded. "Destruction will follow disharmony. The strong live to create others of their kind of equal or greater strength. The weak die to replenish Niah. They do not breed others that are as weak or weaker."

The balance of nature it had been called on Earth, and Tempest was well aware from her studies that that law had proven true. Once the meteor had upset the balance, the entire ecosystem of Earth had crashed. It seemed odd to hear much the same from a being of another race on another world, but she supposed it was human conceit to believe *the people* were the only ones who could understand this immutable truth.

All the same, and despite the fact that he'd made no reference to *the people*, she felt his comments were intended to remind her that *the people* had ignored the law and perished because of it. Or, perhaps, the fact that they'd all died had proven his point. Either way, she resented it on a very personal level, feeling that it was yet another jab at her own weakness, not just the weakness of *the people* in general.

Stature didn't ensure strength anymore than the lack of it implied inherent weakness. "Just because something appears weak, it doesn't necessarily follow that it is," she said tightly. "And I wouldn't think this Zoe you talk about would consider it *your* decision to make. I expect *he* does his own deciding."

Kiran studied her a long moment. "She."

Tempest's brows rose. "She?"

"It is the female who gives life. The Great One, Zoe, naturally, is female. It is *She* who keeps the balance. *She* does not interfere and we are forbidden to interfere."

Tempest was still gaping at him in surprise when he stood, gathered his pack and set off once more without another word. "The female does not just give life and abandon it!" she called after him. "She nurtures her young until it's strong enough to fend for itself!"

Kiran stopped abruptly and turned back to look at her in surprise. "You understand the way of Zoe?"

Tempest gave him a look. Obviously the Niahian's were as conceited in their knowledge as humans, certain no others could be as intelligent, or understand the things they understood. "I understand the nature of the female of the species … I *am* a woman, whatever you think."

Kiran's lips tightened in annoyance. "You are still more child than woman or you would know what I think," he growled, then turned away and started off once more.

This time Tempest gaped blankly at his retreating back for a good two minutes before she shook off her surprise and trotted after him, more thoroughly confused than ever. Her inexperience must be more obvious than she'd thought, or maybe he only presumed she was inexperienced because he could tell she was young? Well, she *was* inexperienced, but she wasn't completely ignorant, whatever he thought. Sexuality had been part of the school curriculum. She'd been thoroughly educated on every aspect of copulation, from the mundane to every conceivable, and some pretty inconceivable, variations.

It was just that, not having any first hand experience, she had a hard time imagining it in association with herself, and theory was different than actual practice.

If she hadn't known better, she would think he was deliberately trying to confuse her. Why couldn't he just say he did, or did not, like her in a sexual context? One minute he would say, or do, something that would make her think he did, and the very next minute, he'd dispute it.

As interesting as the puzzle was, she set it aside after a while when it occurred to her to wonder what might lie ahead. She hadn't been given to thinking about the future as a destination, or as something she need plan for. She could barely remember a time when she had looked beyond the next meal. Before, she supposed she'd really been too young to consider what sort of life she would have when she left her parents' domicile to make one for herself. She had tried to imagine sharing it with first one and then another of her classmates, but she hadn't really been able to fix it in her mind. It had been hazy, almost dream-like and she'd always ended up picturing her parents instead.

Now she began to wonder what sort of life Kiran had. He had said they never stayed in one place long, but it was hard to imagine traveling endlessly. Surely, they must have some settlements somewhere on this vast world?

She shook the thought off finally, realizing that she could not plan any sort of future when so much was still unknown to her. Perhaps, if Kiran did not want her for a companion, she would find one when he returned to his own people?

She needed a companion. She hadn't realized it before, because she'd had no choice but to live alone, but she was used to being surrounded by people. She needed the stimulus of interaction with other beings as much as she needed water and food.

She supposed it was her own needs that had prompted her to befriend the grat as much as her realization of its needs. The thought made her glance back. She didn't know whether to be glad or sorry when she saw it was still trailing them.

Kiran wasn't going to like it.

On the other hand, it was easy to see she couldn't really depend upon Kiran for companionship and the grat seemed pretty determined to adopt her.

Deciding it was probably thirsty, she stopped and poured a little water from the water bag Kiran had given her to carry into her drinking vessel. Kiran glanced back at her, but said nothing when she took a sip from the vessel. When he turned around and kept walking, she waited until he'd started down the next dune, then backtracked. The grat stopped abruptly when it saw her coming, flattening itself against the ground. She halted a few feet away from it and held the vessel out, swirling the water. After a few moments, the grat lifted its head and sniffed. The nostril slits quivered and it licked its lips, but it didn't move any closer, despite Tempest's efforts to entice it. She frowned. "Fine! When you're thirsty enough maybe you won't be so shy."

Tipping a few drops onto the sand, Tempest rose, turned and strode after Kiran, but she made no attempt to catch up to him, trailing several yards behind him and glancing back now and then to see what the grat would do.

When she'd moved away, it surged forward, sniffing the ground where she'd dropped the water, digging at it a little frantically. Finally, giving up, it followed, keeping its distance, but never dropping far behind. Tempest waited an hour before trying again. When she saw Kiran topping another rise, she stopped, waiting until he disappeared over the top. She squatted then, holding the vessel out once more.

She wasn't particularly thrilled about the idea of having to drink after the grat, but she had nothing else to offer water. If she poured it out, it would just soak into the sand. She sipped it while she waited for the grat to make up its mind whether to approach or not. Finally, thirst got the better of it and the small beast crept forward, its head lifted, its nose twitching as it caught the scent of the water. Lowering the vessel, Tempest held it out.

The grat stared at her for several moments. Finally, it startled her by surging forward and slapping the vessel from her hand. Tempest jumped back, lost her balance, and landed on her butt in the sand. She glared at the grat indignantly as it quickly lapped up the little water left in the vessel. "Serves you right! If you weren't so suspicious, you'd have gotten a lot more."

It growled at her when she went to retrieve her vessel. She stomped her foot. "That's mine, you little shit!" she snapped, scooping up a handful of sand and throwing it at the grat. The grat scurried away. Tempest retrieved her vessel, glared at the grat for several moments and finally turned and stalked off. So much for making friends!

Kiran gave her a disapproving look when she caught up to him. "We will not reach the next watering place before dark if you do not keep pace."

"It'd be easier," Tempest groused, "if I had legs as long as yours."

Kiran slid a look down at her that examined her from head to toe. "You would find it easier if you did not stop every few minutes," he pointed out, not unreasonably.

It was on the tip of her tongue to remind him that she wasn't nearly as strong as him, wasn't Niahian, which made the air and pressure of his world more difficult for her, and that she wasn't used to walking all day. It occurred to her, however, that that would be an admission that she'd had no business even trying to follow him. Before she could think of any comment to make, Kiran stiffened.

"Mer-cay!" he snapped.

Chapter Five

Tempest didn't understand the word, but the way he'd said it and his stance indicated alarm. "What?"

Grasping her, he shoved her down into the sand and sprawled on top of her, nearly crushing her. "What is it?" she managed to grunt.

"Quiet!" Kiran said in a harsh whisper.

Tempest obediently went quiet, but she found it almost impossible to draw a decent breath of air with his broad chest bearing down upon her. Then, too, his size was such that her face was also crushed against his chest. She wiggled until she managed to turn her head to one side, but it was still a struggle to breathe. After what seemed like a very long time, some of the tension left him. He eased away slightly, but it was more a lessening of pressure than anything else, for he was still sprawled heavily atop her. Tempest began trying to wriggle away.

"What are you doing?" he asked through clenched teeth.

"Some*thing* is digging into my ribs!" Tempest growled back at him.

"Mer-cay," he spat irritably, rolling off of her abruptly.

Before either of them could say anything else, a whirling dervish landed in the middle of his chest, all four feet splayed, its claws digging into his flesh. Both Kiran and Tempest gaped at the snarling grat.

"Bad girl!" Tempest snapped, recovering first. "Down!"

The grat, responding either to her tone or her waving hand as she shooed at it, leapt from Kiran's chest and trotted off a short distance, then dropped to the sand, glaring balefully at both of them.

Kiran glanced irritably from the grat to Tempest and sat up slowly, rubbing at the perforated flesh from the grat's claws.

"What's a Mer-cay, anyway?" Tempest asked, as much to distract him as because of curiosity.

Kiran glanced at her sharply, obviously torn between amusement and embarrassment. "Excrement."

Tempest bit her lip as that sank in. "Kind of like, oh shit! huh?"

Kiran looked at her curiously a moment. "This means same thing?"

"I'm guessing ... so what was it all about?"

"Mordune. They are enemies of my people."

"And your people are?"

He frowned. "Zoeans.... Children of the life giver, Great One, Zoe."

He said it as if she should have known without him having to tell her. She had studied the mythologies of her own world, but only briefly. She did know though that, basically, all religions had one thing in common. It was the way the ancients had explained their world, come to an understanding about it that comforted them and, to some extent at least, soothed their fears about their mortality. She frowned. "If Zoe is the life giver, wouldn't the Mordune be her children too?"

"Yes, but they do not acknowledge her."

"So.... That's why the Mordune and the Zoeans are enemies?"

"No."

"Well, why?"

Kiran frowned. "I do not know. It has always been this way," he said impatiently, getting to his feet and brushing off the sand.

Tempest rose, too, brushing absently at the sand. "So ... you, the Zoeans, are enemies because of something that happened so long ago nobody even remembers what it was?"

"The Keepers know."

"Keepers?"

"The Keepers of the Memory." Gathering his pack, he set off again. "They are gone now. We must hurry. We still have far to go to reach the watering place."

Tempest grabbed up the things she'd been carrying and hurried after him. "I'm just trying to understand."

"You are Earthling. You do not believe and you scoff at anything that is different from your own beliefs."

Tempest glared at his back. "Niahians, of course, are above that."

He threw her an irritated glance over one shoulder. "Yes," he said haughtily.

"Right!"

He didn't look back that time, but she could tell from the set of his shoulders that her parting shot had hit home.

Darkness fell before they reached the oasis Kiran was seeking. He stopped finally, scanned the darkness ahead of them and finally sat down. "We will wait here until Talore rises to light the way."

Tempest took that to mean the great red moon, which was far brighter than its tiny blue sibling and always crested the horizon first. She settled, grateful for a chance to rest, if only briefly. Her stomach rumbled.

She thought Kiran hadn't noticed, but realized in the next moment that it was a vain hope.

"We would have food if you had not fed it to that beast."

"Did I complain?"

"Your belly complains for you ... mine also."

Tempest shot to her feet and stalked away, settling again with her back to him when she'd put some distance between them. Her heart skipped a beat when she caught a glimpse of movement out of the corner of her eye, but she realized almost at once that it was the grat. Poor thing. It was probably hungry too. She held out her hand. "Sorry, no food."

To her surprise, the grat eased up close enough to sniff her fingers. In the next instant, it bit down on one of her fingers. Tempest yelped and popped it on top of the head. "You can't eat me, you little shit!" she snapped as it scurried away. After a moment, she thought about the water skin. Slipping the strap down her arm, she opened it and took a few gulps of water directly from the spout, then filled her drinking vessel and held it out. The grat reappeared, sniffed loudly, but made no attempt to approach her. "If you want it, you'll have to come get it."

The grat eyed her distrustfully for some time, but finally began inching a little closer. When it poked its snout into the vessel and began lapping the water, she reached over with her free hand and stroked its head. It jumped back at once, studying her suspiciously. Finally, the draw of the water became too much for it and it eased forward again. Again, Tempest stroked it, examining its fur with her hands. To her surprise, much of the fur was soft against her fingertips. There were stiffer hairs, more like tines, along its back and she realized that it was the tines that lifted when the grat felt threatened, not the soft fur that covered the rest of its body.

It jerked beneath her touch, but ignored her until it had finished off the water. When it had lapped up the last drop, it scurried off again, though it did not go far before it lay down, staring at her. "I should name you," Tempest murmured thoughtfully. "What do you think?"

It merely blinked at her, glanced toward where Kiran sat and then looked at her again.

"Kiran Junior, you think?" Tempest offered with a giggle, thinking that it would irritate the hell out of Kiran. "You're a pretty girl, though. I think I'll just call you Kirry."

The grat lifted its head, looking at something just over her shoulder and Tempest glanced around to find that Kiran had risen. "It is unwise to waste water."

Tempest's eyes narrowed. "I'll drink less."

"We will all drink less," Kiran said coolly. "The water skin was for me alone. I had not expected to travel with anyone."

There wasn't much she could say about that and she glanced away guiltily. "If I'd known you would be reminding me every few minutes that I was in your way, I'd have stayed where I was," she muttered angrily when he turned away once more.

"I should not have to remind you," he retorted, grabbing up his pack angrily and slinging it over his shoulder again.

"You *don't* have to remind me," she shot back at him, "but, apparently, you just can't help being an asshole."

He stopped, dropped his pack and turned to face her, planting his hands on his hips. "This is an insult?"

"It's not a compliment!"

His eyes narrowed as he fought a round with his temper. "I know you do not understand, but I must reach the sacred Temple of Zoe before the Great Darkness falls upon us or many generations will pass before we again have the chance to make Niah green as it once was. I can not afford to be turned from my Hymria, or slowed.

"I tire of wandering! I want that which has been promised, fruitfulness for my world so that I can leave a better world for my young."

Tempest gaped at him. "You have children?"

Kiran gritted his teeth in frustration, thrusting his fingers through his tousled hair. "I have no young. I have no mate. I can not seek them until I have taken the sacred journey and completed my task!"

Surprised by his vehemence, Tempest took a step back. Kirry immediately leapt to her feet, growling low in her chest. Kiran turned to glare at the animal for a moment and finally turned away, snatched his pack from the ground and stalked off.

After a moment, Tempest followed him.

Neither of them spoke, focused upon their own thoughts as they made their way across the desert and came at last, after several hours' walk, to the watering hole. The grat, no doubt sensing it would find both food and water in the oasis, raced ahead of them once it spotted the telltale jumble of rocks. When they'd found a spot Kiran approved--a tiny, rocky, but slightly flattened area surrounded by large boulders--Kiran directed her to build a fire while he hunted for food. Shrugging as he left without another word, Tempest spread the bedding out and climbed back down to the desert floor to dig for niahten. When she decided she'd collected enough to build a fire, she gathered it in a bundle in her arms, climbed back up the rocks with an effort, and arranged a small pile.

Pulling her igniter from her pocket, she flicked it patiently over and over until it finally produced a flame big enough to start the fire. As soon as the niahten caught, she shoved the igniter back into her pocket and began piling small pieces around the tiny fire she'd started and finally sat back to watch as the fire spread slowly and grew.

She sighed. Either her igniter was worn out or it was almost out of fuel. Except for the rags she was wearing and her memories, it was all that she had left of the colony. Before long, she would have nothing but memories, and even those were fading.

Try though she might, she couldn't summon the image of those she'd loved, not clearly anyway. When she thought about her parents, her younger brother, her best friend, Georgia, she could remember things they'd done together, things they'd said, but she couldn't really visualize their features, couldn't remember what their voices had sounded like.

She wondered if anything remained of the colony or if it had been plundered by the natives of Niah, or destroyed by the wind storms and the endless dust. She was torn between a yearning to return, to find something familiar, and a fear of the same--fear that the disease might still linger and strike her down--fear that she would find nothing at all remained and would have to accept that, not only everyone, but everything that was familiar to her was lost forever.

Chapter Six

Kirry landed beside her so abruptly it startled a squeak of fright from her. It was several moments before she even realized it was the little grat, for it was carrying the carcass of a dead animal in its jaws and looked like something out of her worst nightmares. A rumbling sound that reminded her of incessant snoring issued from the small animal's chest as it dropped the limp carcass at her feet, sauntered over to a rock and leapt up on it, then sat and began to lathe its forefeet with its tongue.

Tempest stared at the animal in puzzlement for several moments, then looked down at the carcass. A faint smile curled her lips as it occurred to her that it was an offering. "You brought me food?"

Kirry, naturally enough, only stared at her. Finally, she blinked and returned her attention to her grooming.

Tempest chuckled, but reached for the carcass cautiously. When Kirry continued to ignore her, she got up and looked around until she found a chip of stone with a sharp edge and went to work cleaning it.

Kiran had thought it best not to make their campsite too close to the pool of water, and he'd taken the skins to fill them, so she had no water either to clean the food, or her hands. When she'd finished, she laid the meat carefully on a stone and shoved it into the edge of the fire then cleaned her hands the best she could by scooping up sand and rubbing it between her hands.

To her relief, Kiran returned shortly, carrying the skins and a small animal. "We will not have much from this, but it is late. The animals had already come to drink and scattered."

Tempest smiled. "Kirry brought something, too."

Kiran gave her a curious look, then glanced at the grat before moving toward the fire to place his own kill on a stone to cook. When he saw there was already meat cooking, he turned to look at Tempest, who was busy washing her hands. "There is meat here."

Tempest let out a gurgle of laughter. "You didn't believe me?"

Kiran frowned, glanced from Tempest to the grat and back again. Tempest could tell from his expression that he thought it was some sort of trick she was playing on him.

"The grat killed this? Then brought it to you?"

Tempest chuckled. "She did! Dropped it right at my feet." She glanced at the grat. "She's such a clever girl. Aren't you, Kirry?"

Kiran didn't look at all pleased when she glanced at him again and Tempest frowned. "What's wrong?"

He shook his head slowly, still frowning, but finally dismissed it. "The Mordune were here. I do not believe they will come back, but I think it best if we kill the fire once we've eaten."

Tempest felt a shiver of dread. "What will happen if we meet up with them?"

"We will not meet them if we are careful."

That wasn't terribly reassuring. "What if we're careful and we still meet up with them?"

Kiran frowned. "I will protect you."

That wasn't really very reassuring either. She had no doubt that he was a competent warrior, maybe even much more than just competent, but she had a feeling that there had been a number of Mordune, too many for one man to have a chance against. Not that she wouldn't do her best to help, but realistically, she knew she couldn't be much of a deterrent. Unlike Kiran, she had no weapons. One laser pistol--if she'd had the forethought to take one with her when she'd left the colony and not disposed of it as she had pretty much everything else--could have evened the odds considerably, but there wasn't much point in thinking about it. She had no idea how Kiran's archaic-looking weapons were even used, and she was fairly certain they had been designed for the size and strength of a Niahian man in any case.

"The Zoeans war with the Mordune?" she asked hesitantly.

Kiran shrugged. "At times we clash."

"But nobody knows why?"

Again, he shrugged. "It was long ago--before the growing things died and Niah became desert."

Tempest's eyebrows rose. "You think it might have had something to do with the change in the planet? Like a great war, I mean, that killed everything off?"

"Even the Keepers of the Memory do not know."

"How do you know they don't know?"

"They have never said."

"That doesn't mean they don't know, only that they're not telling if they do know," Tempest pointed out.

Kiran frowned, obviously more irritated than thoughtful. "They are the Keepers of the True Memory. They are careful to preserve only what happened. They would not tell untruths."

"Hmm."

Kiran glared at her. "You are not of this world. You know nothing of our people. You are not in a position to judge."

"Maybe not," Tempest said tightly. "But from what I *have* seen, the people of this world aren't a whole hell of a lot different than *the people*, which means they not only lie sometimes, but they also only see their own side of things, which isn't always the complete truth. My father told me that history was recorded by the victors, and they always told everything from their own side. He said it was natural to want to take pride in the things they'd done and that I should always look at both sides before I made a judgment because, without actually meaning to lie, they might gloss over the ugly things ... or just leave them out.

"If it isn't the whole truth, then it's partly a lie."

Kiran gave her a strange look. "Your father was wise for an Earthling."

Tempest rolled her eyes, but she couldn't help but smile. It was a backhanded compliment if she'd ever heard one, but it was actually pretty amusing to have someone from such a backward world comment on the intelligence of Earthlings, who'd been far superior, at least technologically.

"This amuses you?"

Tempest shook her head. "Pride goeth before a fall," she quoted, with no idea what the origins were, except that there was a lot of wisdom in it.

"This means?"

"Be careful you don't trip over it and learn humility the hard way."

He flushed slightly. Tempest wasn't certain whether it was from annoyance or embarrassment, but she thought it was terribly cute to see such a big, brawny warrior blush. "You are young to have such wisdom."

Tempest felt her own color heighten, partly from pleasure at the compliment, and partly because she knew it wasn't strictly true. "I was taught a lot, but, truthfully, I haven't had much chance to practice, or experience, the things I learned. Mostly I just know because I was told.

"How did you learn to speak my language anyway?"

"From the others."

Tempest's heart seemed to stand perfectly still in her chest. "There are others? Like me?"

He smiled faintly. "There are none like you. But yes, other young of the star people. The Zoeans took them in to raise with their own young."

Tempest tried to quell her disappointment. "My age?"

He shrugged. "I do not know. Perhaps. I can not judge the age of Earthlings well. They are far smaller than Niahians."

"Males?" Tempest asked, trying to keep the hopeful note out of her voice.

Kiran frowned, looked away and finally shrugged. "Young males."

Try though she might, Tempest couldn't contain the thrill of hopefulness and relief that surged through her. In all the time since she'd left, she hadn't dared even to allow herself to dream there might be others of her own kind, that she might find people she'd known. The colony hadn't been so large, though, that she hadn't learned most of the faces, even though she hadn't really known everyone. She firmly tamped the hope that any of her friends might have made it out alive. It was enough just to know she wasn't alone.

Overwhelmed with joy, she rushed to Kiran and flung her arms around him, hugging him. "Thank you! Thank you!" she cried, laughing and kissing him all over the face.

Kiran caught her arms, pushing her gently away, and Tempest sat back on her heels, embarrassed now at her impulsive affection, but too happy to feel much discomfort over it. She smiled up at him. "I'm sorry. I'm just so happy," she added, feeling a surge of tears from out of nowhere.

Kiran's hands tightened on her forearms. She hadn't even realized that he'd never released her until that moment. Lifting her arms, she placed her palms on his chest for balance. To her surprise, when she tried to push away to rise, Kiran pulled her closer instead. She looked up at him, both the laughter and the tears of relief abruptly dying. An odd sort of breathless tension took its place as she stared into his eyes.

His expression was harsh, his eyes gleaming with some heated emotion that she was both drawn to and afraid of. He seemed at war with his own emotions and desires, as uncertain as she was. After a moment, however, he closed the distance between them, brushing his lips lightly across hers.

Tempest gasped at the strange sensations that poured through her, felt her heart gallop painfully against her chest wall, felt a tingling rush of heat that made her skin prickle all over. Her fingers curled into his flesh as if they had a mind of their own. Her entire body seemed strangely alien to her.

A tremor went through him as he brushed his lips lightly back and forth against her own. He lifted his head after only a moment, pulled a little away from her.

"They will not make you feel as I can," he said harshly.

Tempest stared at him blankly. "They won't?" she asked, having no idea who he might be referring to.

"Were I not bound by my vows, I would show you," he murmured, his voice husky with promise.

Tempest merely stared at him, unable to jog her sluggish brain into making any sense of what he'd said. She couldn't, in fact, get beyond anything but disappointment that he had only given her the barest taste of a real kiss. Naturally, she'd done some experimentation, despite her parents' warnings that 'kissing leads to capitulation', but she had not believed them because none of the times she'd tried it before had made her feel like this, had made her the least bit interested in carrying it any further.

Now, she completely understood what they'd meant, because she really hadn't wanted him to stop and she would have allowed him to do most anything he had wanted to do.

He released her abruptly and moved away and Tempest shivered at the absence of his warmth. Sluggishly, her brain kicked into gear again and she began to wonder what, exactly, he'd been saying, offering.

After a moment, she rose, almost like a sleepwalker, and moved back to the bedding, sitting on it and covering herself with the blanket. The tiny fire had given off little warmth and it had been allowed to die to embers. As she watched, Kiran removed the food carefully and moved over to sit beside her on the bedding, offering her a portion. She took it, but found she'd lost much of her appetite. She ate anyway, knowing she would be hungry later if she didn't eat, and there would be nothing to eat. Almost absently, she tore off a small piece of her own food and tossed it to Kirry. The grat sniffed it, rolled it around with her paws as if she was playing with it, but, obviously, she'd already eaten her fill.

When she'd finished eating, Tempest rose and wandered off to relieve herself and to find the watering hole so that she could wash up and drink her fill before sleeping. Kiran was stretched out in the bedding when she returned and she stopped abruptly, surprised. He hadn't offered to share the bedding with her since that first night, leaving it to her while he lay on the other side of the fire from her with nothing at all to protect him from the night air.

They had no fire tonight, though, and she supposed it was as much for that reason as any other that he'd claimed a portion of the bedding for himself. After that brief hesitation, she moved toward him with as much unconcern as she could muster, crawled beneath the blanket and lay down on her back, staring up at the stars.

"You are afraid of me now?" Kiran asked, rising up on one elbow to study her in the shadows.

Tempest glanced at him in surprise. Was she? She didn't think so. She wasn't afraid of sex, if that was what he was thinking. Before the disaster, she'd looked forward to it with eagerness, impatient to explore the new experience. When he'd kissed her, she'd felt nothing but anticipation, hadn't really given a thought to what might happen next. If he'd decided to have sex with her, she was fairly certain she wouldn't have objected at all.

Now she wondered if it was even wise to consider it. For all she knew the Niahians might have taboos regarding copulation that could mean serious trouble for her ... for both of them. It was all very well to think about seeking, or accepting, companionship from someone who was not of her own kind when she'd had no choice, but he'd said there were other Earthlings. Wouldn't it be best to stick with her own kind, particularly since she knew and understood the ways of her own people?

And she had no means of birth control, she realized suddenly. She hadn't reached the age of consent before the disease struck, so she hadn't been given the implantation that prevented conception. That was something else to give serious consideration to.

"No," she answered him finally. "I'm not afraid. I know you wouldn't hurt me."

He sighed gustily, a mixture of relief and irritation. "I should not have kissed you."

Tempest smiled faintly. "Probably not ... but I expect it was my fault anyway. I gave you the wrong idea. It's just ... I was so relieved and happy, I didn't think before I did it."

Kiran frowned. "This...."

"Affection," Tempest supplied when he seemed to be searching for the right word. She sighed. "I used to have so many friends, and my family, too. I don't think I even realized how much I missed kissing and hugging, holding hands ... just being able to touch somebody else and feel close to them. I guess it's like you said, Niahians and Earthlings are a lot different in their ways and customs ... worlds apart, literally."

"We are not so different that we could not learn," Kiran pointed out.

Tempest shrugged. "I don't know. I can't picture an Earthling taking a vow of chastity for any reason," she said with a chuckle, then was immediately sorry she'd said it, and worse, laughed. Obviously, it was really important to him. She hadn't meant to insult him or his customs. "Sorry. I know it's important, but you see what I mean?"

"No," he said grimly.

She reached up and patted his arm. "Never mind. It doesn't really matter now, does it?" She sighed happily. "Oh, I just can't wait to see them! I'll bet we could go back to the colony." She frowned. "I should go alone first. If the lab's still working, I could run some tests … I used to help my parents in the lab. I'm sure I can remember how to test for immunity. Well, I suppose I should check to see if the virus is still active first."

Kiran studied her a long moment and finally lay back. After a moment, he put his arm around her waist and dragged her toward him, fitting her against his length. "Sleep. We must rest while we can."

Tempest was a little surprised, but she was perfectly willing to snuggle closer to his warmth. "I don't know if I *can* sleep," she said, yawning.

"It will be difficult for me, as well," Kiran said wryly.

Tempest chuckled sleepily, having discovered that his warmth and her full stomach combined with the day's trek had tired her more than she'd realized in her excitement. Now that it was dissipating, she found it harder and harder to stay awake.

She felt Kiran's hand in her hair, stroking her head. "I like the sound of your happiness," he murmured.

"Hmm. Laughter. It feels good to laugh. I can't even remember the last time I felt like laughing."

"I am glad that I brought this back into your life."

Tempest nuzzled her cheek against his chest and gave him an affectionate squeeze. "Me too."

Chapter Seven

The day was bright with sunlight when Tempest woke. She sat up with a jolt of anxiety, looking around.

Kiran was sitting across from her, studying her.

Tempest combed her fingers through her hair. "I've overslept."

Kiran shrugged. "I thought it best to allow you to rest until you woke of your own accord."

"Oh." Tempest scrubbed her hands over her face, trying to shake off the dregs of sleep. "Thanks! I guess we should get going, though."

Be the time she returned from the watering hole, she felt more alert, but also more aware of the soreness of her muscles from her unaccustomed exercise. Kiran had broken camp when she returned. Without a word, he handed her the water skin, hefted his pack and started the climb down the rocks.

He wasn't the talkative type, but there was something about him that seemed different. He didn't seem to be angry--exactly. He seemed withdrawn, she finally decided, as if his mind was elsewhere. She dismissed it after a while, following her own thoughts, allowing her imagination to run wild with plans for a future with the other survivors of the disaster.

Even if there was no longer any sign of the disease that had killed so many, or if, by some lucky chance, she and the other survivors had built up an immunity to it, it was going to be hard, emotionally speaking, to go back to the colony, bury the dead and take up the lives they'd had before. She felt certain, though, that that was what they should do. As many times as she'd heard the adults bewail the loss of so much of their technology in the crash, it was still vast when compared to what the Niahians had, and more than that, a part of *the people* that needed to be preserved.

It was mid-afternoon before they stopped to eat again. Tempest, still caught up in her own world, was surprised when Kiran stopped, and tempted to try to persuade him to keep going since she now had her own reasons for seeing that Kiran finished what he'd set out to do as quickly as possible. He seemed rather disinclined to talk, though, and she realized that she needed to pace herself, despite her impatience, so she kept her thoughts to herself.

They stopped only briefly in any case, since they'd had a late start to begin with. Tempest felt more than a little guilty about it. He'd emphasized how important it was for him to reach his destination in time. It didn't matter what she thought about it, or that she couldn't see what difference it made when they got there.

It was important to him, and because he had been kind enough to allow her to tag along, he might not reach this sacred place he'd told her about, not when he was supposed to, anyway.

Realizing that, Tempest made an effort to keep pace with him, pushing herself as much as she dared to try to make up the time he'd lost. He glanced at her curiously several times and finally spoke. "You can not keep this pace. You will exhaust yourself."

Tempest shook her head. "No," she said a little breathlessly. "I'm used to it now. And we need to make up the time you lost waiting for me."

"We will not make it up if you faint and I have to carry you," he pointed out.

Tempest chuckled. "Good thing I'm not prone to fainting. I did once, though. The first time I killed something to eat, I puked and then I passed out cold when I cut its throat and it bled all over the place."

His brows rose questioningly and Tempest shook her head.

"It's the difference between knowing how and actually doing it. Like I said, I learned a lot, but actually *doing* it is something else altogether."

"You had not prepared food before you were forced to leave the place of the star people?"

Tempest frowned. "Actually, nobody had had a lot of experience with it. When we crashed here--well, not me. I was born later-- they managed to retrieve a lot of our supplies. It was a controlled crash, you understand--damaged the ship beyond repairing it, but they managed to set it down without killing many people. Naturally, they rationed supplies, but they mostly lived off of them while they were building the colony. They knew, eventually, the supplies would run out and they'd have to start growing, or catching, food, but nobody really had much of an idea of how to do that--they had to learn. On Earth, you see, everything was processed, packaged, ready to add water or heat or eat just as it was, right from the package. And then, too, they had to test everything to see what could be eaten by humans that wouldn't kill them.

"Luckily for me, they'd figured all of that out before … before everybody got sick and started dying. I'd gone out to hunt and gather plenty of times, but mostly the young people just went to help carry things back, not to actually do it--the killing and preparation, you know."

Kiran shook his head. "This is very strange."

Tempest drew a deep breath with an effort. "I understand that it would seem that way to you. Violence almost completely destroyed our world, however, and we had worked very hard to learn *not* to be violent. Unfortunately, violence is part of survival and it was hard to learn to take care of ourselves when we found that we *had* to kill if we wanted to live."

"We, too, are a peaceful people."

Tempest glanced at him, but she didn't argue the point. She was sure that, comparatively speaking, the Zoeans were peaceful. They were still, of necessity, far more war-like than *the people*, far less civilized.

She wondered quite suddenly if the Niahians were rebuilding, as well. It made sense, now that she began comparing the two different civilizations. Everyone at the colony had assumed that Niah was merely a primitive world, undeveloped, its inhabitants only just climbing toward true civilization.

Kiran had told her very little, but from what he had said, it seemed to indicate that something global had happened to his world. The Keepers of the Memory might indicate ancient records that dated back to a time when this world had been entirely different, perhaps much more civilized. He'd suggested as much, but she'd thought it was just tales, passed down from generation to generation. She hadn't considered, until now, that it might actually be true and that his world, having been virtually destroyed, the survivors had had to start once more, virtually at the bottom of the chain of evolution to build again.

For the first time since she'd met him, she felt a genuine curiosity to know what it was that he had been sent to accomplish. Apparently, it was something he, and all of his people, believed would bring their world back to what it had been before.

It still didn't make sense to her, turn it though she would. Planets, if they weren't totally destroyed, usually regenerated, but they did it slowly, over time. Everyone believed, given time, the Earth would one day be habitable again, maybe not for many generations, but eventually.

But, short of moving the whole planet to a different orbital path, and perhaps seeding it, she couldn't imagine anything that would bring about a sudden change.

Kiran abruptly drew her from her thoughts by grasping her arm. She looked up at him in surprise, then followed the direction of his gaze.

In the distance, just topping a tall dune, she saw men--perhaps a dozen of them, mounted on beasts. She could tell nothing about them at this distance except that they were wearing long reddish robes that blended surprisingly well with their surroundings. If not for the beasts they were mounted on and the fact that the fabric was flapping around them, she might never have noticed them at all.

Pushing her into the sand, Kiran covered her with his own body. Tempest grunted as the air was forced from her lungs by the impact. "What are you doing?"

"It is the Mordune," he whispered harshly.

"Yeah, but why squash me?"

"Your flesh is white," Kiran pointed out testily.

She wasn't *that* white! In point of fact, she was more red by now than anything else ... not brown, like the Niahians, but definitely not white--not anymore. She found she didn't really have the breath to argue with him, however.

After a moment, he rolled off of her and began dragging her down the other side of the dune. "You think they saw us?" she gasped.

"Yes," he said grimly.

Tempest's heart seemed to stand still. "What do we do now?" There was no place to run to. No place to hide.

"We wait. If they did not see us, they will pass us by."

"But, if they did...?"

"They might still pass us by."

"And they might not." Waiting wasn't much of a plan in her book.

"They are mounted on aquestens. If they were on foot, as we are, we might have a chance of evading them."

He might have a chance. He didn't need to say it for her to figure out that having her along was enough to doom both of them. "You go then. I'll ... uh ... hide here. I'm not Zoean, not an enemy. Maybe they'll just ignore me."

"You are female."

"You think they could tell that from that distance?"

"I could."

"That's because you know," Tempest pointed out testily. "You didn't know at first."

"Because I could not see you well."

"Arguing isn't going to get us anywhere."

He smiled faintly at that, studying her sharply for several moments. Abruptly, he grasped her, pulling her tightly against his length. Before Tempest could even wonder what he was doing, he dipped his head and pressed his lips firmly to hers. A combination of surprise and pleasure jolted through her, making her toes curl in the sand. She gasped, grasping his shoulders. He touched his tongue to her lips, testing the sensitive flesh where her lips met, tasting her and then plunging past that barrier to taste and explore the exquisitely sensitive inner surfaces of her mouth.

Tempest was both shocked and enthralled at the intimacy of his touch, captivated by the rough rake of his tongue along hers. His taste, his scent, filled her with a delightful sense of floating, a dizzying rush of heat. The muscles low in her belly clenched, a warm wetness flooding her sex.

When he released her almost as abruptly, Tempest swayed dizzily, opening her eyes with an effort.

"I will not allow harm to come to you, little grat. I swear it. Stay close."

Tempest smiled at him a little vaguely, still too caught up in the sensations he'd created inside of her to spare much thought for danger, real or imagined. "I'm not a grat," she said teasingly. "I am a storm. Remember?"

Kiran frowned, studied her searchingly for several moments and finally thrust her away from him. Turning, he pulled his weapons and planted his feet wide, waiting.

Thrust abruptly back into reality, Tempest realized belatedly that it wasn't merely her heart she heard thundering in her ears. It was the approach of riders, many riders.

Almost as if her mind had conjured them, they crested the rise at that moment. Shrieking like demons, waving their own weapons threateningly, they plunged down the dune to where Kiran stood waiting--one man against nearly a dozen. Tempest's blood seemed to freeze in her veins, her muscles seized, leaving her little more than a breathing statue as the horde thundered down upon them. Her mind screamed at her to run, but she couldn't command her feet to move.

The first clash of metal against metal shook her from her stupor, but by then it was far too late. The Mordune surrounded them, jockeying for a position to trade blows with Kiran. Seeing that she was unarmed, one man shot past Kiran's determined blows, grasping a handful of her hair. She screamed, grabbing his hand. Almost in slow motion she saw Kiran glance toward her, saw

Kirry race toward her from out of nowhere and launch herself at the man who'd grabbed her.

"No!" Tempest screamed, reaching toward Kiran as if she could stop the vicious blow of the man who'd taken advantage of Kiran's distraction.

Kiran ducked, swinging at the same moment and, to Tempest's relief, managed to block the blow. She was released abruptly, and landed in a heap on the sand. Looking up, she saw that Kirry was moving over her assailant so fast she was little more than a blur of motion as she shredded the man's flesh from his back, arms and head. She was tempted to urge the little beast on, but as another Mordune surged forward, his arm raised as if to cleave the little grat in two, she jumped to her feet and reached toward the grat. "No! Kirry!"

Startled, the grat's head jerked toward the sound of her voice. In the next instant, it leapt off of the man, even as the other man swung at it. Landing in the sand at her feet, Kirry whirled, all four legs braced, her ridge of fur standing on end as she growled threateningly at the men surrounding them.

Someone shouted something. What, Tempest had no idea since she couldn't speak their language, but as abruptly as they'd attacked, the Mordune withdrew.

Gasping for breath, Tempest turned to look at Kiran. He was kneeling in the sand, bleeding from a dozen cuts on his arms, his thighs and chest. She rushed toward him, falling to the sand and examining his injuries. Several looked dangerously deep and she turned to glare at the Mordune.

To her surprise, they had not gone far before they had turned their mounts around once more. Now, they merely sat perfectly still, staring, arguing amongst themselves.

She stared at them, wondering what was happening. Not for a moment did she believe Kirry and Kiran had fought them off, although, save for one or two, all were wounded, just as Kiran was.

Finally, one of the men, who seemed to be the leader, dismounted. He stared at her as if she was some sort of two headed beast. Finally, he fell to his knees, his arms outstretched.

"Long will the children of Niah suffer and find no rest, no succor from strife, but, in time your pleas will be heard….

"And the day will come when mother Niah will assume the form of a mortal creature and appear unto her children--

"She is Niah and she will be as one with all creatures great and small and you will know her, for she will command even the wild creatures.

"Bless us, mother Niah! Make our world green once more!"

He began to sob, bowing low, his arms stretched out before him. Almost as one, the others dismounted and fell to their knees, bowing as their leader had.

Tempest stared at them blankly. "What did he say?" she whispered to Kiran. When she glanced at him, she saw that he, too, was looking at her strangely.

"He says you are the One."

Tempest blinked. "One what?"

"They believe you are the One whose coming was foretold." With an effort, he turned, bowing as the others had. Tempest stared down at him wide-eyed, feeling a blush rise from her toes all the way to the top of her head.

Tempest looked at the other men uncomfortably, wondering what to do. On the one hand, she couldn't help but think it was a very fortunate thing that Mordune had jumped to such a conclusion.

But then, there was one really serious draw back.

She wasn't the *One*.

Chapter Eight

High emotion was something almost impossible to sustain, no matter how dire the situation, but Tempest found it was also impossible to completely dismiss as she and Kiran were mounted with two of the Mordune and taken away. It didn't help that she was worried about Kiran's wounds; that no one spoke her language but he; and that she had no notion of where they were going or what would happen when they got there. She had enough presence of mind, however, to realize that they believed she was some sort of deity, and that fainting, screaming, cursing or crying probably wouldn't fit in too well with the image.

She was scared enough to do a little of all three, and it took an effort to refrain.

The sun was low upon the horizon when they came at last to what looked like a city of tents. From the moment Tempest realized that it was some sort of portable abode, her tension increased tenfold.

It seemed likely that she was about to find out what would happen and she discovered, belatedly, that she'd rather not know. People poured from the tents as they approached, standing silently, watching, listening as the leader gestured wildly with his arms and pointed to her repeatedly. She sat stiffly erect, staring at a point over their heads since she was too unnerved to look directly at them.

The leader had barely stopped speaking when a collective gasp issued from the crowd surrounding them and Tempest turned to see what they were staring at. With consternation if not a great deal of surprise, she saw that Kirry had arrived. She stared at the grat, willing it not to do anything that would cause them more trouble. The grat sat, staring back at her as if waiting for some signal.

Relieved, Tempest returned her attention to the Mordune. Almost as one, they fell to their knees as the raiders had, bowing, wailing. Every hair on Kirry's body stood out and, with a growl, she took off.

Tempest looked at Kiran helplessly, wondering what to do. He moved toward her, reaching up and lifting her from the saddle. She clung to him. "What are we going to do when they find out I'm not who they think I am?" she whispered.

He squeezed her reassuringly. "I will tell them we must go to the sacred Temple of Zoe."

"But they don't believe in Zoe, do they?"

"They call her Niah."

Tempest was only slightly reassured, but, to her relief, when Kiran spoke to them, the Mordune got up almost as abruptly as they'd fallen to the ground and began yelling excitedly. Several women surged forward, surrounding her. Tempest looked at Kiran helplessly.

"I have reminded them that, in your mortal form, you are weakened and in need of food and rest. Go with them. You will come to no harm."

She didn't really have a choice as far as she could see. None of them actually touched her--any who accidentally bumped into her jumped back in fright--but they seemed very determined to guide her away for all that.

"But--you're hurt. What about your wounds?"

"They will be attended."

She didn't want to go off with the women, but she could see she didn't really have any choice in the matter. They led her to the largest tent, which seemed to be in the center of the village, and urged her inside. Once there, the women pointed to a mound of pillows in one corner. Shrugging mentally, Tempest crossed the sandy floor and sat down.

Looking desperate to please, the women scattered in every direction. Two returned carrying something that looked like a huge dish, which they set down near the center of the tent. Following them were other women bearing skins--water Tempest discovered when they began pouring it into the shallow 'dish'. It dawned on Tempest when they began gesturing at her clothing and chattering that they'd prepared a bath for her.

She didn't think she'd ever actually gotten 'in' water to bathe, unless it was when she'd been a very small child. As important as everyone knew cleanliness was, water was far too precious on Niah to use for bathing, unless it was in very small quantities. At the colony, they had built particle baths, such as had been used on Earth in the days before. Since she had left, she had used a damp cloth to bathe, which not only prevented contamination of her tiny water supply, but also conserved it for drinking.

It seemed very decadent to consider doing so now, but the women seemed so insistent she finally got up, stripped her clothes off and approached the bath they'd prepared. One of the women, and older, motherly looking woman, grasped her hand and helped her step into it. Tempest sat a little nervously, closing her eyes as the cool water washed over her hips and knees.

It felt strange to have water lapping around her, but she finally decided she liked the feel of it against her skin. Chattering happily, the women brought sweet smelling creams and rubbed them into her hair and skin, then, to Tempest's surprise, rinsed them away again. She discovered, though, that a faint scent lingered on her skin.

Finally, when they'd finished rinsing her, she was urged to stand up and the woman who'd helped her climb into the bath, helped her out once more, wrapping a large cloth around her.

When she'd taken a seat on the pillows once more, the older woman knelt beside her and began very carefully picking the tangles from her wet hair. Tempest winced, but gritted her teeth. She'd sawed her hair off short with a sharp stone because she had no way of keeping it in any sort of order, but even so the almost constant winds of Niah kept it in a tangle of knots.

She was just beginning to enjoy it when the woman, apparently satisfied, stopped combing and rose. Clapping her hands, she summoned several of the younger women who came forward carrying several small articles--clothing Tempest decided as they urged her to stand again.

Sort of, she mentally amended when she looked down at the 'garment'. She was next door to naked when they'd finished. The top didn't even completely cover her breasts, and it left her back entirely bare. The bottom was no more than two sheer pieces of fabric connected by tiny chains around her waist. It covered her sex--so long as she didn't move, but she could well imagine that one tiny breeze would expose everything she had.

Mentally, she shrugged. It was beautiful for all that and it wasn't as if she'd been covered all that well by her own ragged clothing. These garments at least had the virtue of being pretty.

When they'd finished adjusting the garments, three more women came forward, two carrying some sort of arm bands, the third a strange looking headpiece topped with huge, fluffy feathers. The bands, when placed on her arms, covered her arms from wrist to elbow. They were made of some strange material Tempest was totally unfamiliar with, much like metal, except that it stretched and retracted almost like skin, fitting her arms as snugly as if the bands had been made for her. The headdress was surprising, as well, light like the arm bands, fitting snugly to her skull.

They stepped back when they were finished, admiring their handiwork Tempest supposed, and then quickly formed a line toward the entrance of the tent.

Apparently, Tempest decided, she was to be escorted out again, so that everybody could see her finery. She moved toward the tent flaps the women held back, ducking slightly when she went under for fear she'd lose the headdress.

She halted abruptly when she'd left the tent, dismayed to discover everyone was lined up outside, formed into two long lines, waiting. Kiran, she saw, was waiting near the opposite end of the line of people and her heart gave a little skip of gladness. Steadying her nerves, she focused on him as she walked slowly down the row, ignoring them as they bowed worshipfully before her.

It wasn't easy to ignore. It thrummed in her mind with each step she took that they thought she was someone, something, she was not. She didn't want to think about what they might do if they discovered they'd been wrong, but she couldn't help but worry that she might do something to shatter their belief.

Kiran had said that he would tell them she had to travel to the sacred mountain, to the Temple of Zoe. She sincerely hoped he could convince them to take the two of them there soon. She was very much afraid that she wouldn't be able to maintain a suitably deity-like demeanor for very long at all.

* * * *

Stone faced, Kiran watched with a mixture of awe and pure animal lust as Tempest moved slowly toward him. It was fortunate, for both of them, that Niah was the goddess of fertility, and they believed he was her chosen mate, for he found he was having a great deal of difficulty restraining his restless serpent.

He had thought her a beautiful creature from the moment he had gotten his first clear look at her, but now, dressed in the ceremonial robes of the goddess mother, Niah, she took his breath.

In all honesty, it unnerved him to see her clothed in the gown that had been designed and made and preserved for her coming nearly a thousand years ago.

It fit Tempest as if it had been made for her--a woman far smaller of frame and stature than most Niahian women--and that made him uneasy in an indescribable way.

Of all those present, except Tempest herself, he alone did not believe. He wasn't certain why he didn't believe. It had been written that she would come from humble beginnings, that she would appear in form much like any other Niahian. It had been written that wild creatures would know her, would respond to her commands ... and she would be known as the Storm, for she would bring life-giving water to his world to make it green again.

The Zoeans believed it would not be Zoe herself who came, but her warrior, sent to wrest the water from captivity. He had expected a warrior much like himself, but he wasn't certain that was why he didn't believe.

He was afraid it was because his faith was weak, or he was simply unworthy as Guardian--because he wanted her for himself--and if she truly was the goddess as the Mordune believed, she would vanish once the task was done. She would release her spirit to the heavens once more and discard the living flesh she had assumed to grace them.

He swallowed with some difficulty when she came to a stop before him. With an effort, he took her hand, knelt and bowed his head.

She tugged on his hand and, when he looked up at her, smiled in a way that was both nervous and hopeful. He stood, escorted her to the throne that had been brought for her and then took his place beside her, all without saying a word, for he could think of nothing at all to say.

* * * *

The food was like nothing Tempest had ever eaten before, but it was wonderful. She had to resist the temptation to stash some away for later, which wasn't nearly as hard to do once she realized she had no pockets to hide it in.

She was deeply regretful, however, when she found that she'd eaten all she could hold. The grat, unnerved by all the noise but apparently fearful of allowing her completely out of sight, slunk quietly into the circle after it had grown dark and under the throne where Tempest sat. The first Tempest was aware its presence was when it growled at one of the servers, who apparently came closer than it liked. Tempest moved her legs to one side and dropped a few morsels for the animal.

When she looked up, she discovered that everyone had stopped dead in their tracks to stare.

She glanced uneasily at Kiran. He smiled faintly, nodded, then stood up and spoke … just as if she'd actually spoken to him.

"What did you tell them?" she asked out of the corner of her mouth.

"That the goddess mother Niah loved all of her creatures and was displeased when the strong preyed upon the weak and helpless."

Tempest blushed at the reference to 'the goddess' and tried not to look as miserable as she felt, but the truth was, aside from being a nervous wreck perched in full view of everyone, and studied either openly or covertly by all those present, she was so tired she was afraid she would fall asleep if she had to sit through the hours of entertainment it seemed they had in store for her.

Finally, when she thought she could bear it no longer, the women who had attended her earlier approached the dais that had been hastily constructed for the throne she sat upon. With relief, she stood and allowed them to help her down, following them with gratitude toward the tent where she had been prepared earlier.

Once there, they removed the garments and carefully folded them and set them aside, then brought forth a robe similar to those they wore, except far richer. Made of finely woven and virtually transparent fabric, it had no fastenings but was instead made to slip over one's head. Tempest lifted her arms and allowed them to drop it over her head.

To her relief, they began to file out immediately, leaving her, at long last with the peace to find her rest--or enjoy her fears.

As the last of the women left, however, Kiran entered the tent.

Tempest looked at him in surprise.

"It's allowed? For you to be with me, I mean?"

Kiran's gaze traveled her length before returning to her face once more. Finally, he moved toward her, stopping a good arm's length away. "It is expected."

Tempest didn't know why that surprised her when they had been captured traveling together, but it did. Somehow, she'd thought since they seemed to be under the impression that she was their goddess they wouldn't expect her to share her tent with a mere mortal.

It was a relief to know she wouldn't be left entirely alone through the night with nothing but her fears for company. Sighing, she surged forward, slipping her arms around his waist and laying her cheek against his chest. "I'm so glad. I've been scared silly ever since they captured us."

After a momentary hesitation, Kiran folded his arms around her. "I would have come regardless. I told you that I would protect you." He pulled a little away and tipped her chin up so that she was looking up at him. "I am the guardian of the goddess of storms."

Chapter Nine

Tempest smiled tremulously. "That isn't even *slightly* funny!"

Kiran stroked her cheek. "You have no need to be so fearful. Tomorrow, they will take us to the sacred mountain."

Tempest pulled away. "Do you think we should? So soon? I mean, you were hurt. Wouldn't it be best to rest a few days?"

Kiran frowned. "You wish to stay longer?"

Tempest shuddered. "Not really. I'd be happy to leave tonight, if you want to know the truth, but I don't suppose it would be a good idea to try it. I'm more concerned about you. There was so much blood!"

"Your grat caused me more injury."

Tempest gave him a look. "She didn't claw you nearly as deeply as some of those cuts looked. Maybe I should have a look?"

He shook his head. "I will heal. They were anxious to give the goddess Niah's chosen mate the best of care."

"I wish you wouldn't keep calling…. What? They think…. Why would they think that?"

"Because of your concern for me."

"Oh." Tempest looked around uncomfortably and it occurred to her for the first time that there might have been more to the ritualized preparation for bed than she'd thought at the time. Tiny, flickering lights in clay and oil lamps were 'strewn' about the tent, creating an atmosphere of intimacy. A length of fine cloth had been spread atop the mound of pillows against the far wall. "I suppose that means they don't consider chastity ... important?"

"Our beliefs and those of the Mordune differ as much as they are similar."

Tempest nodded, not entirely certain of whether she was relieved or sorry. The way Kiran was looking at her made her feel warm and soft all over, and she wasn't overly inclined to lie to herself. His kisses haunted her. When she'd experimented with kissing before, she had been almost as uncomfortable about it as she was excited. When Kiran kissed her, she'd felt things she had never imagined she could feel and, despite her lack of actual experience, she suspected that it was far more than 'typical' of such an encounter.

If he had not been the product of a different culture, she would have told him she was interested in sharing her body with him and discovering if they could please each other as well as she thought they might, just as everyone else in the colony had. She had a strong suspicion though, that the Niahians had very different views about sex than *the people*. Given the cultural differences she'd already seen, she was afraid of what the consequences might be.

Historically speaking, among *the people*, the male had always expressed his sexual interests freely and viewed sex as recreation. Even after the social custom of marriage was conceived, it was only the female who was truly bound--for it was the female who was attacked by society if she was discovered sharing herself with a male not her spouse, and that had gone on for centuries. It wasn't until women were finally able to control their reproductive organs that they found the freedom to express their sexuality as the male did. The whole institute of marriage, as the ancients had known it, vanished once it became unnecessary.

It had been invented to begin with by males, to ensure their breeding lines. With the advancements in genetics, that was no longer an issue. The females could choose the best male to produce children with, the male was in no doubt of the child's paternity, and the female could then pursue sex as recreation the same as their male counterparts, reproducing only when, or if, they felt the inclination.

The destruction of the colony had put her in the same position the women of her own world had held centuries ago. Without birth control, she was at the mercy of nature, which was dangerous enough without adding the possibility of cultural repercussions.

The realization vanquished the last of her internal battle between giving in to her inclinations and 'flight'. She shivered and moved away from Kiran. "We should sleep if we're leaving tomorrow."

He studied her for some time after she'd climbed atop the pillows and covered herself. Tempest didn't look at him, but she felt his puzzled, angry gaze. Finally, to her relief, he moved around the tent dousing the lights.

She rolled away from him when she felt the pillows shift as he climbed onto the pillow bed beside her. She could feel tension radiating from him as he lay stiffly on his back, staring up at the dark shadows of the tent above them.

"You have decided to choose a mate among your own people."

Tempest stiffened. Kiran wasn't one to beat around the bush, but she hadn't expected him to be quite so direct. Finally, she shrugged. Then she remembered that he couldn't really see her. "I'm sure it would be best," she replied noncommittally.

"For you?"

Tempest sighed. "Probably for everybody. I don't imagine the customs of *the people* are much like the customs of any of the Niahians. We've been on your world for years now without having a cultural clash. It just seems to me that the best way to avoid problems would be if we continued to keep to ourselves."

He said nothing for several moments. "You could learn the way of our people."

Tempest felt a surge of anger. "Well, maybe I think the ways of my own people are worth saving."

"I would not take that from you," he said tightly, trying to control his own anger.

"Because you can't--anymore than you can give it. It's part of who and what I am. Don't you see that? I would not be me if I hadn't grown up as I did. My culture is part of everything I think and say and do.... Just as yours is."

Abruptly, he seized her shoulder, bearing her down in the pillows as he shifted half atop her. "I will not always be bound by the vows I have taken," he growled.

Tempest swallowed against a little thrill of fear ... and, if the truth were told, excitement. "What do you mean by that?" she asked a little breathlessly, unable to see him well enough in the shadows to read his expression.

"I will be free to take what I want."

Tempest stared up at him speechlessly, wondering if it was a threat ... or a promise.

* * * *

At dawn, the women came once more. Tempest eyed them sleepily, uncertain of whether to be relieved or sorry that Kiran had risen and left the tent while she still slept.

They dressed her once more in the garments she'd worn the night before and escorted her out of the tent. There, she saw that an equesten outfitted with some sort of enclosure waited. The equesten, a hulking, mostly hairless beast with a row of three horns growing out of its forehead, had been forced to its knees, but even so it was almost as tall as she was and she wondered how, and if, she was expected to climb up. Two men that she recognized from the group that had captured her and Kiran, stepped forward, bowed and then, each taking an arm, lifted her into the strange conveyance.

It was a chair of sorts, she discovered, padded with pillows. The seat was set inside a box of sorts, the roof supported by posts, the sides, front and back open. Sheer fabric had been draped all around and once she was seated, these were released, shielding her from sight, cutting off most of her view.

She grasped the edges of the seat as she felt the beast heave beneath her. Her belly clenched as it rose abruptly.

Through the veiling, she saw that the beast she rode was surrounded by a dozen or so others, each bearing a plain saddle. Kiran had been given one to ride, as well, and as they started out, he guided his beast to walk beside hers.

He was still too far away to allow for comfortable conversation. She had a feeling he would be disinclined to talk anyway after what had passed between them the night before.

It puzzled her. He hadn't been at all willing to allow her to follow him off to begin with. That had been her idea and he had made it clear that he wasn't pleased and that it was only because of his good nature that he allowed it at all.

He hadn't really had to do anything at all to make her aware of him sexually. It was more than enough that he was extremely physically appealing, but he hadn't left it at that. He had teased her into heightened interest by appearing to be interested in her.

What really confused her was that he had implied that his restraint was self-imposed. Could it possibly be true? Or was it just something he said to take the sting out of rejection because he really wasn't that interested? Surely, if he was very attracted to her in a physical sense, it would take more than words to hold him back? Particularly when nobody would know but her that he'd broken his vow?

Either it was a prime example of just how different their cultures were, or he was just being kind because he knew she was attracted to him.

She sighed, dismissing it with an effort. It would be better, she was sure, not to think about it. They really weren't well suited at all, on any level, not physically, by nature, or culturally.

She craved the open affection she'd had before, among her own people. She hadn't realized touching was so much a part of her life until it had been wrenched away from her. She and her friends had often shared hugs and purely platonic kisses of affection. She'd shared much the same with her younger brother and her parents. Even her teachers and other members of the community would pat her on the head, or the back or her hand when she'd done something they approved of, or when she was hurt and in need of reassurance.

Granted, she hadn't been around the Niahians enough to know whether or not that was part of their culture, but she had an awful feeling that it wasn't and that that sort of behavior would be looked down upon, perhaps even earn punishment. They seemed very ... self-contained. They didn't seem to suffer from being completely alone. Family groups appeared to travel together, but as often as not, they traveled alone, as Kiran had before she had invited herself to join him.

Except for the few times he'd displayed a sexual interest in her, he hadn't seemed all that inclined to socialize. He had never asked about her family, her friends, or her life before or after the disaster. He'd never shared any of his own background. In all the time they'd traveled together, she didn't know a whole lot more about him than she had learned in the beginning--he was on a mission, and he wasn't even inclined to tell her what that was all about--except to point out that she was slowing him down.

She hadn't really had a plan in mind when she'd decided to follow him. More than anything else, she supposed, she'd been thinking about survival, and desperate for any sort of contact with another being. Somewhere along the way she'd begun to toy with the idea that she might be able to convince Kiran to continue to be her companion or at least take her to a place where she might find one.

It was almost ... human ... that the moment she began to consider other possibilities, he seemed to have changed his mind.

But, maybe she was wrong about that? Maybe she had completely misunderstood him? It seemed probable that his culture allowed sexual freedom for the men, even if women were chattel as they had been on Earth in ancient times. Maybe he wasn't looking for, or expecting, anything else? Maybe he wouldn't condemn her if she indulged her own cravings?

But, what if he did? What if she discovered, as she feared, that she wasn't allowed to and wouldn't be accepted by him or his people if she gave in to her own needs?

She had the possibility of making a life with her own people now, though. She didn't know how likely it was, wouldn't know until she had the chance to find them, but, if they could go back to the colony and start again, would it really matter what the consequences were in relation to the Zoeans?

That was a lot of ifs, though.

Maybe it would be best just to wait and see?

She sighed. It would be really hard to say no if Kiran offered ... maybe impossible.

* * * *

They had been traveling for hours and the sun was almost directly overhead when she saw her first glimpse of the sacred mountain far in the distance. She wasn't certain, at first, that that was what it was, or if it even was a mountain. It looked more like a heavy purple cloud along the horizon. As the day wore on, however, and their escort headed directly toward it, the mountain became more substantial, discernible from the clouds surrounding it--taller than anything she could remember seeing.

Late in the afternoon, they reached the jumble of rocks at the mountain's feet and the party halted at last. Tempest wasn't at all certain she could stand when she was helped down. They'd only stopped twice, briefly, for respite and she wasn't accustomed to sitting in one position for so long.

Fortunately, when her knees buckled and she went down, her escort seemed to take it as a worshipful posture. They, too, bowed and worshipped the sacred mountain. When they rose, a brief discussion ensued between Kiran and the leader. Finally, the leader, after glancing at her several times, nodded. Their escort mounted the equestans once more, turned them, and departed.

"What was that all about?" Tempest asked, watching as they diminished with distance.

"They wanted to wait here for your return. I told them we would not need their escort further."

Tempest glanced at him. "Wouldn't it have made things easier if they'd stayed? At least then we could have ridden instead of walking."

Kiran turned to look at her. "I did not think it wise to chance it. The leader was far too interested in you."

Tempest's brows rose. "Really?" she turned to study the retreating Mordunes. She hadn't noticed. Maybe Kiran was mistaken?

"You regret that he is gone?"

Tempest shrugged. "I regret the loss of the equestans … I think." She turned to look up at the mountain. There was a steep trail of sorts leading up, or at least something that looked like a trail. She didn't see any sign of anything that looked like a Temple, though. "How long do you think you'll be gone?"

Kiran frowned. "We will go together."

Tempest looked at him in surprise. "I thought you said you had to go alone?"

He glanced away. "I do not trust that they will not return."

"Oh," Tempest responded, repressing the urge to smile. "Do you think we can make it all the way up before dark?"

"If we do not linger here."

Tempest glared at him as he shouldered his pack and strode toward the point where the trail began the climb from the desert. So much for thinking there was any possessiveness in his previous remark. He was all business now. Shrugging, Tempest shouldered the water skin and followed him.

Kirry, instead of trailing behind her as she had from the beginning, followed virtually at her heels. Tempest glanced down at the little grat several times uncertainly, wondering if it was really a good thing that the animal was becoming so tame.

It was strange to think the Mordune would consider taming a wild animal as a sign of a deity. As far as she could see, though, that was the only thing it had taken to convince them. Who would've thought it?

Kiran hadn't. She wondered if that meant the Zoeans weren't as superstitious as the Mordune. Or maybe it was just Kiran? He hadn't seemed particularly inclined even to look upon her as a woman, much less a goddess.

She shook her head. It was just so absurd to think of anybody looking upon her as a goddess! Unnerving, too.

The leader of the Mordune had been handsome, not nearly as handsome as Kiran, but very attractive. Under other circumstances, she might have been interested. As it was, she couldn't get far enough from the Mordune fast enough to suit her. She was just as glad as Kiran to see the last of them, even if she couldn't help but think it would've made his task a lot easier to have the beasts to ride.

She definitely wasn't cut out to be a goddess! Being around people who thought she was one was probably the scariest experience she'd ever had.

Chapter Ten

Tempest was bored. It had been so long since she'd suffered from that particular malady that it took a while to figure out exactly what the problem was.

Kiran had found a watering hole about three quarters of the way up the sacred mountain and they had set up camp there. He had been distant. She wasn't certain if it was because he was angry with her still or if it was because he was focused on what he'd come to do, but she didn't try to slip past the barrier he'd erected. As they settled that night, he'd told her that she would have to remain there until he returned. He had left at dawn the following morning.

Kirry, as it turned out, wasn't as much company as Tempest had thought she might be. She wasn't constrained to stay at the campsite and wandered off, leaving Tempest to spend most of the day alone--a good bit of the night, for that matter.

By the third day, Tempest had begun to wonder if something had happened. Kiran hadn't told her how long he expected to be gone.... Not exactly, anyway, but she hadn't really believed him when he'd said he might be gone for many days.

What if he didn't have any vision at all? Would she be stuck here for weeks? Months?

On the morning of the fourth day, Tempest decided she'd had all she could take of sitting around and twiddling her thumbs. Surely it couldn't hurt to do a little bit of exploring?

It would've been easier if she'd known where Kiran would be. Then she wouldn't risk running in to him.

She decided, though, that she'd just keep an eye out for him and make sure she didn't bother him. As she neared the top of the mountain, she slowed her steps, trying to move as quietly as possible. She stopped when she caught her first glimpse of the plateau at the top. Coming up on her tiptoes, she surveyed the area as far as she could see. There was no sign of Kiran, but she caught a glimpse of what appeared to be a building cut from the stone in the distance.

She climbed a little higher, searching the area carefully. She was about to move when she heard something, dimly. It sounded like-- singing. Chanting maybe? She stopped and looked around the area again.

She saw him then and her heart skipped several beats as she ducked down again.

He was standing on the rock above the building she'd seen, his arms outstretched toward the heavens. He was so far away, it took her several moments to realize he wasn't facing the edge of the cliff he stood on. He had his back to it.

She stayed where she was for some time, watching him, but he was too far away for her to tell what he was doing. She supposed he must be offering up prayers. She could see smoke from a fire and wondered if that had anything to do with his ritual. It was cool so far up, but didn't seem cold enough that he would feel that he needed a fire.

Of course, he was much further up than her. Maybe it was colder up there?

He left the edge of the cliff after a while, disappearing from her view.

She frowned, waiting, but he didn't reappear. Easing up a little further, she looked around the plateau. There were boulders, naturally, but it was surprisingly flat and even and she began to study the rock curiously.

She realized after she'd studied it more closely that it wasn't a natural plateau. The top of the mountain had been flattened.

When she judged that an hour had passed and he still hadn't reappeared, she climbed to the end of the trail and began to wander around the summit, pausing now and then to glance toward the cliff where she'd last seen Kiran, stopping to examine the rocks more closely.

The plateau, she finally decided, had been cut away with precision. The stones were all as smooth as glass. Time would have worn away rough edges, she knew, but they looked as if they'd been cut with something like a laser. Moreover, the entire area that she'd paced felt absolutely level. No matter which direction she wandered, she could not sense any dips or inclines.

The realization intrigued her. She felt a surge of excitement at the discovery, certain it must mean that she'd been right when she had considered the possibility that the civilization on the Niahian world had been plunged backwards by some cataclysm, possibly much the same thing that had happened to Earth.

It could mean anything, of course. She really had no idea of how to go about investigating the intriguing possibility. Finally, it occurred to her, however, that there was at least one thing she could check.

Returning to the campsite, she grabbed up the skin of water and made the climb once more. Pausing to make certain Kiran was still no where in sight, she hurried over to the center of the plateau and slowly and carefully poured a little water on the stone, watching it. The water formed a tiny pool, spreading only as she added water. She stopped, watching for several moments, but the water remained where she'd poured it.

Finally, satisfied, she moved to another spot, and then another. In all she tried five separate points. She tried pouring directly onto some of the stones, and between others. The water didn't run at any point.

Pleased with herself, she sat back and looked around. It was flat. It hadn't just seemed flat. No way was that a natural occurrence, not for such a large area. The whole plateau, as far as she could tell, was dead level.

Setting the water aside, she turned to study the 'building' at the far end speculatively, wondering if she could get close enough to examine it without Kiran seeing her.

He would be furious, she knew, if he caught her. She wasn't worried about his anger so much as his displeasure, however. He believed this place was sacred and had forbidden her to come.

She decided to risk it. She could make her way to it along the perimeter of the clearing. There were boulders large enough that she could hide if Kiran reappeared at the summit.

The circuitous route took more than an hour. She stopped every few minutes to look for Kiran, peering from the cover of first one boulder and then another, but finally she was close enough to see that it didn't just appear to have been cut from the stone, it almost certainly *had* been.

She was directly beneath the point where she'd last seen Kiran. Unless he stood on the very edge and looked straight down, he wouldn't be able to see her now, she was certain. She moved out of the boulders and went to stand directly in front of the structure.

Ten columns were evenly spaced along the front. Above them was a stone roof facade, which seemed to support the top of the cliff. Each column was set upon a plinth which in turn had been set upon one huge, smooth stone that formed a sort of porch. A tier of three stone steps, which ran the breadth of the structure, led up to the porch from the plateau where she was standing.

After a moment, Tempest climbed the steps, waiting at the top for her eyes to adjust to the deep gloom cast by the top of the structure. As her eyes adjusted, she realized it wasn't simply deep shadows that made it hard to see the back edge of the porch. It dug deeply into the side of the cliff, perhaps twenty feet. In the shadowy interior perhaps halfway between the steps and the smooth wall that backed it, a misshapen mass rose from the shadows.

She moved toward it, and as she did, the shape became more apparent. It was a statue, she realized, moving closer and peering up at it. Her heart skipped a beat as her eyes adjusted enough that she could see it more clearly.

It looked like a statue of her.

Startled, she took a step back, wondering if her eyes were playing tricks on her.

She almost chuckled when she realized she'd let her imagination get the best of her. The statue was most certainly of a woman, but it could have been modeled after anyone. It looked like her because she was wearing the exact garments the statue was wearing.

Obviously, this was a sacred place to both the Mordune, and the Zoeans. The Mordune had reproduced the garments of their 'goddess' and, apparently believing she was the physical manifestation of their goddess, dressed her accordingly.

There was a plaque near the base of the statue. Tempest crouched, studying the strange writing, but, naturally enough the writing was completely unfamiliar to her. If the Mordune and the Zoeans even had a written language now she would be surprised. It might have been by the ancestors of either, or another tribe altogether.

She moved back a little to study it. The woman was holding what appeared to be a model of Niah in the palm of one hand. A faint smile curled her lips, the sort of loving, indulgent smile a mother might bestow upon a child.

The woman's features looked disturbingly similar to her own.

Tempest shivered and turned to glance behind her. The plateau looked almost blindingly bright now that she'd been standing in the shadows for so long. She was relieved, though, to see that she hadn't been too preoccupied with her discoveries to lose track of time. She must have several hours left before dark.

She had to wait for her vision to adjust again when she turned away from the bright light to study the statue once more.

She could see where the Mordune, and possibly the Zoeans, had come up with the idea of their goddess. To anyone who had no idea what the statue represented, it did appear almost god-like, and the world in the palm of its hand....

She wondered what it had been originally intended to represent. The structure itself indicated an advanced civilization, as did the plateau. It was possible the statue had only been added for the sake of beauty. Or, maybe it meant something like a global government? Trade center?

It was unfortunate she couldn't read the plaque. She shrugged. It might be nothing more than the title of the piece or the name of the artist.

She stared at the darkness beyond, wishing she had some way to produce light. Even if it was possible to get inside, she doubted very much that she would be able to do anything but stumble around in darkness. Finally, she decided to at least examine the wall and moved around the statue. As she did, something at the statue's 'feet' caught her eye and she stopped abruptly, staring at it disbelievingly.

A grat, carved of stone, in the 'attack' stance of the beast, had been placed at the feet of the 'goddess'.

She looked up at the statue again, feeling coldness wash over her.

She stared at it for a good ten minutes, but absolutely no explanation came to mind.

Finally, she dismissed it. Unless she just happened to stumble across a book, written in the language of her own world, it wasn't likely she would figure it out.

Moving deeper into the shadows beyond the statue, she peered up at the wall. There were grooves carved into it, blind windows of stone complete with casements, a tremendous double 'door' near the center. Disappointment filled her when it occurred to her that it looked like nothing more than one giant carving.

She stopped, looking around again, wondering why anyone would build something so huge, and so elaborate, only for decoration. Maybe it was a monument? But, if so, to what? Commemorating the end of a war? Unity?

Maybe the plateau had once been the site of a city, or government center? If that was the case, though, surely there would have been ruins? She'd seen nothing but untouched rock around the edges of the plateau. Surely, even if the Niahians had carried off stones for one reason or another, perhaps to use for something they were building, there would be some traces left of other buildings?

She hadn't really been looking for such things, she realized.

She decided, once she'd thoroughly examined the structure, she would explore the plateau more carefully.

There were more words carved in the header above the door, she saw. She moved closer, peering at them. Abruptly, a faint tremor went through the stone beneath her feet. Tempest's heart jerked to a halt. She stopped, looking around a little wildly, wondering if the structure was about to collapse on top of her. The telltale scrape of stone against stone sent a jagged bolt of fear down her spine, made the hair on her neck stand on end. She whirled toward the sound, feeling her knees go weak.

The 'doors' were moving. Unable to command her feet to move in any direction, Tempest stared in horror as they moved slowly toward her, her heart hammering so hard in her chest she expected it to burst at any moment.

When they stopped, exposing a black hole, Tempest merely stared at it for some moments, too shocked even to think. Slowly, the terror subsided as her gaze flitted over the opening, studied the doors. A laugh that was part relief, part pure hysteria, erupted, and she clapped a hand to her mouth.

Weak with relief, she collapsed in a puddle, covering her mouth with both hands to muffle the laughter she couldn't seem to control.

She'd stepped within a zone that measured motion and tripped the ancient mechanism. It was automatic doors and she'd reacted to as if she had never seen such a thing before in her life.

No wonder the natives were so fearful of the place! No wonder they thought it was 'sacred'. To their minds it was magic.

When she was finally able to control herself once more, she pushed herself to her feet.

It was nothing short of amazing that the doors worked after all this time. She had no idea of the age of the thing, of course, but it had certainly been long enough that the Niahians had regressed and had no memory or record of it.

It was probably not at all safe to go inside. With the doors now open, a minute amount of light penetrated the interior, but it wasn't enough for her to do much exploring. At any rate, what if the doors closed behind her? What if the mechanism on the other side didn't work? She would be trapped.

And Kiran thought she was at the encampment. It seemed doubtful that he would think to search for her here even if he discovered she had vanished and decided to search for her.

Finally, she decided just to move a little closer. The doors had moved very slowly. If they showed any sign of trying to close, she could leap to safety.

As she walked slowly toward the doors, light flickered to life inside. She stopped, took a couple of steps back. The lights dimmed and went out. She moved forward again and once more the lights illuminated the interior.

Everything seemed to be keyed to movement, no doubt to preserve the power source.

She stopped on the threshold, leaning inside to peer around. Lights, recessed in the ceiling, advanced as she did, illuminating a huge room. In the center, a fountain came to life, sputtering droplets of water into the air, which fell back into a tiny pool at the base. The red dust of Niah coated everything in sight. As tightly as it had been sealed, even that hadn't prevented the fine particles from invading.

It smelled of dust and stale air.

After a moment, Tempest stepped inside. The moment she did so, the doors began to close. Unnerved, she leapt out again. The doors paused and began to swing open. Waiting until they were fully open, she started through, again pausing on the threshold.

After moving back and forth several times, she was finally reassured that the doors would respond and moved further inside. A shiver crawled up her spine when the doors closed completely. She turned to stare at them a long moment and finally moved toward them. As she neared, the doors began to open.

Breathing a sigh of relief, she turned her back to the doors and began to wander around the structure. There was little to examine in the room itself. Doors had been set into the walls and lined either side, but, except for the fountain and an occasional table made of stone, there was nothing to see but dust and more dust.

After looking around, she decided to see if the doors to the rooms leading off of the great hall would open as the entrance had and moved to the nearest. Disappointment filled her when it didn't open. She stared at it for several moments, examining it to see if there was a manual catch, but didn't find one. Finally, she put her shoulder against it and pushed. It didn't budge. Shrugging, she moved to the next door.

None opened, but, at the rear was another set of double doors similar to those at the entrance. At her approach, the double doors swung open and lights in the ceiling flickered to life.

It was yet another vast room, but this one was filled almost to overflowing with row after row of tall shelves. Each shelf was filled with box like objects of various sizes. Finally, she picked one up to examine it.

It wasn't a box. It was some kind of recording device she finally decided after examining it for several moments. On the outer surface, she saw symbols similar to those she'd already seen above the entrance and on the plaque beneath the statue. The outer surface, which was hard and stiff, was attached on only one side and when she lifted it she saw that, sandwiched between the outer covering were thin sheets that looked similar to fabric. They were stiff, dry and the edges crumbled when she touched them. They were also covered with the symbols, each, on both sides.

Frowning, she returned it to the space, moved down the shelves and removed another one.

It had to be some sort of recording devices, she decided, deeply regretful that she couldn't decipher the symbols. It seemed odd, though, that there were nothing but these, no mechanical devices for recording their knowledge. She shrugged. That wouldn't help her figure it out either. She didn't know any of the languages of the Niahians--or the language. It seemed possible that they had more than one.

Kiran hadn't seemed to have any difficulty understanding the Mordune, however.

After a while, she tired of looking at the recording devices. They all looked much the same to her and it wasn't likely she would suddenly become 'enlightened' and able to understand what the strange symbols meant.

At the very back of the huge room, she found something that looked far more familiar to her ... a computer.

Chapter Eleven

At first Tempest wasn't certain whether it was her imagination or not. There was no doubt in her mind that it was some sort of mechanical device, but it didn't look like anything she was familiar with--only vaguely similar.

It began to hum as she neared it and a thrill of excitement surged through her as she moved closer to study it. It had been built in a crescent shape. As she stepped up to the open end of the crescent, a light from the ceiling formed a beam on the floor. She chuckled as she saw the shape of two feet etched into the stone. That must be what triggered the hologram, she decided, glancing around at the tiny lights dancing over the structure as she moved inside and walked carefully around the highlighted area, studying it.

She waved her arm under the beam, wondering if that would be enough to trigger the system. Nothing happened. Shrugging, she stepped cautiously on the stone, peering down at the image and discovered she had stepped onto it backwards. The feet were pointing the other way. As she leaned down to look, however, something stung her on her hip. Yelping, she jumped off of the stone and looked down at the injury.

A crescent had been burned on her hip.

"Shit! What the hell is this thing anyway?" she murmured out loud, glaring at the machinery that surrounded her.

It wasn't a damned computer! Rubbing her stinging flesh, she avoided the spot on the floor and vacated the machine she'd mistaken for a computer. Losing interest in everything except her wound, Tempest rushed from the room and headed for the fountain.

Cupping her hand beneath the fine spray, she captured a handful of water and splashed it over her burn.

She was twisting, trying to get a better look at her injury when she heard the doors open. Whirling, she stared guiltily at Kiran, who stood on the threshold, staring at her as if he'd never seen her before.

Tempest was still trying to think up a believable excuse for her behavior when Kiran, looking at her as if stunned, slowly moved toward her.

"I can explain," she said quickly.

As if her words had released him from a spell, he surged forward. "None are allowed to enter the sacred Temple!"

Tempest gaped at him. "I didn't touch a thing.... Well, hardly anything."

Grasping her by one arm, Kiran hauled her back toward the entrance. He stopped jerkily when the doors opened, but after a moment, he strode outside, dragging her with him.

"What have you done?" he demanded angrily when he released her.

"Done?" Tempest echoed, stalling for time.

"How did you enter the sacred Temple?"

Tempest frowned at him curiously. "The same way you did. The doors opened. I went in."

Kiran studied her angrily for several moments and noticed that she was absently rubbing her hip. Catching her wrist, he pulled her hand away. The blood left his face in a rush as he stared at her hip.

Tempest felt a little faint at his expression. "Is it that bad? It hurts like hell, but I didn't think it was that bad."

"I do not understand."

"That makes two of us! I thought it was a damned computer. Then, out of the blue, this laser goes off and burns the hell out of me. What possible use could they have had for a thing like that?"

Kiran stared at her. "It is the mirror of my own. The symbol of the Guardian and the Storm."

Tempest gaped at him. "You've got a burn like this?"

Kiran shook his head. "It is a mark I was born with."

Tempest looked him over. "Where?"

He turned, pushed his loin cloth to one side to expose his leg. On his upper thigh, Tempest saw what looked like a birth mark. Bending, she examined it more closely. It felt smooth to the touch. It looked like a birthmark, except for the fact that there was nothing irregular about it. A series of dots and lines formed a perfect crescent. When Tempest stood upright once more, she realized that it was, indeed, an exact mirror of her burn, in position anyway.

She frowned. There was only one explanation if, as it appeared, Kiran had never been near one of those things.

He'd been genetically encoded.

Kiran shook his head as if waking from a dream. "I do not understand this."

Tempest empathized with his confusion. "I don't understand either, but I can tell you one thing. This is no Temple, sacred or otherwise. It's some sort of repository of knowledge … a library, maybe, or hall of records."

Kiran turned and studied the facade. "It has been accepted as the sacred Temple to Zoe for generations. How could you, an Earthling, know this?"

She studied him a moment and finally took his hand and led him to the edge of the porch, gesturing toward the paved courtyard. "This isn't natural. It was made, by Niahians some time long ago."

Kiran nodded. "This, I know."

"Do you know how?"

"No."

"I studied it before I decided to go inside to explore. It's absolutely, perfectly flat. It wasn't blown away by any sort of primitive explosives and then ground down. There are no markings that would indicate that. It was cut, smoothly, by something like a laser."

He merely looked at her and Tempest felt a touch of frustration. Kiran was no fool, but the technology that had been a familiar part of her world wasn't at all familiar to him.

"Like something we used at the colony."

Kiran nodded. Plainly, he still had no idea what she was talking about, but evidently the Niahians had discovered far more about the strangers among them than vice versa.

"You didn't think we were gods, did you?"

Kiran gave her a look that told her he found that insulting. "We understand that you are much like us--only from another world. The Keepers of the Memory tell of such things."

A thrill of excitement went through Tempest. "They know about traveling to other worlds?"

He nodded. "They have told of many strange things, some that we don't understand. It is the Keepers of the Memory who told of the prophesy. The coming of the star people was the first sign. My birth the second. Even now the stars begin to align for the great darkness, which we were told comes but once in a thousand years. That will be the final sign. Before that, I must find the Storm. Together we are to find the secret valley where lies the temple Zoe built to summon the waters, to cleanse Niah and return the world to a place of growing things."

Tempest frowned. "It's some sort of emergency plan. That must be it!" She glanced back at the building they'd just left. "I don't suppose you know how to read?"

From his expression it was clear enough he had no idea what she was talking about, but she grasped his arm and led him back to the statue, pointing at the plaque. "Do you know what that says?"

His brows rose. He squatted to look at it more closely, studying it. "I have seen these signs before. Not exactly like these, but similar."

"It's the written word," Tempest said, trying to tamp her disappointment. "Maybe not your language, but a language that was once spoken on this world. Each sign represents a word, or a part of a word."

Kiran shook his head and rose, staring up at the statue. "It is your image."

"It just seems to be," Tempest objected, "because the Mordune dressed me to look like the statue."

Kiran glanced at her and shook his head. "The face is yours. And, at her feet, the grat you call Kirry."

An uneasiness crept over Tempest. "It's just a coincidence."

"It is the prophesy. I refused to accept that you were the Storm, even when you told me--even when I saw that the grat obeyed you as if it knew you--because I had expected that the Storm would be a warrior."

"A lot of weird coincidences--look, you were looking for signs, because of what you've been taught to believe. Just because some of the things that have happened could be interpreted as part of the prophesy, doesn't mean they really are part of it."

"You bear the sign."

"I didn't until I stepped into that damned machine!" Tempest said irritably, rubbing the wound at the reminder, although it had ceased to sting and throb.

Kiran looked up at the statue. "How can an unbeliever bring life to our world?"

Tempest bit her lip. "Look, I never said I didn't believe. At least, I think it's gotten all garbled in all the time that's passed. Whatever happened on this world, your ancestors must have devised a plan to help repair the damage. Maybe *they* left, expecting to return later and reclaim Niah. Maybe they were the star people referred to? Not us."

She took his hand. "Let's go back inside. Maybe we can find something that will explain what needs to be done?"

Kiran looked doubtful, but he didn't object. It wasn't until Tempest was inside that another thought occurred to her.

The symbol on Kiran's leg, and now her hip, was important enough that it had been genetically encoded into the gene pool--or at least Kiran's line--as insurance. It must be some sort of security code to gain access to important information. She wasn't certain how, or even why, she'd been able to activate the machine that had burned one into her own flesh, but she knew that must be the purpose of it. Tugging at his arm, she led him to one of the doors she'd been unable to open earlier, pushing at him until he was standing directly in front of it.

When nothing happened, she twitched the flap of his loincloth aside.

An audible click made both of them jump. Tempest chuckled with triumph when she turned and saw that the door had been released. Pushing on it, she grabbed Kiran's hand and led him inside as the lights overhead flickered on. There was disappointingly little to see for all that, but Tempest refused to be daunted. She checked the virtually empty room thoroughly anyway before moving on to the next.

If nothing else, she'd proven, to herself at least, that the mark *was* a security code of some kind and that it would give them access to areas that had once been deemed important. It had to be the key to the 'prophesy' that was so important to Kiran and she was determined to find answers for him if she could.

In the end, despite Tempest's determination, they found nothing of any significance to either of them. They discovered a room filled with maps, but since neither of them were able to understand the markings, they could tell little about them. It might have been maps of different areas of Niah, or some other world.

Kiran said little throughout the search. Tempest was too involved with her own thoughts, and finding answers, to think much about it.

Finally, tired and disheartened, she returned to the great hall. Kiran was standing with his back to the fountain, looking up at the ceiling. She studied him for several moments, trying to decide what he must be thinking, how he must be feeling.

Guilt swamped her with the sudden realization that she had been so caught up in her excitement over the discovery that she hadn't spared a moment for how devastating this would be for him--His whole religion, his society, had been built around misconceptions and half truths.

How would she feel?

She tried to imagine it, but failed. In a way, she supposed it would be something like she'd felt when she discovered her safe world wasn't safe at all, that something invisible to the eye had breached their security and killed them all before they even realized they were dead. She supposed he must feel as she had when everything that had been a part of her world had been snatched away in the blink of an eye, leaving her to try to figure out how to go on when she had no one to show her or tell her how she was supposed to manage it.

It didn't matter than most of her excitement had been because she thought she could figure out how to make the 'prophesy' come true, because it was so important to him.

She had shattered his beliefs and she couldn't even justify it by making everything come out right.

As if he suddenly became aware of her presence, he turned slowly to face her. His face was devoid of expression and Tempest felt a flicker of alarm. She moved toward him, wrapping her arms around his waist. "I'm sorry. I only wanted to help. I've messed everything up, haven't I?"

It comforted her when, after only a fractional hesitation, he wrapped his arms around her, holding her tightly. "You have done what you were destined to do. You have done no harm."

The alarm of before resurfaced and Tempest pushed a little away from him, looking up at him. "But ... there is no magic here! It's science--lost to your world, but still science."

Kiran smiled faintly and lifted one hand to stroke her cheek with his fingers. "I do understand, Tempest. I know the star children believe that all Niahians are backwards savages … I understand that we lost much knowledge … But we do not lack intelligence."

Tempest blushed despite her best effort not to. "I didn't mean that!" she said, knowing it was a lie. They had felt so superior, despite their plight. And she'd thought they were right, the Niahians *were* savages. She hadn't realized that, in truth, the colonists were no better off at all. They still had some of the knowledge that the Niahians had lost, but cut off as they were, they had been destined to regress just as the Niahians had, destined to reach the point where they had exhausted all that they had and could focus on nothing but surviving.

Kiran sighed, stroking her hair. "Fire hair. I have never seen hair this color. It was said that the Storm would have hair of fire."

"But...."

"There is magic here," he murmured, leaning toward her and brushing his lips lightly across hers. "When the doors to the Temple swung open and I saw you here, by the water, I knew it … even though I had never truly believed before."

Chapter Twelve

Kiran's lips felt like magic as he brushed them lightly back and forth across hers. Tempest's eyes slid shut. Consciousness burrowed to the back of her mind with little more than a whimper of protest. Her breath caught in her chest.

It was as if electricity arched from him, reaching down inside of her to set fire to the blood in her veins. Dimly, she recalled that she had lectured herself about the wisdom of yielding to him. It flickered through her mind that what she wanted was probably dangerous in ways she couldn't begin to imagine, but her mind and body only acknowledged that this was something she wanted.

Briefly, his hard mouth melded with her own, clung for a fraction of a heartbeat. Tempest released the breath she'd been holding in a rush as he drew back slightly to look down at her. With an effort, she opened her eyes to look up at him, wondering if he'd been as affected as she had.

His face was taut with restraint. His eyes gleamed with a mixture of need and doubt.

She realized he was waiting--to see if she would deny what she'd felt as she had before?

Like a flock of noisy birds, thoughts flooded through her mind, the voice of reason clashing with the demon of want. His arms slackened around her, holding her loosely, allowing her to know that he would release her the instant he saw rejection in her eyes.

Doubt assailed her. Disappointment warred with a sense of relief.

She realized she'd wanted him to flood her senses so thoroughly that she couldn't think, didn't have to, so that she could excuse herself if she decided later that she'd made the wrong choice.

He wasn't going to give her the coward's way out. He was demanding that she make her choice, now, based solely on her feelings toward him. Frowning slightly, she dropped her gaze to his chest. As she did, she felt him withdraw, not just physically, but emotionally.

Sensing that he would withdraw far away, fearful of losing her only chance, she placed one hand on his chest, just above his heart. It thudded reassuringly against her palm, hard and fast with the feelings he hid. Her own heart echoed that painful song of desire and fear. Abruptly, certainty settled inside of her, bringing a sense of peace. Whatever their differences, and despite her inexperience, she knew they felt much the same.

She moved closer, burrowing her face against his chest, above his pounding heart, closing her eyes and welcoming the sense of being enveloped by his warmth and his scent. He sucked in a shuddering breath as she pressed her lips to his skin, flicked her tongue out to taste the saltiness of his flesh. His hands tightened almost painfully at her waist as she rose up on tiptoe, nibbling a path of kisses and playful bites along his chest to his throat.

A tremor went through Kiran that was part desire, part relief, and partly the effort to hold his desire in check at her tentative exploration. Bending his head, he buried his face against the side of her neck and breathed deeply of her, felt dizziness assail him with a hard rush of desire that engorged his cock. His desire for her had tormented him so long that his mind threatened to shut down altogether as a red haze of madness descended. He could think of little beyond the nearly overwhelming urge to push her to the floor and thrust inside of her until his seed exploded forth, filling her with himself, claiming her for his own.

Anxiety found a tiny foothold in his fogged brain, however, as he tightened his arms around her and felt the delicacy of her form.

Her frailty both fascinated and alarmed him. It made him feel protective and at the same time, huge and clumsy and fearful that he would damage her if he lost control.

He pushed her a little away from him, gulping in deep breaths of air as he struggled to tamp the fire that threatened to engulf him. As he did so, however, he felt her mouth glide across his cheek, seeking his in mute appeal. The rush of her breath from her own desire sent a fresh flood of need through him. Mindless in his need, he covered her mouth with his own, felt his entire being focus upon the point where their bodies met and melded. Desperate for the taste of her, he raked his tongue along her lips, pushed them apart as he imagined parting the soft petals of her woman's flesh between her legs, and thrust his tongue inside the hot, moist interior of her mouth in a desperate prelude to the merging he was trying to hold in check until he felt she was ready for him.

Tempest moaned in pleasure at the shock of sensation that flooded her with his invasion. Slipping her hands up his shoulders, she held on tightly as she went up on her tiptoes to press herself fully against him. She felt his arms tighten reflexively around her. In the next moment, he released the vice-like hold. A hand settled at her waist and then she felt the skate of one callused hand along her back, moving restlessly from her neck, down her spine to the waistband of the garment she wore, slipping past it and cupping her buttocks, squeezing. As if impatient to feel her skin, the hand moved upward again and then down once more, this time his fingers delving beneath the thin fabric even as his tongue moved restlessly over the sensitive flesh of her mouth.

He broke the kiss abruptly, set her away from him.

Shaken, Tempest opened her eyes with an effort, stared at him in confusion.

He scrubbed his hands over his face. They were shaking, she saw. He was breathing hard, fighting to regain control of himself.

"Why did you stop?"

"I can't do this," he said harshly.

The words sent a shaft of hurt through her. "You don't want me?" she asked in confusion.

A look of anguish crossed his features. "I don't want to hurt you," he said tightly.

Tempest was more confused than ever. Did he mean wound her emotionally? Was he saying he feared she would become attached?

Would she?

"Too late," she muttered, trying to keep her chin from wobbling. If he'd left that very first day instead of forcing his way into her life, she might have been spared, but from the moment he'd pulled her close to him to share his warmth he'd bound her to him as surely as if she'd been chained to him.

That was why she'd welcomed the news that there were other survivors from the colony, because she'd told herself they would be her salvation from pain. He so obviously didn't want her in his life. He desired her, at least a little. She knew that, but she also knew he hadn't had a great deal of trouble ignoring his instincts. Surely he wouldn't have been able to wield that much control if he'd really wanted her?

It must be her inexperience, she decided. Knowledge without experience only took one so far. She wasn't skilled enough to drive him past the point of resistance.

If she hadn't been so enthralled with the sensations he was creating inside of her she would've realized she wasn't enthralling him.

She bit lip, trying to control her chaotic emotions. His taste lingered, however, and it only made matters worse. Shivering as the heat of passion abruptly abandoned her, Tempest crossed her arms and, suddenly embarrassed by her own loss of control, turned away. A knot of misery gathered in her throat and she swallowed convulsively against it, trying to dislodge it. She cleared her throat, looking around at the room blindly while she tried to think of something off hand to say. "It's alright," she murmured to herself. "I'm not hurt." It was a lie, of course, but she thought if she said it to herself enough she could begin to believe it.

She heard movement behind her and stiffened, half afraid he'd leave, half fearing he would approach her. Then she felt his warmth behind her, the touch of his hand on her waist. She twisted away from his touch, took a couple of steps before she turned. "Don't," she said sharply, then forced herself to take a deep, calming breath. "Just … don't."

His face hardened. "I only want to protect you."

Tempest swallowed with an effort. She wasn't really interested in hearing his reasons. "From what?"

"From me."

She gave him a look. "How noble of you," she muttered, trying without much success to keep a note of sarcasm out of her voice.

He strode toward her, gripping her upper arms almost painfully. Tempest winced and he released her abruptly. "You are so small, so frail. When I touch you I can not think and if I can not think, I have no control. I'm afraid I'll hurt you."

Tempest stared up at him in surprise. It hadn't occurred to her that he might be afraid she'd break.... Perhaps because she'd never doubted that he wouldn't hurt her on purpose? Or, maybe he wasn't afraid of breaking her bones with his strength and weight as he was that her body was too small to accommodate his serpent?

She'd be lying to herself to say she'd never suffered any qualms, but surely her body wouldn't betray her in such a way? Tease them both, only to discover their bodies were not compatible? She felt a warm wetness bathe her sex at the thought and dismissed her qualms, certain quite suddenly that they could find a way to please each other regardless. Hesitantly, she reached toward him, cupping his cock beneath his loin cloth. He grunted as if she'd struck him, sucking his breath in sharply. "Shouldn't it be my decision?" she murmured, dismissing the doubts that assailed her as she felt the breadth and length of him experimentally, ignoring the frantic lurch of her heart.

He caught her shoulders, seemed to debate with himself briefly, and then bore her down onto the stone floor of the great hall. Tempest gasped at the coolness against her bare back, seeping through the thin garments, but as she felt his welcome weight settle against her, the discomfort fled. Wrapping her arms around his neck, she lifted her lips for his kiss.

A sort of madness seemed to seize him, almost frightening in its intensity. He thrust the narrow strips of fabric of her top to each side of her breasts with shaking hands and covered one trembling peak with a hungry mouth, suckling, scraping her distended nipple with his teeth. Tempest gasped, then groaned as pleasure shot through her with almost painful force. She tensed as he moved his attention to her other nipple, hot moisture flooding her sex as he fastened his mouth over it and sucked greedily.

She clutched him tightly, digging her fingers into his shoulders, then stroking the muscles of his back, gasping for breath, dizzy with the perfume of lust. When he released her nipple at last, he sucked the rounded top of her breast, and then her throat, licked a hot path up her neck and bit gently on her ear lobe. Seemingly determined to devour her, he lifted his head almost at once and covered her mouth with his own, thrusting his tongue inside, raking it possessively along her own, sucking, then thrusting. With each thrust of his tongue inside her mouth, she felt the thrust of his hips, the hardness of his cock against her thigh, the restless stroke of his hand on her body, thrusting her garments impatiently aside.

She moved restlessly against him, her pebble hard nipples brushing against his chest. The motion, the hardness of his flesh against her softness, sent echoes of the pleasure his mouth had created. As if he'd sensed her need, he broke the kiss and moved downward once more, kissing each breast in turn before he moved lower still, nipping her trembling belly with his teeth. Tempest clutched at him, stroking any part of his flesh that she could reach.

She gasped when he buried his face in the apex of her thighs, jerking upward, clutching his shoulders. He ignored the frantic tug, prying her thighs apart, licking her cleft, biting her gently, sucking. Tempest felt as if her heart would explode. Her breathing became so labored it was more like little gasping cries. She felt the tension building in her body toward explosion, knew she was approaching her peak.

Frustration filled her. She didn't want her first time with a man to be like this. She didn't want a clitoral climax. She dug her fingers into his shoulders. "No!"

He lifted his head, his eyes wild with desire. "I want to taste you," he said harshly.

"I need you inside of me," she gasped a little desperately.

His face hardened. He closed his eyes, but in the next moment he was moving over her. She felt him fumbling to release his engorged member, felt the heat of it along her inner thigh as it seemed to search for her opening of its own accord. He cupped her sex with his hand, parted her moist flesh with his fingers and delved inside of her. Tempest arched against his hand, gasping. He groaned. Pushing her thighs wider, he settled between them, holding his weight on one arm as he nudged her with the rounded head of his cock

Tempest clutched him a little frantically, wriggling to align her body with his, eager to feel him filling her, desperate now to feel him becoming a part of her.

Kiran caught his breath on a groan as he felt her flesh part reluctantly and the head of his cock enter her. He panted, fighting the urge to thrust full length inside of her, trying to allow her time to adjust to the intrusion. She moaned, moving against him. He couldn't tell if it was with impatience or pain, but blinding, mind numbing pleasure lanced through him. Her heat engulfed him, her slick passage beckoned and, unable to resist, he pushed.... And made no headway, his thrust merely pushing her along the floor. Gritting his teeth, he caught her around the hips with one arm, holding her as he pushed again and slid slowly deeper. Her fingernails dug into his flesh like talons. The minute pain distracted him, clearing some of the haze from his mind, and he paused, realizing dimly that he'd met the barrier of her virginity. Pushing himself up, he looked down at her.

She opened her eyes and looked up at him trustingly, her eyes glazed with passion and wonder, but uncertainty, as well.

His heart felt as if it would beat through his chest wall as he struggled for control, gritting his teeth to fight the nearly mindless urge to thrust so deeply inside of her he could loose himself in her. "I'm hurting you," he said through gritted teeth.

He was and the pain had diminished the pleasure, but it hadn't diminished her need to feel him deeply inside of her, to cradle his hardened flesh next to her womb and feel his seed spill into her. Lifting her legs, she entwined them with his, arching her hips wordlessly and pushing up against him.

A shudder went through him. Sweat broke from his pores. She could hear him grinding his teeth as if it was he who was in agony, he whose flesh tore. Unable to contain it, she whimpered as she felt the burning, but caught her breath and pushed again.

With something like a growl, he matched her thrust and sank so deeply inside of her she thought for a moment that he would rip her in two. Panting, she held herself still, willing the pain away. Slowly, it subsided and she began to relax, felt her body adjusting to him.

He began moving them, jerkily at first, then with more surety. Pleasure sparked to life once more, twinges of the pleasure she'd felt before, but something else, as well, the sense of being a part of him, a deep satisfaction that was purely emotional that she had claimed him even as he claimed her. The joy fed her tactile senses, sent a rush of delight through her. She felt a rush of warm moisture fill her body cavity, easing his way, felt the muscles of her vagina contract around him. He thrust harder, grinding against her clit in an effort to burrow deeper inside of her. A jolt of pleasure went through her with each grinding thrust, each harder than the one before, each building the tension inside of her.

He went still suddenly, gasping, his cock jerking. The realization that he'd climaxed brought her to explosive fulfillment, as well, as he began thrusting once more, short hard thrusts that pumped his hot seed inside of her. She clutched him tightly, groaning as it swept over her in blinding waves of gratification.

She felt completely drained of energy as it subsided at last. Apparently, Kiran was drained, as well, for he lay heavily atop her now, making it difficult to breathe. She held him tightly anyway, unwilling to let go of the experience so soon.

Like annoying insects, her doubts from before began darting at her the very moment her desire gave way to reality once more. They would not be ignored, buzzing closer until she could hear the tiny complaints in her head. The doubts, or her growing awareness of her surroundings, quickly made it impossible to ignore the discomfort of struggling for breath while she was pinned between a stone floor and the body of a behemoth. Tempest pushed at his shoulders. He merely grunted, but after a moment, he pushed himself up with a great effort and moved off of her.

"Mer-cay!" he exclaimed as he rolled onto his back. "This floor is cold!"

"Hard too," Tempest muttered. "Next time, let's find a soft place to … uh … fuck."

Kiran glanced at her sharply, frowning. "This is not a good word."

It was like being scolded for her slang by her parents, but Tempest forced a chuckle. "Yes, it's naughty. What did you do? Get the Earthlings to teach you all the 'bad' words first?" She thought about it a moment. "Guess that's what I'd do. That way you at least know if somebody's said something nasty to you."

Kiran sat up slowly, studying her. "I did not pleasure you?"

Tempest was never afterwards certain why she did it, except that he seemed to disapprove of her now that she'd had sex with him, but it challenged the immature side of her to do her worst. She crawled over to him and straddled his lap. "Oh yes!" She shoved her hand down between them, cupping his sex. "This is a very nice serpent you've got here. He can crawl in my hole any time."

He frowned, studying her face uneasily. "We should not have done this. We are not paired. I've shamed us both with my lack of control."

It needed only that. Tempest knew there was no reason to feel shame for expressing her sexuality … at least her own people didn't feel that way. To her surprise and anger, however, his disapproval was enough by itself to make her feel ashamed of her behavior. She rolled her eyes. "Oh boy. How did I know this was coming?"

Standing abruptly, she moved away from him, discarded her garments and climbed into the pool beneath the fountain. "I'm sticky," she added plaintively when she saw he was watching her still with a mixture of uneasiness and dawning anger.

"We should talk."

"Let's don't and just say we did, huh? I'd really rather not."

Chapter Thirteen

"Why do you not wish to talk?" Kiran demanded angrily.

Tempest gave him a look. "In all the time I've known you, you've hardly said three words to me. Why do you suddenly want to talk?"

He flushed at the jab. "I need to know why you are angry with me."

Tempest studied him for several moments and finally sighed. "I don't think I *am* angry with you ... not really. I think I'm mad at myself ... but I don't want to talk about that either.

"What are we going to do now?" she asked, changing the subject abruptly as she sloughed as much water from her skin as she could and stepped from the fountain pool. "I mean, about the prophesy?"

Kiran didn't speak for several moments, his gaze riveted to her gleaming, wet body. "There was no true prophesy," he said slowly.

Tempest, who was trying to figure out how to put the garments on once more, glanced at him. "Not mystical, maybe, but ... it was something that needed to be done."

"You believe that?"

Tempest stared at him for a long moment. "I know that whatever it is, it's vitally important to Niah," she said positively. "I don't understand exactly how it got tangled up in religion over the years--it doesn't really matter. What matters is that whoever left this message thought it was important enough to imprint that in your genetic code," she finished, pointing toward the symbol on his thigh.

Kiran frowned. "This part I do not understand."

Tempest bit her lip. There was no way to completely explain such a concept to someone who didn't even have the most rudimentary idea of genetics. She thought about what he'd said about her hair, however, and grasped a strand between her fingers. "You said you'd never seen hair this color? It's carried inside a person's body, the genetic code that makes a person have this color of hair … or your color. It's the reason children look like their parents or their grandparents. That mark on your leg isn't something that would be carried, like skin tones, hair or eye color, the shape of your mouth or nose. It's foreign. It would've had to have been put there, in one of your ancestors. And if someone thought it was important enough to do that, then it's got to be very important."

Kiran's brows rose. "What of yours?"

Tempest shrugged. "OK, so that part is *really* weird. That part I don't really understand. Maybe it was a mathematical probability somebody figured out. Maybe your ancestors could actually see the future and knew what would happen. I don't know except that I found the machine that they must have used in the old days … before whatever it was that happened. Parts of this building were obviously open to pretty much everyone. But there were other areas that we couldn't enter without the code. The doors wouldn't open. Who knows what those rooms were used for before--government most likely.

"That's part of the prophesy, though, so it's something we need to open a door. The part that worries me is that neither one of us understand the written language--I guess they hadn't considered that possibility--but, even if we find our way to whatever place we were supposed to go to, I don't know if we'll be able to figure out what we're supposed to do once we get in."

Kiran thought about it for several moments. "We must return to the Keepers of the Memory. If there is anyone who would be able to tell us, it would be the Keepers."

Tempest frowned. "Was that supposed to be part of the prophesy?" Kiran shook his head and she bit her lip thoughtfully. "We're not going to have time to go back and still make it to the right place at the right time, are we?--Because I don't think there would have been any mention of a planetary alignment if it hadn't been significant."

"We will ask the Mordune for their aid."

Tempest looked at him in surprise, but she didn't argue, knowing he was right. Unless they could get an equestan, there was no way they'd be able to learn what they could from the Keepers and still reach the sacred valley before the alignment.

* * * *

Tempest was glad she had something to focus on that took precedence over her personal concerns. She should have been relishing the memory of her sexual encounter with Kiran. He had been her first. It had been wonderful--though the first was generally not expected to be--but she knew it was because she had grown emotionally attached to Kiran.

The problem was, she was afraid she had misunderstood everything in her inexperience. She had gotten so caught up in the way he made her feel that she'd simply 'assumed' he was feeling the same things. Afterwards, when she'd been clear headed enough to think, it hadn't taken long to realize that Kiran hadn't said anything to indicate that it was more than lust--not that she would've objected to a purely lustful encounter under other circumstances--but the culmination had intensified her emotional attachment to him.

It would've been far wiser to have kept her distance.

It was too late to worry about that now. It was done. And she had no idea how to handle it.

She knew she was being cowardly. She should have just talked to Kiran about it, but she couldn't bring herself to allow the possibility of having her pride further trampled. It would've been wonderful, of course, if he'd professed undying love or something like that, but nothing he'd said seemed to indicate the conversation might be going in that direction.

She was furious with herself. Why was it that it was never enough to *know* something was bad for you? Why was it that people always had to try it, just in case they were wrong? Kiran was a wonderful person. She couldn't blame him. He'd made it clear she was in his way. He hadn't tried to seduce her. He'd done his best to ignore his urges.

Knowing all of that, she'd worked hard to focus on the possibility of a future with people of her own kind, whom she understood and knew would understand her. She really had tried to ignore her growing attachment to him, and her urges to entice him. If she just hadn't pushed it by giving in to the urge to get close to him physically, everything would've turned out all right. He wouldn't have given in. She wouldn't have experienced that oh-so-fleeting moment of triumph when she felt like she'd claimed him … and she wouldn't be feeling sorry for herself, wounded, lost.

She glanced up to discover that Ta-li was watching her. He was the leader of the group of men who'd captured her and Kiran, and it was he who'd volunteered to take her and Kiran where ever she needed to go.

It wasn't too difficult to see he lusted for her. She knew without a doubt what that expression meant now. She wasn't going to flatter herself that it was anything else. He'd been kind and helpful, but she couldn't think of any logical reason why it might be more than that. She hadn't even been able to speak to him--not directly, anyway. He didn't know her language, and she certainly didn't know his.

Not that it mattered.

She was still emotionally attached to Kiran and, in any case, she thought she'd learned her lesson. As she'd known, it would be far better to focus on her own kind ... always assuming there were enough of them left that she had that option.

Smiling at him a little vaguely, Tempest returned her attention to the distant range of mountains that was their destination.

Kiran, accepting her determination to pretend nothing had ever passed between them, had gone back to being withdrawn. Except for necessary conversation, they'd hardly spoken since they had left the mountain and headed for the Mordune encampment. Once they'd reached it, they had made arrangements to leave immediately, and they'd scarcely left the backs of the equestans since.

They were loathsome beasts. They stank for one thing. Otherwise, they were temperamental and stupid. The one she rode tried to stomp poor Kirry any time the poor little thing came anywhere near it.

If they weren't running out of time, she would've preferred walking.

If, she amended, they weren't running out of time and things weren't so uncomfortable between her and Kiran now.

The sun was low on the horizon by the time they drew near enough to see the city of tents dotting the sand below the mountain. Despite everything, Tempest felt her spirits lift. Kiran had said there were Earthlings among them. Maybe she would at least have the chance to see them and find out if it was anyone she knew.

She was dismayed, however, when chaos suddenly broke out in the encampment and men surged forward, bristling with spears and swords. Kiran spoke to Ta-li and then, when Ta-li nodded, guided his beast alongside hers. Taking the leading ropes from Tali's grip, he urged both equestans to take the lead while the Mordunes fell back a few paces.

"What is it? What's wrong?"

Kiran's expression was grim. "We are enemies of the Mordune."

"Oh." Tempest felt stupid. Between her own emotional problems and the task she was trying to help Kiran complete, she hadn't given much thought to the possibility that they might find a poor welcome when they arrived at the Zoean encampment with a party of Mordune.

Kiran glanced at her. "There are many here who know your language. Guard your tongue. It would be … dangerous to say anything that might call our religion into question."

Tempest felt a coldness wash over her. She hadn't thought of that either … now she was going to be fearful of even opening her mouth.

Her heart was still fluttering with fear when Kiran drew the equestans to a halt a short distance from the men who'd come to 'greet' them.

They might know her language, but it was their language they used in the ensuing, somewhat heated, discussion. Finally, with obvious reluctance, they were allowed to proceed with their escort.

Despite her nervousness, Tempest glanced around with some interest as they rode between the tents. Many of the Zoeans, like Kiran, were dressed in loin cloths of animal hide, though here and there she saw women wearing woven robes very similar to the robes the Mordune wore. The 'star children' weren't hard to pick out among the Zoeans.

As Kiran had pointed out, they were far smaller in stature. Beyond that, the Zoeans were almost universally dark haired, ranging from blue black hair to a medium brown. Five of the half dozen humans she saw had varying shades of blond hair, from barely brown to an almost colorless white.

The oldest was a boy who looked to be about fifteen Earth years. She didn't recognize any of them and disappointment filled her.

The older boy looked her over with interest and she smiled at him, realizing that he seemed vaguely familiar. He was younger than her by two or three years, and it had been nearly two since the disaster. He could not have been one of her classmates, but she decided she must have seen him--or perhaps she'd known an older sibling?

Kiran urged his beast alongside hers, glaring at her and Tempest gaped at him in surprise.

He ignored the look, focusing his attention straight ahead.

As if he didn't know he'd blocked her view!

After a moment, she dismissed it. She didn't have time, now, to try to get to know any of her fellow survivors.

They stopped at last before the largest tent, which stood in the center, just as it had been in the Mordune encampment. An old man emerged. Kiran dismounted and moved to help her down. Grasping her around the waist and setting her lightly on her feet, he released her almost immediately, turning and kneeling before the man.

Tempest looked down at him a little nervously, wondering if she was supposed to kneel too. He hadn't said she should. Surely he would've told her, she thought a little frantically.

She relaxed a fraction when Kiran rose once more, allowing her attention to wander while the two men talked. Occasionally, she would hear a word that she recognized, but she wasn't even close to understanding their language. The tone, she understood, and anger was universal. Finally, Kiran bowed once more and grasped her wrist, leading her back to the equestan and helping her to mount.

Tempest was confused. She waited until they had ridden through the encampment and dismounted at the foot of the mountain before she asked him, however.

He was obviously controlling his temper with an effort. "Mikissi will not intervene on our behalf."

"I don't understand. Why would we need him to?"

Grasping her around the waist, Kiran helped her down from her saddle. "The priests will allow no one to enter the temple."

Tempest stared at him. "What temple?"

"The Temple where the Keepers of the Memory live."

"You mean to say we rode all this way and we aren't even going to get to talk to them?"

Kiran's expression was grim. "We can speak through the priests. It has always been the way of things. The priests present the problem to the Keepers and give us the answer once they have consulted them."

Tempest looked at him doubtfully. It didn't seem to her that they would make much progress that way, particularly when they wouldn't be able to ask straightforward questions to begin with. They were going to have to think of some way to find the answers without seeming sacrilegious. "Do you think they'll help us?"

"We will find the answers we need," Kiran said tightly.

He strode away then, spoke to Ta-li for some time and apparently came to an agreement. Ta-li and his men mounted the equestans and, tugging the two Kiran and Tempest had been riding behind them, rode off.

"They will circle the mountain and climb the northern pass. They will meet us at the Temple by mid-day tomorrow."

Tempest felt a touch of alarm. "What are we going to do?"

"We will seize the temple."

"We're going to kill the priests?" Tempest exclaimed, horrified.

A faint smile curled Kiran's lips. "We will hope it doesn't come to that."

As it turned out, to Tempest's immense relief, it didn't. The 'priests' didn't fit Tempest's concept of holy men. They were armed, and made it evident that they were willing to die to defend the Temple. However, they did not expect to be attacked. As she and Kiran presented themselves at the gate, Ta-li and his men went over the wall. The priests were surrounded and subdued before they had fully realized the Temple was under attack.

Once they had rounded them all up and locked them in one room, she and Kiran began their search of the sacred Temple. They found the Keepers of the Memory in the catacombs beneath the main Temple, accessible through a set of doors that only opened to the code of the crescent.

Tempest turned to look at Kiran with startled eyes when the doors opened. "You're a priest of the Temple."

Kiran glanced at her. "Yes."

The implications made her feel ill, but she dismissed them as the full magnitude of it struck her. "They lied to you. The whole thing--all of it was a lie and they knew it for a lie. You weren't born with the sign. They took you to that place.... They must have."

Kiran's expression was grim, but he shook his head. "I do not know. I was not born into the priesthood as they were," he said, jerking his head in the direction of the room where they had locked the priests. "I was brought to them as a young boy after the death of my parents. They said that I was born with it."

Tempest frowned. "But ... if the priests are the only ones who can access this chamber, then they must either know of the code and machine ... or it's in their genetic line. Which means your father, or grandfather, would've been a carrier of the gene."

Kiran shrugged dismissively. "It is not important now. We need to learn what we can from the Keepers and leave before it is discovered what we have done."

It hadn't occurred to her that it might be discovered, at least not while they were still there. She'd thought the greatest danger was in seizing the temple to begin with. She should have realized before that Kiran had a very good reason for sending Ta-li and his men to take another path. "The people come here often?" she asked in alarm.

"When they make camp here, yes," Kiran said, grasping her arm and striding down the dimly lit corridor. It seemed to go on for miles, in a slight, but steady descent.

Tempest's alarm grew as they went. She was fairly certain that it would've unnerved her traveling so far underground, but knowing they might be discovered at any moment, and that there was only one way in, or out, unnerved her far more. It didn't help that it occurred to her that it was a very strange place for anyone to live and she couldn't help but worry that they were risking their lives for something that might not even exist.

They came at last to a vast chamber. As they had at the sacred temple of Zoe, lights flickered on before them, keyed to sensors.

The vast computer at the back of the chamber came to life, as well.

Chapter Fourteen

Despite the fact that she was very familiar with such things, Tempest felt her heart jerk to a standstill as two ghostly men appeared before them and began to speak. Stunned, she walked toward them slowly, not even realizing that Kiran had stopped until she waved her hand through the images and turned to look for the projector. "Holograms. I've never seen anything quite like this, though." She moved away and studied the images and the strange garments they wore.

"What are they saying?" she asked, turning to Kiran.

He frowned. "Some of the words are familiar, but they speak strangely."

Tempest looked at him in dismay. "You can't understand them?"

"Some."

"Ask them what happened to Niah."

Kiran's brows rose, but he asked the question. A hologram of the solar system appeared. The men spoke in droning voices for several minutes. Then the image of Niah was enlarged and they began to gesture at certain points. The image enlarged again, zooming in on particular areas as the dialogue continued. After a few moments, the image of the globe disappeared and a collage of other images began to flash and disappear. Even without a grasp on the language, Tempest began to get some idea of what had happened just from the images.

The planet had become destabilized at some point. It wasn't clear on how that had happened, perhaps because the Niahians themselves weren't certain. One thing was clear, however, and that was that the destabilization had created killer storms, widespread flooding and great loss of life. There'd been a global war, but Tempest couldn't tell whether the war had caused the destabilization or if it had arisen out of the chaos of the breakdown of the ecosystem, possibly because the survivors were fighting over the limited resources that were left.

She was on the point of telling Kiran to stop it when another image flashed into view, zooming in on a map location and then zooming closer still to show a building much like the temple of Zoe. This one, however, was in the side of a mountain that had two peaks. A wide valley separated them.

Kiran tensed. "The secret valley," he murmured.

The image disappeared and was replaced by the interior of a building, the 'temple', Tempest presumed. The two men reappeared, walking in the building and gesturing to points of interest.

"That's it!" Tempest exclaimed. "Tell them to zoom out and show us the location on a map."

The computer complied and Tempest and Kiran both moved closer, examining it. "Does any of this look familiar?"

Kiran frowned, but after a moment he shook his head. "There is no place that looks like this.... Now."

Tempest thought it over. "Tell the computer to show us this place in relation to the hall of records."

Nothing happened. "Try the government center."

The map remained unchanged and Tempest frowned in frustration, then rolled her eyes as it occurred to her that she was using the wrong reference point anyway. "Tell it to show the facility in relation to our current location."

An image was promptly displayed and Tempest felt a spurt of excitement and triumph. "Now overlay with cardinal compass-- now scale the distance."

They studied it for some time. "How far you think?" Tempest finally asked Kiran.

He shrugged. "Two days with the equestans. Five walking."

"Do you think Ta-li will let us take the equestans?"

Kiran was quiet for some time, thinking. "We don't know what will happen when we release this … whatever it is. Perhaps nothing at all, for it is ancient." He looked around as if he'd suddenly become aware of the passing time. "We should leave here. We can decide what we must do when we are in a safer place."

Turning, they hurried back the way they had come. Tempest had to stop several times to catch her breath, however, for the climb back up was far more difficult than the walk down. Finally, they reached the main chamber of the temple once more, however. Ta-li met them, speaking rapidly.

"Mer-cay!" Kiran snapped. "We've been discovered. A group from the encampment is already on the way up."

Abandoning the Temple abruptly, they raced through the outer gates. The Zoeans in the lead spotted them and, shouting furiously, charged. Kiran grasped Tempest's hand and ran. As frightened as she was by the pursuit, however, Tempest was already winded from the long climb back up the corridor. She stumbled, almost falling. Without a word, Kiran caught her, tossed her over his shoulder and rushed onward. The impact of hitting his shoulder knocked the breath from her and black spots swam before her eyes, growing larger until they completely filled her vision and awareness drifted away.

When she became aware of her surroundings once more, she discovered that she was atop one of the equestans, cradled against something hard and warm. She lifted her head and looked up at Kiran, still more than a little dazed. "What happened?"

"We managed to out distance them … most of them. Two of Ta-li's men were killed."

Tempest bolted upright with a gasp of horror. "Fighting?"

"Not much. They stayed to hold off the men in the lead. They were overwhelmed."

Tempest looked at the men accompanying them and the three saddles, now empty, stunned, disbelieving. "But ... we're only trying to help ... everyone."

Kiran's lips tightened. "You are naïve, star child! You did not think they would simply listen, did you?"

She deserved the rebuke and she knew it. She had only considered how devastating it would be to Kiran to discover his religion, indeed the entire society they now had, had been built upon a corruption of truth, and deliberate lies. She hadn't considered that it would create a break down that could end in war. "They will all die," she said suddenly.

Kiran frowned.

Tempest gestured to the rolling desert around them. "The Niahten beneath the desert--This is not desert, or wasn't. This is powdered stone and soil, most of it deposited here by flooding. All of the places you consider temples were built high in the mountains and dug into the rock ... because it was the safest place. I don't understand exactly what this device is that we're supposed to activate, but I do know there's only one way to make this world green again and that's by water ... a lot of water. There'll be nothing to stop it once it's released. If it's rapid and widespread, anyone in the low areas could be swept away.

"We could end up destroying all life on Niah, not saving it."

"Those who believe in the prophesy will be saved," Kiran said with conviction.

Tempest looked at him curiously, wondering what was going through his mind. He'd seemed to accept that there was no true religion, no true prophesy--but rather warnings and instructions from the distant past. "How?"

"The alignment is their sign to move into the mountains for the coming. *They must gather all that they cherish together and wait. When the great darkness falls upon the land, they must offer prayer for deliverance and wait for the light to come again. And afterwards, behold, acres of water shall await them to quench their thirst and the thirst of the land and all living creatures, water will fall from the sky and the land will become green once more with growing things.*"

Tempest digested that for some moments. "All the believers? And they know that the alignment is within the next few days?" She thought it over for several moments, realizing that nothing they could do would make much of a difference anyway. As far as they knew, the alignment had a direct impact on the efficiency of the equipment. If they didn't try now, following the instructions the best they could, it seemed doubtful they would have another chance. And Niah had no communications beyond word of mouth. There was not enough time to reach everyone with a warning. "You said that the Mordune's beliefs were similar, but not exactly the same. Do they know about that part of the prophesy?"

Kiran glanced toward Ta-li and questioned him sharply. Ta-li frowned, asked him something. After a brief conversation, Ta-li turned to his men and spoke sharply at length. Within moments, they began to peel off, each taking a different direction.

"I guess that means no?"

Kiran shook his head. "Ta-li says his people know of the prophesy, but they are not true followers of the religion. Until they saw you, he didn't believe either. He thinks they will follow *the word* anyway, but he doesn't want to chance it. He and his men go to make certain that the tribes take refuge in the mountains."

"They took the equestan that I was riding."

Kiran looked down at her. "You do not need it."

It wasn't going to be very comfortable for her to travel in such close proximity to Kiran for several days, however. Not that there was any point, now, in objecting. His arms tightened around her when she tried to sit up. "Do not move away from me, Zheri Cha."

Tempest looked up at him in surprise, before she could point out that the saddle wasn't really big enough to put a lot of distance between them, he spoke again, smiling faintly.

"I meant in spirit."

"Oh," Tempest said, frowning as she tried to figure out what he meant.

He touched her cheek caressingly with the back of one finger. "Tell me how I have offended. I will undo it if it is within my power."

Tempest swallowed against the sudden lump that had risen in her throat. "I don't think I could explain. I mean, you really didn't offend me. Anyway, it hardly seems the time."

"There may be no other time," Kiran said quietly. "Neither I nor you know what will happen when we enter the secret valley. And we have nothing but time, now."

Tempest had avoided considering the possibility of danger in their task, but she knew he was right. It might well blow up in their faces. She sighed. "I doubt you'd understand even if I tried. We come from such different cultures."

His lips tightened. "I understand more than you realize, obviously."

Tempest frowned. "Obviously *not*, if you're going to get insulted every time I try to explain."

His lips twitched. "Then I will listen and try to understand without making judgment."

Tempest shrugged, but found she couldn't meet his eyes. "In the temple ... when we had sex, you made me feel like I'd done something wrong afterwards. It didn't feel wrong to me, or bad. I felt good about it because ... because I thought.... Well, I guess I misunderstood, that's all." She hadn't realized how hard it would be to try to put it into words. She threw a glance at Kiran and saw that he was frowning.

He sighed finally. "You have decided that you will return to the place of the star people with the others from Earth?"

Tempest shrugged miserably. "I suppose. If they want to and it seems safe to go back." She forced a smile. "It would be nice to be around people that shared a common background with me, to be around things that are familiar."

Kiran was silent for quite some time. Finally, he spoke a little hesitantly. "If the fates allow, I would do my best to build a stone house like that for you."

Tempest glanced at him in surprise. "Why would you do that?"

"To bring joy to your heart once more, like that you feel when you speak of that place and *the people*. When you look upon those of your own kind."

She knew he was referring to the time when she'd seen the other survivors in the encampment. She remembered that he'd placed himself between them, blocking her view, and a little flutter of something unidentifiable went through her. Hope?

"I do not know the things that you know, but I am willing to learn."

"You would do all of this just to make me happy?"

"Yes."

"Why?"

He swallowed a little convulsively. "I ... uh...."

Turning on the saddle, Tempest lifted a finger and began to trace swirls with her fingertip over his chest. "What does Zheri Cha mean?"

Kiran flushed, but frowned, obviously trying to figure out how to translate, obviously distracted by the movement of her finger. He covered her hand with his own, trapping it. "Difficult one."

Tempest sat back. "Difficult one?" she echoed. "As in, pest?"

A faint smile curled his lips. "Cherished one?"

He was teasing. Tempest didn't know whether to laugh or cry, because she couldn't decide if he was teasing, but meant it, or if he was just trying to annoy her.

Irritation won out. Snatching her hand away, she twisted, putting her back to him.

An arm slipped around her waist, pulling her back against him. Leaning down, he began to whisper in her ear, words that were unfamiliar to her, words of his own language. "I suppose that means I'm nothing but trouble," Tempest said irritably when he stopped.

"It means, I do not know pretty words in your language."

Tempest tried to turn to look at him, but he held her snugly.

"I ache with emptiness when you are not near me. I can not think. Sadness fills me. Stay with me, Tempest. Do not leave me. I will be your people."

Tempest sniffed, but despite all of her efforts, tears gathered in her eyes and began to run down her cheeks. Kiran stiffened, tugging her around so that he could look at her, touching the tears on her cheeks. "You do not want this?"

Sniffing, Tempest slipped her arms around his waist. "It's all I ever wanted from the first ... for you to want me."

"I did want you."

"You left me," she pointed out.

He sighed. "Because I believed it was the right thing to do, not because I wanted to."

"I love you," Tempest said. "Whether it was the prophesy, or fate, or just pure luck, I'm so glad you happened along to find me."

Kiran's arms tightened around her. "This ... love. This means you will stay with me?"

Tempest pressed a kiss to his chest. "It means everything you said to me before--I want you. I need you. I'm lost without you."

He captured her face in his hand and urged her to look up at him. He met her half way, kissing her deeply. "I love you, little grat."

And when the many worlds of the star system aligned, the Guardian and the Storm entered the chamber in the temple of the secret valley. Before them, the doors opened and light spilled down upon them. Together they walked to the ancient stone and each placed their hand against the crystals that had been placed there. The world trembled as the great darkness fell upon it. A great rumbling was heard throughout the land as the goddess Zoe threw off the restraints that had been placed upon the waters, and they spilled forth from the depths of the chasm and onto the land, cleansing the world and bringing new life.

The End

TWILIGHT'S END

Prologue

"Legend has it that long, long ago the gods grew angry with the world because their chosen people had not cherished the gifts that they had given them. For many ages, the gods had smiled upon them for their cleverness and the *people* had flourished. The *people* had built great cities filled with wonders unimaginable, cities that reached up into the clows. They had built marvelous machines that flew across the hvens, carrying the *people* from one great city to another like the wind. As they flourished, the *people* learned many things to bring comfort to their lives. They had great healers to bring succor to the ill and even to give them life once more when the evil seeds came upon them and caused them to wither.

"But they had also built terrible wepons to kill, wepons that were so powerful that they could level whole cities of their enemies with great fire that turned all before its wrath into ash.

"In time the *people* grew lazy, weak, slothful. They had raped the life giver, the mother Eirt, and taken so much from her that she became weak and sickly. The strong preyed upon the frail, the clever upon the weak of mind, the young upon the old.

"A day came when those who called themselves god sayers, who worshiped in the temples of the gods, were overcome with a fever of the mind. They began to believe themselves to be the hands of the gods. Ignoring the teachings of their gods, they took vengeance and judgment upon themselves. They killed in the names of the gods, destroyed, did all that they could to deprive those they considered unlike themselves of the right to life and liberty, for they had come to believe that only *they* knew the true way, only *they* had the right to the gifts of the gods, only *they* had the right to prosper. All had to believe as *they* believed, or it was their duty as the hands of the gods to smite them down and destroy them.

"The gods grew angry and fearful of these tortured souls, fearful for their wandering children. For, like doting parents, they had felt joyful when their children had grown wise and strong and begun to make their own way, to walk alone. They had forgiven their follies, knowing that in time they would attain the wisdom to use the gifts they had given them wisely.

"When they saw that the blasphemers, those whose minds had been eaten with a sickness that made them believe that they were higher and more favored than the other children, would inherit the Eirt with the blood of their brothers, they looked for a way to protect the *people*. But they could find no way pluck them from the path of destruction of those who called themselves god sayers. They saw that the only hope for their children was to wreak their anger upon all, to cleanse mother Eirt and allow the *people* who survived the chance to learn from their mistakes and to begin again.

"For many days, they rained fire upon the land to cleanse it. And when the great cities of the children sank beneath the sea, they blew their breath upon the land to cool the fire, making of it a frozen land. In time, when they saw that only a few of the *people* remained and they were miserable with cold and hunger, they took pity upon their children and blew their breath upon the land again and brought warmth to mother Eirt.

"And they wept for what they had had to do to their children, bringing green growing things to the land so that the *people* were no longer hungry. It was then that the *people* discovered that the gods had left one gift to their children on mother Eirt to show them that they were forgiven and that they would be allowed to prosper again. They placed this gift upon the lifeless plain, where none could deny that it was a gift from them, and them alone, for it sprang from the withered, lifeless soil in that place where nothing else grew. And this is why, each year, we travel to that holy place and offer prayer and wait for the sign that we are smiled upon once more. Each year, at the time of the spring solstice, the gods lift their eye upon us to see if we have learned our lesson and are worthy of the gift they left us."

The children around the fire were silent as the village Speaker ceased his sayings, their eyes wide as their imaginations ran rampant, scurrying to conjure the wonders the old man spoke of.

"What gift did the gods leave us?" one of the younger children asked in an awed voice.

Most of the older children tittered nervously at the child's audacity, but others glared at the child for interrupting their favorite tale, fearing the Speaker would grow angry and refuse to finish the telling.

The village Speaker merely smiled at the child, however. "We do not know. There are many legends that surround the holy place, but we can not say which are true, or if any are true, for few have ever dared approach beyond the ridge that surrounds it."

The child frowned. "Then how do we know that this is a gift of the gods?"

"We know," the Speaker said with finality.

Rebuked, the child was silent for several moments. Finally, ignoring the elbow his older brother plowed into his ribs, he spoke again. "What is the gift?"

The speaker smiled as if he had been waiting for the question. "Renewal."

The child looked awed at that for several moments, but then frowned. "What is renewal?"

The Elder chuckled. "You will not understand if I tell you."

"Tell me!" the child demanded. "I can not understand what I am not told!"

The Speaker studied the child with a mixture of censure and approval in equal measure. "The gift of all that was lost."

The child's jaw dropped. He considered that for many moments and finally frowned as he discovered a flaw. "But--the holy place is quite small! It is hardly bigger than my father's lodge. How could it hold so much?"

"You ask too many questions, Khan!" one of the older children said angrily. "We will not hear the rest of the legend if you make the Speaker angry with your silly chatter!"

Khan, stood abruptly, glaring at the older boy, silently daring him to take action beyond the use of his tongue.

The Speaker studied the child with both amusement and interest, for Khan was sturdily built for all his tender years, brave and wise beyond his years, and showed promise of being a great warrior some day, a leader of the *people*, possibly even greater than his father was.

Summoning Khan before his youthful determination could lead him to openly challenge the older boy, Notaku 'growing bear', who was easily twice his size, the Speaker bade the child to sit at his knee.

"The legends say," the Speaker continued, "that one day a great warrior will be born unto the *people*, a leader with wisdom, and skill, and strength, and without fear. And this great warrior will pass unharmed beneath the watchful eye of the gods and pluck the gift that they have left for us and open it for the *people*. But the unworthy shall not pass."

Khan digested that in silence before another question rose to his mind that demanded answers. "How will he know he is the chosen one?"

"The gods will not smite him down as they did others who tried, lackwit!" Notaku snarled angrily.

The Speaker placed a hand upon the thin shoulder of Khan before he could leap up to face the challenge.

Khan tamped his anger with an effort, but the Speaker was pleased to see that he could master his anger and find wisdom. "This is true, Speaker?"

The Speaker shrugged. "Yes. Some have grown bold in their prowess as warriors and come to think of themselves as *the chosen* and they have tried to open the gift of the gods and failed-- because they were not worthy."

"I saw one!" Rikard, Khan's elder brother volunteered excitedly. "He approached the dwelling of the gods and the box sang to him at his touch and then the red eye of the gods fell upon him and burned him to dust!"

The Speaker gave Rikard a chiding look. "Because he had strength and fearlessness, but not the wisdom! The chosen will be gifted with all three.

"Go now, young magpies, for it grows late and you will need rest if you are to grow into strong warriors."

The children glared at Khan, certain his questions had ruined the mood and cut short the tales the Speaker wove for them, but they bowed respectfully to the elder and scurried toward the lodges of their fathers.

Khan watched them with a mixture of resentment and uneasiness. "They are angry with me for asking questions," he said, looking up at the Speaker. "It was wrong?"

The Speaker smiled, patting his shoulder, and then guided the child toward the lodge of his father protectively. "It is never wrong to gather knowledge, for knowledge leads to wisdom, and one can not find that without questioning the world around them. You are not bound by what others believe. Seek the knowledge you desire, Khan. The gods will favor you."

Chapter One

Khan stared up at the stars in the sky above that had slowly been moving into the alignment of the spring solstice, wondering what had possessed him to come to this place again. As a child, he had come with everyone else each year to gape in wonder at the 'gift' the gods had left them and to offer up prayers. As a youth, he had come because it was demanded of him. As a young man, he had come out of curiosity.

He had known thirty and four winters, however, and he had long ago ceased to believe in the legends, realizing that they were merely tales the Speakers passed on to each new generation to teach the young the folly of the *people* in the past so that they would not make the same mistakes their fathers had made.

In his time, he had seen many warriors, desperate to earn the respect of the people and the right to leadership, approach this thing that rested in the lifeless valley and vanish into dust when the baleful eye of the gods fell upon them.

In his time, he had lost his wonder of the tales told around the campfire and begun to believe that it was not meant as a gift to the *people* at all, but a warning.

Whatever it was, it could not be intended for the *people*, he reasoned, for all who had tried to open it had perished.

And yet, deep down, he knew why he had come.

He had come to collect the gift of the gods, or dispel the myths surrounding this place, to turn the *people* away from the old beliefs, because so long as they believed they had only to wait and they would be given all that they had lost, they simply waited. They would not seek the knowledge that had been lost that only awaited rediscovery. They would not work to lift themselves from the struggle to merely survive and begin to build something better for future generations.

Hope was all well and good, but not when it encouraged the *people* to simply wait like children for the gift to be presented to them. There was nothing good about their stubbornness to cling to the old ways and their refusal to learn and grow.

He had been camping on the ridge for days before the faithful began to gather to witness the event. In those days while he awaited the event, he had carefully and methodically delved his memories of each attempt that had been made before, those he had witnessed himself, and those that had joined the legends from generations past, trying to find the pattern of their failure so that he could find success.

The people of many tribes and from distant places had gathered upon the ridge before he found the key he had been seeking.

The singing box, he realized finally, dealt death because those who had tried to play it had not found the song that would open the gateway.

The magnitude of that epiphany sent a surge of triumph through him until he realized that he did not know the song that would, nor any way to discover it. No one was given a second chance. When they plucked the wrong notes, the gods, or whatever guarded the dome, smote them.

He considered that for a time and finally arrived at the realization that since it was the red eye of the watcher that smote them, he must find a way to keep the eye from seeing him if he was to gain the time he needed to find the right notes. When his thoughtful gaze at last fell upon his shield, excitement and purpose filled him, for he knew he had discovered the way.

He had found the shield in the forbidden land. It was smooth, and thin, hard like stone, but stronger than stone. The shield protected him in battle with its strength, but like water, it also reflected images, making him virtually invisible when he remained still.

Grimly, he rose at last when he saw the tentacle of the gods begin to rise above the dome to look about the land. Grasping his shield, he slung it across his back, hefted his long knife and made his way down the ridge, ignoring the murmurs of the worshipers as they saw his intent. When he had planted his feet firmly on the cool soil of the lifeless plane, he drew his shield from his back and positioned in along his forearm by way of the leather thongs he had attached to it.

All who had gone before him had approached the place of the gods as worshippers and supplicants. He strode across the plain as the warrior he was, boldly, guarding himself from the watchful eye with his battle shield. When he had reached the dome that rose from the sands, his heart was pounding with the same mixture of excitement and dread that he felt when he rode into battle astride the back of his nay beast.

Surprise flickered through him when he saw that the dome was stone much like the stone that the people found in the fields they cultivated. This was smooth and rounded, however. Thin lines that he realized were cracks formed a strangely regular pattern upon it. Sparing a wary eye toward the tentacle, he situated his shield to protect him and reached out to touch the stone with his hand. It was cool, but beginning to warm already from the sun as it breached the horizon and began its upward climb.

Gods had not created this, he thought derisively. It was much the same as the dwellings that he had found when he had explored the forbidden lands and discovered the remnants of those who had spawned the legends, the corrupters of Eirt. Satisfied that at least some of his guessing had proven to be truth, he moved around the dome until he found the gateway and the singing box. Ignoring both for the moment, he aligned his shield carefully, so that each time the eye passed his way the shield would reflect its gaze way from him.

When he was certain that he was protected from the death gaze, he stroked the nubs on the singing box. Each made a different sound and he matched them with those he had recalled, eliminating the songs that had spelled death for the others.

Time passed. He began to feel cramped and stiff from crouching in the same position as he stroked the singing box, calling forth notes in every order that came to mind, trying to use the sounds to evoke songs the *people* knew. Impatience and discomfort began to play upon him, but he persevered determinedly. Slowly, the sun climbed upward, until it burned him, and still he stroked the nubs. In time, the sun passed above him and ceased to singe his skin but his other discomforts only grew more pronounced.

The time came when Khan at last lost patience with the singing box. He began to pound on it with his fist and finally took his long knife and struck it, tearing it from its resting place. Abruptly, the gateway opened. Stunned, Khan merely stared at the gaping black mouth for several moments.

A voice called from inside.

"Intruder alert! Intruder alert! Activate bio-pods. Begin resuscitation."

Frowning at the strange words, Khan threw one last glance at the death eye and stepped beyond its range, into the gaping cavern. He froze once he had entered. A bluish glow began to brighten the throat, until he could see the length and breadth of it. Dancing lights of different colors joined the bluish glow, among them the red eye of death.

As one reached out toward him, he moved his shield swiftly to block its touch. Heat blossomed on his shield, but began to dissipate almost at once. More careful now, for he hadn't anticipated that the death eyes would be inside as well, he began to move slowly along the tunnel-like room, watching for the death eyes, using his shield to block them each time one reached for him.

The strange, detached voice continued to chatter, dogging his steps. "Intruder is in the upper corridor of the emergency exit route. Intruder is approaching the hatch."

Khan frowned, wondering what would hatch. He had to move constantly, repositioning the shield because of the death eyes, but he had scanned all that he could see to search for threats, the walls, the strange ground beneath his feet, the roof of the cavern. He had not noticed any eggs of any kind.

He reached a second gateway and stared at it in consternation for many moments. Finally, he placed his back against it, holding his shield toward the tunnel where the death eyes stalked back and forth angrily, searching for him. He had just decided that he was as protected as he could manage when one of the eyes reached out and touched the ground near his feet, within a hair's breadth of his toes. He jerked the digits back even as heat seared the tips, grinding his teeth against the bloom of pain. Sweat broke from his pores as the certainty grew upon him that there would be no returning the way he had come. The death eyes had discovered his ploy. Even now they were searching for a way to reach around the shield they could not penetrate.

As he twisted his head from side to side to examine what he could see of the gateway, he saw another of the singing boxes. For several moments frustration, fear, and anger threatened his composure. This one was smaller than the one outside with fewer nubs, but he had no idea if that would make it easier to find the song, or harder.

He was tempted to simply destroy it as he had the first, but the gateway had closed the moment he stepped through, trapping him inside. He had no idea what this one might do if he destroyed it, as well. It might open as the first had, allowing him to enter, or it might simply bare its teeth and crush him when he tried to jump through.

Dragging in a deep breath, he sought inner calm and began to stroke the box.

To his relief and surprise, he found the song after only a few tries and the gateway behind him opened. He studied it suspiciously for a moment, looked inside for any sign of threat and finally leapt through. The moment he did so, the gateway closed. He stared at it in consternation, but realized fairly quickly that whatever trouble it represented, at least the gate prevented the death eyes from the other corridor from touching him. He had scarcely stepped into the new tunnel when the blue glow surrounded him as it had when he had stepped through the first gateway.

Having repositioned his shield in front of him the moment the gate closed behind him, Khan peered cautiously around his shield, surveying the new tunnel for the death eyes.

None appeared. He remained still and watchful, certain that they were only waiting for him to relax his guard. When enough time had passed that he began to feel the cramping of his muscles from crouching on the icy stone beneath him, he decided that the death eyes must not be able to reach so deeply inside.

Or perhaps, as the old ones claimed, he had passed the test of fire and been accepted?

He didn't believe that. The voice was still complaining, making it clear that it watched him still.

Lowering the shield cautiously, inch by inch, he scanned the tunnel carefully. When the red eyes still did not appear, he finally rose from his cramped position and followed the tunnel. This tunnel was short and ended at a hole. Focusing his gaze downward, he saw that there were strange shaped branches embedded along the side in a regular pattern. After glancing over his shoulder one last time, he slung his shield on his back and shoved his long knife into the sheath also strapped across his back. Sitting down on the hard surface, he tested the odd shaped protrusions and discovered that they did not bend beneath his weight.

Realizing that they had been carefully placed to help in climbing, he began a slow descent, pausing now and again to study the dimly lit tunnel below him for any new threat. He could see flickering light below, almost like firelight dancing in the wind except that the colors were different--blue, white and yellow. He reached the bottom without further incident, however, and paused as the blue glow began to brighten the area around him, making the harshly flickering lights that crawled along the walls dim by comparison.

It was a single room, he saw, somewhat larger than the main room of his lodge, perhaps twice as large. In the center of the room rested a strange object that looked to be made of ice or crystal such as the *people* occasionally found in the Eirt, but far larger than that, nearly as long as he was lying flat, nearly as wide as his shoulders were broad. The dancing lights reflected off of it, and yet he could see even from where he stood that there was something inside.

Curious, he moved closer.

He had covered perhaps half the distance between the standing tunnel and the object when the voice surrounded him again.

"Beginning final phase."

He jumped, freezing in his tracks and searching the area swiftly, expecting to see the death eyes once more. When they did not appear, he relaxed fractionally and returned his attention to the crystal.

Smoke filled it, hiding what he'd glimpsed before.

Dismay filled him. He strode toward it quickly, certain the fire would consume whatever it was before he had the chance to see it but he realized almost immediately that there was no heat, no sign of flame--only the smoke.

Frowning, he reached out and touched the surface. It was cool, not cold like ice, but smooth, unlike the crystals he had seen. The hard shell of crystal retreated from his touch, drawing upward, like a threatening hand. He stared at it hard, wondering if this was some new threat, watching to see if it would move again. When it didn't, he flicked a gaze toward the hollow that had been revealed.

The smoke swirled and writhed along something pale and pink. His attention caught, he stared unblinkingly as, inch by inch, the flesh of the creature emerged from the swirling mist and he found himself staring down at the most beautiful, perfectly formed woman he had ever seen in his life.

His heart seemed to stop dead in his chest for several painful moments. He found himself holding his breath as he allowed his gaze to drink in the smooth, flawless, almost pore less skin, the curve of hip and thigh and the deep red of the triangle of hair that covered her woman's mound, the narrowness of her waist, the rounded globes of her breasts. The same dark red hair curled around her still face, winding like a vine along her body and ending near her ankles.

Slowly, the wonder dissolved, driven back by the realization that she could not be real. It could not be anything but a likeness of a woman, he decided, carved from some lustrous stone. After a moment, he scrubbed his damp palm against the skins of his loincloth and lifted his hand to touch her. He almost jumped back when he discovered that her flesh was warm and supple, not cold and hard as he'd expected.

She was not only real, she was alive. It could not be otherwise or she would not be warm to the touch. After a moment, he lifted his hand from her arm and stroked her cheek, feeling his heart beginning to pound once more as he felt the softness of her skin, her warmth.

But he frowned in confusion. She slept the sleep of the dead. She had not stirred at his touch. He could not even see that she'd drawn breath.

Finally, he nerved himself to lean closer, to see if he could hear what he could not see, breath.

He was almost nose to nose with her when she opened her eyes and stared up at him with unfocused eyes. Her lips parted and she dragged in a long, slow breath.

Startled, he straightened abruptly.

A duet of low growls greeted the movement and Khan felt the fine hairs on the back of his neck lift. Very slowly, he turned to face the menace that had crept up behind him while he stood staring in helpless awe and adoration at the goddess he had discovered at the heart of the temple of the gods.

Chapter Two

Khan had never seen the likes of the two creatures that had hunkered down threateningly not ten feet from where he stood, looking as if they might leap at him at any incautious move. They were two of a kind. Each had a head nearly as big as his. Each, although crouched, their limbs drawn up closely to their bodies, seemed to be as long as he was tall, and very likely was of a similar weight, as well, or possibly heavier. Each was covered all over with short, light brown hair that grew close to their bodies. And each opened their mouths in a parody of a smile to reveal a great many wickedly sharp teeth.

Ever so slowly, Khan began to move his hand toward the hilt of his long knife. His fist had scarcely closed about the hand grip, however, when something soft and warm closed over his hand. A jolt went through him, but he didn't dare take his eyes from the threat before him.

"Heel, Sachi! Nomi!"

A mixture of relief and warmth spread through Khan at the sound of the musical voice that had uttered the words, warmth at the pleasantness of the sound, relief that the beasts instantly became docile, sitting back on their haunches and staring at the space beyond his shoulder as if awaiting further command.

"Who are you?"

Khan slowly turned his head at the question, but he didn't particularly relish the thought of turning his back on the beasts. The goddess, he saw, had sat up on her knees to face him. "It's all right. As long as you don't threaten me, they won't attack."

Khan frowned. He didn't like to doubt the word of a goddess, but he didn't have a lot of confidence that the beasts wouldn't pounce the moment he presented them with the target of his back. "I am the chosen one," he said flatly, because he wasn't at all certain that he was, and he didn't particularly care for the idea of lying to a goddess.

"Really?"

He heard movement behind him and realized the goddess was struggling from the crystal that had entombed her. "Jesus fucking Christ! Why is it so cold in here? And where the hell did all this hair come from?"

She uttered a gasp and sprawled headlong on the floor beside him.

He glanced down in consternation and saw that her glorious hair had tangled around her legs. Keeping a wary eye on the beasts, he knelt beside her, grasped her arm and helped her to rise.

"Shit! No wonder I'm so damned cold. What happened to the clothes I was wearing? How long have I been in the bio-pod, anyway?"

Khan looked her over curiously, wondering why she was angry, wondering why she seemed to be asking him questions--as if he was supposed to have answers. All he had were questions of his own.

"I am not Jesus fucking Christ," he responded apologetically. "I am Khan, and I do not know the answers to your questions."

She blinked at him several times, slowly, and began to chuckle. Khan didn't particularly care for the fact that it seemed to be something he'd said that had set off her amusement, but he liked the sound of her laugh. Warmth blossomed in his belly and he had to fight the urge to smile back at her.

Waving her hand at the two great beasts, she dismissed them. "Sachi! Nomi! Go!" When they had retreated to the far end of the room, beneath the tunnel, Khan saw with some uneasiness, she looked him over with interest. "So--you weren't sent to wake me, were you?" she said in a chiding voice.

Uncomfortable beneath her frank, knowing stare, Khan shrugged. "I am the first to pass through the gateway in memory. If there were others, it was long ago, beyond even the memory of the Speakers."

"Speakers?"

"The elders who keep the stories of the *people* and pass them from generation to generation."

She looked dismayed and he felt uneasiness move through him again, wondering what he had said that had disturbed her. After a moment, she seemed to dismiss whatever it was that had disturbed her and began to struggle with her hair. When she'd disentangled herself from the wild mass, she tossed it over her shoulder and began to stride purposefully about the room, touching the walls. Khan watched her, perplexed, and even more uneasy when a low hum replaced the deafening silence of the chamber. The blue glow disappeared. It was replaced almost instantly with blinding white light, brighter even than the sun. He stared down at his arms in dismay for several moments, fully expecting the flesh to begin to cook from them. Nothing happened. He didn't even feel warmth from the light.

Realizing finally that he had no reason for concern, he dismissed the wonder of lights brighter than the sun that did not burn and allowed his gaze to follow the woman hungrily, wondering if she actually was a goddess and would make his manhood wither if he so far forgot himself as to seek her favors.

"What name may I call you?" he asked finally, wondering even as he did so if it was allowed for him to address her without first being addressed by her.

She glanced at him over her shoulder before returning her attention to the strange squares of light along the wall. "I am Dionne. That means divine queen. In mythology, she was the mother of Aphrodite, the goddess of love," she said, smiling at him in a way that made his heart stammer erratically. She went silent abruptly, tapping one of the squares. "This can't be right," she muttered.

Curious, Khan crossed the room to stand behind her and leaned closer, peering at the object that held her attention. He could see nothing about the strange, dark lines that should upset her, however. "What is it?"

Her head whipped around at the question. Khan hadn't realized how closely he'd leaned toward her until she did so and the tips of their noses brushed. Disconcerted, they moved apart.

It seemed to take her a moment to gather her thoughts. Finally, she tapped the square crystal with the strange markings. "According to this, I've been entombed here for almost a thousand years. This is wrong. It shouldn't have taken more than a couple of hundred at the most. God only knows if any of the materials are still viable after this length of time--if that's even accurate. I certainly don't."

Khan stared at her. He hadn't understood half of what she'd said. It wasn't because of her strange accent. Most of the words she'd spoken up until then had made sense in his mind. The words themselves were strange to him and he could put no meaning to them. There was one part of her speech that he thought he did understand though. She had said the gods would know, but she didn't. Did that mean she was not one of them, he wondered, feeling a surge of hopefulness. "Which god?"

She blinked and then frowned. "Uh, I didn't actually mean god. It was just a figure of speech. Didn't you hear what I said?"

"Yes."

"You don't understand, though, do you?" she asked shrewdly.

He felt his face color with embarrassment, abruptly feeling like a child who couldn't entirely understand the conversation of the adults around him. He dismissed the urge to lie, however. "No."

"Never mind," she said soothingly, lifting a hand to stroke his cheek. "You can't be expected to." She studied him thoughtfully for several moments. "You're an intelligent fellow, though, aren't you? You couldn't have had the security code, but you figured out a way in." She looked him over from head to foot. "And not a scratch on you."

He stiffened as she examined him curiously but with a marked lack of passion--reinforcing his impression of before. After tracing the totem tattooed on his cheek and studying him with a strangely intense look, she appeared to dismiss it. Lifting one of his arms, she studied his hand and fingers, testing the flexed muscle of his upper arm. Dropping the arm to his side once more, she ran her palms over his chest and belly and finally squatted down in front of him to examine his legs with the same curious, almost detached, interest as she had his arms.

Two conflicting emotions washed through Khan like a tidal wave--desire--and anger as it dawned upon him that she was examining him in the same manner that he examined the nay beasts they captured to tame. When she stepped around behind him and he felt her hand squeeze one of his buttocks, he whirled abruptly, catching her wrist. "I am not a beast," he growled threateningly. "I am a man."

He'd forgotten the two beasts that guarded her. At his tone, or his sudden movement, they growled ominously in threatening chorus.

Dionne merely stared at him in surprise. "And you are a most handsome, wonderfully made ... uh ... man," she responded in a soothing voice. "Besides being such a clever fellow. Teeth?"

Furious by now, he gritted his teeth at her, curling his lips back in a snarl.

She patted his cheek. "Good fellow. Very nice teeth."

The comment and her careless caress knocked the wind from him, making speech impossible. He glared at her, fuming, but she dismissed him after a moment, tugged her wrist free of his grip and moved back to the wall to stare at the strange, shifting lines again.

Khan would have departed then to lick the wounds to his pride except for several minor problems. One, the beasts now lay beneath the tunnel he'd come in. And two, he couldn't recall if the singing boxes had been on the inside of the gateways as well as outside and didn't particularly relish the idea of trying to hold the two beasts off while he struggled with the singing boxes to get out.

Most importantly, as wounded as his pride was, he was loath to leave the gift the gods had left specifically for him, however disconcerting a creature she was, and he wasn't at all sure he could get her past the snarling beasts without leaving some of himself behind.

Of course, he had long since ceased to believe in the legends or the gods the *people* worshipped, but that was entirely beside the point. Goddess or not, annoying or not, he wanted the woman. He'd found her and he wasn't going anywhere without her.

She sighed finally. "Everything looks fine, as hard as that is to believe after all this time. Evidently they did a far better job than anyone imagined." She glanced at Khan. "I'm cold," she complained, moving toward him again and grasping the lower edge of his loincloth. "I don't suppose you have one of these, or perhaps something a little longer that I could have to cover myself? The clothes I was wearing fell apart from age and I expect everything else is in much the same condition, unusable."

He stared at her a full minute while her question sank in and produced the answer to his dilemma. He relaxed fractionally, feeling a smile tug at his lips as he realized he wouldn't have to figure out how to get her past the beasts. "At my lodge."

She smiled at him hopefully. "And food?"

"Yes. Skins to keep you warm and plenty of food to fill your belly." Until he could fill her belly.

She seemed to consider for several moments. "But no sanitation to speak of, I'm thinking, certainly not what I'm accustomed to. I'd have thought humans would have bounced back far better than they appear to have."

He frowned at the unfamiliar words she used. The sadness that came into her eyes disturbed him even more. "Uman?"

"Human," she enunciated very slowly and carefully. "Yes, that's what you are."

He didn't particularly like being corrected, especially not in that tone, which implied that he was a simpleton. He gave her a narrow eyed look. "I am Unan, of the Kota nation."

"Mmm, well the language has been corrupted a lot in the past several hundred years, but, the correct word is human." She looked thoughtful for several moments. "Kota? Lakota, maybe? You look like you could be a descendant of some of the first North American people, which I don't mind telling you I find curious. Very curious. We had expected the races to mix and individual racial characteristics to disappear. I will have to do some research before I proceed--well, I would anyway, but this is something we hadn't expected.

"For now, we seem to be communicating reasonably well, all things considered. Will you take me to your lodge now? Oh, and I'll need to speak with the –uh--headman? Leader?" She frowned. "Chief?"

"I am Chief," Khan growled irritably.

Her face brightened with pleasure. "Oh! Well, this has turned out far better than I would've expected considering everything that went wrong," she said brightly. "If you could just give me a few minutes? I suppose I'll have to grow accustomed to bathing in natural bodies of water, but I'd as soon make use of the facilities here before we go."

Khan frowned. He was ready to go at once. He had already stayed far longer in the strange place than he liked. It made him uneasy. Before he could forbid whatever it was she was talking about, however, she touched the wall and vanished through a hole that opened and closed so fast it almost seemed as if she'd been gobbled up. Stunned, he simply stared at the wall for several moments, and finally moved toward it, feeling along the surface with his fingertips. He found a fracture finally that was regular, about the width of a hair and roughly the size of the opening to his lodge. He did not immediately find a way to open it, however.

When he could find no edge to grip or pry against, he found the edge of the opening and began to feel along the wall. The wall opened as abruptly as it had before. He was too surprised by his success to react immediately, though, and before he could recover, it had closed again. When he found the spot the second time and the mouth opened, he leapt inside before it could close again and looked around, his attention caught by the sound of running water.

He surveyed the strange room, but he was less curious about the room than the whereabouts of his woman. When he'd finally determined the direction of the sounds, he moved to a wall that was much like the one where she had entered, running his palm over the smooth surface until he was rewarded with an opening.

He leapt through immediately, glancing around in surprise at the heated cloud of mist that filled the room. The current of air that had followed him whipped at it, sending drifts of mist swirling away and creating a path before him.

The goddess Dionne was bathing in a water fall erupting from high on one wall. Desire flooded through him like fire as he stood watching the water flowing over her beautiful body, making her skin glisten, making his mouth water with a thirst that set his mind on fire.

For several moments, his mind filled with the image of closing the distance between them and pulling her against his length to fill his senses with her. In that vision, she responded with a desire for him that equaled his for her, moaning with pleasure as he lowered her to the stone at her feet and covered her body with his own.

He'd already taken a step in her direction when another image entirely filled his mind, of her curiously passionless examination of him in the other room. That banished the previous images so quickly that he felt more lightheaded at the rush of blood *from* his groin than he'd felt when the blood rushed *to* it.

Baffled irritation replaced his ardor of moments before.

She was a strange creature. He wasn't certain what to make of her beyond his admiration of her flawless beauty. Her gaze when she looked at him was frank, open, interested--even curious. She seemed to suffer no fear of him, and yet at the same time she was cool and distant. One moment she enchanted him with her lively chatter and husky chuckle, the next she insulted him by behaving as if he was an inferior animal--or a superior animal, not a man.

It seemed inescapable that she considered him beneath her in some way, perhaps every way.

He frowned, partly from anger and partly in confusion. She had not claimed to be a goddess, and, truthfully, he simply did not believe in such magic anymore. He had seen nothing to support such thoughts, and much to disprove it.

As much as he did not understand about this place, he *did* understand that there was no magic here. He had seen similar things when he had found the city of the old ones in the forbidden lands. Those things had not worked, but in breaking they had revealed that they were things made by the hand of man.

He suspected she was from that long forgotten world and time, not a goddess, but he could not quite figure out how it had come about that she had emerged from that thing that held her alive, young, and strong.

After a few moments, he shook those thoughts off. It would take time to unravel it in his mind, if he could do so at all. He wasn't as interested in understanding in any case as he was in staking his claim to her.

She jumped when she emerged from the water and discovered him as he reached the edge of the platform she stood on. "Almost done. I just have to dry." She stepped off the platform and onto another. Air began to rush around her.

Her complete obliviousness of his intent halted him in his tracks as nothing she could have said. Nonplussed, he watched as the air pelted her from every direction. After a few moments, his curiosity gained the upper hand and Khan lifted a hand to feel the air, discovering with surprise that the air was warm against his skin.

As he watched her, she gathered the long mane of hair in her hands and began twisting it to wring the water from it. "I don't understand this. The chemicals were supposed to retard this sort of growth. Of course, I was in the bio-pod far longer than anticipated, but the nails didn't turn into great gnarled tangles," she added, studying her fingers. "But I don't suppose it really matters now. I feel fine. I'll do a bio scan in a day or so and check everything," she added thoughtfully.

When she stepped from the second platform, she strode past him to a table attached to the wall. Above it was a surface that reflected her image. Khan moved closer, peering at it and finally placed his hand on the reflecting surface that produced a perfect image, without any blurriness or wavering. As he watched her, she opened a cavity beneath the table, which he saw was a box of some kind. After a quick search of the unfamiliar contents, she took a strange devise from it that resembled two knives joined at approximately the center. Slipping her fingers into the curls at one end, she grabbed the hair trailing down nearly to the floor and began to work the knives up and down over the lock she held in her hand.

The beautiful hair began to fall all over the floor.

"No!"

She glanced at him in surprise. "It's just hair. It grows."

"It is beautiful. You can not simply destroy it," Khan said, outraged at the sacrilege.

"Thank you. It'll still be beautiful short and far less trouble." She hesitated though, studying his expression a moment. "Shorter. I'll leave it to here for now since it seems to upset you," she added, examining the new length, which stopped near the tops of her thighs. "Besides, it's something to cover me until I can find clothes," she added, more to herself than to him.

When she had raked a comb through it and removed the tangles, she turned to him again. "Now we can go."

Frowning, still both angry and more than a little unhappy that she had cut so much of the beautiful hair, Khan followed her in tightlipped silence as she left the room and returned to the main room. Summoning the two beasts, she crossed to the other side and reached up to touch the wall again.

Since he now knew what that meant, Khan, who'd been stalking along in angry, wounded dignity, sprinted forward to keep her from disappearing again. He misjudged the distance, however, and slammed into her backside when she halted abruptly, apparently waiting for him. The impact launched her forward, but he managed to catch her before she sprawled out on the floor.

Peeling his palm off of her breast, she threw him a reproving glance over her shoulder and headed down the tunnel they had found themselves in. It was a short tunnel, far shorter than the two he had used to find her. At the other end, she stopped and began to play the signing box. Nothing happened.

Khan glanced around a little uneasily, wondering if her notes would summon the death eyes again, but there was no sign of them, and he finally decided that that was because it was her playing the song. She belonged here. The death eyes somehow knew that, and they would not rain death so long as she was nearby and might be hurt.

She frowned and played the tune again. The structure groaned, like an animal in agony. Very slowly a crack opened. As it did so, sand began to pour through. Fortunately, the gateway only opened a matter of inches.

Dionne stared at the sand in consternation. "How did this get here?"

Khan shrugged. "This lodge rests in the lifeless valley. The sands shift like waves upon the water."

She stared at him, obviously thinking. "This may explain the elapsed time," she said finally. "The computer was to analyze the surroundings and awaken me when the world renewed itself. There was no anticipation that this would become desert." She studied over that for a time and finally moved past Khan, heading back the way they'd come. "We'll have to go out the way you came in."

Khan followed as before, trying to tamp his impatience. A thought occurred to him as they reached the main room, however, that he found lightened his mood considerably. "The beasts will not be able to come."

She was staring at the ceiling, he saw. "Lois. Disable the security. We're going out."

"Affirmative."

Khan glanced at the ceiling, but saw no one. "She is coming also?"

Dionne bit back a smile. "No. Just us. I told her so the lasers wouldn't activate and turn us into a pile of ash."

Khan's brows rose, but he knew she must be speaking of the red death eyes. It was much as he'd thought. She commanded them. "But not the beasts."

"Them, too. Cougars can climb. They're here to protect me. I couldn't leave them if I wanted to, and until I see how hostile the world is, I don't particularly want to. "

Khan frowned, not particularly pleased by the comment, but then he wasn't convinced that the beasts she called cougars could climb the tunnel.

He allowed Dionne to go first, thinking that he could catch her if she slipped and fell. He very quickly discovered the situation had both advantage and disadvantage. He almost fell himself when he looked up and saw her cleft winking at him with every movement she made. For many moments, he simply froze, mesmerized, feeling a blinding wave of lust move through him. It wasn't until she stopped and looked down that he came to himself. He glanced down, as well, partly on impulse because she did, and partly because he didn't want her to know that he'd been simply staring at her woman's place, transfixed.

When she began to move again, he returned his attention to the object of his fascination, missed the next rung and nearly took the quick way down. Catching himself with an effort, he concentrated on making certain he had a firm hand and foothold before he allowed himself another look. He was breathing like he'd run many miles when he reached the top, however, his blood pounding in his brain and his groin until he felt like one or both might explode. She looked him over curiously, and not very approvingly. "You're not as fit as I would've thought," she commented.

He wasn't certain what she meant by that, but he strongly suspected it wasn't a compliment. Ignoring the comment since he couldn't think of anything to say in his defense, he leaned out to look down the tunnel. He was less than delighted to discover she had been right about the beasts. They didn't seem any too happy to make the climb--he could see the one in the front shaking--but neither beast seemed to be having the trouble he had expected and hoped for.

Three

The moon had risen when Dionne stepped from the bio-lab onto the soft sand of the desert. It was full. Dionne stared up at it for several moments, feeling a relief she hadn't expected. The moon, at least, had not changed. The world obviously had, a great deal, but the glowing mass above her was a reference point, a familiar landmark that gave her a sense of belonging.

Whispers and gasps from hundreds of human throats dragged her back to the present and she searched for the origin of the sounds with interest. A dark ridge rimmed the desert in a crescent shape. Along the top of it, she could see shifting shadows, some merging into unrecognizable blobs, others standing apart, silhouetted by the moon's glow.

Uneasiness moved over her at their stillness. She glanced at the man, Khan. "Tell me your people don't have some sort of taboo about nakedness."

He stared at her uncomprehendingly and she searched her mind for other words he might be more familiar with. "Will my being the way I am create violence?"

Something flickered in his eyes that was a combination of comprehension and, possibly, amusement. "Only if I have to kill them for staring at you."

Startled, Dionne merely blinked at him as she tried to follow his line of reasoning, wondering just how barbaric the customs were. "You would kill them for looking?"

He looked disconcerted that she had taken him so literally. "I will not *like* it. But since I have nothing to cover you with, I can not see that there is anything I can do about it."

She considered that for several moments and finally decided that there might be a possibility that he was feeling possessive about her for some unfathomable reason. That was not good and could lead to more complications that she would have to deal with.

Perhaps she should consider moving on when she had the things she needed?

She could not do that at once, though, she realized. There were tests she needed to run, studies to be done. In truth, she would need a guide to take her where she needed to go next since the geological and atmospheric changes had altered the landscape into a place completely unrecognizable to her, and very likely she would need more protection than the cougars could give her.

She would have to reserve judgment until she had studied the situation, but there seemed little in the way of civilization left--or progress made in that direction since the collapse of it.

An escort under those circumstances seemed essential to accomplish her mission. She was not to awaken the others until she had carried out phase one and two of renewal. They were the major part of phase three. It seemed to her that her chances of success would be greatly increased with the escort and protection of a man of Khan's stature, who was not only impressively tall and muscular, but who also happened to be a leader of his people.

"It is a very good thing that I did not cut my hair too short then," she responded finally, striving to infuse a positive note into the remark. "It will offer some coverage. Which part of the female body most incites the males?"

He stared at her blankly.

She combed her memory for other words and since it was impossible to guess what words might have survived, what words might have been corrupted, or what euphemisms and slang might currently be in use, she reeled out all that came to mind. "What part of my body is most likely to attract the attention of the males with--uh--mating in mind? Sexual intercourse? Copulation? Fucking? Scrogging? Bumping uglies?"

He studied her speculatively and she saw that gleam in them again. "Your toes," he said finally.

Dionne blinked at him as she assimilated that. "My toes?" she echoed.

He nodded. "The top of your head--and all between."

"Truly?" Dionne asked, studying his expression. "Oh! You are being facetious? This is humor? Funny? Joke? To make one laugh?"

He smiled wryly. "Only in part."

Dionne thought that over for a moment. "Perhaps we are going about this wrong. Which part do *you* want me to cover?"

"*Every* part," he responded promptly, but before she could demand to know how she was to accomplish that, he caught her hair and pulled it forward over her shoulders, carefully smoothing it over her breasts and belly. To Dionne's surprise and discomfort, her body responded to his touch with immediate arousal.

She directed her mind elsewhere until he seemed satisfied and removed his hands.

As they climbed the rise above the desert floor, people gathered near the edge to stare down at them, but the moment Dionne stepped onto the plateau at the top, they scattered back. Stunned, Dionne looked around at their frightened expressions and finally looked up at Khan.

He stepped behind her, placing one large hand on each of her shoulders. "This is the goddess Dionne. She has come to bring the Eirt to renewal."

"Oh but...," Dionne began, startled by the announcement.

He calmly placed one hand over her mouth, cutting her off. "This is what they expect," he said, low, against her ear. "They will be more comfortable with your presence if they see it as the favor of the gods."

Dionne nodded understanding, but she wasn't entirely comfortable with the role he'd bestowed upon her.

"These beasts are her guardians. They will not harm you so long as you do not approach the goddess Dionne without permission."

The people crowding in a circle around them stared at the two cougars for several moments and abruptly went to their knees, bowing their heads low to the ground. Dionne stared at them for several moments in confusion before enlightenment dawned. She sent Khan an accusing look. "This is not acceptable," she whispered, both irritated and unnerved by their behavior. "I can not do what I was sent to do if the people are afraid of me and falling down to worship every time I am near them."

Ignoring her comment, he caught her arm and led her away from the group, who skittered to one side to make a path as they approached. Dionne glanced back several times, wondering if the worshipful would follow and relieved when she saw they weren't. At the bottom of the low hill, she saw animals grazing--or perhaps sleeping. As they neared, one of the animals lifted its head and whinnied. "This nay beast is mine," Khan said, leading her toward it.

"Nay?" She repeated blankly, searching her mind for the source of the strange name which wasn't even a corruption of the original name. "You call it for the sound it makes?"

He nodded. "My people have captured these for many generations and trained them."

Dionne sent him a wry glance. "Poor beasts. They were destined to be beasts of burden, I suppose. They were called horses in my time, but they did not roam free so there was no need to capture them--and they had not been used as transportation for several hundred years."

He looked a little put out by her comments--those he understood--and she realized with a touch of amusement that he thought his people had come up with the idea.

It wasn't the most ideal sort of transportation, particularly since she was bare bottomed and the horse had nothing but a very coarse blanket over its back. The horse's hair might actually have been less uncomfortable.

When Khan had settled her, he vaulted onto the horse behind her. Grasping leading strings in one hand, he settled the other at her waist. Dionne tried to ignore the hand. She also tried to ignore the groin plowing into her buttocks, but it was difficult since the bouncing gait of the horse bumped them together, made more difficult by the hard erection he developed within moments.

It's erectile tissue, she chastised herself. Blood flows to it, engorging it and making it harden and stand erect in reaction to stimuli. It's involuntary, like my nipples, and not something to be disturbed about. It could mean a lot of things besides lust.

The hand upon her waist kept slipping lower and lower until it was resting along the top of her thigh, however, and she couldn't convince herself that that was an accident. Gritting her teeth, Dionne grasped his hand and moved it to her waist once more. The second time his hand landed in her lap, Dionne swiveled around to look up at him suspiciously.

He gave her a questioning look, but there was something in his eyes that suggested she was right. The incident was not accidental. She moved his hand to her waist again.

He slipped it from the curve at her side to the center of her stomach, splaying his palm over her belly and pulling her snugly back against him until his erection was plowing the cleft of her buttocks. Dionne's belly executed a strange little flip flop. The distinctive heat of desire swirled inside of her.

She cleared her throat uncomfortably. "This is not--not allowed."

His hand slipped lower until his fingers tangled in the curls at the apex of her thighs, the tips lightly brushing her nether lips. Dionne's heart skittered to a halt and then began to beat rapidly.

"Not permitted,' she said shakily. "Forbidden?"

"Why?"

His voice was husky. The heat of his breath wafted along the channel of her ear, stirring nerve endings to life. His fingers slipped lower and Dionne found she was having trouble breathing as one thick finger parted her flesh and brushed lightly along her clit.

She was having even more trouble thinking. "I am the arc of humanity," she managed finally. "One of the--uh--chosen. Even--even if I wanted to," she said unsteadily, which she discovered with more than a little surprise that she did, "I couldn't."

After a brief hesitation, his hand slid upward. Dionne had just managed to drag in a breath of supreme relief when his hand kept going, settling finally, possessively, over one breast. He placed his mouth over her ear, tracing the contours of the shell lightly with his tongue. A cascade of delight showered her, every nerve ending from her neck to her toes coming to attention. "Why?"

"You wouldn't understand. I can't explain it so that you would understand," she said a little desperately.

His hold loosened slightly. "Try."

There was anger in his voice now. Dionne licked her lips, but her mind was chaotic and she realized she was hardly up to using the terms *familiar* to her. She couldn't think of a simpler way to say it. "I am a bio-engineered superhuman. Each of the eggs I carry in my body is specifically designated as a match for only the finest specimens this time has to offer. Each has a specific DNA code that represents the preeminent minds the world of my time had to offer. My primary mission is to help to seed the Earth with the life forms necessary to ensure the resurrection of mankind's civilization by yielding the genius of its past.

"No man can be allowed to touch me unless he meets the criteria set forth by the founders of the resurrection project.

"It is why I was designed. It is the primary reason that I am here.

"I can not belong to one man. I belong to mankind."

She couldn't believe that he could possibly have understood half of what she'd said, but his hold upon her loosened and, to her immense relief, his hand settled lightly along the curve of her waist once more. She didn't look back at him. She didn't have to to know that he was angry. The tension that had come upon him as she spoke told her that.

Uncomfortable with his anger, she searched her mind for something to say that might smooth matters between them. "I--regret anything that I may have done that led you to believe...." She broke off. "I'm sorry if I--if I made you think...."

He didn't respond and she allowed the half finished sentence to trail into silence, wondering why she had even tried to explain something he couldn't possibly understand.

"I have not asked you to be my woman," he said after several moments of uncomfortable silence.

Chapter Four

Embarrassment filled Dionne at that remark and she felt her face redden, but relief filled her, too--and, surprisingly, a good deal of regret. Khan appealed to her in many ways and she seriously doubted there was any man living that would appeal to her more. As sorry as she was that things were the way they were, though, she knew how vitally important her mission was, and she had accepted the role she would play in this new world. She couldn't simply discard it at whim.

She threw him a smile over her shoulder that was only slightly forced. "No, you hadn't, and I see that I misunderstood. Well! I'm glad that's out of the way."

Regardless of her efforts to smooth the situation over as diplomatically as possible, she couldn't help but be aware of the awkwardness that had arisen from it. They made the remainder of the ride in silence that wasn't at all comfortable.

Dionne managed to dismiss it from her mind only when they at last reached the village. To her disappointment, however, the moon was setting and there was not enough light to see much detail. The structure Khan took her to was like all the others surrounding it as far as she could see, though, and much the same size, and she found that she was anxious to study it.

The animal skin that covered the doorway wasn't very promising.

Her excitement plummeted.

Once they were inside, Khan lit the room with a lamp that appeared to be a pottery bowl filled with some sort of fat. Sadness filled her as the dull glow chased the shadows into the corners and she looked around for the first time. After centuries of struggling to build a civilization of such promise, nature had overcome after all, pitching them back to their beginnings.

The structure appeared to have been constructed of mud and sticks. The floor of the lodge was nothing more than hard packed dirt, covered with mats here and there that appeared to be made of woven weeds of some variety. In the center of the lodge a ring had been formed with stones and, as Dionne watched, Khan arranged wood in the center and set fire to them. Looking up, she saw that there was a smoke hole in the roof of the structure--not even a chimney.

Sighing, she glanced around for a place to sit. She should not have been tired after 'sleeping' a thousand years, but the uncomfortable ride on the back of the horse had seemed to drain her of energy.

Or maybe it was the magnitude of her task?

Finding a mound of furs along one wall, she sat down on it, drawing her knees up and propping her back against the wall of the lodge as she idly studied the implements and tools that she could see, only dimly aware of Khan as he built the fire and moved a clay pot, which she supposed contained food, close to the heat.

This scenario had been considered a possibility, but unlikely. The devastation wreaked by catastrophic natural disasters would have caused a break down in governments, military, all services, the loss of power and fuel. Pockets of survivors would have been isolated and forced to survive as best they could on what ever could be found, but even after widespread destruction and loss of life, there should have been food stores to feed the survivors for many, many years, and along with those stores of food there should have been many other things--the building blocks of civilization, things that could have been gathered and used to bring order again.

Perhaps there had been. Maybe after the worst had passed, the survivors had scavenged and found the remains of their civilization and lived off of it while they could, but it was obvious they had done nothing else. There could not have been much of a push to regain what was lost or civilization would not have continued its spiral downward until it reached bottom.

She pushed that thought aside.

This was not 'bottom'. It might be close in her eyes, but they had established communities, leadership, family units, made tools, domesticated animals, begun processing natural materials into useful household items.

She wondered about the shield and sword that Khan carried, however. Aside from those, she saw nothing that indicated these people had re-learned metallurgy.

"You found those," she said abruptly, trying to tamp the hopefulness that surged through her, realizing almost at once that they might be nothing more than scavenged materials from a civilization long dead.

Khan turned to look at her and then followed her gaze. After a moment, he returned his attention to what he had been doing near the fire. "Yes."

"Where?"

He said nothing for several moments. Finally, he rose and moved to one wall. Taking a garment from a hook, he approached her and dropped it into her lap before he settled on the skins at a little distance from her.

Dionne lifted the garment and studied it in the flickering light. It was very simply made and constructed out of some sort of animal skin. The pungent, but not unappealing scent of leather tickled at her nostrils. Her first thought was that it was a short shift, but she'd seen nothing to indicate he lived with a woman and finally decided it was simply a tunic--his tunic. He was big enough that she discovered once she'd pulled it over her head and adjusted the tunic, though, that it was fully long enough to fit her like a shift, reaching halfway down her thighs.

Smoothing a hand over the tunic, she sent him a grateful smile. "Thank you."

He nodded without glancing at her, his gaze focused on the dancing fire. "I found the shield and shining long knife in the forbidden lands."

Dionne sucked in her breath sharply at that. "Forbidden?" she gasped.

He nodded. "The Speakers tell that evil dwells there, strange beasts and stranger things that belonged to the gods when they dwelt among us. There, death awaits the unwary. None go there."

"Except you?"

He studied her a long moment and finally shrugged. "Yes. I was--curious and I do not believe in the gods, the old ones, or the ones the *people* worship now--not anymore anyway." He smiled faintly. "Then, I suppose I did, but I did not believe they would punish me for my curiosity. And when I went, all that I saw there had been fashioned by the hand of man, not gods, so I ceased to believe, or fear. I took what pleased me and they did not smite me."

Dionne covered her face with her hands, shaking her head. She saw that he was frowning when she looked at him again. "Those things--all of those things--were made by the people and what had survived the destruction should have been gathered for the use of those left. It was the things they needed to begin to rebuild. Why would it have been forbidden?" she muttered to herself, studying over the puzzle.

It occurred to her after some thought that the 'evil' and the 'death' spoken of might have been disease. With the enormity of loss of life, there had probably not been enough survivors to bury the dead. Sanitation would have vanished. Disease would have been rampant.

Somehow, the warnings to avoid the cities must have evolved into these myths over time and they had never gone back, which meant they would not have had the tools to rebuild. They would have begun again with little more than intelligence between them and a state very like cavemen--perhaps even that had been a handicap of sorts, for they had evolved so far beyond their animal instincts before disaster they would not have had those basic senses to guide them.

Or, quite possibly, since so very much time had passed, they had suffered a number of setbacks in trying to regain what was lost?

She shook the thoughts off. It was a moot point. Whatever had gone wrong was done and over with. She had this point to start with and she could not allow the enormity of the situation to overwhelm her. It would take generations to bring mankind back to that point that they had achieved pre-disaster so that they could go forward, but she had the means to give them a tremendous push in the right direction and help them advance rapidly in the generations to come.

She would begin by carefully assessing what was missing from the building blocks of civilization and ascertaining that the race had not suffered a serious setback in mental capabilities. From what she'd learned of Khan, she didn't think so, but it must be thoroughly checked to make certain that he was not a genetic fluke. If the race had regressed, she would not be able to provide them with enough knowledge to prepare them for what they needed to do.

She studied Khan as he rose and filled two pottery bowls with food from the pot nestled in the fire he'd built, wondering if it was wise to enlist his help beyond what was absolutely necessary. She thought perhaps it wasn't given his interest in sexual congress with her, but she found it comforting even to have the illusion of an ally.

She cleared her throat as he handed her the food. "I need to return to the bio-lab tomorrow. Will you take me?"

He frowned at his food. "I must lead the hunt tomorrow for food."

Dionne sighed, nodding that she understood. "Sachi and Nomi can show me the way."

He looked displeased at that comment. "I will take you."

She stiffened at the command, but carefully refrained from looking up at him. She could certainly see the need for him to hunt for food if supplies were running low, but her task was equally important. She had no intention of awaiting his convenience, and no real need to have him escort her. She had only asked because she could have made the trip faster on the horse, and also because she had wanted the comforting presence of another human being. "Oh," she muttered noncommittally, uncertain of whether he would try to force the issue or not if she seemed uncooperative.

She could feel his gaze upon her and knew he was studying her for any sign that she intended to ignore his command, which she did, but after a time he seemed to dismiss it. She doubted, particularly since he was the leader of his people, that he was used to having his commands questioned, or dismissed, but he would have to accustom himself to the fact that she wasn't one of 'his' people and not subject to his rule.

It occurred to her after several moments that Khan had presented her with an opportunity to observe and collect data that would be far better than simply asking questions. "I could go with you," she suggested tentatively.

Khan frowned. "Women do not hunt."

She should have expected as much, but outrage still surfaced. "Excuse me?"

"It is dangerous. You must wait here with the other women."

"I am not *like* the other women!"

"But you can not ride a horse. You can not use the weapons. And you will scare the beasts away with your chatter."

Dionne's eyes narrowed at the look of superiority on his face. It occurred to her that she probably deserved it--or he thought she deserved it. He'd accused her of treating him like he wasn't a man, which could only have meant that she'd wounded his pride. She didn't like it any better to think the shoe was on the other foot now.

Particularly since he was right. She didn't know anything about hunting and she certainly had no idea of how to use the weapons they might have. On the other hand, she didn't intend to hunt. She only wanted to go to watch.

He looked thoughtful when she'd pointed that out. She could almost see the wheels of his mind turning--that he realized he had the opportunity to prove to her that he was not one to be so lightly dismissed. It took an effort to curb the desire to smile.

It was comforting, actually, to realize that the species hadn't changed as much as she'd thought. Men still wanted to impress women with their manliness.

"I will take you if you will give me your word that you will stay out of the way and be quiet."

Stifling both resentment and the temptation to smile in triumph, Dionne promised.

There was only one bed--or pallet, she discovered when they'd eaten--the furs she'd planted her butt on. Khan tricked her into climbing beneath the furs, however, merely pointing to them when she asked where she was to sleep.

She assumed it meant he was giving it to her, not that he intended to *share* it with her. She'd barely settled when he grabbed the edge of the fur she was using for a cover and climbed in beside her. She went rigid with tension instantly. Disconcertingly, he merely presented her with his back and composed himself for sleep.

The suspicion that he was only waiting for her to let her guard down occurred to her, but when she realized from his deep, even breathing that he'd gone to sleep, she finally dismissed it and sought her own rest.

She'd hardly drifted away, it seemed, when she was awakened by something plopping solidly on the furs that covered her. Since her mind instantly supplied the possibility of some sort of creature, she jackknifed upright as if her body was ejected by springs, slapping at the spot where the unknown thing had landed.

A deep chuckle emerged from the darkness. "The boots are dead already."

Dionne blinked, struggling to focus her vision, and finally detected a darker shadow among the shadows. Khan was crouched beside the pallet. "Have you changed your mind about the hunt already?"

He'd like that, Dionne thought indignantly. She could hear it in his voice.

All the same, it didn't seem to her that there was much sense in hunting when it was still dark outside.

"No. I'm coming," she said, searching blindly for the boots he'd dropped on top of her and then flinging the fur back. Lifting them one at the time, she peered at the boots and finally decided there didn't seem to be a right and left. They looked identical. Shoving her foot into one, she searched it for some way to tighten it around her calves and discovered lacing. When she'd pulled it taut and tied it, she grabbed the other boot and repeated the process.

She discovered when she'd finished that Khan hadn't so much as moved a muscle. When she looked up at him and then followed the direction of his gaze, she saw why.

The tunic he'd given her was up around her waist and she wasn't wearing any under pants. She closed her legs so quickly her thighs slapped together like a hand clap.

Stiffly, he rose to his full height. "I will heat food while you take care of your needs."

Dionne, still more than half asleep, merely gaped at his back as he moved away from her and squatted down in front of the fire, stirring it to life with a stick. It dawned on her finally what he meant, however, and she struggled to her feet, looked around the lodge and finally went outside. The sky seemed lighter, though it was obviously still very early. No facilities magically appeared, however, and finally she went to search for privacy among the bushes.

She couldn't eat. The food had actually tasted very good the night before, but her stomach simply couldn't face meat stew this early in the day.

Khan disapproved, but he didn't argue.

The other hunters looked both surprised and disapproving when Khan settled her on the front of his horse as he had the night before and vaulted up behind her. He ignored them, settling one hand on her waist to steady her and kicking his horse into a brisk trot that quickly left the village pathways behind.

The cats followed. Dionne ordered them back--twice--but she strongly suspected they merely fell back, disappeared into the brush, and continued to follow despite her command to the contrary.

Dismissing them from her mind, she peered around at the dark forest, trying to figure out how Khan knew where he was going. Finally, she decided the horse could obviously see well enough to miss the trees even if she could barely penetrate the gloom.

No one spoke. She couldn't decide if it was because they all knew what to do and where to go, if it was because they were afraid talking would frighten the animals away--which didn't make much sense to her considering the noise the horses made--or if it was simply a disinclination to talk because they were as wickedly tired as she was.

Finally, when she'd begun to think the jogging of the horse was going to drive her spine through the top of her skull, Khan pulled back on the reins, lifting an arm in signal to the others.

Everyone stopped and dismounted. From their horses, the men gathered bows, quivers with arrows and spears.

Dionne's stomach clenched as she studied the stone tips of the weapons, trying to imagine what it would feel like to have something that dull rip through one. Being bludgeoned to death might almost be preferable.

Swallowing a little sickly, she made a mental note--long range killing capabilities, and spears for close contact, possible defense.

On foot, they moved away from the horses. Dionne followed as quietly as she could, but she couldn't help but notice that the men moved like ghosts. Her own progress was marked by a good deal of rustling and kept earning her censorious glances. She shrugged apologetically, and focused her attention on her feet, trying to move more carefully and quietly. That helped until she smacked into a tree and nearly knocked herself senseless.

Khan grabbed her arm, examined her head and then, obviously fighting the urge to grin, signaled for her to follow him, placing her feet as he did.

Resentment surfaced, but she did her best to comply--no easy task considering how much longer his legs were than hers.

They stopped at last at a slight rise. The hunters flopped onto their stomachs and began to sort of 'slither' along the ground. Frowning, Dionne did her best to imitate them, wondering even as she did if this was some joke they'd concocted between them.

She wouldn't have put it past them.

She hadn't noticed them conspiring against her, however.

"Moos," one of the men near her whispered on a breath of sound.

Moos? Curious, Dionne crawled up beside Khan and peered around at the meadow just beyond the tree line. Cows. They'd returned to the wild. As scruffy and rangy as they looked, however, she could see that that was what held their attention.

No one moved. It occurred to her after a while that they must be waiting for one of the animals to wander a little closer, within range of their arrows. She fell asleep waiting and missed the kill.

Fortunately.

Watching them bound across the meadow and stab it with the spears was bad enough. She stayed where she was as they settled down and began to skin and butcher it.

She was glad she hadn't eaten. Dry heaves were bad enough.

After wrapping the bloody chunks of meat in pieces of the animal's hide, they trudged back, looking tired but pleased with their kill. Dionne managed a tight smile when she saw that Khan was looking at her expectantly. "Moos--uh--cow. Is this what you usually hunt?"

Khan frowned, obviously not convinced that she was suitably impressed. "When we are fortunate. They are not easy to find. But one will fill many cook pots for days."

They had no means of preserving food. They would have to spend most of their time hunting, she realized.

They were all liberally coated with the animal's blood. She was surprised the horses would even allow the hunters near them, but apparently they were used to the scent of blood. They whickered and shifted uneasily when the meat was settled across their backs, but they didn't try to bolt.

Khan gathered moss and leaves and dabbed at the blood, but he was still sticky with it when they mounted again.

Dionne did her best to ignore it, but she was immensely relieved when they reached the village again.

Hearing the returning hunting party, the villagers began to pour out of their lodges, smiling and laughing and chattering excitedly when they saw that the hunt had been successful.

Leaving the other hunters to distribute the food, Khan urged his horse through the village and along a narrow path at the other end. "Where are we going now?" Dionne asked curiously.

"To bathe."

The comment pleased her in more ways than one. It would be a relief to be rid of the sight and smells of the hunt. She was also happy, though, to discover that good hygiene hadn't died with civilization. It was an excellent sign and probably accounted for the overall good health of the Kota people she'd seen.

He took her to a small stream. Instead of stopping when he reached it, however, he turned his horse and followed the bank. Rounding a sharp bend, they came upon a wide area where the stream had formed a pool.

Dionne looked at it with a sense of delight. A hot shower would have been better, but the pool held its own appeal. Khan scooted off the horse's rump and swung her down, catching her arm to stop her as she headed toward the pool. He pinched a fold of the tunic between two fingers. "This will draw up if it becomes wet."

Dionne looked down at the tunic a little doubtfully then twisted, trying to look at the back. She couldn't see any blood, but she strongly suspected it was there just the same.

A splash brought her attention back to the pool just as Khan surfaced.

His loincloth had been deposited, she saw, on a large, flat stone near the water.

Shrugging, she pulled the tunic off, dropped it beside the loincloth and waded in.

The water was cold, icy in fact. Chill bumps erupted all over her, depriving her of all desire to join Khan in the water. Undoubtedly, the pool was spring fed, nothing else that she could think of would account for the temperature of the water.

Squatting down, she began to dab at her hands, arms and legs. Gasping each time she splashed cold water over her warm skin. She didn't know how Khan could stand it, couldn't imagine how anyone could ever get accustomed to such a drastic temperature change.

She was surprised he wasn't on the bottom after such a shock to his system.

Having disappeared again for several moments, he emerged a few feet from her. When she glanced up, she saw that he was watching her disapprovingly. "You will not get very clean only splashing in the water."

"I wouldn't get very clean without soap anyway," she retorted, deciding to ignore him.

It was a mistake. She'd though he had decided to get out. She didn't realize until he grabbed her that he meant to make certain she got in. Uttering a gasp that hovered between fear and outrage, she wrapped her arms and legs around him before he could toss her into the water.

Grinning, he merely fell backwards.

The cold water sucked the breath from her lungs. She came up sputtering and coughing and trying to shove her wet hair from her face. When she managed to catch her breath, she saw that Khan was studying her worriedly.

It was just as well for him that he wasn't grinning like a jackass. She glared at him, balling her hand into a fist and taking a swing at him.

Surprise registered on his face. He leapt back out of range only a split second before she could connect. The move sent him off balance, however. His arms pin wheeled, failed to right him, and he disappeared under the water again.

Satisfied, Dionne trudged from the water and bent to retrieve her tunic. She sent a threatening glare over her shoulder as she heard him break the surface again.

"You are angry."

"You are so observant!" she snapped, refusing to turn around as she heard the wet slap of his feet against the stone as he climbed from the pool.

She tensed as his arm slid around her waist while she was still struggling to pull the tunic over her wet skin.

"I am sorry."

"You should be!" she retorted, but she was slightly mollified by his tone. He did *sound* contrite. She sent him a petulant glance over her shoulder, studying him suspiciously for any sign that he hadn't been sincere. Seeing none, she relaxed fractionally. When he released her, she straightened the tunic and sat down on the rock to pull the boots on again.

Khan, she saw when she finally glanced at him, had his back to her. She saw that he'd grabbed a handful of damp moss and was dabbing at the blood that had spattered the leather loincloth.

Guilt began to replace her anger.

There had been no malice in what he'd done, far from it. Right up until she'd snarled at him, he'd been smiling.

He'd been flirting with her, she realized abruptly. The realization created a chaotic mixture of remorse, pleased surprise, disappointment--and more irritation.

She felt mean and that irritated her. "The water's cold," she finally said uncomfortably. "I wouldn't really have minded otherwise."

He glanced at her as he finished tying his loincloth in place, reddening faintly. "It was--a childish trick. I am too old for such silly games."

She couldn't agree more, but that only made her feel worse, particularly since she could no longer be in any doubt that he *had* been flirting.

They were both subdued as they climbed onto the horse again. When Khan settled behind her, he placed a palm on one of her cheeks, urging her to look at him. "I would never cause you harm," he murmured, his expression earnest.

She searched his gaze. "It didn't once cross my mind that you would."

She saw as they passed the point where the path intersected with the stream that the other hunters had come to bathe--which she decided probably explained why Khan had taken her to the pool.

He'd already said he didn't like the other men looking at her body.

The cats were stationed on either side of the opening to Khan's lodge when they returned, looking for all the world as if they'd been waiting patiently for her return.

She didn't believe it for a moment, particularly since Nomi was grooming her paws.

She could hardly object. They'd needed to find food themselves, after all, since the food supplied for them was back at the lab.

She wanted nothing so much as to crawl back into the furs and catch up on the sleep she'd lost in joining the hunt. She ignored the urge, however, and spent most of the day strolling around the village, observing the day to day lives of the Kota people. Without a good deal of surprise, but with considerable pleasure, she discovered the fields where they grew food. She'd seen that they were not nomadic and surmised they had some skill in cultivating, but it was still very happy to discover evidence that she'd been right.

She was too exhausted by the time she finally climbed into Khan's furs to spare much thought for his intentions.

He was gone when she awoke the following morning. Stretching, she pushed the furs back and tugged the boots on that Khan had given her. Deciding he must have left to hunt again, she got up and studied the crude structure.

The light filtering through the smoke hole in the roof still left the interior in dimness, but she could see more than she'd been able to see before. She would've liked to explore, but her body's needs drove her from the lodge to search for privacy to relieve herself.

The villagers looked at her curiously, but also fearfully, as she strode through the village, but she thought perhaps that was largely due to Sachi and Nomi, who escorted her.

When she'd taken care of her needs, she directed the cats to lead her back to the bio-lab and struck off at a brisk walk. Along the way, she studied the flora and fauna, identifying what she could. Not surprisingly, there were new varieties that were unfamiliar and she made a mental note to analyze them for their usefulness. It seemed probable that nature, in attaining balance, had produced new life to replace what was lost, but whether the replacements would work as well in the chain as its predecessors had was another matter.

Regardless, she reminded herself that retaining balance was as crucial as identifying the building blocks. If she touched off another imbalance in nature, her efforts could be for nothing.

The security pad had been destroyed. She'd been too unnerved at the discovery of the gathering along the ridge above the bio-lab to notice when she and Khan had emerged from the lab. She looked up at the cam. "Lois, open the hatch and deactivate security."

The door opened and she strode down the corridor to the junction and descended.

When she reached the main room, she immediately moved to the sensors to begin a check. "Activate the bots, Lois, and have them clear the debris from around the lab. It'll be impossible to move all of the equipment I'm going to need via the emergency access tunnel."

"Processing request." There was silence for several seconds. "Dionne?"

"What?" Dionne asked absently.

"There is no egress for the bots."

Dionne frowned, glanced up from what she was doing and considered it for several moments. "They'll have to go out the way I did," she said finally. "Program the bots to use a wench and pulley to pull themselves up the escape shaft. They can get what they need from storage."

"Affirmative."

When the bots came in some twenty minutes later, Dionne broke off what she was doing long enough to watch their progress. Once she'd seen that the first had no difficulty hauling itself up the shaft, she returned to her work, pausing now and then to rub her aching head, tired eyes, or the cramp of a muscle.

The news wasn't good and she checked and rechecked the data each time she discovered another seed that was no longer viable. There was no denying the readouts, however, and by the time she'd made it through a quarter of the seeds entrusted to the care of the bio-lab, she'd determined a loss of 30 percent.

Dropping her tablet to her side, she glanced around the bio-lab, wondering if the same would be true of the units that lined the other three walls.

She jumped when her gaze encountered Khan, who was standing at the foot of the escape shaft, his arms folded over his chest, his entire stance aggressive with anger. "I told you that I would bring you," he said when he finally had her attention, his voice tight with barely suppressed anger.

Dionne's brows rose and then descended as she probed her mind for the memory. "Yes, you did. I remember," she responded agreeably. Returning her attention to her tablet, she moved to the next wall of units.

"Then why are you here?" he demanded after several stunned moments of silence.

"I decided not to wait," Dionne said without turning.

"It is not safe for you to wander the wilderness alone," Khan growled.

Dionne sent him a wide eyed look of surprise. "You are angry," she observed unnecessarily.

He glared at her. "Because you endangered yourself when there was no need."

Amusement dawned. "There was no danger. I am the goddess Dionne," she said with a touch of humor. "At least, that is what everyone seems to think. Anyway, I had Sachi and Nomi."

"Dumb beasts! You are lucky they have not turned on you."

Dionne stopped and turned to study him. "They are not dumb beasts. They were genetically engineered, as I was, and given a good deal more than natural to their species, including higher intelligence. Beyond that, they were trained in stasis. If they had the ability for speech, they could speak. They can't, but they have no trouble at all understanding and they are programmed to follow my orders without question--unless the order would endanger me."

"They made no attempt to stop me from entering," he pointed out.

She shrugged. "Then they have decided you can be trusted."

He looked more irritated rather than less when she countered every objection with a perfectly reasonable response. After a moment, he changed tactics. "Why are you here?"

"Because I must be here to begin the job I was sent to do."

He fumed for several moments. "*What* are you doing?"

"Checking to see how much still lives. So far I'm seeing at least a 30 percent loss and these seeds may well be irreplaceable."

"Seeds?"

"Mmm." She glanced at him. "Of all living things that inhabited the Earth in the days before the asteroid struck the planet and brought about global extinction of many species, plants *and* animals. The planet stabilized long ago--I can only guess, but probably at least 500 years ago--but many different things were lost and I don't know yet what will be needed--maybe none of what I have here, maybe all."

Khan frowned, glancing around at the walls with a new understanding, and the realization that it wasn't merely walls but containers. He still didn't see how, or even why, this place was so important to her. He didn't completely understand how the seeds would have been gathered and kept, but he had no trouble understanding that Dionne considered this to be her place, or that she would not willingly leave it.

"We do not need these things," he said finally.

"You don't know that," Dionne responded. She saw when she glanced at him that he was glaring at her.

"We live well enough with what we have," he said tightly.

She studied him for a long moment. "If you believed that, you wouldn't have come here the first time," she said shrewdly.

Instead of responding, he glanced around at the lab. "If you must come here, then I will bring you--and I will take you back to the village when it is time to rest."

Dionne thought that over for several moments. The truth was, as primitive as the conditions were in the village, the lab was very little more comfortable and did not have the draw of human companionship. On the other hand, she strongly suspected she hadn't convinced Khan that she could not allow him to consider her his woman, particularly after the way she'd responded to his touch. He might be a barbarian, but he was no fool. He hadn't failed to notice, she was sure, that her reaction was extreme for someone who claimed no interest in him. "I should probably just stay here," she said. "Really, I've seen enough of the village and I have so much to do here before I can begin the studies of the outside world that it's pointless to stay in the village and travel back and forth."

"No."

Taken aback, Dionne simply stared at him for several moments. "No?"

"It is not safe for you here--alone. If you stay, I will stay also."

Dionne couldn't decide whether to laugh or cuss at his highhandedness. It occurred to her presently, though, that it would be better all around if she stayed on his good side. Even if she refused his help in every other area, her task would be far harder than it needed to be without his cooperation. As leader of his people, he could bring them to her, or turn them against her.

Still, it went against the grain to simply bow to his orders.

Apparently, he read the belligerence in her expression for he abruptly changed course again.

"We will stay here. If this place is of such importance, then it, too, will need to be guarded."

Chapter Five

Dionne studied his expression, unhappily aware that she wanted him to stay with her. She didn't particularly feel threatened by the world she'd woken in. She didn't lack confidence that, if there was a threat of any kind, the security measures available to her would amply do the job they had been designed for.

She could've simply accepted the undeniable truth that she was accustomed to being surrounded by people. She'd never had any family beyond those directly involved in the project, but, until she'd gone into the bio-pod, she had rarely experienced more than a few minutes when she was completely alone.

Regardless, she couldn't lie to herself that the idea appealed to her only, or even mostly, because she wanted human contact.

Khan intrigued her.

It wouldn't have bothered her if that interest had been purely on a scientific level, but she knew very well that it wasn't.

There was danger in her curiosity.

She was keenly aware of that, but she had also evaluated the situation both scientifically and in regards to his importance to her mission and concluded that he was of tremendous value to her in those respects--something she couldn't just dismiss because she was afraid of the temptation he represented to mate before she was called upon to do so, and without any consideration for whether or not he was a suitable selection.

She would simply have to do what was best for all concerned and curb her personal interest in him, she decided. "That will be good," she responded finally. "I should be finished with my preliminary studies this week, and then I will need to investigate changes in the environment."

She lost him after the capitulation, she saw, but she couldn't decide whether it was because he hadn't understood the remainder, or he simply wasn't interested. "The cats will protect me, but stores *are* limited and it will actually be better for me if I have someone to--uh--someone with survival skills."

The look he gave her at that comment was sardonic--which left her in no doubt that he'd understood the gist of it, but he didn't seem to resent her assumption that he would take care of her. Or, to do him justice, delight in the admission that she wasn't certain she had the skills she needed to survive a hostile environment without help.

He was surprisingly intuitive and intelligent, which, she supposed, was at least part of the reason she found him so fascinating. "Would you be willing to allow me to run tests on you?" she asked impulsively.

He frowned, his gaze moving over her speculatively.

"They wouldn't hurt," she added quickly. "At least, there might be a little discomfort, but nothing intolerable." She waited tensely for his answer, wondering if he hadn't understood, wondering if he *had* but didn't particularly care to be a lab animal.

"This is to help the *people* in renewal?" he asked finally.

Surprise flickered through her. She beamed at him. "Yes. Yes, it is."

He nodded assent.

Dionne was so excited her hand shook as she set the tablet aside that she'd been using to record her findings. Grasping his hand, she led him to the door to the examination room and activated it. He laced his fingers through hers, matching palms with her as the door opened and they stepped through. Dionne's hand tingled from the warmth of his. She glanced down at their clasped hands, a little surprised that so simple a touch could seem so intimate, could stir to life things better left buried and ignored.

His hand dwarfed hers. His dark skin contrasted dramatically with the paleness of hers. Why such things would appeal to her on a purely carnal level, she couldn't understand, but neither could she deny the quickening inside of her that she didn't particularly welcome. Smiling uneasily, she carefully extracted her hand and gestured toward the examination table.

He simply stared at it, his expression unreadable, but as she watched, she saw his gaze move over the table and then lift to the scanner above it. His expression was eloquent of suspicion when he looked at her again.

He was not as trusting as she'd thought he would be.

She lifted a hand to stroke one of his arms soothingly. "I won't hurt you," she promised.

Something flickered in his eyes. The next moment, so swiftly she hadn't even realized his intention, he caught the hand she'd extended and jerked her up against him.

She gaped up at him in surprise. He caught her face in one hand that was so huge his fingers curled around both sides of her jaw, making it abundantly clear to her that she hadn't properly appreciated the sheer enormity of the man. "I--am--not--a--beast," he said in a low growl, very slowly, very succinctly.

Dionne felt color climb slowly into her cheeks until her entire face felt hot. "I didn't imply that you were," she said a little unsteadily, realizing almost the moment she said it that she had, in fact, on a subconscious level been treating him as if he were, or more accurately, a clever child.

She could see from the look in his eyes that he didn't believe her polite lie.

Her eyes widened as he dragged her higher against his body, lowering his head until they were almost nose to nose, his expression rife with intent. Dionne sucked in a breath to order him to release her at once, but she didn't get the opportunity to use her tongue--that way. The moment she opened her mouth to speak, he covered it--with *his* mouth.

She was so stunned at his audacity that her mind went perfectly bereft of cognitive thought. Her senses did not shut down with thought malfunction. On the contrary, it seemed the moment the reasoning side of her brain went into a state of catatonia, her primal side took over completely, focusing more acutely on reception. Warmth was the first sensation that registered as his mouth closed over hers with an aggressiveness that evoked a rush of adrenaline and made her heart palpitate so frantically that her lungs had to struggle to provide her with enough air. Faintly, the scent and taste of some kind of mint assaulted her as he thrust his tongue boldly past the barrier of her lips and the taste of him exploded across the sensory buds on her tongue. His own unique taste, laced with his potent male pheromones, flooded her mouth with the first rake of his tongue across hers and jetted through her by way of her laboring heart and lungs like a drug injected directly into her blood stream. It produced almost instantaneous euphoria. A wall of erotic heat enveloped her like flash fire.

Warning sirens sounds, but failed to communicate more than a whimper of protest above the clamor her body instantly set up for more. Weakly, she pressed a hand against his hard chest in objection, but her body felt strangely boneless and it took an unbelievable effort even to offer that much protest.

She forgot the need, and the reason, to object almost as quickly as it arose to her.

His hunger communicated itself to her in the way his mouth moved over hers and his feverish exploration of her mouth, summoning forth a response from her body she was helpless to deny even if it had occurred to her to try. Aroused, the hunger within her matched his, then surpassed it. Her fingers curled reflexively against his hard chest. Too weak to hold herself up, she almost seemed to melt against him, drinking in the sensations that were pelting her from every direction.

He lifted her more tightly against his body, turning. Her mind reeled dizzily at the movement. Disoriented, she felt as if she were falling. Instinctively, she wrapped her arms around his neck, clinging as he lifted her.

The cool steel of the examination table sent a jolt through her as he settled her buttocks on it, but before her mind could formulate a protest, he wrenched her thighs apart, wedging his hips between them.

Something as hard and thick as his forearm nudged her nether lips, parted them. Sparks of electricity shot through her in a debilitating rush as he moved against her and she felt the roughness of his loincloth teasing the sensitive bud he'd discovered. She shuddered, but the sensations enthralled her, called to her and she didn't even attempt to resist as she felt his hand settle on her buttocks, bringing her closer, holding her tightly as he arched against her.

Her belly clenched, quaking with an unidentifiable need as a powerful force gripped her, lifting her a little higher each time he thrust against her until she discovered that she was moaning into his mouth.

Her body convulsed without warning, almost seeming to explode with euphoric sensation.

Almost as abruptly as he'd begun the assault to her senses, he ceased, as if he'd discovered what he had wanted to know. Lifting his mouth from hers, he swung her from the examination table, setting her away from him, and finally releasing her. Wobbly kneed, Dionne felt herself sinking toward the floor. She sprawled there in a puzzle of jolting, sizzling nerve endings, too stunned to register pain if there had been any, too shocked even to figure out what had happened for many moments.

The chill from the floor finally penetrated the heated cocoon that had enveloped her, sending an almost painful shiver through her. Dazed, she looked around in confusion.

Khan, she saw when she finally glanced upward, had climbed upon the examining table. He was staring at the ceiling, his expression grim. Vaguely embarrassed, but too distressed to feel much of anything, Dionne struggled to command some strength in her jellyfish corpse and finally managed to get up.

He exhibited no signs of either arousal or distress. Her gaze, as if magnetized, immediately zeroed in on the part of his anatomy he'd had wedged against her cleft and she saw that he'd either already tamed the beast, or he hadn't actually been particularly stimulated to start with.

Feeling more disoriented than anything else, Dionne looked around a little vaguely for some place to sit down before her wobbly knees gave out again. Nothing immediately presented itself and after a few moments she gave up the search and settled for trying to remember what she had intended to do when she'd come into the examination room.

Khan glanced at her curiously, prompting her.

Examination, she thought a little vaguely, still looking around a little helplessly while she searched her mind to figure out what kind of examination she'd had in mind.

Finally, she simply lowered the scanner and, after studying the keypad for several moments, trying to jog her sluggish brain into providing her with the information of how to use it, punched in the code for 'thorough'.

Once the scanner was activated and began its slow advance, she remembered that there was a rolling stool beneath the table and dragged it out to sit down. As the scanner inched its way down his body, the weakness began to dissipate. Her mind opened the same way, thoughts rushing in like water flooding over an opened dam.

She glanced at Khan, discovered he was still staring at the ceiling and then looked away again before he could sense her scrutiny and meet her gaze.

Something irrevocable had happened, she finally realized.

Without any attempt at penetration, Khan had marked her as his female. As surely as any other animal in the animal kingdom, the human male was capable of instantly addicting any female of his choice with a powerful dose of his pheromones--the more he wanted her, the more potent the injection and the harder it was to break the 'habit' when the female found that those pheromones appealed to her. Neither knowledge of human mating habits, or scientific evaluation of the situation, was going to break the addiction.

She wondered a little vaguely if he was truly that attracted to her, or if she'd provoked him past caution and control by inadvertently wounding his ego.

It didn't really matter now. She was in a hell of a mess, not to put too fine a point on it.

Chapter Six

By the time the scanner had completed its programming, Dionne had recovered enough to remember that her intention had been to discover if his brain was sufficiently developed to handle the inner cerebral teaching device. If his brain was too primitive, the ICTD could have the opposite effect intended and cause damage.

When the computer finished processing, she pulled up the brain scan and forced herself to concentrate on the read out, going over it three or four times before she managed to actually comprehend what she was reading and evaluate it. She'd already absently punched memory dump before it occurred to her that she should have saved the data for future reference, particularly since she hadn't even glanced at anything beyond the data regarding his brain development. "Shit!" she muttered, irritated.

She saw that Khan was looking at her piercingly and formed a tight smile intended to reassure him. "Nothing. I just should have saved the data to study it."

He tensed to rise from the table.

She placed a hand on his chest to stop him and then snatched it back immediately as if she'd been burned.

He settled back, however.

"I want to try a little primary programming--if you'll let me."

He frowned, which wasn't surprising. She knew he couldn't possibly understand the ICTD. "It's--uh--sort of like the village Speaker," she said on sudden inspiration.

His expression immediately changed to comprehension and interest.

"It will tell me about your world?"

She couldn't help it. Every time he displayed his understanding and intelligence, it gave her a thrill of hopefulness. "Yes--uh--not just at first. There are other things you have to understand before that."

He didn't look especially pleased by that information, but he relaxed, waiting for her to explain. He looked confused and a little suspicious when she pushed the scanner out of the way and pulled up the cranial cap. Uneasiness slithered through her when she tamped the urge to reassure him as she had before, but as leery as she was now of physical contact, she couldn't avoid it completely. She had to settle the device securely on his head and make certain the nodes were correctly placed. She did her best to ignore the feel of his hair beneath her fingertips, the warmth and smoothness of his skin. Her belly was shimmying inside by the time she'd finished, however.

Their gazes met when she straightened at last.

With an effort, she broke the contact, focusing on the tattoo on his cheek while she fought the urge to offer reassurance he didn't really seem to need despite the fact that this entire situation had to be so alien to him he would almost have to have some anxiety about it. "This mark," she said finally, as much to distract his mind as because of her own curiosity. "Why did you place it there?"

He lifted a hand to touch it. Before she realized his intention, he moved his hand from his cheek to her breast and stroked his finger along the area where her own skin had been tattooed. Even through the heavy leather, she felt his touch like a firebrand. "It is like this."

Swallowing a little convulsively, she resisted the urge to jump back. "Yes. That's why I'm curious. It's the logo of the resurrection project--an ancient symbol of life eternal. Did you--did you happen to see this--drawing when you were exploring the forbidden lands?"

"It tells my line. I wear it as my father did, and his father, and the father before."

Dionne's heart seemed to stand still in her chest as it leapt into her mind to wonder if there was any possibility at all that Khan was a descendant of one of the members of the renewal project. It seemed doubtful that he would know it, though, even if the possibility existed--but his intelligence certainly hinted at superior genetics.

"You don't know the origin, though?" she prodded, still hopeful.

He frowned thoughtfully, but finally seemed to dismiss it. "Only what I told you."

Dionne sighed in disappointment, but forced a smile. "I'm ever optimistic that I will discover something that will make my task easier."

Moving to the computer console, she thought it over for several moments and finally programmed the system to terminate after remedial instruction. She was afraid to give him too much at once, regardless of her impressions of him or the readouts. It was a gut reaction, she knew, and based more on emotion than science, but she couldn't help it. The fear that she might injure him simply couldn't be dismissed. He tensed when the programming kicked in and she caught his hand in the instinctive urge to reassure him. His fist tightened around her hand for several moments. Finally, his hold relaxed, however.

She found that she was reluctant to remove her hand regardless of the fact that she knew the crisis had passed. She liked the feel of her palm against his, the feel of his fingers. She studied them. The temptation was nearly irresistible to examine his long, tapering fingers with her own. Chastising herself, she moved away finally and returned to sit on the stool, watching him until the ICTD completed its cycle and shut down.

He'd passed from consciousness into something similar to a dream state. It was normal, something to be expected, and yet she found she couldn't resist the temptation to place her fingertips on his neck. His heartbeat was strong but slow in his relaxed state.

Irritated with herself, she moved away from him finally. Since it occurred to her then that at least a part of her weakness could be accounted for by the fact that she hadn't eaten since the night before, she left him sleeping and went into her quarters to scrounge for food.

It hardly deserved the title. The idea, she supposed, had been to discourage any inclination she might have to remain holed up in the bio-lab when it was of utmost importance that she leave it as soon as possible. Some concession had been made for comfort since the possibility existed that she might encounter a hostile environment that could jeopardize her mission. It was the bare basics, however. If she had discovered that conditions were still too unstable to make it possible to implement the plan, she was to have gone back into the bio-pod, making living quarters non-essential.

There had been clothing. That was piled in the bottom of the locker now, though, and little more than dust mixed with severely degraded scraps of material. The narrow bunk still folded out and retracted into the wall, but the mattress on it was in no better shape than the clothes. The base of the bed, as well as the chairs, tables and shelves, which had been constructed of plastics and metal, were still in usable condition, but hardly comfortable. Except for the separate facilities for bathing and sanitation--separated because of the dampness inherent in those facilities, not for the sake of privacy--the entire living quarters was contained in one, small room.

Moving to the wall that housed food storage and preparation equipment, Dionne removed a couple of the meals and examined them. Deciding it still looked edible, she added water and programmed the computer to heat the food to a temperature high enough to kill any bacteria.

The food actually smelled appetizing as it began to heat. Satisfied, Dionne left it to finish the cycle and returned to the examination room. Khan, she saw, was sitting on the edge of the table. She surged forward, reaching up for the ICTD device protectively, discovering almost at once that she couldn't reach it.

Khan slipped off the table. As he did, his body slid along hers, bumping her. He caught her waist to steady her. Rattled, Dionne focused on retrieving her precious equipment and moved away from him the moment she had it, carefully placing it back in storage.

"I smell food."

The comment drew her attention back to Khan.

She moved back to him, studying his eyes. "How do you feel?"

"Hungry."

She smiled, but although she didn't see anything that she felt was cause for alarm, she wasn't completely reassured either. "You won't be impressed, but I left two ration kits heating."

He followed her back to the 'residence', studying the container of food skeptically for several moments before he nerved himself to try it. Dionne chuckled at the expression that crossed his features when he tasted it. "It's designed more for nutrition and energy than taste."

"I noticed," he said wryly.

Pleased that he didn't seem to be having any difficulty following her conversation, Dionne nevertheless decided not to question him and concentrated on her own food.

When they'd finished, she disposed of the containers in the recycler and left him exploring the living quarters while she returned to the main lab to take up her readings once more. He came out a little later. She sensed his gaze upon her, but she didn't look up until she realized he was leaving the bio-lab. She frowned when she realized he'd disappeared up the escape tunnel, but repressed the impulse to ask him where he was going.

She would have preferred that he remain close by until she could be certain he hadn't suffered any ill effects from the ICTD session. Ordinarily, that wouldn't have been anything to cause much concern. The device had been in use for years. It wasn't intrusive and problems arising from its use were extremely rare.

This wasn't a typical situation, though, and she'd been distracted when she should have been totally focused on the test results. She could have missed something.

She was sorry when that thought occurred to her because that made it even more difficult to concentrate. Finally, she managed to push it to the back of her mind and focus on her task reasonably well.

She would have made far more progress if she could have managed the absolute concentration she'd had before Khan had suddenly shown up in the bio-lab, but she discovered she couldn't block him out completely. Random thoughts flickered into her mind at the most inconvenient moments--the way he'd made her feel when he'd moved so intimately against her; the way he'd looked at her; the way his hand had felt in hers; the way she'd felt when he'd kissed her--causing her to have to redo far more tests than she should've had to.

After a time, her determination to persevere began to have the desired effect and she managed to concentrate so fully on what she was doing that a sudden thud behind her startled her so badly she nearly dropped her data tablet. Whirling to scan the lab for the source, she spotted a large, furry bundle at the foot of the access shaft. Curious, she set her tablet aside and crossed the room to investigate. By the time she'd reached the shaft, Khan was half way down it.

Uncertain of whether he'd seen her or not, she decided to pretend she hadn't noticed he'd come back--she didn't know why she wanted to. It was just an impulse that she followed without delving too deeply.

She was standing in front of the wall unit, staring at it blindly, her focus on the sounds behind her, when she at last heard the thud of Khan's feet hitting the floor tiles. Casually, she glanced in that direction.

She might have saved herself the effort. Khan had already bent over to retrieve his bundle. The muscles in his upper arm bulged as he lifted it. Her gaze zeroed in on that indication that the pack was heavy, but somehow her mind didn't really focus on anything except the rippling of the muscles along his back and arm as he hefted it.

Without once glancing in her direction, he turned and strode toward the door that led to the living quarters and disappeared.

Dionne tapped her fingers restlessly on her tablet for several moments, struggling with the urge to follow him and see what he was doing. Finally, she decided to wait to see if he would come out again.

She struggled through three more tests before she reached the point where her curiosity got the better of her. Setting her tablet aside, she strode purposefully to the door of the living quarters and went in. Khan was no where in sight and neither was the bundle. The skin that had been used to form the bundle had been smoothed into a pallet on the floor near the far wall. An assortment of pottery jars and bowls now resided on the table where they'd eaten earlier. The smell of cooking food drifted lazily, enticingly through the room from the cooking unit.

She went to stare through the glass at the food, but, as tempting as the smells were, she was far more interested in what Khan was doing inside the facilities--which was the only place he could possibly be.

After several moments of indecision, she moved to the door and stuck her ear to it to listen. She could hear water running. Instantly, visions of Khan showering collided in her mind with the display of muscles she'd seen earlier.

She stared at the door activator--hard, fighting the temptation just to take a peek.

It would be for the sake of science, of course. She'd checked him for obvious defect before, but she hadn't thoroughly examined him.

After tapping the wall just beneath the pad indecisively for several moments, she moved her hand very deliberately behind her back and turned away from the door to pace--and think.

Nothing inventive came to mind as a reasonable excuse to go in.

Would he believe it, she wondered, if she pretended she hadn't realized he was using the shower?

Maybe she could take a scientific approach? She just came to check to make certain he wasn't suffering any ill effects from his session with the ICTD.

It was eating her alive to see what he looked like naked, damn it!

There was the chance that he might take her intrusion as an invitation to do more than just touch her, or kiss her.

The memory of his caresses and that wholly devastating kiss clinched the matter. She'd crossed the room, punched the access pad, and breezed into the facilities before she had the chance to think better of it.

It was just--almost--as she'd imagined it would be. Khan was standing beneath the spray, his hair as black as a starless night and plastered in clinging, water molded locks to his neck, and back, and shoulders. Rivulets of gleaming water ran down his magnificent body, setting off little explosions of heat inside her as he twisted and turned, rinsing the bubbles of soap from his hard, muscular frame. Her mouth watered as she allowed her gaze to follow the gleaming waterfall over his naked chest and down his rippled belly where her gaze snagged on the thick member protruding from his pubic bush.

His phallus had felt huge when he'd been rubbing it along her cleft, but it had been hard then--she thought--and she'd figured it had just felt huge when it reality that wasn't the case at all.

It was nestled unthreateningly along his thigh now, and it was *still* long and thick.

It was at this point that the actuality deviated drastically from the scenario she'd imagined.

Instead of breezing into the room and stopping short, as if she was surprised to discover him in the shower, or taking the scientific 'I'm not fazed' approach, she went into a temporary state of Zen meditation, as if she'd hit a brick wall, her jaw sagging until her mouth dropped open. When her eyes began to sting from staring, she blinked, slowly. It was enough to bring her out of her entranced state sufficiently for her to realize that Khan was facing her when he hadn't been before, and he was standing perfectly still, not bathing. Unnerved, she glanced upward and discovered that Khan was not only well aware that she'd come in on him, he was staring at her with an expression of cool amusement, waiting, she finally realized, for her to say something.

"Uh," Dionne managed to get out. "I was wonder--you know, I think I should probably just wait until you're through here," she finished, whirling on her heel and beating a hasty retreat.

Chapter Seven

As disordered as her thoughts were, one thing taunted Dionne as she struggled to pretend she was busily at work once more in the lab, one ear cocked to see if Khan would follow her. She wasn't working. Her mind was where it should never have gone to start with.

It was all right to get caught up in her work. It was even all right to be fascinated with the people and culture she'd found upon awakening. This was her job. She was supposed to care. She was supposed to focus every ounce of her being on bringing about renewal.

No one, least of all her, had expected her natural urges to get in the way.

She supposed all of them should have taken into account that she might be superhuman and bio-engineered for a specific purpose, but she was also of an age where her own mating instincts were strongest.

There'd been no avoiding that, of course. Her age was as critical to her mission as anything else. She was the fail-safe of the project. She had to be at her peak reproductive years in case it was found necessary that she produce the genius needed to rebuild.

"Hungry?"

Dionne jumped at the question and whirled to look at Khan. He didn't wait to see if she meant to follow him, but turned as soon as he'd caught her attention and went back into the living quarters. She debated with herself for a few moments, tempted to simply ignore her stomach when attending it meant facing Khan so soon after that uncomfortable episode. Finally, deciding it wasn't something she could avoid, she set the tablet aside again and followed him.

The food he'd prepared was obviously food he'd brought with him, and not the over processed food from storage. The fact that it was virtually identical to the meal he'd prepared the night before--some sort of stew--was further evidence if she'd needed it. Regardless, it tasted better than the meal she'd had earlier and she was starving.

They ate in silence. Khan seemed relaxed enough, Dionne thought resentfully. For her part the silence was an uncomfortable one. She managed to attain a semblance of calm after a few minutes, however, since it occurred to her that Khan had obviously decided to pretend the incident hadn't occurred.

When they'd finished, she took the pottery bowls and bone utensils he'd brought and washed them since he'd provided the meal. She saw when she'd finished that he'd settled on the pallet of furs and was idly polishing his shield and sword with a piece of thin, cloth-like leather, his brow creased in a frown of concentration, or thought. She cleared her throat. "Headache?"

He glanced toward her at the question, but finally shrugged. "Nothing I can't handle."

Someone else's pain was hard to gauge. A mild headache from a session with the ICTD wasn't uncommon, though. After searching his face for signs of strain, she relaxed fractionally. Obviously, it wasn't much pain--or he was handling it well. She decided, just to be on the safe side, to wait a few days before trying it again.

Upon consideration, she realized that would probably be best all around--for all of them, when the time came. There hadn't been any specific protocol laid down for education, but she thought that even if their minds were capable of handling the volume of information she was to feed them, culturally and emotionally it could present a serious shock.

From what she'd observed despite her sexual preoccupation with the test subject, he appeared to have assimilated the information very well. He was already learning his way around the habitat--he hadn't seemed to have any problem figuring out how to work the cooking unit or the bathing facilities and he was not familiar with either.

She was a little worried about the fact that he hadn't commented on the changes he must have noticed, but then he had not struck her as the talkative sort and the ICTD was not going to change his personality--not unless something went drastically wrong.

Since he seemed disinclined to socialize and she was not tired enough to seek her rest yet, she decided to go out for a breath of fresh air. She debated with herself briefly when she reached the main lab, but finally decided to just climb out the escape hatch as she had before. The bots had been busy for hours and might well have cleared the main door by now, but they might not have.

She saw when she reached the exit hatch that the bots had actually made quite a bit of progress. A small hill of sand was slowly growing perhaps a quarter to a half mile from the habitat as the bots circled the building, pushing the sand away from it a few inches at the time. They had already uncovered almost half of the bio-lab. In another day, perhaps two, she would be able to use the main entrance of the lab, which would allow her to move some of the heavier equipment out to begin environmental testing.

She was mentally fatigued from spending so many hours testing. Her feet and legs hurt from standing all day. A hot shower would relieve much of the strain, but she was loath to go near it while Khan was still awake. If he decided turn about was fair play she might end up doing something she would regret forever.

After a while, she sat down at the mouth of the exit tunnel, staring up at the stars while she mentally went over her list of things to do. It was important to be careful and methodical in the way she went about executing each phase, but impatience rose inside her as she considered how much time it would require.

She needed to locate the other bio-pods. There were twelve in all. Each contained a bio-engineered woman like her, the women the project had given the exalted title of Mothers of Mankind.

Everything had been very carefully evaluated and calculated to the nth degree. Each 'mother' carried four eggs that had been cloned, carefully implanted, and programmed for first release in pairs. They would be 'immaculately' conceived, would not need fertilization by a male donor. Once the 'army of deliverance' was produced, a male would be selected for them from among the survivors according to a strict selection procedure that would ensure superior stock as their own genetically enhanced eggs were released naturally.

If all of them still lived, her importance as keeper of the treasure of humanity would not be critical to the future of mankind. She was the project's fail-safe, however. So long as she did not know, until she was certain that all twelve were still viable, she didn't belong to herself. She couldn't make her own choices.

Even if all twelve had survived as she had, she was not to take the liberty of simply choosing any male that took her fancy. As with the others, the selection would be made for her according to the male's genetics.

It was ironic, actually, that no one had considered the 'human' element while they were so carefully formulating their plans and tabulating the results. The entire project had been conceived in a time when man's civilization had become threatened by the destabilization of their world--a destabilization that they were at least partly, if not entirely--responsible for. They'd come to realize that the world was rapidly reaching a critical point where one major natural disaster could cause all their work to collapse like a house of cards. The meteor had been the *coupe de grace*.

She supposed, given the dire situation and the limited time they had to complete their project it was only understandable that they'd focused on survival of the species and reclamation of their civilization, not the lives of individuals.

She sighed despondently. It didn't really matter why. She'd been given a sacred trust. She would have to focus on that and set her personal feelings aside until and unless such as time as she had fulfilled her part. She would be much better off not even thinking along the lines she'd been thinking in the meanwhile.

* * * *

Since he showed no signs of problems of any sort, Dionne coaxed Khan into a second session with the ICTD on the third day. He was not pleased when he demanded a third session with the ICTD the following day and Dionne refused, explaining that, for safety's sake, she felt that it was best to allow at least a day to lapse between sessions.

She had mixed feelings about it. It was heartening that he was eager, almost hungry, to learn, unsettling that he seemed both angry and suspicious of her motives when she insisted on waiting, and distressing in a way that she didn't really want to analyze to watch him change before her eyes.

The changes were fairly subtle, but profound nevertheless.

By mid-week Dionne had finished her testing of the seeds and was ready to begin environmental studies. Here her job was somewhat easier. For the most part, the equipment gathered the data through a series of sensors, analyzed the information and fed the results into a growing data bank.

Khan followed her step for step, tense, alert, and armed to the teeth. His behavior unnerved her far more than wandering about the wilderness. She knew that there were most likely animals that roamed the woods that presented a potential threat, but she had Nomi and Sachi. The noise she and the equipment made and her scent were enough to drive most any wild thing deeper into the woods. The cougars were there to protect her if any wild animal should feel threatened enough to attack.

Khan's people had struck her as peaceful and since the gathering outside the bio-lab when she'd emerged had included several tribes, she assumed the populace was, for the most part, peaceful.

Khan greeted that assessment with an expression that was difficult to read. "Precisely how did you arrive at that conclusion?"

Dionne was in the process of collecting plant specimens. She stopped what she was doing and lifted her head to gape at him. For several moments, she was so pleased at his improved vocabulary and diction that she didn't even consider what he'd actually said. "Conclusion?" she echoed finally, realizing that she'd missed the gist of the question.

Khan glanced around and finally squatted beside her so that they were face to face. "This is a dangerous conclusion you've made, and based on nothing but the most rudimentary observations. *None* of the tribes are peaceful when compared to what you're accustomed to. Our survival is primarily dependent upon the food supplied by nature. If we don't guard our territory, other tribes will encroach and we will suffer for it."

"Oh," Dionne responded, blinking rapidly as she considered the information. "That's going to make things more difficult. I'd assumed I would be able to interact freely with the specim--people and gather my data."

Something flickered in his eyes at her near slip. Feeling a twinge of color surge into her cheeks, she looked away, focusing on carefully placing the specimens she'd collected in the hopper of the analyzer.

"I will just have to figure something out," she said finally. "It's important that all survivors be tested for sicknesses, inoculated against disease, and analyzed for genetic defect before we can proceed to phase three," she said absently.

Khan stood, staring down at her. His gaze seemed to burn into her. "And phase three is?"

She frowned, bracing herself for the anger she expected. "The introduction of superior genetic stock. The 'mothers' were bio-engineered to ensure quality, but there wasn't enough time or money to pair them with their male counterparts. It was all the project committee could do to produce the twelve they considered a bare minimum of what was needed--and the one they had designated as their fail-safe and project leader."

"And this is phase one?" Khan asked after a fairly prolonged silence.

Dionne nodded without glancing at him. There was a tightness in his voice that hinted at displeasure if not open hostility, but she didn't feel up to any sort of confrontation. "Phase one: I am to collect data for analysis so that the main computer can determine if any necessary building blocks are missing--in order to create a new civilization, the natural resources must be there to be collected and used--but they must also harmonize with what is here to avoid creating an imbalance like the one that contributed to the downfall before.

"Once that has been determined, I'm to implement phase two-- which is to begin reintroduction of key species of plants, insects, and animals, location of necessary ore and mineral deposits, and education of the survivors via the ICTD devices--assuming their brains have not regressed and they have the capacity for learning what's needed. If there has been some regression, then I must *still* do what can be done and hope that the introduction of superior stock will eventually produce the desired results."

"Timing is critical. In order to maximize the benefits of the project, it's important that everything be in place at the right time for utilization. If the clones reach maturity before the tools and building blocks are in place, their genius could go untapped."

"For now, you will confine yourself to my tribe and tribal territory."

Dionne surged to her feet. "That isn't part of the plan," she said, keeping her voice even with an effort. "Renewal is for mankind, not merely a handful."

Khan gestured to the world around them. "Did they envision *this* when they were formulating the 'grand design'? Did they consider the human factor, human nature--at all? Did they consider that the only possibility of survival, the only ones likely to survive, would be those strong enough--animal enough--to use their instincts? These traits that ensured survival will also make it next to impossible for you to implement the 'grand design' on a full scale. They are wild, untamed, and dangerous. They will not simply walk into your lab like--domesticated cattle and allow you to do whatever you like--or need to do.

"I am chief of my tribe. Most will trust me enough to do as I ask of them--but not all. Even in my own village there are those who will refuse and those who will have to be coaxed.

"Among the tribes that are our allies, some cooperation is also possible. Beyond that, the only way you will collect your 'specimens' is by force, which will result in a great deal of bloodshed and loss of life.

"This is not a lab where all the animals are contained in cages awaiting their fate."

Dionne stared at him in dismay, knowing he was right. She was a scientist, and as alien to his world as if she'd been dropped here from a world across the galaxy. She knew what to do and how to do it in a lab setting, but how was she to carry out her assignment in the real world? This savage Garden of Eden?

Chapter Eight

It took a full week for Dionne and Khan to work their way across the wilderness that separated the bio-lab from Khan's village. Khan used his tracking skills to determine the points most frequented by the denizens of the forest seeking water and after carefully de-scenting the probe, they set it up near enough to the spot to track and record the animals as they came to the stream to drink. Khan and Dionne spent much of those nights perched on a platform Khan had constructed high in a nearby tree, so that they could guard the probe from the possibility of human intervention and observe the variety of species that inhabited the woods.

Setting the probe near the water supply was Khan's contribution to Dionne's efforts after she'd observed that it could take months or years to catalogue them all if she could do little besides sit in the woods for hours at the time and hope an animal wandered by.

As helpful as Khan's suggestion was in rapidly accumulating necessary data, the job was still a miserable one. The platforms Khan constructed at the various sites were small, barely wide enough for one, much less the two of them, forcing them into a false intimacy that Khan seemed to find as uncomfortable as Dionne did. When one added the limitation of movements, the impossibility of even talking as a diversion, the cool night air, and the long, muscle cramping hours they had to perch there, Dionne arrived at the conclusion that very few situations could even come close to it in terms of absolute misery.

The one thing Dionne had in plenty was time for thought. Part of that was expended on the problem Khan had pointed out with the project. The other part revolved around Khan, much to her dismay.

Since the day he'd done--whatever it was he'd done that had made her feel so desperately achy and needy that had culminated in such a wonderful explosion of ecstasy, he hadn't made any attempt to repeat the experiment--at all. Of course she supposed that might be partly her own fault, because she'd gone out of her way to keep as much distance between them as possible after that. But it seemed to her that he'd accepted her refusal of intimacy far easier than he should have if he'd truly been attracted to her to start with.

He didn't strike her as the sort to be easily dissuaded. He'd been interested enough up until that last devastating encounter that he'd ignored her weak protests and introduced her to a whole new world of sensations.

Why had he simply backed away then? Shouldn't he have been as desperate to experience it again as she'd was?

She supposed she shouldn't complain. She'd said no. He'd backed off. That was that. It was much better than the alternative.

It made working with him easier.

It was irritating as hell to have to suffer alone.

He seemed very different since he'd begun the sessions with the ICTD. She wasn't certain she approved of the change, but she couldn't quite put her finger on what it was about him that was different, or more precisely, that she didn't consider an improvement. There was nothing she could see that seemed symptomatic of neurological problems, and she felt no particular anxiety that he'd been injured in any way.

That thought did lead her to one she began to think might be closer to the answer.

He'd erected a wall of indifference, she finally decided. It was the sort of premeditated, carefully contrived emotional distance people manufactured to protect themselves from something, or someone, that was hurtful.

She glanced at him at that thought, but her eyes had adjusted to the gloom as much as they were going to and she couldn't make out much more than a vague outline of his face. The movement attracted his attention, however, and he turned to look back at her--questioningly, probably.

There was no point in asking him what she'd done, she realized. It was very unlikely that he would tell her anything at all. Most likely, he would pretend he hadn't any idea at all of what she was talking about.

Mentally, she shrugged. It was probably the rejection thing. That was always a low blow, no matter how carefully worded. It didn't make anyone feel any better to be told that it wasn't them, it was something else, because they never believed it--mostly because everyone knew that kind of excuse was almost always just a polite lie.

The confusing thing about that theory was that Khan understood far more than he had in the beginning. The ICTD had not only brought him through basic education, but it had familiarized him with the civilization she had been born to. Surely he had learned enough to understand the importance of what she'd been sent to do?

But perhaps that was it? He'd been interested, but now he realized that her mission was too important to jeopardize with personal feelings and he had distanced himself emotionally because he knew it could come to nothing?

She looked away from him again after a moment, staring down at the creek running along the forest floor. It took an effort to put him from her mind when it was his body heat keeping her warm and she could feel the brush of his arm along hers, or his hip butting hers whenever either of them shifted to a more comfortable position.

She was fortunate, she realized, that it had been Khan who'd awakened her and that he had not simply abandoned her when he'd realized her mission prevented her from giving him sexual gratification. She'd made a great deal of progress and most of it was due to him.

His insight about the current situation wasn't something she could dismiss either. She supposed it had been in the back of her mind all the time and that was why she'd had to fight a sense of hopelessness all the while she went through the motions of her assignment. She *had* considered the magnitude of the problem. She had also realized that the scientists had not really considered the human equation as they should have. She just hadn't considered how much of a road block this barbaric society would present to her.

There were certain points of the original plan that were critical, even though she saw that executing it as it had been laid out for her probably wasn't going to work. It seemed probable that she could bring Khan's people out of the wilderness, possibly some of his tribe's allies--and likely no more. That was enough for a start, but even she could see that reaching so few would mean that she'd only succeeded in dividing the civilized from the uncivilized, which could create as many problems as it relieved.

She began to think it might have been better if she had not argued with their belief that she was a goddess. At least if they'd believed that they would have been concerned about displeasing the goddess, which, theoretically would have made them all more cooperative.

That thought led her to an idea she hadn't considered. She dismissed it at first, knowing it was unethical, probably immoral, but it kept returning, impossible to ignore.

She glanced at Khan again. "What if--assuming they're still alive--we allowed the people to believe the 'mothers' were goddesses?"

Khan frowned thoughtfully, seemed to consider it, then shrugged. "It would be dangerous."

Dionne pursed her lips in irritation. "As you pointed out, everything on this world is dangerous now, completely savage and uncivilized. I need to get them into the different tribes if they're going to do any good. If the people believe they are goddesses, or gifts from the gods--whatever--aren't they more likely to try to please them? Something could be worked out. I know it's--morally wrong, what I'm saying, but wouldn't the end justify the means?"

Khan studied her in silence for several moments, his face taut. "Exploit their beliefs, you mean? Use their ignorance and child-like trust to manipulate them?"

Dionne felt her face redden. "You think it's less wrong to deprive them of what we could give them? To give the gifts only to your people?"

His lips tightened with his own anger. "How much of a 'gift' is it to bring dissatisfaction to people who were reasonably satisfied with the lives they had? To show them what might have been? What they don't have that they should?"

Dionne's jaw slackened in stunned surprise. She'd thought Khan, at least, would understand that she only wanted the best for everyone. She hadn't thought for a moment that he was actually against everything she was doing.

She lurched to her feet so abruptly she almost went off the platform and had to grab the trunk of the tree to steady herself. "If you had no interest in learning, why did you risk your life to enter the bio-lab? If you were completely satisfied with the life you had, why did you go to the forbidden land? How do *you* know what they want?"

"They are *my* people," he said quietly, though the words were no less angry for being spoken low.

Dionne swallowed against a lump that suddenly formed in her throat. "They are *my* people, too!"

Her exit was nearly a grander one than she'd planned. The climb down the tree was treacherous enough under any condition. Angry and hurt, she was too distressed to pay as much attention as she should. Halfway down, she stepped on a branch too thin to hold her weight. It snapped. Fortunately, she had a good handhold and caught herself, but she scraped a good bit of hide off on the rough bark. Muttering curses under her breath, she did her best to ignore the burning scrapes and made the remainder of the climb more carefully. She was still shaky from the near fall when she reached the ground, however.

Khan landed on the ground only a few feet from her, having dropped the last several feet. Ignoring him, she stalked angrily along the narrow path they'd followed to the stream. Nomi slid from the brush along the path and fell into step on one side of her. A few minutes later Sachi wedged himself between Khan and Dionne on the narrow path, nearly pushing both of them down.

Dionne barely glanced at either cat, but a sense of satisfaction filled her that Sachi had so effectively distanced her from Khan. They walked the two miles to the bio-lab in offended silence. When she reached the bio-lab and realized that Khan had fallen back, Dionne stalked through the entrance and ordered the door closed before Khan could reach it.

To all intents and purposes, it was *her* lab. He could take himself back to his damned lodge if he was so frigging satisfied with living in a hut!

He came in through the escape hatch, glaring at her when he landed at the foot of the shaft. As startled as she was that he'd not only climbed the building and entered it despite the fact that she'd slammed the door in his face, arriving in the main lab at the center of the building at almost the same time she did, Dionne wasn't about to let him know he'd unnerved her. She merely glared back at him and stalked through the lab and into her quarters. Without pausing, she headed for the shower, peeling the tunic she wore off as she went and tossing it to the floor. She was chilled, despite her anger, and her palm, forearm and thigh still stung from scraping them on the tree.

She knew the very moment Khan entered the bath behind her. A chill draft breezed through the room, pebbling her skin despite the warmth of the water rushing over her. Ignoring him, she pulled off the thong she used to bind her hair and began to unravel the braid she'd bound her hair in to keep it out of her way while she worked.

Despite her determination to ignore him, Dionne jumped when she turned and discovered Khan had followed her into the shower.

"We should talk," he said quietly.

"And the point of that would be...?"

He curled his fingers around her upper arms quicker than thought, pushing her back against the tiled wall. The cats, who'd apparently followed him, uttered a low, threatening growl--which he ignored--but made no attempt to come any closer than the door since they had an antipathy for water. Apparently they were as certain as Dionne was that, despite the aggression inherent in the move, he didn't actually intend her any harm or they would've ignored their dislike of water and attacked anyway.

"Send them away," he growled, his face mere inches from hers now.

Dionne swallowed with an effort at the effect his close proximity was having on her, instantly at war with herself. There was threat/promise in every tense line of his body that her own body instantly responded to with hopeful excitement. Sending the cats away would be tantamount to capitulation, however, and she was not only not willing to allow him to compromise her position as mission failsafe, but she resented what appeared to be an arrogant assumption that he could 'fuck the meanness' out of her. She was not being unreasonable. She didn't particularly consider that he was either, but the hard fact was that they had two diametrically opposed opinions on this matter and nothing he could do or say was going to change her mind. "Why?" she finally managed to ask, although the word emerged as little more than a squeak.

His gaze moved over her face caressingly. "I think you know why."

"This won't resolve anything," she responded a little shakily.

His gaze moved over her face. "Wrong again," he muttered, covering her mouth in a kiss that instantly sent a tidal wave of need through her as if a dam had burst. A sound that was part need, part despair escaped her, but she opened her mouth to him, glorying in the dizzying rush that decimated rational thought as his tongue raked across hers with restless possessiveness.

She'd wanted this, *needed* it.

She grasped his waist, pulling him closer, slipping her hands beneath the back waist of his loincloth to cup his buttocks. A shudder went through him. He pushed a knee between her thighs, lifting her up until she could wrap her legs around his hips. When he cupped her buttocks, pulling her sex tightly against his erection, the pleasure was so exquisite she felt faint. Her heart lurched, galloped frantically. Pulling her hands from his breechcloth, she ran her palms over his back feverishly, drinking in the feel of him, his bare chest against her own, his strong back against her palms.

When he dragged his lips from hers at last, they were both gasping hoarsely with need. Nuzzling her neck, he dipped his head toward her breasts. Dionne hooked her hands over his shoulders, arching up to meet him. "We can't--can't have sex. We can pleasure each other, though."

He stiffened, lifting his head slowly to look at her.

Dizzy, disoriented, it took a supreme effort to open her eyes and gaze back at him.

A frown flitted across his face. Something indecipherable flickered in his eyes and vanished. He eased slightly away from her, allowing her to slide to her feet, forcing the tension from his body with an effort. Finally, he released her and stood away, studying her for several moments as if he'd never seen her before. She shivered when he stepped away from her, turned and strode from the room without another word.

Frustration and confusion creased her brows as she watched him leave and it occurred to her to wonder if she'd completely misread him. Maybe it hadn't been his intention, or belief, that he had only to seduce her to bend her to his will? Maybe his anger had merely moved him to passion, broken through the wall he'd erected?

But why then, if that were true, had he acted like she'd slapped him when she'd offered to pleasure him?

The look he'd given her disturbed her far more than she liked, as if she'd betrayed him somehow, as if he'd seen something in her that he hadn't seen before--and he hadn't liked it.

Maybe he had, but that wasn't her problem.

Fighting the urge to weep, or scream obscenities, Dionne plunged beneath the pounding water, hoping it would soothe the ache that was still pounding inside of her, knowing it wouldn't.

She had never made any attempt to represent herself falsely only to appeal to him. She had been completely open and honest with him from the first, whether he'd understood her or not. She was attracted to him, had been almost from the very beginning, but she had known even before she went into the bio-pod that she must be utterly and completely committed to her task. She couldn't allow anything, or anyone, to distract or divert her from what needed to be done.

She had wanted him though, desperately enough to offer what she could even knowing how risky it was to allow that much, because, in her heart, she'd known that would only make her want him more, not quench the fire.

Even when she'd told him she couldn't allow penetration, she had desperately wanted it. It was scary how badly she'd wanted him to ignore her protests and do what he wanted with her, unnerving how weak her will was where he was concerned.

Pushing the incident from her mind with an effort, she turned the hot water up until it was next to scalding and finished her shower. By the time she was done, much of her tension had dissipated and exhaustion had set in. Khan was no where in sight when she returned to the living area and reluctantly donned the tunic once more. She stared at his furs longingly for a few moments, almost sorry now that she'd established a boundary between them by silently refusing to share his bed furs, but after a moment she dismissed temptation and moved to the hard platform that was her own 'bed'.

Chapter Nine

For the first time in his life, Khan stood on a rise and stared at his village without the warmth and excitement of homecoming that he'd always felt before when he returned after a long absence. He saw it now through a stranger's eyes--her eyes--and the emotion most dominant inside of him was shame and embarrassment. There was order about the place, but the shelters were crude--their entire culture was painfully primitive. The people covered their nakedness with the skins of animals they'd killed or poorly constructed garments woven of reeds--both of which carried the unpleasant stench of decay. For the most part, the children scampered about the village naked, squatting to relieve themselves whenever and where ever the mood struck.

The primitiveness of conditions made him feel vaguely ill and he almost hated Dionne in that moment for removing the veil from his eyes, for making him see his life for what it really was--one step away from the animals they killed and ate for food.

The sense of shame went deeper even than that.

From the moment he'd set eyes on her he had wanted her to a point of near desperation. As leader of his people, as a warrior who had earned respect, his self-esteem had been high enough he had not considered it inappropriate to aspire to so fine a creature. It made him cringe inside now to imagine what she must have thought.

Small wonder she had behaved toward him as if he were simple minded, little more than a beast. Her kindness was almost worse than open contempt would have been. At least then he wouldn't have made such a complete fool out of himself. If she'd shunned him, he would still have been angry, but it would have been enough to turn him away from her, to kill his interest.

Several of the villagers noticed him at last and straightened from their tasks. Smiling as recognition dawned, they waved and called out a welcome.

Khan's anger waned. He returned the greeting and started down the slope into the village. Children swarmed around him, chattering excitedly, pelting him with questions about the 'goddess' and the 'temple'. Smiling with an effort, he evaded their questions, but good-naturedly. The adults were more polite and restrained, but he could see that they were as curious as the children.

Somehow, he made it through the village without losing the false smile he'd pasted on his face and, with relief, ducked at last through the entrance to his lodge.

He needed time to think--and enough distance from Dionne to think clearly. Wryly, he supposed he should have considered finding a place far from anyone at all, but he had not been near the village in almost two weeks. Regardless of the things that had changed, one thing had not. He was still Chief of his people. They still needed him. There were bound to be problems and/or disputes that had arisen since he had left them that needed his attention.

The problem looming largest in his mind, however, was Dionne herself.

His brothers, if they'd known what had transpired between him and Dionne, would call him a fool. She'd offered to give him pleasure. He should have taken it. Even *he* thought he was a fool for not jumping at the chance, particularly since he hurt all over for refusing.

The moment the words were out of her mouth, however, he'd known exactly what she *hadn't* said.

He might or might not be up to her stringent standards. She wanted him. She was willing to share her body with him--to a point, to give and take pleasure, but when it came right down to it, she was still going to choose her mate according to the damned computer.

It was just as well he didn't know where the main processing unit was. He might have been tempted at that moment to destroy it.

She would never have forgiven him for it. He was fairly certain he wouldn't have been able to forgive himself either.

There was always the chance, of course, that the computer might consider him suitable.

He shot to his feet at that thought, pacing his lodge like a caged beast, trying to outrun his shame and anger that he was so desperate to have her that such a thought could enter his mind.

Furious, he decided at that moment that he should have nothing else to do with her. If she was so coldly clinical that she could consider seeking her pleasure with him and then going to whatever male the computer decided was her best match she wasn't the woman he thought she was.

He was in love with a mirage--a woman that didn't exist beyond his mind.

He was a damned fool.

Grinding his teeth, he pressed his hands against his pounding skull, as if he could expunge her from his thoughts. It didn't work. His mind continued to churn with hurt and anger.

He should have taken her right then, taken *exactly* what he wanted and left her to figure out how to expel his undesirable seed before it could go near her precious eggs.

He needed to kill something--an outlet of some kind before he exploded. Erupting from his lodge, he stalked toward the stream. The chill of the water as he dove into the pool took his breath, but it also extinguished much of the fire in him. He swam back and forth across the pool until the tension finally began to subside.

When he emerged, he discovered Chala was waiting for him.

Dismay and desire collided inside him, making his belly clench painfully.

They'd been lovers off and on since they were little more than children.

He needed an outlet for his frustrated desires and he didn't doubt for one moment that Chala was more than happy to oblige.

Without a word, he knelt on the ground beside her and covered her body with his own. She smiled up at him, slipping a hand between them to massage his flaccid member. "I thought you'd claimed the goddess as your woman."

He frowned, covering her mouth with his in a deep kiss to shut her up before she said something that completely pissed him off.

Her mouth was not nearly as sweet as Dionne's.

Resolutely, he pushed that thought to the back of his mind.

Her hands on him were far more practiced, knowing. By the time he broke the kiss, he was relieved to discover his cock had risen to the occasion. He was nibbling a trail toward one pert nipple when she decided to talk again.

"You always did know just how to give me pleasure," she murmured, writhing beneath his caresses.

He tried to ignore that, too, fighting the urge to plant one hand over her mouth, but the comment so closely echoed the one Dionne had made that the desire he'd been struggling to build died and his erection with it.

Grinding his teeth, he buried his face between her large breasts, trying to resurrect his fallen warrior.

It was too much to hope she hadn't noticed.

Shoving at his shoulders, she jumped to her feet the moment he rolled away, glaring down at him--or, more accurately--his cock.

"That--witch has placed a spell on you!"

Khan sat up. "Just go, Chala, before you make me say something we'll both regret."

Snatching up her dress, she dragged it over her head and stalked off. He lay back, when she'd gone, wondering just how long it was going to take her to spread her tale of woe through the village.

Realizing finally that he didn't particularly care, he got up tiredly and pulled his breechcloth on once more. Half way back to the village bathing spot, he passed her entwined with Notaku. She sent him a triumphant smile over Notaku's shoulder.

Contrary to her obvious hopes, Khan didn't feel even a twinge of jealousy, or envy that she'd decided to bestow her favors on Notaku instead.

He did feel some disgust--mostly with himself.

He didn't know whether to be more disgusted by the fact that he couldn't arouse any interest in another woman because it made him feel guilty as hell, or more disgusted that he would even feel guilt.

Dionne had been clear enough that she didn't consider herself his woman.

Before his ongoing state of unrequited lust could rouse his temper once more, he turned his thoughts to the other matter regarding Dionne--the argument that had led to his most recent brush with madness.

Beyond the desire to fuck her senseless, which hadn't actually required a lot of thought, he'd thought of very little besides their dispute from the time it had finally erupted and he wasn't one bit closer to deciding which of them were right. His first critical view of his village had been more of a jolt than he'd anticipated. Now he understood why Dionne had looked so devastated, so hopeless when he'd brought her here.

He felt much the same.

Would it be better for them to feel as he did now, he wondered? Or better to let them cling to their pride in their accomplishments, meager though they were, and their happiness with what they had?

He was not left alone with his thoughts long. Almost as soon as he reached his lodge again, the village elders gathered outside, requesting council. He invited them in and listened with determined patience as problems were presented for resolution. The session tried his tolerance as it never had before. Ordinarily, the slow progression from one problem to the next, the long discussions of each as each of the elders presented their opinion on the matter, at least held his interest. This time, he found his mind wandering. Toward mid-day, women filed into his lodge bearing food. Debates continued even while they ate.

Khan ate little of the food himself. He'd noticed with the first bite that the meat that was the main ingredient was borderline spoiled. It wasn't likely to hurt him. He'd been in the habit of eating just this sort of thing his entire life and knew that was the reason the food was overcooked--to ensure its safety--and well seasoned with wild herbs to mask the taste--but he was aware of it now in a way that made it difficult to swallow.

It was late in the afternoon that he heard a stir of excitement in the village that caught his wandering attention. With a sense of relief, he cut the council short and left his lodge to see what the commotion was about.

The villagers, he saw, were hurrying toward the opposite end of the village. Pushing his way through the flow, he strode quickly along the main path toward the rise where he'd entered the village that morning.

He stopped abruptly when he saw Dionne sitting on the rise overlooking the village.

When everyone had gathered, she stood up and looked out over the crowd. For several moments her gaze locked with his, and then moved on. The villagers fell silent beneath her gaze, tensed, obviously unnerved by her presence. Finally, as if some silent communication had drifted through the gathering, they knelt and bowed to her.

Even from where he stood, Khan could see that worshipfulness embarrassed her and he wondered what had made him think even for a moment that her motives were less than pure, that she might abuse her position and use it to exert power over the simple people she was dealing with.

"For many generations you have gone to the lifeless plain to worship and pray to your gods to favor you with the gift of renewal," she said finally.

Khan tensed, wondering if he'd misjudged her--again.

"I've come to offer you the gift. It's the gift of knowing all the things that were learned long, long ago in the days before the world was covered with ice. This knowledge will change--everything, but it will also give you the chance to build a better life for your children and their children.

"I can not take it back, once given, so you must think hard before you decide to make this choice whether you want to know, or if you want to go on as you have, as your fathers did.

"If you want this gift, if you are not afraid to change if it will make your children's lives better, then you need only come to me on the lifeless plain and I will give it to you. It's your choice."

From the moment she'd begun to speak, the villagers had sat up to listen. Slowly, as if they weren't entirely certain it would be allowed, they stood. The warrior, Notaku, was the first to stand. "You are not a goddess," he said, almost challengingly.

Dionne turned to look at the bear of a man, sensing hostility in his manner even if she hadn't noticed the tone of his voice. "No, I'm not," she said calmly. "I'm the one entrusted with the task of bringing the gift."

Notaku sent Khan a challenging glance before he returned his attention to her. "You've not chosen a man."

The look as much as the undercurrents she detected in his defiant stance, drew Dionne's attention to Khan. She sensed immediately that there was longstanding hostility between the two men that had nothing at all to do with her. Very likely it was tied to Khan's position as Chief, but the warrior seemed determined to make her the latest bone of contention.

"I can not," she said finally. "Not until I have done what I was sent to do." She studied him for several moments, wondering if she dared go further, but finally realized that she had little choice if she was to do what she'd set out to do. Khan was opposed to the plan. It seemed unlikely that he would help her now, and now that she had a better understanding of the situation, she realized she would need help if she was to have any hope of surviving long enough to complete her task. "First I must find the others--like me. They were--uh--hidden in a place far from here--many days ride. I will need strong, fierce warriors to take me there."

A wide smile curled the warrior's lips. "I will take you."

Oh shit!

Dionne managed a thin smile in response. Before she could either accept or reject the offer, however, Khan spoke for the first time. "No one would trust you--alone--Notaku, to take her there safely and return. She speaks of the forbidden land."

Notaku reddened at the insult, but at Khan's last remark, the color left his face abruptly. His skin turned a sickly hue. "I am brave and strong enough to take her," he said with forced bravado.

Dionne couldn't help but notice that no one else volunteered. She didn't know whether it was the mention of the forbidden land, or the possibility that they might find themselves caught up in the middle of a dispute between Khan and the warrior, Notaku, who struck her as brutish and dangerously stupid.

"I will not accept the help of any warrior not brave enough to face the tests, or wise enough to accept the gift," she said firmly. "I will go alone if I must."

Having said what she had come to say, she turned to depart. Notaku had made her uneasy, however, and she made certain she summoned the cats in full view of all the villagers before she left.

She had not gone far when Khan caught up to her. She could tell even before he spoke that he was angry.

"What was that all about?" he demanded tightly.

"Giving them a choice."

He was silent for several moments, obviously wrestling with his temper. "I meant the invitation to Notaku, but we'll leave that for the moment--I would have spoken to them myself."

"Without trying to influence their decision in any way?"

He ground his teeth. "And you didn't?"

She colored faintly. "I didn't lie to them."

"You did suggest, oh so subtly, that their refusal to accept would be tantamount to denying their children a better life."

"Which it would be."

"What gives you the right to judge?"

"What gives *you* the right?" she demanded, stopping abruptly and turning to face him. "When I look at them I see sickness, squalor, hunger--all things that could be prevented if they only knew how."

"It is all they have ever known. They accept the cycle of life because they know no different. You have no right to play god with their lives, to make them yearn for things they will never have when they are satisfied with the world they know."

Dionne struggled to contain her outrage and failed. "*You're* not playing god with their lives?--at all?"

"I had no intention of doing so. I only wanted time to consider what would be best for all. That is why I was chosen as their Chief--to make the decisions according to what was best for everyone."

"It isn't *your* decision. It's theirs! You make weapons and go out and choose which animals you will kill to fill the cook pot and which ones you'll use to make yourself more comfortable, but that isn't playing god?"

He gave her a look. "That is a matter of survival--ours or theirs."

"It's *all* a matter of survival *and* the quality of life. You use the tools and knowledge you have to see to your comfort and survival. If someone gets sick, or hurt, you do what you can to help them get better, to make them well. This isn't playing god. It's no different at all. And no one person has the right to make the decision for everyone else--*that's* playing god, taking it upon yourself to make someone else's decision for them only because you don't approve of their choice or methods."

He was silent for several moments. "We can not agree on this."

"No, we can't."

"Because you are stubborn and will only see one side of this."

Dionne glared at him.

"We will agree to allow them to make their own decision without *either* of us trying to influence their choice."

Dionne wrestled with her temper for several moments and finally capitulated. "Agreed. I only came anyway to tell them they had a choice--because I realized that you were right and it was just as wrong of me to try to trick them into doing what I thought was best for them as it was for you to try to convince them not to accept the gift."

The final jab resurrected his temper, but instead of taking up that gauntlet, he backtracked to his earlier complaint. "It was not wise to invite the warriors to battle for your favor," he said.

Dionne's jaw dropped in stunned surprise. "I did no such thing!"

"Maybe not intentionally...."

"Not at all! You were the one who pointed out that it would be dangerous to travel alone."

"I'd intended to take you when you were ready to go," he said tightly.

Dionne stared at him in surprise for several moments. "And I was supposed to know this? You made it pretty clear that you didn't approve of the project at all."

"I don't."

She shook her head. "I don't understand you at all. Why would you even consider helping me if you don't approve?"

He seemed to wrestle with himself for several moments. Finally, he merely shrugged. "I released you into this dangerous world. I'm responsible for your safety."

It was unreasonable for that statement to hit her like a fist to the solar plexus, but it did, and she found she had to struggle against the pain even to catch her breath. "Because you released me?" she managed to ask finally.

"Yes."

Nodding, she turned away, paused for a moment to get her bearings and then headed a little blindly in the direction of the bio-lab. He felt responsible for her. All this time she'd struggled with her own demons of desire, certain that his staying with her was an indication that he felt something for her--even when he'd retreated behind that cold wall of seeming indifference--*because* he had. She'd misinterpreted everything.

When she'd questioned his presence at all--which she really hadn't because she'd just been so damned grateful that she wasn't facing such a daunting task alone--she'd thought it was desire that kept him close, the hope that she'd change her mind.

It hadn't occurred to her once that he thought she was so weak and helpless and ineffectual that she couldn't take care of herself.

She was so caught up in her misery that she wasn't even startled when his hand curled around her arm and dragged her to a halt. She merely lifted her head and stared up at Khan blankly. "What?"

"It will be safer for you if I take you."

Dionne blinked at him several times while that slowly sank in. "Actually, it isn't at all necessary. Never let it be said that scientists don't consider practicalities at least occasionally. There are weapons in the lab. I have the cats, too. I'm sure the maps will be almost as useless as the global positioning assistance since the geology of the landscape has altered so drastically and there probably haven't been manmade satellites orbiting the world in centuries, but the bots should be able to pinpoint the general area.

"I'm not even certain now if there would be any point in going." She frowned. "I may need to consider whether it would be better to scrap the project at this point, seal the bio-lab, and re-enter the bio-pod to wait for a more receptive time."

Chapter Ten

Khan's hand tightened reflexively on her arm. The emotions that chased across his features were hard to decipher, however, and Dionne wasn't in any mood to try. "You're not seriously considering going back into that thing? You're lucky you survived this long."

"Actually, I haven't decided what I'm going to do. But aborting the mission is my decision. I'm team leader. I'll have to give it some thought."

When he released her arm, she resumed her trek, but the new possibility supplanted her hurt and confusion, pushing them to the back of her mind. By the time she'd reached the bio-lab, she had arrived at one conclusion. She was too emotionally involved with Khan to make an objective decision. Everything about her association with him clouded her judgment. If it hadn't, she would have considered the possibility of aborting and trying at some unspecified future time much sooner.

She was tired and hungry when she reached the lab, but none of the food in storage was so tempting that she found it hard to resist and she decided to put off preparing a meal until after she'd input the data.

Dragging a stool over to the console, she plopped down on it and sat for some minutes trying to compose her thoughts. "Lois?"

"Yes?"

"I need you to run a scenario for me."

"Awaiting data input."

"This is to be matched against the Renewal Project overview."

"Affirmative."

"We overshot the projected implementation date by approximately 700 years. There are no survivors, as was anticipated, with any memory of the pre-disaster world. Although the populace shows no signs of physical or mental regression in so far as learning capabilities or physical attributes that would preclude the use of modern tools, culturally they have regressed to a stage of tribal hunter/gatherers.

"Actually, I can't be certain that they've *re*gressed to that point. It's possible that they have *progressed* to this point and conditions were more primitive before. From what I *have* learned it seems that they have been perched on this plateau of development for several generations at least with no appreciable progress.

"They have the ability to make tools from stone, bone, and wood. Their skill in pottery making seems fairly sophisticated. The study subjects do not appear to be nomadic. They have land under cultivation, but little in the way of domesticated stock. They seem to have built permanent dwellings in a fairly organized village structure. The dwellings are constructed of clay mortar, some sort of animal hair, and stick. I had originally interpreted the absence of fortification of any kind as a sign that the people were peaceful, but I have learned that this is not the case. Tribes are territorial and fight to protect their hunting grounds...."

In took her several hours to dredge up every scrap of information she had noted in her observations of Khan and his people. It surprised her that she'd observed as much as she had without actually being aware of it.

When she'd finally run dry of information, the computer asked for more.

"Number of subjects in test?"

Dionne frowned, scanning her memory for an approximation. "Approximately twenty five family units--one tribe."

"Area?"

She hadn't a clue. "Calculate a territory of about thirty to fifty square miles per tribe. Oh, and there seems to be very large tracts of land that are considered uninhabitable. The bio-lab sits in 'the lifeless plain' a large desert. And the 'forbidden land' seems to include major cities of my time--so you should subtract that from the equation."

"General attitude regarding tests?"

Dionne considered that. "Overall, negative."

"General attitude regarding ICTD?"

"Hostile."

"General attitude regarding introduction of enhanced genetics subjects?"

Dionne thought that one over for several minutes. "I don't think they'd have any problem finding someone to fuck them," she said dryly. "Testosterone levels are through the roof here." She paused, considering. "I think the probability is high that the 'mothers' would not be able to integrate smoothly into the culture. Ignorance and superstition about them could contribute to battles or outright war--the subjects are very territorial."

"Calculating probabilities."

Sighing, Dionne got up and headed for her quarters. She jolted to a halt when she saw Khan had followed her, but after a brief pause continued without acknowledging him.

It was really starting to get on her nerves that he kept sneaking up on her like that.

Not that it would be hard to evade her notice, she admitted. As distracted as she'd been lately a five hundred pound gorilla could probably sneak up on her.

And, of course, Khan and his people survived on their ability to move quickly and silently, which gave him a distinct advantage.

Selecting a meal at random, she shoved it into the cooking unit, tapping her fingers on the countertop impatiently while she waited the two minutes it took to heat.

When it was done, she settled at the table to stare at the food and stir it with her fork. God she missed real food!

She missed real clothes, too. Not that she wasn't grateful just to have something to cover herself with, but miserable was still miserable. The tunic was scratchy and stiff and chafed her skin where ever it happened to rub her.

It occurred to her after a moment that it wasn't even hers. She'd 'borrowed' it from Khan. She'd done her best to keep the thing as clean as possible, but there was no washing leather. She'd checked with the computer. If she'd washed the thing it would probably look like a choker by now.

"That was a harsh assessment," Khan said, settling in the chair across from her.

She looked up at him in surprise, then frowned thoughtfully. "It wasn't accurate?"

His lips tightened. "You don't know that they will be hostile about the ICTD or that they will refuse to be tested."

She blinked, several times, rapidly. "It was an assessment based on prior experience and observation of expressions and body language when I made the offer. I don't have anything else to go on."

"Then the results will not be accurate."

She considered his remark thoughtfully and finally dismissed it. "The computer is only tabulating the statistical probability of success or failure. The more data the better, of course, and the more accurate the data the more accurate the prediction, but I'm only looking for something to support, or disprove, my own assessment of the situation."

She took a bite of the rapidly cooling food and chewed it, chasing it with water. When she decided she'd had enough to stave off starvation for a little while without becoming ill from trying to eat when her stomach was a knot of nerves, she left the table to dispose of the container and clean the fork.

"You're not seriously considering going back into the pod?"

Dionne turned to study him, folding her arms over her chest and leaning back against the cabinet. She found his attitude almost as confusing as it was annoying. What did he want from her? What did he expect her to do if she couldn't complete her mission in this time? Just give up? Did he think she could, in good conscience, simply discard all the hard work so many people had put into this project to ensure a future for mankind?

"You do understand that I was especially bio-engineered for this task? That it is the only reason for my existence at all?"

"It doesn't matter why, or how, you came to be, only that you are a human being and have the right to life that everyone else enjoys."

"It *does* matter why and how. I was conceived in a lab, gestated in a lab, reared in a lab. This is all I have ever known--this and the people who programmed me to carry out the task they knew they wouldn't be around to take care of themselves. What I do *after* I have completed my assignment is their gift to me." She shook her head. "I never asked you to agree with me, or to help me. I don't need you to help me and I certainly don't want or need you standing in my way. Go back to *your* people and leave me alone. I have work to do."

He followed her back into the main lab, but she was acutely aware that he lingered as she called up the computer again. "Have you finished processing, Lois?"

"Affirmative. Probability of completing one hundred percent of Project Renewal, zero. Probability of completing ninety percent of project successfully, zero. Probability of completing eighty percent...."

Dionne drummed her fingers on the desk top, fighting the urge to tell the computer to stop.

"...Probability of completing fifty percent of assignment, thirty percent...."

Deciding she'd heard enough when the computer reached twenty percent, she stopped the readout and got up to pace. To her relief, she saw that Khan had at last departed. Dismissing him from her mind, she considered the possibilities without emotion. "You're saying the probability of reintroducing specific plants and animals is good?"

"Affirmative."

She considered that with a slight budding of hopefulness. It wasn't much, to be sure, but if she could successfully introduce the necessary species into the chain the building blocks would be there when needed.

It was risky.

But then the whole enterprise was a calculated risk, and currently the odds were very much against the more complex aspects of the operation. "What is the probability of seed failure if I leave them for another one hundred, two hundred, or three hundred years?"

The computer calculated the odds and read them out.

"That good?" Dionne responded glumly. "We've already lost more than we could afford to considering the percentage that's bound to be lost once transplantation is implemented. I don't think we can afford to wait."

She rubbed her neck, realizing she was exhausted. "I want you to run the data I collected and determine what should be grown based on your findings."

"The test area was to have been a one hundred mile radius of the lab. The data is not sufficient for a high percentage of accuracy."

Dionne shook her head. "Calculate it anyway. I want to get started. We can abort later if additional data contradicts. I'm going to have to locate the other bio-pods anyway to see how many--or if any--of the others survived. I can collect more data along the way."

"Affirmative."

Dionne sighed tiredly. Now all she had to do was to figure out how to elude Khan and do what needed to be done. She couldn't delude herself any longer that he would help. If he knew what she had in mind he was far more likely to try to stop her.

Chapter Eleven

Khan settled his back against the cold stone, and drew his knees up. Below him, he could see the bots still tirelessly moving sand. They had cleared the area around the lab, but the sand continued to shift and they'd begun pushing it further and further from the building until they now had a small mountain of sand built up near the northern rim of the stone ridge.

The cool air and solitude cooled his temper after a while and reason reasserted itself.

She hadn't been deliberately insulting. In her mind her assessment was an impartial evaluation of the situation and he supposed it was reasonably accurate, whether he liked to admit it or not. He was fairly certain she hadn't realized that he'd followed her. She'd been too furious after their last argument to be aware of much of anything beyond her anger.

Which meant he couldn't even comfort himself with the thought that she'd insulted him just to get a rise out of him. That would've infuriated him, but it would've made him feel better if he could've believed she'd been trying to provoke him.

It stung nevertheless. True or not, intentional or not, her opinion made him wonder if he wouldn't be better off just beating his head on the wall of the lab.

He would've liked to think she was the only one being unreasonable, but he hadn't been thinking very rationally, or behaving very rationally, since she'd come into his life and turned it upside down.

He'd never considered that he had a jealous or particularly possessive nature, but there was no other way to account for his anger and frustration at her single minded, unwavering devotion to her cause. It surrounded her like a solid stone wall, unbreachable. Nothing he could say or do penetrated that absorption or diverted her one inch from the 'plan'.

There had been a couple of times that he'd actually seemed to pierce that barrier--not by much--but enough to keep him ever hopeful that the next time he'd actually reach her.

He was bone weary, afraid to close his eyes most nights for fear she'd take it into her head to wander off in the middle of the night to collect specimens and happen upon an animal that didn't appreciate the intrusion, or fall into the hands of his enemies--or any randy young warrior for that matter. His grip on his own self-control in that respect was wearing dangerously thin. He'd begun to fear that the beast inside him was going to escape and he was going to do something he would regret if she didn't stop behaving as if he was a stone, impervious to the fact that she constantly waved it in front of him, just out of reach.

He scrubbed his hands over his face and palmed his chin thoughtfully, contemplating the sickening roiling motion of his gut.

It dawned on him finally that he was just plain scared, in a way he had never known fear before.

It was his powerlessness in the situation that made it nearly unbearable. He'd faced the axes, spears, and arrows of his enemies. He'd faced animals with twice his strength, or more, but each time, no matter how afraid he was, he'd never really doubted that he would win in the end. He'd trusted his skill, his strength, his speed, and his wit and known he would triumph over his foe.

This time was different. This time his foe was himself. And the worst of it was that the more desperate and anxious he became, the worse he behaved. He'd pushed and prodded and lost his temper and behaved like a complete idiot one time too many.

She was going back into that damned coffin. He knew it in his gut, and he would be dead and long forgotten before she walked the Earth again.

Nothing he could do or say was going to divert her. If he'd learned nothing else about his goddess, he knew she was absolutely as immovable as a mountain and as predictable as sunrise.

Her gift was for everyone and she meant to find the way to bestow it.

Reluctantly, he admitted it was a gift in more ways than a curse--although he'd spent a good deal of time considering it more a curse than a gift. He'd been too wrapped up in his misery to consider it anything else for a long time. The knowledge had made him take an uncomfortable look at himself and he'd been so certain she must hold him in contempt that it had taken him a very long time to realize that she didn't, never had. She had treated him like a clever child, which he'd found insulting, but she had never looked at him with anything other than pleasure and hopefulness.

Now, when he looked at the world around him, he saw promise--just as she did, not progress, but a vast potential for it.

If she left him--if he couldn't find a way to stop her--the light of promise would go with her.

She'd seen, though, that the *people* had no real interest in the gift she'd offered. They hadn't understood--or they'd been afraid, or distrustful.

He frowned at that.

Maybe it had been more than that.

He had been insulted that Dionne had treated him like a child, but it occurred to him that his people weren't insulted in the least. They willingly gave up all responsibility to him. They didn't want to make decisions for themselves. They didn't want to shoulder responsibility for their own welfare.

For generations now, they had done nothing more than the tasks assigned to them, trusting that he, or his father who was Chief before him, would handle the difficult problems.

He frowned, considering it, realizing at last that they had given him permission to make decisions for them and that it could not be wrong to do so now. The gift *was* in their best interests. They might not like it. They might not appreciate it, but it would be better for them in the long run, no matter how unhappy it made them to begin with.

A great weight seemed to lift from his shoulders at that moment. A tentative smile curled his lips.

Dionne would not feel she had to go if she could carry out her assignment now. She had to know that it wouldn't accomplish as much as it would have if they'd been more advanced, but she hadn't seen that as an impediment as long as she could bring them forward with the gifts she'd brought.

Doubts immediately swarmed his mind, but he dismissed them. Whatever his motives--and he knew they weren't entirely pure--there was nothing wrong with his reasoning.

He would order them to present themselves and take the gift of knowledge, and when he was done, he would bring the other tribes that were his allies to her. And if that was not enough, he would take his warriors and round up his enemies and drag them to her.

And when she had discharged her burden, she would be able to focus on her own life.

Feeling better than he'd felt in many weeks, he rose at last and stretched. As eager as he was to start at once, he could not start until morning.

It occurred to him as he made his way back into the lab that Dionne would be happier if she believed that the people had listened to her and come willingly to accept the gift she was so joyful about giving them. He would wait until he was certain that she was fully occupied with her latest project and then he could be easy about leaving her. He knew from hard experience that once she'd made up her mind to do something there was no distracting her from it.

She was curled up in a tight ball on the platform she slept on when he reached her living quarters. He studied her for several minutes, fighting the temptation to join her.

It was a bad idea, a very bad idea. As long as he kept a good distance between himself and her he didn't have nearly as much difficulty controlling himself. When he got too close, his body went up in flames and his mind followed, leaving him so mindless with need he was a danger to his own future.

When he'd settled on his pallet, though, he could do nothing but stare at the ceiling and think about climbing in beside her.

She was asleep. Chances were she wouldn't even wake up.

If she did, she'd give him a tongue lashing if nothing else.

He got up anyway, grabbed the fur he used for cover and stalked across the room. She mumbled in her sleep when he crept onto the bed beside her. He froze, holding his breath. When she quieted again, he stretched out beside her, spread the fur out over both of them and let out a sigh of pure pleasure as her warmth and scent washed over him.

He'd just begun to relax and feel drowsy in spite of the heat of arousal simmering just beneath the surface of his calm when she rolled over and burrowed up against him, kneeing him in the groin.

It knocked the breath right out of his lungs. He gritted his teeth against the pain and nausea that washed through him and very slowly and carefully pushed her knee away from his groin, which was now throbbing with pain instead of hopefulness. By the time the pain had completely subsided, his tension had, as well, soothed by the softness of her body pressed so trustingly against him and her warmth.

Chapter Twelve

It was with great reluctance that Dionne roused. Despite the heavy weight lying across her, she hadn't felt so warm and comfortable in so long she couldn't remember the last time. An annoying tickle finally got the best of her, however, and she cracked an eye for a bleary look to see what it was.

It wasn't a lock of her own hair. The hair lying across her nose and cheek was as black as a night sky. The pleasant aroma tickling at her senses was Khan's scent, as easily identifiable as her own, and impossible to ignore since she had her nose plastered to his chest.

Confused, she eased away from him slowly and opened her eyes.

The warmth was his body and the fur covering them.

Her heart skipped a beat. Had she climbed into his pallet with him?

She'd thought about it, more than once. She hadn't acted on it because she'd known he would think it was an invitation for more, but maybe her subconscious mind had led her from her own bed to his pallet? Sleepwalking?

She moved a little further away and stole a peek up at his face.

He was staring straight at her, his expression carefully neutral.

Still groggy and disoriented from sleep, Dionne pushed herself up on one elbow and looked around.

She was still in her own bed, she discovered, so either Khan had been the one sleep walking, or more likely, he'd simply decided to climb in with her.

His motive for doing so eluded her, but she found she was reluctant to ask. It was all she could do to get out of bed when she first woke. She wasn't up to verbal sword play.

She almost rolled off the bed when she turned over. She'd forgotten how narrow the platform was and Khan was taking up more than half the space. He caught her, holding her until she'd managed to get her legs under her and her feet squarely on the floor. When he released her, she pushed herself upright and wove a slightly drunken path into the bathroom to perform her morning ritual.

By the time she emerged, Khan had disappeared.

Plunking her hands on her hips, she glanced around the room, a slight frown pulling her brows together. No answer to the puzzling question of why she'd woken up with him wrapped around her magically appeared and finally she dismissed it.

Lois was ready with the report Dionne had asked her to compile. As the computer read it off, she took notes with her tablet. When she'd finished, she returned to her quarters to study it while she nibbled at a breakfast meal.

The list was longer than she'd anticipated. She wondered if that was why so little progress had been made, if resources had just been too unavailable to promote building.

She could remedy that much at least.

Rising, she disposed of the container, crossed the main lab and took the lift down to the lower level. It was divided into a garden area and a hatchery/incubation area. Ignoring the plants for the moment, she consulted her list and started with the animals that had the longest gestation period.

Khan wandered down in the middle of the afternoon and propped against the wall to watch her. She found it distracting. It kept popping into her mind to ask him why he'd decided to sleep with her the night before, but each time it did, she dismissed it. She wasn't certain of what his answer might be but she was pretty sure it wasn't something she wanted to deal with at the moment.

He'd been watching her for nearly an hour when he finally pushed away from the wall and approached her, offering to help.

She'd just managed to dismiss him from her mind and focus on her task and it took her several minutes to shift gears again. After staring at him blankly while the question slowly sank in, distrust surfaced. "Thanks, but no."

He frowned. "You have a long list. It would be quicker if you had help."

"Hmm. Probably, but you aren't trained and these embryos are delicate--besides being borderline critical from being frozen so long. I've already lost more than I could really afford to lose."

He studied her for several moments. Out of the corner of her eye, she glanced at him a few times but she couldn't see any sign that he was angry about her distrust. On the contrary, he looked pleased for some reason she couldn't quite fathom--probably, she thought with more than a little irritation, because she'd admitted she'd already lost a lot of the stock.

Why it was he seemed so hopeful that she would fail, she couldn't entirely grasp, but it had begun to seem like an indisputable fact to her.

"It could take months without help," he said tentatively.

"Hmm."

He left when he saw he wasn't going to get a more definitive answer, but he kept popping in from time to time to check her progress.

It was almost as annoying as it was comforting. After their last argument she'd expected him to disappear for good. She'd flat out told him to go, after all. Considering his nature, she was surprised he hadn't left, but she supposed his pride was at war with his absolute certainty that the world was his responsibility.

And more specifically her.

His determination to guard her whether she wanted to be watched or not was beginning to get annoying.

She didn't know why he persisted in making her life so difficult!

Shrugging her impatience off with an effort, she focused on her task until she'd successfully implanted the first batch and watched the cells begin to divide. Satisfied, she sat down with her tablet and began to calculate the length of time it would take her to reach the bio-pods and return. Assuming she could locate them without too much difficulty, she decided she should be able to make it back to the bio-lab in plenty of time to start the next batch--the median range gestations.

She was going to have to hike the distance, not that she minded walking, but it would've been faster if she had had some sort of transportation.

She dismissed it. There was no sense in whining over things that couldn't be changed. She had no experience with horses even if asking for one wouldn't be a dead giveaway that she intended to travel, and there weren't any other options. She could take one of the bots with her to carry what she would need to take with her.

She didn't feel nearly as lighthearted, or excited, once she'd settled her plans as she felt she should have. Partly, she supposed it was because the prospect of going off alone was almost as scary as it was exciting. Partly, she knew it was because she was afraid of what she would find at the end of her travels--that her fellow time travelers had not made trip with her. Mostly, though, it as because one thing had been nagging at her since she had decided that she would have to rethink the renewal project.

Khan.

On a purely scientific level, she knew her decision was a sound one, and the computer's projection of one hundred to two hundred years also seemed reasonable. That would allow a number of generations to pass and, hopefully, a good bit of progress for the human race. There was a better chance the people would be more receptive and not as superstitious or distrustful.

Khan wouldn't be there, though, and she couldn't take him with her even if he wanted to go.

She couldn't bear thinking about it. Ever since it had dawned upon her that he would not be there to try to foil her plans, to annoy her, to protect her, she'd been working frantically, as if she could outrun the thoughts if she worked feverishly enough.

When she had started, she'd hoped that she could fully launch the project and her responsibility would be ended. Once she had done all that was humanly possible to ensure success, she would *have* to let go and hope for the best. Even if it transpired that the 'mothers' hadn't made it and she was obligated to contribute her eggs to the cause, there might have been some chance for them to have a future afterwards, a life together.

She supposed she hadn't really believed there would be, but some chance was better than none. Some hope was better than no hope.

It didn't really matter now and it was best just not to think about it. It seemed to her that the entire project had been doomed from the start. The members of the project had done everything they could to encapsulate a brilliant future for mankind, but they hadn't spent enough time considering the most important factor in the equation, man himself and his unpredictability.

That didn't bear thinking on either, though.

She would just do what she could and try not to worry about what she couldn't do.

She could and would reintroduce key species of plants, insects, and animals. There were obstacles to be overcome even there, but the insects and animals would be the easiest. The incubators were designed to 'program' specific behavior during development. Without parents to teach them, they would need the programming in order to survive in the wild. But the programming would also see to dispersion of the various species.

The plants would be a little harder. She would be taking seeds with her, however, and would use the trip to locate the pods as an opportunity to sow them over as wide an area as she could manage.

She was afraid of what she was going to find when she located the other pods, but she had to know. She would have to reprogram the pods anyway, assuming the women still lived. There was no way to remote program from the main lab.

Regardless, if they were alive, she couldn't take the chance that they would awake in such a primitive society. They would be easy prey for the barbaric culture that existed now and their lives could be in jeopardy, not just the project.

Khan was asleep when she finally returned to her living quarters. She studied his form in the semi-darkness for several moments and finally went to take a shower to help her relax. When she emerged, she headed resolutely toward her bed without glancing at Khan's pallet. She found, however, that she was wide awake the moment she lay down and, after staring at the ceiling for at least an hour, she finally sat up again.

Khan had rolled over, she saw and was now facing in her direction. She stared at him hard but as far as she could see he was deeply asleep. Capitulating finally to the urge that had brought her out of bed, she crossed the room and knelt beside his pallet, very cautiously tugging at the skin to find a way to burrow under it.

Khan flipped the fur back in invitation. She stared at him uneasily, embarrassed and without any believable lie to explain why she was trying to crawl into his pallet with him. "I was cold."

"The furs are warm."

Hesitantly, she climbed beneath the fur he held up, lying stiffly beside him while he straightened it, covering both of them. Finally, she rolled onto her side and presented her back to him. Both of them lay perfectly still for some time, rigid with tension.

Finally, with a sound of impatience, Khan wrapped an arm around her and dragged her close. Heat instantly enveloped her and it wasn't altogether shared body heat. Khan merely settled himself comfortably, however, and after a few minutes she heard his breathing slow to the deep, even rhythm of sleep.

Sighing with a mixture of disappointment and relief, Dionne forced herself to relax, as well, but it was still a while before sleep finally claimed her.

He was gone when she woke. Lazily, she turned over and snuggled deeper into the furs where he'd slept. Faintly, she detected, or thought she could detect, Khan's scent on the fur. Sheets and a pillow would've been better. Still, it sent a pleasurable glow of satisfaction through her only imagining she could smell him next to her.

That thought brought her more awake than she really wanted.

Groaning, she rolled out from under the fur and headed for the bathroom, wondering where Khan had gotten off to. When she'd eaten and there was still no sign of him, she decided to stroll outside for a look.

There were fresh tracks leading away from the lab in the direction of Khan's village. She knew this because the bots hadn't had time to eradicate them, not because she'd picked up any of Khan's tracking skills.

A faint smile curled her lips. He'd decided she was occupied in the lab and probably wouldn't even notice he was gone.

If he ran true to form, he wouldn't be back until dark.

There was a lot to be said for a man who was, at least occasionally, predictable.

Entering the lab once more, she set about preparing quickly for her journey. The storage room contained the gear for 'field' trips. Fortunately, the project managers had shown remarkable foresight here. The gear was locked in an airtight, climate controlled pod much like the one she'd traveled a thousand years in. Even better, the materials used to construct the equipment were super synthetics. There'd been some deterioration, but not enough to make any difference.

Summoning one of the bots, Dionne loaded the camping equipment into the bot's half ton shovel. The hiking boots hadn't survived the passage of time quite so well, but after walking around in nothing but the leather moccasin boots for so long Dionne figured the calluses on her feet were thick enough to protect her from the cracked and pocked synthetic insoles.

Having shoved her feet into them and locked the catches, she stared at the equipment that remained in the locker. After a very brief hesitation, she removed two pistols and one rifle, checked them to make certain they were still safe and fully functional and added them to her pile along with enough ammunition packs, she figured, to start--or stop--a revolution.

Almost as an afterthought, she added a pulley and wench, in case she encountered any terrain the bot had trouble with. In a general way, it wouldn't. The bots were equipped with three options for mobility; a track system, retractable wheels and, for climbing over uneven terrain, a tripod 'walking' system.

From her habitat, she took a case of rations. It was probably far more than she would need, but she preferred to err on the side of caution than be forced to the necessity of having to hunt and kill food. After adding three gallon containers of water, she gathered the case containing the electronics she figured she would need and the seeds she intended to disperse.

Her heart was beating unpleasantly fast as she left the habitat, partly from anxiety that Khan would return early and catch her, and partly from pure adrenaline excitement.

It was irrational and she knew it. Everyone she had known in the short life she'd had before she had been entombed was long gone. There would be no familiar faces, no people, no buildings. The city she had known would be nothing more than ruins now. Nothing that she remembered would be recognizable.

Reason held no sway over her emotions, however.

In her heart, she was going home.

Chapter Thirteen

The people who had been hired to construct the lab were from the opposite side of the country, and the site chosen had been as far from human habitation at the time that it was built as was possible. The decision had created a good many problems and slowed construction to a crawl, and often a complete halt, when materials that had been purchased from some distant manufacturing company were delayed in arriving.

The scientists had still considered it well worth the aggravation.

If it couldn't be constructed in secrecy, then the next best thing was to make certain that no one near by knew of its existence. If no one close enough to reach it knew of its existence, then vandalism once authority broke down was less likely.

The city was seventy five miles north, north east of the site--by the roads that had existed at the time. By Dionne's calculations, walking as the crow flew, she should be able to make the trek in three to four days.

She didn't know whether Khan would decide to come after her or not, but she figured the more distance she put between herself and the lab the less likely he was to catch up to her, and the less likely it was that she would have to deal with an unpleasant confrontation.

If she was right and he didn't return until dark, he wouldn't be able to start out after her until the following morning. He might be able to track her, but she figured by then she would be closer to the 'forbidden lands' than the lab and even he should agree that she might as well finish the trip she'd started.

He wasn't always entirely reasonable, however.

Thrusting that thought aside, she focused on covering as much territory as possible, only stopping a couple of times to rest for a few minutes and catch her breath. Near dusk, she stopped to eat a quick meal, unearthed a flashlight and kept going. The cats, Nomi and Sachi ranged further and further as the night drew in, but Dionne wasn't overly concerned about their disappearance. Their senses were sharp. If there'd been any sign of a threat they wouldn't have wandered off.

It was nearly midnight by the time she decided she'd made enough progress for her first day and stopped to make camp. Using the bot's floodlights to see, she dragged the pop out tent from the bucket, set it up and staked the corners, then dragged out a thick sleeping bag.

She didn't like using the lights even the short length of time it took her to set up, but she also didn't like the idea of setting up her tent on top of anything that crawled or bit. The cougars bounded into view just as she'd finished. Relieved when she hadn't even realized she was tense, Dionne ordered them to guard, crawled into the tent and passed out from sheer exhaustion almost before she'd settled in the bag.

The first light of dawn awakened her--not because of the light but because every animal in the forest woke up chipper and ready to face the new day. Groaning, Dionne covered her ears to block out the noise. The movement, slight though it was, sent pure, undiluted agony through every muscle and bone in her body. She moaned then in pain, but she was thoroughly awake.

Uttering little grunts of discomfort, she unzipped the bag, rolled out of it and rolled it up. Tucking it under one arm, she picked up the laser pistol she'd cuddled for comfort the night before--the very short night--and crawled out of the tent.

The cats had disappeared again, but the ground where they'd lain was still warm. She knew they couldn't have been gone long.

Vaguely irritated, she dismissed it after a moment and set about packing the tent and bag and stowing them in the bucket with the rest of the equipment. She wasn't particularly hungry, but she figured she might as well eat before she set out again.

She discovered the blisters on her feet before she'd walked a half a mile.

So much for calluses.

She wasn't going to be able to walk at all without excruciating pain if she didn't do something before they got worse, she realized. She had three choices as far as she could see. She could sacrifice a piece of the tent, a piece of her sleeping bag or a piece of Khan's tunic. She was more inclined to sacrifice the tunic, but upon consideration decided the leather would probably chafe her feet as badly as the boots. Any part of the tent was absolutely out as far as she was concerned. There were bugs. It might not be the bugs the scientists had considered a necessary ingredient for success, but they were still here and still in abundance.

Feeling very much like a martyr, she used the laser pistol to cut two wedges from the top end of her bag and stuffed the fabric into the boots for padding. The blisters still hurt like a sonofabitch, but she thought the padding might keep them from getting worse.

The sun had just risen above the tops of the trees when she made a discovery that took her breath for several painful moments.

She was standing on top of a mountain that shouldn't have been there.

Completely disoriented by the discovery, Dionne simply stood on the ridge, staring out over the unfamiliar landscape.

Her first thought was that it explained why every muscle, bone and sinew in her body felt like someone had been trying to draw and quarter her. She must have started climbing near dusk when she was already too tired to pay much attention to anything around her, she decided, trying to account for the fact that she hadn't noticed.

Her second thought was that it was going to take a good bit longer to reach the city than she'd anticipated. The climb down into the valley shouldn't present too much of a problem, but crossing the river gorge at the bottom was going to be a real treat.

Shaking off the shock, Dionne started down the graduating slope, wondering if she would even reach the gorge before dark.

She did, but there wasn't nearly enough light left to allow her time to look for a way across the gorge. Rather than stumble along in the dark and risk injury or death if she happened to wander too close to the gorge, she set up camp while there was still enough light to do so, ate yet another cold, tasteless meal and climbed into the tent before the biting bugs could suck her dry.

Unlike the night before, sleep was slow to come.

It should have been easy to drift off. She was tired, not as totally exhausted as the day before when she had been pushing herself so hard to make progress, but still tired. She was still sore from the unaccustomed exercise, but she'd walked off most of it and the discomfort was minimal. The rush of the water in the gorge below created a soothing background noise that filtered out the unfamiliar sounds of insects and animals, making it easier to relax, but her mind was still active, wandering from one thought to another.

Her current problem teased at her for some time, but she knew she would have to look for a resolution. Thinking about it wasn't going to help her find a way across.

There had to be one. Khan had told her he had been to the forbidden lands and she didn't think he would have swum across with the horse.

The minute she allowed his name into her mind it conjured a welter of other thoughts and she found herself wondering if Khan would come after her at all.

Not that she wanted him to. She had important business to take care of, whether he considered it important or not.

She did wonder, though.

It had been a mistake to cuddle with him in his furs. She'd known at the time that it was. She just hadn't been able to resist the temptation to be near him.

She'd told herself that it was only creature comfort she was seeking. The bed was hard and she'd had nothing to cover herself with and, despite the regulated temperature inside the lab, she grew chilly at night when she wasn't moving around enough to generate much body heat.

All of that was true and the furs were more comfortable, adding a modicum of padding between her and the hard surface of the floor, blocking the currents of circulating air and helping her to stay warm. That had only been part of the reason, though, the smallest part, and she knew it no matter what lies she told herself.

She'd been hoping Khan would take advantage of the situation and relieve her of the responsibility of resisting. She wanted him to kiss her as he had before, to caress her with his hands, to possess her completely. It was scary how much she wanted him to and how desperately she wanted any kind of contact at all--or just his presence nearby. As long as she could glance up from her work from time to time and see him, she was content.

It was wrong of her to want it, and worse still for her to want to shift her responsibility for her behavior onto him. She was a scientist, and an adult, not a child. It wouldn't make her less guilty to yield to his persuasion.

She knew he thought she was obsessed with her work. She supposed it looked that way from his viewpoint, but she had a responsibility that was unprecedented. At the time it had been given to her she'd felt nothing but pride and humility that it had been entrusted to her care. She couldn't just discard it now because of her personal feelings. To do so would be criminal, unthinkable in the scope of its consequences.

It could mean the extinction of mankind.

She didn't think that it would. She thought, in time, humanity would pick itself up and start again, but she couldn't possibly be certain of that. They were vulnerable now in their ignorance as they had not been for ages, almost completely at the mercy of nature, disease, famine, even their own propensity for violence.

If she gave up on them without even trying, gave up because her desire was leading her astray, they could fail to prosper and that would be entirely her fault.

She didn't want to have to live with that knowledge. It would be hard enough to live with failure if she tried and didn't succeed. The knowledge, the guilt she would feel, that she hadn't even tried would be unbearable.

But the feelings Khan had stirred in her had escalated to debilitating proportions and she didn't know anything to do except fight it with obsessive determination. Every time she let down her guard, even a little, the desire to give up and embrace everything Khan promised grew stronger.

She would find herself staring at his hands and remembering how strong and warm they'd felt when he had clasped her hand. Images would fill her mind of his hands skating over her caressingly. Sometimes when he spoke to her, she would watch the movements of his lips and remember what it had felt like when he'd kissed her and she'd find herself wondering if it would feel like that if he did it again. She would remember what he'd looked like standing under the shower and think how good it would feel to be pressed so tightly against him that every inch of his skin touched every inch of hers.

And when she wasn't thinking about those forbidden things, she was listening for the sound of his voice, the sound of his footfalls, feeling his presence nearby, expanding her senses just to detect a trace of the faint scent of his body if he moved near enough she thought she might.

She placed her palms over her ears as if she could block the sound of her own thoughts.

She shouldn't even allow herself to *think* such things. It only made her want more what she knew she had no right to want.

Chapter Fourteen

Dionne woke more tired than when she'd lain down to sleep. It took more of an effort than usual to drag herself up and push onward. The cats, she discovered when she emerged from the tent, had wandered off again.

Irritation immediately surged through her. They were supposed to stay close and guard her, damn their hides! She had the weapons, but she didn't want to be forced to use them to protect herself. The huge cougars would be enough, if they were nearby, to discourage anyone or anything from considering aggressive behavior, she knew, but they had to be in view to have that effect.

Depression settled over her shortly behind the anger. She knew what they were doing. They were looking for territory to claim. They were preparing to settle and breed offspring.

They were not going to be any happier than she was about going back into the bio-pods.

Sachi and Nomi appeared only minutes behind her call, reassuring her that they hadn't wandered far and making her feel guilty for being so angry with them. She caught their attention and spoke directly to them. "You have to stay close by me," she said firmly. "I need you two here to prevent the possibility of threats."

The cats exchanged a look, as if they were communicating silently. Finally, almost seeming to shrug, they lay down, watching her as she moved back and forth from the tent to the bot, collecting her gear and stowing it. When she'd finished, she moved as close to the edge of the gorge as she dared and studied the walls in both directions. Seeing no access to the bottom within range of her own vision, she summoned the bot closer and had it analyze the problem.

The bot used laser sighting to calculate the elevations and produced the information that the fall was to the south. The cliffs surrounding the gorge should decrease in depth to little more than twenty feet over the next five to ten miles.

"Shit!" Dionne greeted that information with irritation.

There was no hope for it, though, she knew. She was going to have to detour ten or twenty miles and there was no sense in dragging it out. In fact, the faster she moved, the more quickly she could make up the lost time.

She struck off southward, following the lip of the gorge. The ground was hard and strewn with rocks and pebbles--too hard for vegetation, which crept no closer than fifteen to twenty feet at any spot, forming what looked like a natural roadway along the edge of the gorge. It was relatively flat and smooth, however, free of anything but scrubby vegetation and sloped downward in a fairly gradual decline. She found that she was making far better time than she had on either of the two days previously, for the downward slope of the mountain she'd negotiated the day before had been steep enough that it had been almost as hard to traverse as the climb upward had been.

Settling down to rest and eat not long after the sun had passed its zenith, Dionne considered her progress with slightly more optimism. At the rate she was going, she figured she would only lose one day off her calculations--not even that if she considered that she'd added a full day for just this reason. Instead of hiking back up to the point across from where she'd met the problem, she could strike off at a tangent and recover some of the detour, she decided.

Her blisters had burst, leaving raw, exposed skin. She didn't even need to take off the boots to know that and decided it would be best not to. At the moment, she was reasonably comfortable. If she disturbed the injuries by pulling her feet out and shoving them back into the boots she was going to pay for it.

She glanced around at the landscape speculatively.

Two days and no sign of Khan. She supposed he'd either not been able to track her or he'd decided not to try. He would've caught up to her by now if that wasn't the case.

Sighing in disgust at the direction of her thoughts, she got up and struck off again.

Less than an hour later, she heard the clatter of hoof beats behind her. Her heart leapt into her throat, threatening to choke her, but gladness filled her. She slowed, listening intently and finally turned to search for the rider.

He was still a good distance from her, but closing fast.

It wasn't Khan.

"Sachi! Nomi! Come!" Dionne called loudly when she glanced around and discovered the cougars had disappeared again.

Within moments, they came loping toward her out of the brush some twenty feet from where she stood. "On guard!"

Both cats skidded to a halt and changed directions, moving to a position between her and the rider.

He dragged back on his reins when he saw the cats. Pebbles flew in every direction as the horse he was mounted on screamed, rearing up and flailing its forelegs in the air. The rider, caught off guard, rolled off the horse's back and hit the ground so hard Dionne winced as the smacking sound of flesh against stone echoed along the canyon like a clap of thunder.

He growled in fury as he scrambled to his feet.

His horse, riderless, beyond his control and scared witless by the cougars, tore off in the direction from which it had just come, bucking and kicking.

His chest heaving, Notaku glared at her, thrusting the long, stringy locks of his pale hair out of his face. "I came to take you to the forbidden lands," he said, his voice still tight with anger he was trying hard to control.

Dionne studied him critically, but she thought his hostility went way beyond anger at being thrown from his horse and fear of the cats. There was something in his expression she completely distrusted. Then again, she hadn't trusted him from the moment she'd set eyes on him. Everything about him screamed 'brute and bully'. He was a huge man, taller even than Khan and broader of shoulder. Fat overlay the bulging muscles of his body, indicating a tendency toward self-indulgence and laziness.

She just plain didn't like him.

"Thank you, but I don't need an escort. I have Sachi and Nomi to protect me--and my own weapons."

He reddened with anger. "You are just a woman," he pointed out. "You need a man to protect you."

That settled it. If she'd had any doubts whatsoever in her mind, his insulting remarks clenched it.

He'd thought she would be easy prey without Khan around. That was as crystal clear as if he'd said it plain out.

Dread clenched at her stomach at the thought of Khan, the fear instantly surfacing that he might have had something to do with the fact that Khan hadn't shown up.

"If I'd felt the need for a *man*, I would've asked Khan to bring me," she said pointedly.

He wasn't as stupid as he looked. She could tell from the way his eyes narrowed that he realized she'd just insulted his manhood. His next words confirmed it. "I am a better warrior and hunter than Khan!" he growled, but he seemed to think better of his display of temper. With an obvious effort, he tamped it and attempted a smile of reassurance that looked more like a grimace of pain. "He is too busy arguing with the council of elders to come. He sent me."

He must think she was a complete moron if he thought she'd believe that lie. Even if she hadn't seen the hostility that existed between the two men with her own eyes, she knew Khan well enough to know that he would never delegate her care to anyone else, much less a man like Notaku--who represented everything Khan despised.

Notaku was the sort of man who expected his enormous size and show of aggressiveness to intimidate others, and very likely it was a tactic that worked most of the time--except with Khan, which was probably why he hated Khan so much. She doubted very much that he had the balls to back up his bluster. Of course, frightened people were usually far more dangerous than the brave hearted.

"That was kind and thoughtful--of both of you. But as you see, I'm more than halfway there already--and no problems. You can go back and tell Khan I didn't need help."

His eyes narrowed. After a moment, his gaze shifted from her to the cougars and he studied them speculatively. She didn't like the gears she saw turning in his head. They were watching him steadily for any threatening move, but at the moment they appeared completely docile.

He was trying to decide whether or not he would have time to shoot both before they could reach him.

She didn't really care for the idea of turning her back on Notaku, but she couldn't allow this standoff to continue either. She'd dismissed him. She had to make a pretense, at least, that she'd believed his lies and considered the matter settled. With an effort, she turned away. "Sachi! Nomi! Come!"

Trying not to give the appearance of flight, Dionne resumed her march along the lip of the gorge. She counted out five minutes and then ten. Finally, she turned to see if the cats were following. As she turned, Notaku began to back slowly, warily, away from the cats, who were still sitting where she'd left them. She stopped to watch until Notaku disappeared into the brush at the foot of the mountain, searching, she supposed, for his mount--which might well be halfway back to the village by now.

After about twenty minutes, Sachi and Nomi came trotting up behind her and she relaxed finally, realizing Notaku must have retreated beyond range of his scent.

She discovered she was trembling with reaction. The encounter had unnerved her far more than she'd been willing to let on and she doubted very much that she'd seen the last of Notaku. He'd been embarrassed by the way things had gone down. He wouldn't take that sort of humiliation well. Whatever his intentions had been--and she strongly suspected they'd included claiming her as his woman and subduing any protests she might think to make-- she had a real enemy now. She doubted very much that he would simply give up and head back to the village.

He was either ghosting her, maintaining a distance that prevented the cougars from catching his scent, or working up his rage and sense of mistreatment and thinking up ways to punish her once he caught her.

Chapter Fifteen

Khan lost his temper. He had not been completely easy in his mind since he'd left Dionne. He had thought she was too occupied with her project to pay much attention to his absence since she hardly seemed to notice his presence, but he'd begun to feel uneasy almost from the moment he left. He'd shaken the vague, indeterminate feeling over and over, but each time it came back stronger than before.

There was something about the way she'd been behaving that just didn't sit right, but, turn it though he might, he couldn't figure out what it was and he'd finally pushed it to the back of his mind when he'd reached the village and summoned the council.

The talks had started promisingly enough. When the elders had gathered, he had very carefully explained what Dionne had proposed to them, in terms he knew that they would understand.

The remainder of the day had been spent hashing and rehashing every tiny detail and discussing every conceivable outcome of every change. Khan's patience had worn to a thread long before the elders had taken their leave to consider their opinion in the leisure of their own lodge.

He'd swallowed his impatience with an effort. There was nothing unusual in the request to 'sleep on it' and this matter was far more important than anything that they'd considered before.

He could not seek his own rest. He had to fight the urge to return to the lab and make the trip back to the village the following day. After tossing and turning for hours instead of sleeping, he finally managed to convince himself that he was worrying about Dionne for no rational reason. Beyond that, if he left instead of prodding the elders the chances were that they would spend another entire day rehashing everything--or a week.

They were in no hurry.

Despite the few hours of sleep he'd managed, Khan felt reasonably relaxed when the talks resumed the following morning, primarily because he'd convinced himself that the issue would soon be settled and he could return to the lab. By noon, he had a pounding headache, however, and his patience was fading fast.

It wasn't the umpteenth request to explain the benefits to the *people* that finally pushed Khan into exploding. It was the realization that the elders were doing nothing at all but stalling because they were afraid that enlightenment of the *people* would diminish their importance as the respected elders and wise men in the community.

Shooting to his feet, his face as dark as thunder, Khan had virtually roared at them and ten ancient jaws had dropped in stunned dismay. "Out!" he'd growled furiously, pointing to the door of the lodge.

Without waiting for them to comply since it looked as if they were too stupefied to move, he strode from the lodge and addressed the villagers that were loitering near his lodge to hear the decision of the council. "Go, now! Tell everyone in the village that they are to gather there," he said, pointing toward the rise where Dionne had stood to speak to them, "for they are going to the holy place where they will *joyously* receive the gift the goddess Dionne has offered!" He lifted his head then and issued the tribal war cry. The moment he did the warriors of the village scrambled to gather their weapons, raced from their lodges and mounted their horses. They met him at the ridge, but there was confusion on their faces as they looked around for a threat and saw none.

"Every man, woman, and child will make pilgrimage to the lifeless plain. See to it that there are no stragglers!" He summoned his five brothers then and informed them that they would be the first to receive the gifts. None of them looked particularly thrilled to discover that they were volunteering to go first, but it was a hard and fast rule within the family that they never questioned their Chief's authority--publicly. Privately, Khan had found himself and his brothers at odds almost as often as they agreed on anything.

Too impatient to wait for the villagers, who would be making the trek on foot, Khan nudged his horse to a trot. His brothers, after exchanging questioning glances, shrugged and followed suit.

The first thing that Khan noticed when he arrived at the lab was that there was only one bot. Surprised, he pulled up on the reins, bringing his horse to a halt, and surveyed the landscape.

"What is it?" Rikard, his older brother asked uneasily.

"There is only one bot?"

"What's a bot?"

Khan pointed. "A machine."

Rikard stared at the machine for several moments in horrified fascination before glancing around nervously. "Do you think it is waiting to attack?"

Khan threw a disgusted glance at his brother. "No, I do not. And I do not like it at all that there is only one when there should be two." Kneeing his horse into motion, he raced the short distance to the lab and leapt from the horse's back before the animal had even come to a complete halt.

He knew the moment he entered the lab that Dionne was gone. He searched the building from top to bottom anyway, becoming more angry and worried as he did so. When he finally emerged once more, he saw that the villagers were assembling on the rise above the lab, just as they had for generations when they had come to worship.

"She's gone," he said flatly.

His brothers, who'd remained mounted, exchanged a look of confusion. "The goddess?" Rikard asked hesitantly. "Where would she go?"

Khan ground his teeth, but it didn't take more than a split second for the answer to present itself to him. "The forbidden lands."

"Why would she go there?" his youngest brother, Tin demanded, appalled.

Khan ignored him. "I should have known she had something in mind when she kept looking to see if I was still here," he muttered angrily, realizing she'd made a complete fool out of him--again. More correctly, he supposed he'd made a fool out of himself, thinking with his little brain rather the one that actually worked-- because he'd thought her seeming preoccupation was with him, that she was finally thawing toward him, when the reality was she'd only been waiting for him to leave. "We will have to go after her," he added, climbing onto his horse once more.

"In the forbidden lands?" his brothers chorused.

Khan fixed them with a sweeping glance. "To hell if necessary."

He didn't wait to see if they would follow. Instead, he turned his horse and kicked it into a brisk trot. After a moment, his brothers turned and followed. They paused on the ridge and Khan looked out over the villagers. "Dionne is disappointed in you. You will wait here until I return to show her that you are repentant."

He glanced from one face to another, making certain that each realized that they would know his displeasure if they did not do as they'd been told. After a moment, a frown drew his brows together. He scanned the people again, hoping he was wrong and it was only anxiety that was clouding his judgment. Finally, he turned to his brother, Rikard. "Where is Notaku?"

* * * *

He attacked her from behind as Dionne stepped from the tent. Still sluggish from just waking, it took her several critical moments to collect her wits about her, but in that stream of random data transfer, her brain instantly connected 'attack' with 'Notaku'. One hand covered half her face, cutting off her air supply. The other was cinched so tightly around her waist, trapping her left arm, that it was almost like being squeezed by a boa constrictor.

The cats had vanished again--or he'd killed him. If they'd been anywhere around they would have been all over him before he could get so close.

Reacting automatically to the threat rather than consciously, Dionne swung her free arm upwards and back. The pistol she held in her hand went off on impact, firing harmlessly skyward, but the metal connected hard enough with the side of his head that his grip loosened fractionally. It was enough to give her the chance to bite down on the hand covering her nose and mouth hard enough to draw blood. At the same time, she lifted one leg as high as she could and slammed it backwards, catching his shin bone with her hiking boot in a glancing blow.

The moment he reacted to the pain by snatching at his hand, trying to free it from her teeth, she released her grip, screaming at the top of her lungs to summon the cougars.

He retaliated by cuffing her hard enough along the side of her head to send her flying. The landing stunned her almost as much as the blow itself. She lost her grip on her pistol. The weapon struck the stone and went skittering away as she landed. Shock slowed her reactions and paralyzed actual thought. It was instinct that sent her scrambling toward her pistol to retrieve it, but she felt as if she was plowing through a thick liquid. Each movement seemed to take minutes to complete. She could hear her own thundering heartbeat, the rush of air in and out of her lungs as she struggled to catch her breath and very little else.

She heard Notaku scream even as she curled her fingers around the pistol and her heart clenched reflexively. Expecting another attack any moment, she dropped to the ground and rolled onto her side instead of trying to regain her feet. Blinking to clear her vision, she saw that one of the cougars had returned from its morning stroll--Nomi, she thought. The great cat was standing on her hind legs, her teeth clamped onto Notaku's shoulder. "Subdue him, Nomi! Don't kill him!" she gasped out, though the words sounded slurred even to her own ears.

The cat had heard her, though, and obeyed reluctantly, releasing its grip on his shoulder and dropping to all fours. With an effort, Dionne staggered to her feet just as Notaku, who'd recovered with surprising speed from the attack, lifted a stone ax and swung at the animal. Nomi ducked, but Sachi surged forward, leaping and snapping at Notaku's arm.

He switched hands, swinging again. Sachi leapt away and Nomi surged forward. Horrified, Dionne lifted her pistol, but she couldn't find a clear shot between Notaku and the cats, who swirled and surged around him, looking for an opening to relieve him of his weapon. "Don't touch them, you bastard! I'll blow your head clean off your shoulders!"

She had no idea whether he heard her or not. Before she could make good on her promise, or disarm him, which she would've preferred, a high pitched whine zipped past her and a wooden shaft buried itself into the center of Notaku's chest with a sickening sucking sound. His eyes widened. A look of panic crossed his features. Slowly his fingers uncurled and the ax fell from his hand. Just as slowly, his legs quivered and buckled. He went to his knees and fell face forward on the hard ground.

Still too shocked to fully comprehend what had happened, Dionne merely stared at him open mouthed for a full minute. Finally, she turned to follow the path of the arrow.

Some thirty feet away, near the trees that edged the wide stone outcropping that formed the sides of the gorge, sat three men on horseback. As she turned to look at them, they began moving slowly toward her--whether from wariness of the cougars, who immediately loped forward to stand between her and the oncoming riders, or to reassure her that they intended no threat, she wasn't certain. They halted while they were still some distance away.

The man in the forefront scanned her encampment and the area around it before addressing her. "Are you injured, my lady?"

Dionne blinked at the sound of his voice, several times, slowly. Of its own accord, her gaze traveled over the chain mail and steel helmets the men were wearing and fastened finally on the crossbow the rider in the forefront still held across his saddle horn.

Metallurgy, advanced weaponry, her mind computed, wrestling with the puzzle of finding herself face to face with a group of men far in advance of the villagers of Khan's tribe. An evolutionary fluke, she wondered? Or the natural chain of events of advancement? It was a historical fact that the need to find bigger, better, and more efficient weapons for killing was as responsible for the advancement of civilization as the desire for creature comfort--maybe more so.

"Are you badly hurt, my lady?" the man repeated, more slowly this time, enunciating each word carefully.

Dionne lifted a hand to her cheek and then looked down at herself, searching for any sign of injury. There were scrapes and bruises all over her arms and legs, but nothing was broken. She shook her head. "I don't think so."

Turning, she went to check Notaku for signs of life. Sachi and Nomi followed her step for step, sitting back on their haunches when she knelt to examine the man. She gave them both reproving glares. Neither had been where they should have been or Notaku wouldn't have had the chance to attack her.

Placing her fingers along his throat, she checked him for a pulse and discovered with little surprise that there was none. The bolt had caught him in the heart, killing him almost instantly.

Anger surfaced. He shouldn't be dead. Not that she wasn't grateful that the men had rescued her and saved the cougars from harm, but she would've preferred that he be subdued and taken alive. Whatever his intentions had been--and she knew they hadn't been good--death was still a high price to pay for stupidity and meanness, and there would've been at least some hope of rehabilitating him if he'd lived.

Tamping her anger, Dionne returned her attention to the men who'd come to her rescue. She noticed that all three were studying Sachi and Nomi warily. "They're trained to guard me. They won't attack unless I'm threatened--or I order them to."

The man holding the crossbow, who had risen in his saddle as if he was considering dismounting, appeared to lose interest in doing so. "I am Sir William of Lockley. This is Lord Harry and Sir David," he added, gesturing to the two men slightly behind and on either side of him. The two men nodded curtly at the introduction, but they seemed far more interested in scanning the wooded area nearby.

Either they suspected a trap--which seemed likely--or they were making certain they wouldn't be interrupted. It was possible that their motives for helping her weren't purely altruistic, but Dionne found it hard to believe that she was of that much interest.

She felt her pounding head, wondering if the blow had been worse than she'd thought. Advanced well beyond the others she'd met, but, medieval? "Where did you come from?"

Sir William smiled faintly, but lifted an arm and pointed to the north east. "The Monarchy of Albany."

Dionne was stunned speechless for several moments, but then a thrill went through her that made her feel almost lightheaded. "Albany?" she echoed. "You said monarchy?"

"Aye, under the rule of our blessed queen, the mighty sorceress Eugenia."

Dionne didn't know whether to laugh or cry. "Genie?" she gasped, breathless with rising excitement. "She's your queen?"

The men exchanged curious and highly suspicious glances. "You know the queen?" Sir William asked, disbelief evident in his voice.

"Yes! I think I do! She was--she was the sorceress--uh." Dionne paused, frowning as she tried to think what sort of tale might have been invented to explain the sorceress' awakening. "--who slept for many years?" she finished.

Sir William's dark blond brows rose in obvious surprise. "You *have* heard of her. Your pardon, but I'd thought you were one of the savages from the forbidden lands. The--uh--garb."

"The forbidden lands?" Dionne bit her lip, trying to fight a totally inappropriate urge to smile. She couldn't help but see the irony of it, however, that virtually the same superstition had arisen on both sides, virtually ensuring that neither side knew about the other and developed completely independently of each other.

Sir William studied her a little uneasily, as if he was wondering if she was entirely sane since she kept repeating everything he said. She didn't blame him. She felt more than a little off balance.

Before either she or Sir William, who'd done all of the talking-- and apparently the rescuing--could say anything else a band of screaming demons erupted from the trees just south of where they stood.

Dionne's heart seemed to stand still in her chest as she whirled to look.

Khan was leading the war party.

Chapter Sixteen

When Dionne glanced back at the knights, she saw that they'd drawn weapons. Their expressions were grim, but determined. She threw up a hand. "No! They're friends!"

Sir William's eyes narrowed, his suspicions evident in his expression now. "They're savages!"

"I knew it was a bloody trap," Lord Harry growled.

Terror filled Dionne. There was going to be a battle, a bloody one. The knights were outnumbered by about two to one from what she could see, but they also had weapons capable of killing at a longer range with far more accuracy than the long bows Khan and his men had.

Gripping her pistol, Dionne whirled away from the knights and began jogging toward the band of men racing toward her. "Stop! Please don't do this! They're friends!"

Either they were still too far away to hear her or, more likely, they were making so much noise themselves with their war whoops that it drowned her out. She couldn't see that anything she'd shouted, or her frantic waving, had any effect on them beyond, maybe, making them ride faster.

Fear and frustration filled Dionne, but it also inspired her. She had to prevent a confrontation. If anyone was hurt, the violence would escalate out of control.

And Khan was in front, the most likely to be killed.

"Disarm! Subdue!" Dionne yelled as she raced toward the bot and jumped into the bucket. "Lift! Now!"

Behind her, she heard the snarls and screams of the attacking cats, and the responding shouts of the men, but she didn't have time to check to see if the cats had been successful or not.

When the bucket stopped rising, she stood up, trained her pistol on the ground between the oncoming riders and herself and switched the pistol to high power, cutting a gash in the ground with the laser. It wasn't much of a gash, but the laser blast itself was enough to bring all of the warriors, with the exception of Khan, to a screeching halt. Khan kneed his horse and leapt the shallow gash in the ground.

The whine of a bolt sizzled past her. "No! Oh God! Khan!"

Without waiting for the bot to lower the bucket, she half jumped, half fell out, racing toward him. He dragged back on the reins, fighting the horse to a standstill as she neared him. Dionne looked up at him fearfully, expecting to see blood, the hilt of the bolt protruding from his chest--imminent death. Instead, she saw that Khan had caught the bolt with his shield. The tip had nicked him as the impact drove the shield backwards, toward his body, but she saw little more than a trickle of blood.

She released a sob of relief as Khan leaned from the horse, wrapped an arm around her and dragged her across his lap. Wrapping her arms around him tightly, she burrowed against him and promptly burst into tears. "You scared me! I thought you'd be killed! Don't *ever* scare me like that again!" she wailed.

It wasn't until Khan nudged his horse forward that Dionne realized he'd barely acknowledged her, that his body was still tensed for action. The realization instantly sobered her. "They saved me from Notaku!"

Khan paused, glancing down at her and lifted one hand to touch her cheek lightly. "*He* did this to you?" he growled furiously.

"He caught me off guard. They must have heard the fight and came--Notaku's dead."

Khan relaxed fractionally, but walked his horse closer to the armor clad men, now lying on the ground. Both of the cats and all of the men were bleeding from battle wounds, but she saw that Sachi and Nomi had obeyed. All three men were disarmed, and they looked very subdued. Sachi and Nomi had their forepaws planted on two of the men's chests. The third looked unconscious--or dead.

She stared at the man hard until she saw that he was still breathing.

"I am Chief Khan of the Kota people. I thank you for protecting my woman," Khan said gruffly, his arm tightening around Dionne in silent communication.

Dionne twisted her head to gape up at him in stunned surprise anyway. It didn't occur to her to dispute his claim. He wouldn't have done it, she knew, if he hadn't felt that it was necessary. Ignoring the feeling of warmth that washed over her at his claim, she looked away. Glancing down at the men from Albany, she saw that Sir William was eyeing the two of them speculatively. His expression was still hostile, however.

"We were happy to come to the lady's aid--I would be happier still if you would call these beasts off."

Before Dionne could do so, Khan stunned her again. "Sachi! Nomi! Release!"

His command wasn't nearly as surprising as the fact that the cats obeyed him instantly.

Recovering from her surprise, Dionne glared at the cougars disapprovingly.

She decided to deal with them later, however. She had more pressing matters that needed her undivided attention. "These men are from the Monarchy of Albany. My--uh ---sister, Eugenia is their queen. I was about to ask them to take me to her."

All four men looked at her with varying degrees of disbelief.

Sir William had struggled to a sitting position, but made no attempt to get to his feet as the warriors who'd come with Khan rode up, surrounding the men on the ground. "The queen is--your *sister?*" Sir William demanded incredulously. "She has never spoken of you," he added suspiciously.

Dionne gave him a look. "You didn't mention that you were so close to Eugenia," she said coolly.

He reddened. "I have no claim of close ties to the throne beyond my loyalty to my queen, but I can not imagine why she would never have mentioned a sister."

"She thought I was dead," Dionne said promptly.

Sir William and Lord Harry exchanged an uncomfortable glance. Sir David, only just coming around, merely groaned.

"What are you up to now?" Khan whispered harshly near her ear. "I've no intention of allowing you to walk into the clutches of our enemies."

Dionne gave him a look of exasperation. "Which is exactly why I didn't tell you I was coming to start with. I have to go--there. I think I know the woman they're talking about and if I'm right, she's one of the 'mothers'."

"Mothers?"

"The project?" Dionne prompted.

Something flickered in Khan's. "They are like you? To serve the same purpose?"

"Of course! I told you!"

"You did not tell me! If you had, I would have come to find them long since," Khan retorted in exasperation. "How many others?"

Dionne shrugged. She was still trying to remember if she actually *had* forgotten to give Khan that little detail. "Maybe I should explain later--in private."

"Explain now," Khan said implacably.

"There were twelve--besides me. *They* each carry clones. Once they were revived, they were to produce the people that would be the keys to rebuilding. I am the thirteenth, the failsafe. If the others did not survive, then that would be my role. Though I carry no clones, my own eggs are genetically enhanced to breed superior off-spring."

She could hear Khan grinding his teeth. "I would not have forgotten that. You told me you could choose no one because you were the arc of humanity. You implied in that that you were the only one capable of serving that purpose."

"Oh," Dionne said. "I think, maybe, I didn't tell you about the others because I wasn't certain they'd survived and I wouldn't have a choice if they hadn't."

He glared at her.

"I didn't see any sense in considering it a possibility until I knew. I *still* don't know. Nothing has changed. Nothing *will* change until and unless I find them and they still live. I have to go to the forbidden lands to find out."

Nearby, someone cleared their throat. The noise distracted Khan and Dionne from their argument.

"We can take you to the castle, but I can not guarantee that the queen will see you. If it is as you say, she will welcome you. If not...." He shrugged.

"You will guarantee her safety or she will not go," Khan said implacably.

"But I have...." Khan cut her off by covering her mouth with his hand. She glared at him, but subsided.

Sir William studied him speculatively for several moments. "We can not guarantee anything," he said finally. "I can not predict how the queen will react, nor protect your lady if the queen is displeased by her claim."

"Then you will go to your queen and you will tell this: The goddess Dionne has risen from the sleep placed upon her in the temple that bears this sign," he said, pointing to the dragon tattoo on his cheek. "And you will describe Dionne to her. If she wishes to speak with Dionne, she will come to meet her where our lands adjoin. This will be neutral ground under the treaty of peace. I will give my word as Chief of my people that they will not attack-- unless we are attacked."

Sir William frowned, obviously insulted that Khan would even consider offering *his* queen an ultimatum, but finally shrugged. "I will relay the message." With an effort, he and the other two men mounted their horses. His gaze flickered curiously over the shield and sword Khan carried once he'd settled in his saddle. Recognition dawned as he studied the weapons and his expression changed radically. "How did you come by those?" he asked sharply.

Khan's eyes narrowed, his face hardening. "I took them from the man I killed."

Dionne gaped at him. "You said you found them!" she gasped accusingly.

"I found them on the body of the man I slew," Khan responded, shrugging.

"You ambushed him, you savage!" Lord Harry roared furiously.

Khan turned to look at the man who'd spoken. "He attacked me. We fought. I won."

"You bested Gallahad!" Sir William demanded, disbelief evident in his voice.

"He did not give me his name," Khan said dryly. "But if you are so curious to know how I bested him, I will gladly show you."

"You could not have bested him in a fair fight," Lord Harry growled, turning red with fury.

Khan's eyes narrowed at the insult, but he kept his temper with an effort. "I do not cheat, and I do not lie. But you are right. The fight was uneven. I had no long knife, no shield, and none of the shiny metal to protect my flesh that you wear."

Sir William held out an arm, stopping the other knight before he could surge forward and take up the challenge. "Wait. You will get your chance another time to avenge Gallahad's death--if the queen does not lock you in the tower prison. First, we will go to her and see if she knows this woman."

With obvious reluctance, the three knights turned and rode away. Khan watched them until they disappeared and finally looked down at Dionne. "You and I have much to discuss."

Chapter Seventeen

Communicating with hand signals, Khan ordered the warriors who had accompanied him to follow the knights to make certain they didn't double back. When they'd ridden off, he sheathed his sword in the holder slung across his back. After breaking the tip off of the bolt stuck in his shield, he slung the shield onto his back, as well, and dismounted, reaching up for Dionne to help her down.

Despite her uneasiness about his remark, Dionne placed her hands on his shoulders readily enough. "I'm so relieved you weren't hurt," she said as she slipped from the horse's back, feeling a renewed rush of thankfulness and horror at the bolt that had been protruding through the center of his shield. If he had not had it, or been swift in bringing it up to shield him, he would be dead now, just as Notaku was.

Disconcertingly, instead of simply setting her on her feet, Khan pulled her close so that she slipped along his body slowly until her toes were barely touching the ground. "I am relieved that you were hurt no worse than you were," Khan responded, his voice tight with a mixture of emotions. He dipped his head toward hers, hesitating when his lips were mere inches from hers.

Dionne stared at his lips for a heartbeat and abruptly yielded to the surge of need that washed through her, a mixture of desire and gratitude that he hadn't come to harm when he'd thrown his life into the breach to come after her. His breath sawed out of his chest in a gust of relief and urgency as she closed the distance that separated them. A tremor went through him as he pressed his lips to hers in a series of feather light caresses, his lips moving over the tender surface of hers as if searching for the perfect fit.

The moment she felt the heat of his mouth molding firmly over hers, felt the roughness of his tongue slide along the seam where her lips met, the more tender emotions that had spawned her capitulation yielded to a fiercer force, a burning thirst that seemed unquenchable. Opening her mouth to him, she twined her arms around his neck, straining upward to meet him, pressing herself tightly against him so that she could feel his length against hers.

As wonderful as it had felt when he'd kissed her before, it dimmed by comparison. This was better than before, she thought dimly as a thrilling rush of desire swept through her, enthralling her with the keenness of the pleasure his touch evoked, leaving her breathless and dizzy.

Her body quickened almost instantaneously, responding to the thrusting rhythm of his tongue as his explored her mouth with a thoroughness that left no nerve untouched, unprovoked. She pressed harder against him, feeling the blood pulsing in her breasts, her heartbeat thrusting against his chest wall. The muscles low in her belly clenched and unclenched with restless need, bringing her body to dew point.

It he'd taken her to the ground at that moment, no thought of denying him would've entered her mind regardless of the consequences. She thought for several moments when she felt his embrace loosen that that was exactly what he had in mind, then she, too, realized that the pounding rhythm she heard wasn't just her own heartbeat. It was hooves.

Reluctantly, she drew away as he lifted his lips from hers to identify the oncoming riders. Still feeling weak and disoriented, every nerve in her body sizzling like broken live wires, it took Dionne longer to steady herself. Belatedly, she released her death grip on his neck and allowed her arms to drop to her sides, trying to look unconcerned as she turned to look, as well.

Relief and irritation collided briefly when she saw it was no threat, but the returning warriors.

One glance at their faces was enough to assure her they hadn't missed the tender embrace and that she looked as thoroughly aroused as she was. Embarrassment flooded her cheeks with color.

"They headed north," the eldest of the five said gruffly.

Khan nodded, nudging Dionne's chin up with his index finger. "These are my brothers. Gray hair is Rikard, the eldest."

When Dionne nerved herself to look directly at him, she saw that his hair was nearly as black as Khan's, though there was a narrow streak of white hair sprouting from the left quadrant of his hairline at his forehead.

"The fat one is Lex, who is just younger than I am." Shorter and stockier than the others, not fat, Dionne noted with amusement.

"The ugly one there is Mato." The most handsome of the five.

"The long skinny one is Nigan and the infant there is the youngest, Tin."

Despite her discomfort, Dionne couldn't help but smile as his brothers reacted to the introductions with varying degrees of irritation, indignation, and amusement.

The 'infant', Tin, was plainly indignant at having his manhood called into question--still young enough to be prickly about it, obviously. Mato merely grinned since he couldn't help but be aware that he about as far from ugly as it was possible to be. Nigan and Lex both looked irritated, but only mildly and Rikard, who was undoubtedly the most laid back of the five ignored the insult altogether.

"I didn't know you had brothers!" Dionne exclaimed in pleased surprise. "Do you have sisters, too?"

Khan gave her a look. "Thankfully, no."

Since it was abundantly clear that he was implying that females were trouble, Dionne glared at him.

He stepped away from her. "Gather her belongings. We will pull back across the gorge to the border and wait to see if the queen from the forbidden lands comes."

There wasn't much to gather. "I can do it," she said firmly.

She didn't particularly care for Khan's highhanded attitude, or his assumption that she would follow his orders like everyone else appeared to. On the other hand, he *was* Chief--not of her, but the leader of his people nevertheless, and she knew it wouldn't be diplomatic to challenge him in front of his brothers.

Besides, if there was less danger to them by pulling back, she wasn't about to insist on going on and possibly ending up getting someone killed.

Especially if that someone was Khan or any of his brothers.

"What is this?" Tin asked as she folded the tent. Dionne looked up to see that he'd dismounted and was studying the tent curiously.

"A pop tent. It's designed so that one person can quickly and easily set it up and fold it again when they get ready to leave."

His brows rose, then descended in a frown as he squatted down to examine it more closely. "What sort of hide is this?"

Dionne looked at him, but she didn't currently feel up to trying to explain something she doubted he would understand. She shrugged. "It isn't animal hide at all. It's synthetic fibers--made by my people."

She lost him at synthetic, but he seemed to dismiss it, taking the tent once she'd folded it and looking around, as if for a pack horse. She pointed to the bot. "Just drop it in the bucket. The bot carries for me."

Nodding, he moved toward the bot cautiously. Dionne stopped to watch him as he examined it, fighting the temptation to order the bot to move, just to see what his reaction would be.

Apparently, he decided it wasn't a threat. After looking it over thoroughly, he dropped the tent into the bucket since it was obviously the only place that could hold anything, then rapped on the side of the bucket with his knuckles. The metal rang. His brows rose in surprise, but it seemed he liked the sound. He rapped on it several more times, then looked up at his brothers, grinning.

Khan was glaring at him. "If they did not know where we were, the noise you make would certainly alert our enemies."

Tin's face fell almost comically. He reddened, glared at his brother and stalked back to his horse, mounting it sulkily.

Hiding a smile, Dionne carried her rolled sleeping bag to the bot and dropped it into the bucket. Ordering the bot back the way they'd come, she glanced at Khan questioningly. Leading his horse over to her, he caught her waist and lifted her onto the horse's back, leaping up behind her.

The return trip was faster, although Khan didn't push the horses to more than a fast trot. As before, it took a while for the bot to wench itself across the narrow point of the gorge, but Khan and his brothers merely swam their horses across.

The climb up the other side on horseback was even more unnerving than climbing on foot. Dionne would've preferred to dismount, but Khan didn't give her the chance to voice her preferences. As soon as the horse emerged from the water, he kicked it and sent it surging up the narrow, steep trail in a series of bouncing jumps that nearly unseated her.

They made camp as soon as Khan had found a spot he deemed suitable. Again, Dionne wasn't in total agreement with his decision. The land near the gorge was far more flat. Even near the edge of the trees, the ground began to slope upwards, but Khan refused to set up camp in the open.

Rikard did not stay. Even as they dismounted, he nodded to Khan in silent communication and rode off.

Curious, Dionne turned and looked at Khan questioningly.

"He goes to summon the others."

That didn't entirely answer her question. "You think they'll be needed?" she asked uneasily.

"I would rather have them and not need them, than not have them."

Dismay filled Dionne at that comment. She knew nothing about war--and she very much hoped that she wasn't about to learn.

Chapter Eighteen

Two days later, Mato, who'd been sent to watch for the arrival of the strangers of the forbidden lands, returned to their camp to report that many men and horses pulling strange boxes were slowly advancing toward the gorge. His face grim, Khan left camp and went to see the army for himself.

He looked more thoughtful than alarmed when he returned, however.

"What is it? Did they bring an army?"

Khan shook his head, still obviously puzzled. "Warriors, yes, but many who do not appear to be warriors. We'll wait and see."

Confused, worried, and curious at the cryptic nature of Khan's report, Dionne tried to pry more information out of him without success. The following day, she saw the first of the men emerge on the opposite side of the gorge. Using teams of horses, the men began to drag felled, denuded trees from the forest on the other side and lower them into the gorge. By the time darkness settled, ending their labor for the day, Dionne realized what they were doing.

"They're building a bridge," she murmured to no one in particular.

"The question is, to what purpose?" Khan responded.

The answer arrived almost a week later in the form of a royal procession. The procession halted before it reached the bridge, which men were still working on like fighting fire. An encampment was set up.

It was all Dionne could do to contain her impatience. She knew it *had* to be Eugenia, otherwise why would the queen come?

Khan refused to budge from his position, even when his own warriors arrived. He'd said they would meet on neutral ground and he meant it, and to see to it that Dionne didn't decide to ignore his orders and go off on her own, he moved into the tent with her.

That move threw her into complete disorder. Despite the kiss the day he'd rescued her from his enemies, he'd kept his distance since. She hadn't been able to figure out why, unless it was because of the lack of any real privacy to pursue the matter further, but she certainly hadn't asked. She'd just been relieved that temptation wasn't close enough to make her forget herself again.

When Khan decided the best way to keep her out of harm's way was to guard her closely--very closely--he very effectively diverted her from what was happening across the gorge. A mixture of dread and excitement had filled her the first night he crawled into the tent with her, but she realized fairly quickly that he'd brought his furs to sleep in--which seemed to indicate his intentions weren't what she'd hoped for.

Without a word he stretched out beside her and composed himself for sleep.

She lay tensely for some time, staring wide eyed at the ceiling of the tent while she tried to think what she could say if he seemed interested in kissing her again. Nothing came to mind, but when the minutes dragged into an hour she finally realized she didn't need to. Some of her tension dissipated just from weariness, but she found she still couldn't sleep.

"Why did you tell Sir William that I was your woman?" she asked finally.

Khan didn't answer for so long that she thought he would pretend to be asleep--She knew he wasn't any closer to sleep than she was--whether from the same reason, or because he didn't dare close his eyes and sleep until he knew *she* was asleep, she didn't know, but she was certain from the rhythm of his breathing that he wasn't asleep.

"I didn't like the way the men were looking at you," he finally responded.

Dionne was surprised at the admission, vaguely pleased and flattered, and confused all at the same time. She hadn't noticed anything about the way the knights had looked at her to indicate desire. She had not been in any condition to pay close attention at the time, of course, but it had seemed to her that there was more suspicion and uneasiness in their expressions than anything that might remotely be interpreted as desire.

"Oh. I see," she said finally, although she didn't, not really. "But--you could've made up any sort of story. It wasn't really necessary to tell them that."

"Are you saying you liked the way that pretty faced boy was looking at you?" Khan growled.

Amusement surfaced despite the anger in Khan's voice. "Which one was the pretty faced one?" she asked, all innocence.

"The one with the yellow hair and big teeth."

"Oh. Sir William."

"Well?"

"What?"

Khan ground his teeth. "Go to sleep, Dionne."

Dionne rolled onto her side facing him. She knew she shouldn't, but she couldn't resist the urge to touch his face. "I like your face much better."

He placed his hand over hers, pressing her palm against his cheek and finally turned his lips into her palm, nibbling at the tender skin. Goose bumps raced up her arm and scattered across her body. Her nipples puckered as blood engorged them, making them stand erect.

To her relief and vague disappointment, he went no further, however. Removing her hand after a moment, he placed it on the fur between them, covering it with his own. "Sleep," he commanded.

When the bridge was completed at last, thoroughly inspected and tested, the royal procession was reassembled and crossed the gorge with slow dignity. Dionne's feelings were mixed. Khan had thoroughly impressed upon his men that the meeting was to promote peace and no warrior was to fire upon the party unless he detected intent on the opposite side to break the truce and ordered them to attack. But even she, who hardly knew the men at all, could see that they were on edge and she knew it wouldn't take much to set them off.

She strongly suspected the knights on the other side were of pretty much the same mind.

And doubts surfaced about her own beliefs. What if she'd been completely wrong? What if she'd attributed the advancement of the people of Albany to the woman she'd known and it had had nothing to do with leadership of someone from a more advanced civilization?

Was it even possible that it could be the woman she remembered?

Dismay filled her when the coach carrying the queen halted at last, the steps were let down, and the coach began to disgorge women dressed in elaborate medieval costume.

She studied the face of each as they stepped from the coach, but couldn't detect the faintest familiarity. Finally, when four women had lined up outside the coach, a woman dressed far more elaborately than any of the others was helped down. This, Dionne realized, must be the queen--but she was old!

Dionne sent Khan a glance filled with distress.

He frowned. "Is it not her?"

Swallowing with an effort against a knot of misery and dread that felt like it was the size of an egg, Dionne peered more closely at the woman. Vaguely, a tenuous sense of recognition surfaced, but she wasn't certain if it was because she was trying so hard to see something familiar in the woman's face, or if she truly had. "I'm not--not sure," she said finally.

Khan took her cold hand in his, squeezed it reassuringly, and urged her forward. Dionne sent him a wavering smile of gratitude and allowed him to lead her to meet the queen. As she drew closer, the certainty grew in her that she hadn't been mistaken, but that only threw her into more confusion.

Her knees were quaking when they finally stopped little more than an arm's length from each other. "Genie?" Dionne said a little doubtfully.

Tears welled in the old woman's eyes. "Dee! Oh god! Dee! It *is* you!"

Dionne wasn't certain whether she threw herself into the woman's embrace or vice versa. But one moment they were merely staring at each other in stunned amazement and the next they were hugging, laughing and crying, and both trying to talk at the same time.

"Your majesty?"

Sniffing, Eugenia pulled away reluctantly, though she retained a firm grip on Dionne's hand, and turned to look at the man who'd spoken to her. "It's all right. This is Dionne." She glanced at Dionne and winked. "My sister. We've got a lot of catching up to do. Have the servants set up a comfortable place where we can talk."

The man, who looked to be perhaps forty, nodded and signaled to those at the rear of the procession. Slipping her arm through Dionne's, Eugenia looked around and finally led Dionne a little distance from the carriage. Khan and the man who'd escorted Eugenia trailed them, examining each other with a mixture of curiosity and thinly veiled hostility.

"This is Lord Neville--my son," Eugenia said when she noticed the tension between the two men.

Shock went through Dionne, but she recovered herself quickly. Catching Khan's hand, she tugged him forward. "This is Chief Khan of the Kota, my...." She hesitated fractionally, trying to decide what she could say without making an assumption about Khan that might be potentially embarrassing for both of them, or insulting him. "...dearest friend and companion."

She felt a jolt travel through the hand she held and glanced up at him searchingly, but she couldn't tell from his expression whether the introduction had angered him or merely come as a surprise.

Eugenia's eyes danced with amusement. "Your dearest?"

Dionne tightened her grip on Khan's hand when she felt him trying to withdraw. "More dear to me than I can say. It was he who freed me, and he has remained by my side and protected me from my own foolishness ever since."

Eugenia smiled. "Then he is very dear to me also," she said, offering her hand.

Khan stared at it a moment and finally withdrew his hand from Dionne's and shook the queen's hand. Genie chuckled.

"What ... what happened?" Dionne asked when the introductions were completed.

Genie waved the question away. "When we can sit and talk comfortably," she said significantly.

Dionne studied her for several moments, trying to grasp what it was Genie was trying to convey, but she finally nodded, knowing Genie had no intention of telling her more until she was more comfortable that they wouldn't be overheard.

The servants were swift in carrying out their orders. Within twenty minutes, they had set up a pavilion, covered the stone with thick carpets and brought comfortable chairs and tables, arranging everything very carefully.

Lord Neville escorted Eugenia to a chair as soon as the servants began scampering away. Dionne and Khan followed, taking seats across from Eugenia. Genie glanced at her son several times and finally possessed herself of his hand, holding it tightly.

"As I'm sure you've already guessed, I was released from the bio-pod long years ago--by Neville's father, Prince John. I was--terrified, let me tell, to find myself in this--backwards society. It was disconcerting to be looked upon as a sorceress, but I didn't try to correct the misconception. It seemed--safer than trying to explain the truth."

Dionne understood that much without difficulty, but part of the story was still confusing. "What convinced them that you were a sorceress?"

Eugenia shrugged. "The bio-pod itself, in part. The weapon I used to try to frighten them off. As scared as I was, I couldn't bring myself to actually harm anyone. Then there was the--ah--immaculate conceptions--particularly the first."

Dionne nodded, understanding. "And Lord Neville is...?"

Eugenia shook her head fractionally. "Not one of the first twins."

"I see," Dionne said, nodding.

Eugenia chuckled. "I'm not sure you do," she said wryly. "The--uh--experiment was a *complete* success. Two by two the first were born--and thereafter, also. There were times when I thought some very bad thoughts about the lab technicians who'd come up with the brilliant *plan*. But it was at least a little easier for me than it might have been. When John and I were married, there were wet nurses and--an entire staff of servants to take care of the babies I filled the royal nursery with."

Dionne glanced quickly at Khan, then settled back in her chair to digest that.

"How many?" she asked finally.

"Twenty eight in fourteen deliveries," Eugenia supplied, not without some pride.

"Oh my god!" Dionne was horrified. In their own time, such things simply did not happen. There had been birth control to prevent women from having one child after another. Historically, she knew that hadn't been the case. Women had produced until they no longer could, or died, which ever came first. She also knew that it was no part of 'the plan' to limit the number of children the 'mothers' produced. They wanted the women to 'seed' civilization with off spring carrying superior genetics. But an abstract vision of the plan hadn't prepared her for the shock of actuality.

Eugenia shrugged. "There was no help for it. I was--alone."

Dionne blinked at that, brought back to the conversation with a jolt. She felt a little ill as the full implications of that comment sank in. "The others?"

"Only you know the location of all the bio-pods," Eugenia said, shaking her head. "The two entombed with me...." Her chin wobbled faintly. "The other two bio-pods were destroyed when part of the building collapsed. Neither Deborah nor Amelia made it. I was the lucky one."

Dionne quelled the urge to cry as images of the two young women rose in her mind. They truly had been sisters in every way that counted. All of them had been bio-engineered and they had grown up together in the lab nursery, been trained together for the roles they would play.

Eugenia smiled sadly. "I truly was lucky, not just because I survived, or the fact that the collapse was what eventually led to my discovery, but because it was Prince John who found me and set me free. I loved him, very much. In spite of everything, I've had few regrets about my life. The only real regret I've ever felt was that circumstances prevented me from following the plan as it was intended to be implemented and the knowledge that I couldn't make the difference I'd hoped to."

Sensing that Khan was looking at her, Dionne glanced at him. She couldn't read his expression, but she thought she saw understanding in his eyes.

Eugenia grasped her hand, capturing her attention again. "You can, though. Nothing seems to have gone as the project founders hoped, but we can still make a difference to these people. *You* can make a difference. The lab? Is it ... intact? Functional?"

Dionne nodded. "Actually, we did excellently well all things considered. We lost nearly forty percent of the batches, but the rest seem to be in good to excellent shape."

Eugenia smiled. "Then I will send my children to you. They are--really exceptional. They only need the ICTD. There's still time for them to make tremendous progress."

Dionne frowned. "The others?"

Eugenia looked uneasy. "We can't change what's happened, but we can prevent the project from being a complete failure if we act quickly. Tell me where to find them and I will send men to remove the bio-pods and bring them to you--if they still live."

She studied Dionne for several moments, growing angry and distressed when Dionne still seemed reluctant and doubtful. "We have mine!" she said urgently. "Don't throw away what we have for something that might not even be possible! Surely you can see that even what we have now is better than nothing at all?"

Dionne could see it, but she couldn't just abandon the guidelines of the project without considering every angle carefully. "I think you are probably right," she said slowly, soothingly. "But I still have to consider everything. Just give me a little time to think."

Eugenia stared at her for several moments in frustration, but finally nodded. "You're right. I don't like it, but I know you're right. And I know you'll do what is right for everyone."

She rose from her seat. "I'm old," she said almost apologetically. "I'm going to return to the encampment to rest and give you time to reach a decision--but please consider this, we have twenty eight brilliant minds that need only knowledge to reach their full potential."

Chapter Nineteen

Dionne slept on it. Long before the sun crested the distant horizon, she knew what she would do. She had no data to either defend her position or oppose it, but she had realized that the plan simply could not be implemented as conceived. She had to do what she felt was right in her heart.

It occurred to her that her heart might be leading her astray, but she dismissed it. Bio-engineered or not, scientist or not, she was still merely human, and subject to her emotions. She would do what *felt* right, and accept whatever came of it, because she knew she had done the very best she was capable of.

Eugenia didn't appear to have suffered a great deal of doubt over the outcome. Either that, or she was simply hopeful. She'd summoned her children, explained to them the best she could and told them to prepare to go with Dionne to receive the gift of knowledge.

Dionne answered the questioning look Eugenia gave her with a smile and the locations of the other nine pods. Only she had been separated, left in sole possession of the most critical lab of all. A shortage of money more than anything else had determined that the others would be secreted in four other locations by threes.

Summoning her best men, Eugenia and Dionne went over the locations with them, described what they were to find and how to transport it, and the men departed to search for the 'ladies of the casks', the long lost sisters of Queen Eugenia.

Feeling more at peace with herself than she had in many months, Dionne joined Khan at the head of the procession that was returning to the lab. She was surprised that he seemed a little cool and distant, and disturbed by it, but even that didn't dim the sense of hopefulness that filled her as they began their trek to the lab.

Despite the fact that they traveled now with horses and carriages and she'd made the trek to the forbidden lands on foot, it took almost as long to make the return trip as it had before because of the difficulty in getting the carriages over the mountain.

In some respects, Dionne's spirits lightened the closer they came to home base, but she couldn't help but notice that Khan grew quieter and more distant and nothing she could think of to say would draw him out.

Her good spirits began to wane under that dark cloud, until she felt almost as miserable as she was puzzled.

Why, she wondered, was he so withdrawn? Was he that set against the implementation of the plan? She didn't know why, but she'd thought he might have changed his mind, that he had come to see how much it would benefit everyone, and that he would be happy about her decision.

She supposed his coolness was indication enough that she'd been wrong.

She was still confused. He had seemed very upset when she'd told him she was considering abandoning the project and returning to the bio-pod to wait for a more opportune time to implement it. She had thought that meant that he was as tortured by the thought that they would not be together at all as she was.

Now she had the chance to discharge her duty and still have something for herself, him, and it seemed he didn't care at all.

Almost without exception, everyone was tired and on edge by the time the tediously slow procession at last hove into sight of the ridge overlooking the lab.

Dionne, who was riding at the front with Khan and his brothers, gasped when she saw that the Kota had gathered at the ridge above the lab. She glanced at Khan. "They came!" she said, breathless with excitement.

Something flickered in Khan's eyes. He sent his brothers a warning frown. "I see," he said finally.

His reaction dimmed her excitement. "You're--not pleased?"

His lips curled into a smile that did not reach his eyes. "I am pleased for your sake."

"But...." She stared at him in dismay. "It isn't *for* me! It's for them!"

It was an uneasy, distrustful group that gathered outside the lab and settled to make camp. Dionne chided herself for allowing the atmosphere of impending doom to kill her excitement, but it distressed her nonetheless and she was glad when she escaped the crowd and entered the quiet of the lab, away from the uneasy whispering, the distrustful glances.

Dismissing it with an effort, she hurried to the lab first, to check the progress of the embryos. Relieved when she saw that everything was proceeding as expected, she returned to her quarters, indulged herself in a long hot bath and collapsed in exhaustion on her bed.

She began testing the following day. As Eugenia had claimed, her offspring were excellent specimens and Dionne began the ICTD sessions, alternating those sessions with testing the Kota, Khan's brothers at the forefront.

She was pleased to discover that, despite the fact that they had not advanced as far as Eugenia's people, there was no significant difference in physical or mental development.

A week later, a troop of Eugenia's men arrived carrying three of the pods and the anxiety in the back of Dionne's mind that none of the others had survived was eased when she programmed the computer to revive them and they emerged in perfect health.

Two weeks passed before the remaining pods arrived, but the six women resting in the bio-pods emerged as strong and healthy as the others and Dionne's cup of happiness overflowed.

Until she had revived them all, she hadn't realized she'd feared from the time she first climbed into the bio-pod so many years ago that she would never see any of them again. Despite the work they all faced, when Eugenia arrived with the last of the pods, they gathered in Dionne's quarters to celebrate their reunion and mourn the loss of the two who hadn't made it.

Eugenia entertained them long into the night with anecdotes of her life among the medieval society she'd emerged in. When it came Dionne's turn to tell her own story, she realized she had very little to share. Her experiences were mostly confined to reminisces of Khan, and she found she didn't really want to share that.

When she looked for him the following morning, she discovered that he was no where to be found. Frowning, she probed her mind for the last time she'd seen him and realized that she hadn't seen him at all since shortly after they'd returned.

How could she have been so tied up as to have failed to notice that he had gone, she wondered in dismay?

A sense of urgency gripped her then. She had to find him, to see him and assure herself that he hadn't abandoned her.

Leaving the others in charge of the lab, she struck off for the Kota village.

Khan was not in his lodge, nor anywhere in the village that Dionne could discover. Dismayed, fearful, she called the cougars and ordered them to track his scent, watching in anxiety as the cougars wandered back and forth and around and around, crisscrossing each other's path. After watching them for some time, it was borne in upon her that too many days had passed. His scent had faded and even the cougars couldn't help her.

She stood in the middle of the village indecisively, trying to think where he might have gone but nothing came to mind. She was too distressed to think beyond the horrible sense of loss.

She was trudging unhappily through the village, heading back the way she'd come, when she heard a sound that stopped her in her tracks. Her heart skipped several beats, surging with hope when she realized it was the sound of hoof beats that had finally penetrated her abstraction. Crushing disappointment filled her when she saw that it was Rikard. She went to meet him anyway, hopeful that he would know where to find Khan.

"I can't find him," she said, trying to keep the thread of desperation out of her voice.

His lips tightened. "He is gone."

Fighting the urge to wail like a lost child, Dionne simply stared at him while she mastered control. "He left? Without even saying goodbye?"

Some of the anger seemed to leave him. He shook his head. "He left many days ago. If you had cared you should have sought him out then."

Giving up the impossible task of controlling her emotions, Dionne blinked as tears filled her eyes. "I do care! Please! If you know where he's gone, tell me! I need to talk to him."

His expression hardened, but she could see indecision in his eyes. "He loves you. Even I can see that he would gladly move heaven and Earth to have you, but you are not for him and he knows this. If you care about him as you say, leave him in peace. In time, it will be easier for him to accept."

Dionne stamped her foot. "I don't want him to accept, damn it! I love him! Why would he leave now, when we can finally be together? I don't understand this at all."

Rikard's lips tightened. "Did you tell him?"

"I did! I told him he was my dearest friend and companion in the world!"

Rikard gave her a look of disgust. "Then I don't wonder that he left, only that he stayed as long as he did!"

Dismay filled Dionne. "I said it wrong?" she asked unhappily.

Rikard gave her a look of disgust. "I have never seen two people who made more of a muck of things. He has been so fearful that you would flatly refuse him, he was afraid to take the chance and ask, and you have been too busy saving the world to consider saving your part of it. I suppose, though," he said grudgingly, "that it is only human to screw up the one thing most important to you both."

Dionne reddened, but she didn't try to deny his accusations, merely continued to look at him hopefully.

He studied her thoughtfully for several moments. "Go back the lab. I will find him and persuade him to take one more chance. *You* will know what to do when he comes, or you aren't the woman I think you are. If you two screw this up, I wash my hands of you!"

She wanted to argue, to demand that he take her to Khan at once, but one look at his face was enough to assure her that he couldn't as easily be persuaded as Khan was--and Khan had been next to impossible to budge an inch. Nodding miserably, she watched until he'd turned his horse and disappeared and finally trudged back to the lab.

By the time she saw the lab, hope had surged back and she entered the building purposefully. Ignoring the activity, she headed straight for her quarters.

She paced a while, trying to rehearse what she would say to Khan, but her nerves were on edge and nothing brilliant actually materialized. She'd said so much that had turned out all wrong already that she wasn't certain anything she could come up with would make any difference at all.

She kept thinking about what Rikard had said, though. When it finally dawned on her what he'd meant, she stopped dead in her tracks and looked around the room, trying to think how much time had passed. It didn't help. She couldn't think, couldn't begin to calculate the time that had elapsed since she'd spoken with Rikard.

Pushing that aside, she rushed to the locker where she'd stowed the clothing Eugenia had brought with her as gifts to all her 'sisters'. As thrilled as she'd been with the presents and Eugenia's thoughtfulness, she hadn't worn any of it. The dresses were beautiful, but hardly the sort of thing to wear in a lab. The leather tunic Khan had given her was far more suitable.

She'd already decided on a dress when it occurred to her that it wasn't exactly seductive--beautiful, but not alluring. Besides that, it would take too long to get out of the damned thing. That was what Rikard had hinted at, she knew. The only thing she could do now to convince Khan that she was in deadly earnest was to prove to him that she considered him far more than merely a friend and companion, dear or otherwise.

Naked seemed a little too blunt. Khan might not object, but he might also think that she was taunting him and bolt.

Grabbing a sheer wisp of a nightgown, Dionne charged into the bathroom and bathed frantically, leapt from the dryer while she was still sticky and fought with the nightgown until she'd managed to settle it. The mirror was fogged up. Deciding not to wait to see what she looked like, in case she lost her nerve, she dashed into the main living area and began pacing again, trying to calm her frayed nerves, trying to decide how she should approach her seduction of Khan.

Chapter Twenty

When he was certain that Dionne had done as he'd told her and not taken it into her head to try to follow him, Rikard circled the village and headed for the stream where he and his brothers had often gone to swim as children. There was a small pool upstream from the shallow area where the villagers usually went to bathe and collect water for drinking and their cooking pots.

As he'd hoped, and indeed expected, he found Khan sitting on the great flat stone they liked to sun themselves on, staring blindly at the rippling waters of the stream.

Khan tensed when he heard his approach, but he didn't turn to offer a greeting.

It was indication enough that he was intruding and unwelcome, but Rikard ignored it. Dismounting, he left his horse to graze and strode purposefully toward his younger brother.

Khan turned to glare at him when he finally stopped beside the rock.

It wasn't a promising beginning, Rikard thought wryly. "She noticed you were gone."

Several emotions chased each other across Khan's face. Finally, a wry smile curled his lips. "I should be flattered, I suppose, that it only took her a couple of weeks. How goes renewal?"

"Well," Rikard said, frowning.

Khan nodded, but it was obvious he had little interest.

"Why did you leave?"

"It was time--to let go."

Irritation surfaced. "I've never known you to back down from anything in your life! What is it about this woman that defeats you?"

Khan glanced at his brother angrily before focusing his enraged gaze on the river again. "Futility!" he growled. "I'm not such a fool as to continue to fight for something that was lost even before I started. I would not have tried at all if I had known I could change nothing. I didn't understand ... then." He sighed tiredly. "I knew when she told me that she considered me a friend and companion that she was telling me that was all I could ever be. As much as I value that, I can *not* endure it. Sooner or later I would lose what little sense I have left and do something completely unforgivable."

Rikard looked heavenward, seeking patience. "You misunderstood," he said, resisting the urge to call his Chief a fool. "She's dying...."

Khan's head snapped around so quickly, Rikard heard a bone in his neck pop. The color washed from his face even as he surged to his feet. "What?"

Rikard gaped at him, so stunned by the abrupt transformation in his brother that his mind went completely blank. An unholy amusement settled in his gut when he realized Khan had completely misunderstood him. He ought to take pity, he knew. Khan was liable to kill him--or try--when he realized what he'd done, but he could see nothing short of a bomb under his ass was going to galvanize Khan into taking action now when he'd met so much opposition for so long. "She begged me to find you, to tell you she needs you."

Khan looked like he might faint for several moments and Rikard suffered another qualm. Shrugging inwardly, he dismissed it. "Take my horse," he said helpfully.

"Poor choice of words," he muttered when Khan had disappeared. "I suppose I should have said, desperate instead of dying---of course, if he'd let me finish the sentence...."

After considering it thoughtfully for a few minutes, he wondered if he ought to find Khan's horse and try to catch up to him. A little more thought convinced him that Khan was probably halfway to the lab by now and the attempt would almost certainly be pointless, besides putting him closer to ground zero than he really wanted to get. That possibility convinced him he'd be far better off to find Khan's horse and make himself scarce for a while--just until Khan and Dionne had settled things.

* * * *

Dionne took one look at Khan's face when he burst into her quarters and felt as if the world had dropped out from under her. He looked--devastated. The moment that thought popped into her head a dozen images of disaster collided in her mind, each worse than the one before, and she thought for several moments that she would faint. "Khan?" she asked weakly, too unnerved by the haunted look on his face to ask him what terrible thing had happened.

She didn't know whether she rushed to him or vice versa, but she found herself caught up in a crushing embrace.

"Are you all right?" they asked, almost in perfect unison.

Khan relaxed his death grip on her and pulled away enough to look down at her. His expression was puzzled. "Shouldn't you be lying down?"

Dionne blinked at him in confusion. "I should? Is it that bad?"

"Rikard said you were--you needed me," he said slowly, obviously baffled, although to save her life Dionne couldn't figure out why.

"You're all right?" she asked tentatively.

Anger was starting to glint in his eyes. "Except for having been scared out of ten years of my life, I'm fine," he said tightly.

Dionne went back to blinking. "Who scared you?"

"You!"

Her jaw dropped. "I don't understand. I just told your brother I needed to talk to you."

Khan's temper went into slow boil. "I'm going to kill him," he growled, setting Dionne away from him.

Dionne gaped at him as he spun on his heel, but when she saw his intent, she raced him to the door, planting herself firmly in front of it and spreading her arms to either side to block his retreat. "Lois! Lock the door!"

"The barbarian is inside," Lois pointed out.

"Lock it, damn it!"

Khan stopped, his eyes narrowing on her face. "I'm not in the mood for games, Dionne. I warn you, I'm well beyond the limits of endurance. Move--before I do something we'll both regret."

Alarm fluttered in Dionne's breast, but she stood her ground. "I just--wanted to talk," she said a little lamely, unnerved by the look in his eyes as his gaze traveled her length, slowly, before returning to her face.

When he reached for her, Dionne knew he meant to move her out of his way. She also knew that if he left she might lose her chance to reach him. "I love you," she said quickly.

A jolt went through him. His expression changed from anger to one almost comically blank. "What did you say?"

Taking advantage of his shock, she surged toward him, wrapping her arms tightly around his neck and lifting up on her toes to kiss him. "I--love--you," she said slowly, emphasizing each word with a light kiss along his jaw. "Make love to me--make babies with me--make a new world with me."

He caught her waist in his hands, lifting her, and she thought he meant to thrust her away. Instead, he pushed her against the door, corralling her with his own body, as if he more than half feared she would change her mind. Twisting his head, he sought her mouth blindly, settled his lips over hers in a kiss filled with a need that went beyond desperate yearning.

Relief surged through Dionne. Desire followed upon its heels in a heady rush of heat, weakness, breathlessness. The threat of abandonment past, she loosened her hold on his neck, stroking his silky, inky black hair, his back and shoulders, opening her mouth to his possession, kissing him back with a fervor that rapidly overtook his need in terms of urgency.

She dragged in a shaky breath when he lifted his lips from hers and kissed her cheek, her neck and then dragged his lips upward to suck the lobe of her ear. The heat of his breath on her ear lifted the flesh along her neck and arm in tight little pinpoints of sensory perception, making her more keenly aware of the feel of his flesh against hers. Her nipples responded, coming erect with the blood that engorged them. The same heated tide engorged her sex, echoing the frantic pace of her heart.

Sighing with pleasure, she turned her head, pressing her face against the side of his neck to breathe in his scent before she nibbled a trail of kisses along his neck to his ear and investigated it, teasing the sensitive flesh with the edge of her teeth.

A shudder went through him. He sought her mouth again, sliding one hand between them to cup her breast and massage it briefly before he slid his hand down over her belly and between her thighs, curling his fingers against her cleft. A jolt like an electric current went through her as his finger found the tiny nub of her clit and rubbed it. Gasping, she rocked against his finger. Her brain went into total melt down.

Drowning in a sea of her own need, she slipped one hand downward to cup his sex, as well, rubbing her palm over his erection through the leather and finally digging beneath his loincloth to touch the heated, silky skin of his sex. His cock jerked as her hand closed around it.

Breaking the kiss, he buried his face against her neck, breathing raggedly as he ran his hands over her, searching a little frantically for a way to free her from the nightgown. He found the ties in the back at last and fumbled to untie them. The ties tangled and knotted, frustrating his efforts. Dionne encountered a similar roadblock when she discovered the tie of his breechcloth and jerked on it.

Thwarted, they abandoned the effort for the moment, stroking each other through the barriers that confined them, sharing a long, hungry kiss before, almost as one, they turned their attention to trying to disrobe each other again.

Tugging at the fabric, Khan managed to push the shoulders of her nightgown far enough down her shoulders to unveil the upper slope of her breasts. Stroking the soft skin with his hand, he followed with a trail of open mouthed kisses. Finding he could tug the gown no lower, he returned to the source of his frustration, wrestling with the ties again for several moments. Tiring of fighting with the knot, Khan wrapped the ties in one fist and gave it a sharp tug. The sound of rending fabric followed and the gown loosened. Dionne murmured a halfhearted protest. "This is my only nightgown."

He grunted, nibbling along her shoulder as he pushed the gown down to her waist and covered the tip of one breast with his mouth, instantly depriving Dionne of any interest in the gown at all. The tug of his mouth on the acutely sensitive nub induced a riot of drugging sensation. Her belly quivered and tightened. Moisture gathered along the channel of her sex.

Enthralled, Dionne went perfectly still, her fingers kneading his flesh where she clutched him. She gasped when he lifted his head and captured its twin, evoking an even more profound explosion of sensation.

A feeling of desperation began to invade her senses as he continued to divide his attention between the two tender nubs. Scarcely aware of what she was doing anymore, Dionne threaded her fingers in his hair and tugged. He lifted his head and looked up at her for a moment. Straightening, he covered her mouth once more, thrusting his tongue between her parted, gasping lips and exploring the highly responsive inner flesh of her mouth.

A shiver went through Dionne as the hard muscles of his chest brushed across her acutely sensitized breasts along the way. The feel of his bare skin against hers was captivating. Frustration invaded her as she slipped a hand downward again, encountering his breechcloth. Blindly, she felt for the tie again, struggled with it briefly. Finally, she gripped the tie and gave it a sharp tug. She was rewarded with the sound of tearing leather and the loosening of the barrier.

"This is my only loincloth," Khan growled against her lips.

Pushing the breechcloth from his hips so that it fell to his ankles, she cupped her hand over his bare flesh, stroking his engorged flesh.

He sucked in his breath sharply. A shudder went through him.

Grasping her waist, he lifted her up against the door, thrusting his hips forward and grinding his cock against her cleft. Dionne moaned as the rough caress touched off jolts of piercing delight, wrapping her legs around his waist to steady herself and give him better access.

She slid downward.

He caught her buttocks in his hands and pushed her up the door again.

She looped her arms around his neck and tightened them to hold herself up.

He ground his hips against her and his hard flesh bumped along her tender cleft, producing a wild combination of pleasure, frustration, and enough pain to pierce her absorption. She sucked in her breath sharply.

"I hurt you?"

"No," she lied, nibbling at his ear lobe. "Don't stop."

Either he didn't believe her or he simply gave up on getting the leverage he needed. Tightening his arms around her, he kicked his breechcloth from his ankles and moved to the tiny counter of her kitchenette and propped her buttocks on the icy surface. Dionne yelped, jerking away from the cold instinctively.

Glancing around with a look desperation, Khan spied the furs across the room at last. Carrying her to them, he dropped to his knees and bent over, half lowering her and half falling onto the pile. The air left her lungs in a grunt as he landed on top of her. She tightened her arms before he could pull away, however, sticking her tongue in his ear.

His breath hissed sharply through his teeth.

Dragging his arms from beneath her, he brushed her hair from her face and locked his lips to hers in a brief, gusty kiss before shifting to one side of her and sliding a hand down her body as far as he could reach. Encountering the nightgown at her waist, he lowered his head to her breast, teasing the nipple most accessible to him with his lips and tongue as he gathered the fabric in his hand. When he'd unveiled the skin beneath, he skated his hand upward along her thigh.

Dionne gasped, arching her back as she felt his fingers thread the curling patch of hair on her mound and then part her nether lips. His thick finger slipped back and forth briefly along her cleft, gathering and spreading the moisture of her desire, and finally settled on her clit.

The desperation that had waned slightly in the search for a place to lie together, burgeoned, quickly outstripped the need of before. Pushing at his shoulders until he leaned away, she lifted her hips, shoving the nightgown down until she could fight free of it, and then grasped his wrist, spreading her thighs wide as she guided his hand back to her cleft.

He settled his knee between her thighs, moving over her and replacing his hand along her cleft with his swollen member. Gasping, Dionne caught his shoulders in her hands, lifting up to meet him so that his thick cock plowed along her cleft, bypassing the point that ached for him.

Gasping against her throat, he pushed her hands away, caught his cock in one hand and guided it home, wedging the head in her opening.

She gritted her teeth, pushing against his exploratory thrust until she felt her flesh reluctantly parting to accept his intrusion.

They paused to catch their breath, their bodies clinging with the moisture of their labors. Supporting himself on his elbows, Khan nuzzled her neck and one ear. "You said you were the failsafe," he murmured, his voice harsh as he struggled against his need.

Dionne wrapped her arms tightly around his shoulders. "Make me your woman, Khan. Please."

A shudder went through him. He lifted slightly away from her, watching her face as he claimed her, inch by excruciating inch, embedding his hardened flesh a little deeper with each smooth thrust until he encountered a barrier. Dionne gripped his buttocks as he began to withdraw, digging her fingers into the firm flesh in determination. He hesitated a moment and thrust again. She arched to meet him, squeezing her eyes tightly at the slight burning as he breeched her hymen and letting out a gasp of relief and pleasure as he sank fully inside of her.

A thrill went through her to feel him so deeply inside of her.

Khan held still, sought her mouth with his, kissing her until he felt moisture gathering along her channel, felt the hard clenching of her vaginal walls relax fractionally to ease his way. The response of her body to his wrenched the last of his control from him. Breaking the kiss, he began to move with purpose, seeking the prize that hovered just beyond his reach.

Pleasure bloomed inside of Dionne again the moment he began to move, expanding rapidly. She countered his rhythm, focusing her all on scaling the fullest spectrum of delight as each thrust touched off another wave higher than the one before. She reached crisis, reached a point where she could contain no more pleasure, teetered briefly on the edge and let out a cry of purest delight as she plunged over the precipice in an explosion of mindless bliss.

Her crisis touched off his and she could feel his body jerking inside of her with his convulsions of rapture.

The eruption of tension sapped every ounce of strength from her. Feeling a glorious sense of repletion, she ceased to struggle against the weakness and lay limp beneath him as he shuddered and went still, a smile of utter satisfaction curling her lips.

Gasping for breath, he levered himself off of her and collapsed on his side beside her, removing the bulk of his weight from her, although he made no attempt to move completely away, leaving nearly half of his body draped across her.

Slowly, her heart and lungs ceased to labor with the aftereffects of supreme excitement. She was drifting lazily when he roused enough to lift his head and look at her.

"No regrets?"

It took an effort to lift her eyelids to look at him and even more of an effort to lift her hand to caress his cheek. "I've done all that could be expected of me, all that I can for mankind. As you pointed out, I have the right to take something for myself."

He swallowed audibly, his gaze searching her face. "I don't want you to feel regrets. I don't want to have to live with the guilt that I interfered when I shouldn't have. It would be--unbearable to think you regretted being with me."

She caressed his cheek. "I may regret some things, but I'll never regret choosing the best this world has to offer for myself."

The End

Printed in the United States
40409LVS00002BA/127-657

9 781586 087289